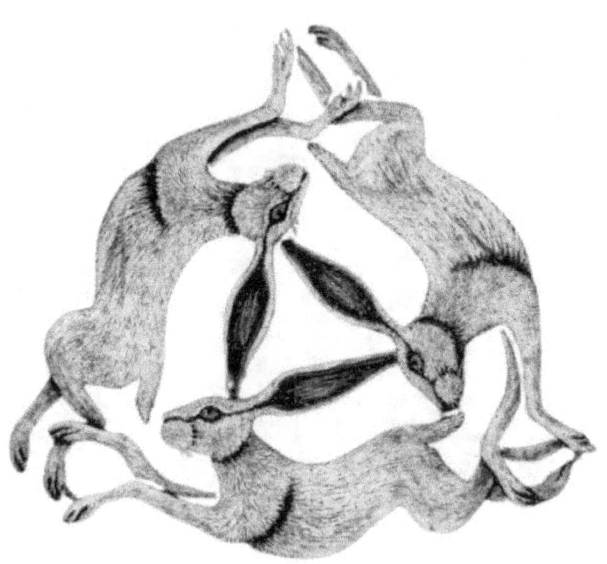

THE GREAT DANE

Suanne Laqueur

Hardcover ISBN: 979-898802-1-650
Paperback ISBN: 979-898802-1-667
eBook ISBN: 979-898802-1-674

This book is dedicated to all of us.

At one point or another, all of us have wondered who we are.

All of us have scratched at a label put on us, feeling it didn't quite fit.

All of us have felt pressured to be something we're not.

All of us have wished we were someone else.

All of us have looked in a mirror and been confused at what we see.

All of us don armor to do brave things: a change in voice, a different accent, a favorite sweater, high heels, a good luck charm.

All of us are fluid.

I used to think all of us hear a voice when we talk to ourselves, but I've since learned this is only some of us. But whether or not you have an inner monologue, the book is for you. The journey is for you. The quest and the game and the mystery and the solution: all for you.

Also for me.

And especially for Beatrix and Celeste.

"*The Three Hares motif is marked by ambiguity, but it could be that this was intentional. Perhaps the hares could represent friend or foe depending on the choices made by those who looked at them.*"

—*The Three Hares: A Curiosity Worth Regarding*, by Tom Greeves, Sue Andrew and Chris Chapman.

"Come, my child," I said, trying to lead her away. "Wish good-bye to the poor hare, and come and look for blackberries."

"Good-bye, poor hare!" Sylvie obediently repeated, looking over her shoulder at it as we turned away. And then, all in a moment, her self-command gave way. Pulling her hand out of mine, she ran back to where the dead hare was lying, and flung herself down at its side in such an agony of grief as I could hardly have believed possible in so young a child.

"Oh, my darling, my darling!" she moaned, over and over again. "And God meant your life to be so beautiful!"

—Lewis Carroll

A NOTE ON THE ARTWORK

Ethan Hasen's pencil sketches are from the private collection of Dr. Saskia Hasen-Strong and used by permission.

Depictions of The Naomi Road *are courtesy of the Montresor Gallery in New York City and also used by permission.*

The Naomi Road *is a collection of 52 postcards hand-drawn by Ethan Hasen, mailed between 2016 and 2017. All are addressed to Danelaw Strong in Birch Island, New York, USA. The message side of each card contains a single fingerprint beneath a quote from the Book of Ruth, Chapter 1, verse 16:*

"But Ruth replied to Naomi, 'Don't urge me to leave you or to turn back from you. Where you go I will go, and where you stay I will stay.'"

PROLOGUE

"But how could you live and have no story to tell?"
—*Fyodor Dostoevsky*

FABULOUS PIPPLE

December 31, 2015
Grandview-on-Hudson, New York

"So how'd you two meet?" Dane asks, licking a drip of hummus off the side of his hand.

Robby glances at Jack and the tips of his ears turn red. "You sure you want to hear this story?"

Dane's glance volleys between the blushing husbands. "Sure, why not?"

"Well," Jack says, rubbing the back of his neck. "As is wont to happen in my world, I had to go to the ER because I had a certain..." He turns his hand over in the air a few times. "Sexual plaything lodged in my..." The hand circles again.

"Ah," Dane says. "Gotcha." He takes a suave bite of celery and hopes it isn't obvious he's clenching his butthole.

"And the nurse, who was a total sweetheart by the way—"

"She came to our wedding," Robby says.

"And got us a lovely toaster," Jack says. "Anyway, while she was talking me off a ledge, she told me not to feel too bad because there happened to be another man in the ER with the same problem."

Robby wags an index finger in the air. "Representing."

"She introduced us. We commiserated. And that's how we met."

"Love at first dildo extraction."

"Except it was Jack's second."

"All right, we don't need to share *everything* about the encounter. Whoa, Dane, are you okay?"

Dane is doubled over now, the laughter splashing in his chest and the tears rolling down his face. Teeth clamped together to keep the mouthful of celery and hummus from spewing everywhere.

"Breathe," Robby says, thumping Dane's back. "Want a little dick with that choke?"

Huff Jensen comes by with a tray of drinks. "Hey, hey, don't break my brother-in-law. I've just spent long and arduous months putting him back together."

"Told him how we met," Robby says.

"Oh, the dildo story. You guys are so basic." Huff hands Dane a napkin to wipe his eyes. "Stop clenching your butthole."

LIKO GREENMAN STANDS ON the far perimeter of this exchange, hearing Jack and Robby's how-we-met story for the third time tonight. With each telling the dildo gets bigger, the nurse shifts between male and female, and the wedding gift is either a toaster or a blender. But Jack and Robby always end up together so what's the harm with a little embellishment. They've earned it.

So instead of listening, Liko is watching Dane.

Liko doesn't know the man's name is Dane. They haven't been introduced and Liko hopes they aren't. Not just yet.

Liko doesn't think of himself as an introvert. He likes parties. He's not afraid to join a group he doesn't know. He makes small talk easily and more than once he's been referred to as a social tether—someone who becomes the mothership of your party mingling and you often make your way back to him or her, just to catch your breath, process, collect yourself. Liko digs being that person. A beacon of social safety. *Come stand next to me. Join my conversation. Or just stand here and siphon off some peace.*

But this dude… The man whom Liko doesn't yet know is named Danelaw Strong… He looks at Liko once, just a glance across a crowded room with a pair of illegally blue eyes, and Liko introverts.

Panics, if we're being honest, he thinks. He retreats a few steps to the living room's bookshelves. Pretends to peruse. Glances at Dane, who is looking at him. Liko looks away, puts his nose into a random book, and introverts further.

Weird. He's not even my type.

Liko likes to be thrown around a bed if he's in it with a man. Bears are his type. Dane is not a bear. In fact, it's pissing Liko off he can't get a bead on this guy, and that he's even trying to classify Dane with body type slang is pissing him off more.

Dane stands in his circle of conversation, head turning from one person to another. He's a short man, so his chin is tilted up. His sandy hair is buzzed tight and he pulls the extreme style off well. Dressed in jeans and a V-neck sweater. A beer in one hand, the other fingers tucked in his front pocket. He looks at the person on his right, and he's a poet. He looks the other way, and he's a construction worker. He's whip-thin and sparse, then he moves or turns or shifts and he's all fit muscle. Unsmiling, he looks early forties, tired after a long day, feeling his years. Then he smiles and he's barely out of his twenties, rawboned and bristling with energy.

What is happening? Liko thinks.

Dane's looking at him with those ridiculous blue eyes. Liko is used to being on the receiving end of eye compliments because his own are an intense purple-gray. Honest-to-God Liz Taylor violet peepers. Dane is competition. His gaze and Liko's are two bucks circling each other, each believing they are the fairest of all, and they ought to take it outside and decide.

Or upstairs.

Don't panic, Liko thinks, looking away.

He can't get words to stick to his reaction. His ex-wife would probably call it a trauma response.

Don't be dramatic. You're digging someone. It's been a while. Enjoy it.

He can't. This isn't enjoyable. He needs to get back to a mothership but he has no tether. He looks at Dane across a galaxy, walking free in space, placing his feet on nothing, aware of time and gravity and vastness and how everyone is an infinitesimal, insignificant speck of dust with no control over anything. At the mercy of a conniving Universe who likes to put her cheek on the heel of her starry hand while the other fingers delicately move two motes into place.

You. Annnnnd you. Say hello.

Trust me. I know what I'm doing.

Some people you meet do an effortless end run around your psychological constructs (or worse, around your chemical ones). One encounter and they're suddenly wandering the emotional hinterlands of your soul, where the line between sad and wretched, or happy and manic, can't be seen with the naked eye. These damn people not only see everything, but they make you feel shit to your bones.

The stupidly blue gaze of this impossible twink-otter-construction worker-poet is slipping under Liko's skin and throwing arms wide to encompass his entire emotional spectrum, right out to the hinterlands and beyond.

Some call this love at first sight.

Liko Greenman calls it *Pump the brakes, you moron.*

In his twenties, Liko would fuck this guy in the next five seconds. Liko is fifty-four now and knows it's wise not to eat this proffered delicacy in one sitting. He doesn't even have to taste it.

Fine, Universe, you obviously have a plan. Noted. I'll take it from here. On my schedule, thanks very much. Bitch.

So Liko Greenman walks away from the party. Grabbing his jacket from a pile on a bed, he goes up the stairs and down the hall to its end, where he opens a door to the attic steps. From the attic he opens another door, climbs a ladder and steps onto the widow's walk. A railed-in space of maybe five feet by seven feet, with two Adirondack chairs, a little table, and Huff Jensen's telescope.

Liko sits, remembering his first time visiting this beautiful house. Six months ago, when Liko was newly divorced, still bruised and smarting, and finally finding his feet and feeling he could play nicely with others. Huff and Maisie were throwing a housewarming and invited Liko over early to help with preparations, let him establish himself as a host instead of a guest. Before anyone else arrived, Huff took Liko upstairs and showed him the way to the rooftop haven.

"We tell everyone the roof is in need of repair and it's not safe to come up," Huff said. "But it is. And if it gets to be too much tonight and you need to get away, don't go home. Go here first. Just sit alone and listen to the party. Pace like the widows of old and watch the water. Okay?"

Liko didn't pace that night, for he'd found himself content. Still profoundly wounded by his ex-wife's betrayal, but the hurt graciously moved over and let a peaceful happiness swell in his chest, alongside a dash of petty smugness: Janelle had left the marriage so Liko not only got the house, he got all the cool friends and their sympathy, plus this magnificent rooftop vista.

Suck it, bitch.

With a bottle of beer and the cut-off crusts of Maisie's famous cucumber sandwiches, Liko sat and gazed at the panoramic view of the Tappan Zee Bridge. Not waiting for a ship to come in. Not making wishes on the first stars that peeked into sight. It was a pure moment of not needing anything and Liko liked to practice leaning into such mindful, content times. He watched the sunset, blissfully unaware that Madame von Universe, the conniving bitch, was manipulating Danelaw Strong into his path.

Tonight, in the last minutes of 2015, Liko steps onto the widow's walk again, neither mindful nor content. He clutches the rail and shivers, butthole clenched tight. Behind his closed lids he sees a million shades of blue. He puts an eye to the telescope, looking for the Universe.

"What are you doing," he whispers. "What is this? Who is he?"

The Universe just shrugs.

Nothing for it, so Liko sits down, reaches for his vape and proceeds to get *really* fucking high.

It's an excellent party and Dane feels he's doing quite nicely. After a year of eating, sleeping and breathing a complicated widowhood, his grief invading every aspect of daily life, he's playing a little experimental game: How long can he go at this fiesta as an unattached man with no past to speak of?

So far, so good. It helps that the Jensens have an eclectic, diverse circle of friends. What Dane's late wife would've called "fabulous pipple." Dancers. Musicians. Artists of all ilk. Advocates. Entrepreneurs. Survivors. All of them superb conversationalists. They make it easy for Dane to reinvent himself as a superb listener.

That's amazing. No no, you're not boring me at all, this is fascinating. Tell me more...

Dane's daughter Saskia murmurs out the corner of her mouth, "All right, Dad?"

"All right." Dane smiles at her, full of pride. She's gotten so beautiful. The kind of beauty forged in adversity.

"I could've used a pre-party to warm up my conversation," Saskia says. "I need a can of D5W to get a word in with these fabulous pipple."

"WD-40," Dane says. "D5W is an IV drip solution."

Saskia rolls her eyes. "Whatever."

"Rhodes scholar, my ass."

"Silence, please."

Huff Jensen comes up behind Dane and puts arms around his shoulders. "All right?"

"All right," Dane says, telling the truth.

The party continues to unfold, and Dane finds his own social tether: a travel agent named Nando. "Hernando," he first introduces himself. "As in Jesus Hernando Christ."

They don't hang out exclusively all night but keep circling back toward each other to share intel and snacks. Nando's love of food borders on a vocation, and he reconnoiters with a plate and a beatific smile. "Dane, you gotta try this. It's tits."

They laugh a lot between bites. Like a forgotten dream, Dane remembers what it's like to be *on*. Slightly astounded to remember he can be a charming person.

"Man, your eyes are ridiculous," Nando says, scraping up the last of some artichoke dip. "You just stand in bars with those baby blues and take numbers?"

Dane laughs. A little guiltily, because only one of his eyes is truly blue. The other is a contact lens.

A quiet but haughty voice in his head clears its throat and says, *They are* my *eyes, thank you very much.*

Dane smiles down at his plate, blinking his lids slowly. Thinking, *Quiet, you. I'm being charming.*

Suddenly Nando extends a hand toward Dane's head. "May I?"

"What?"

"Touch your hair."

"Oh. Sure?"

Nando runs his palm from Dane's forehead to his crown, along the short, thick nap of closely cut hair. Then back again. "That's tight."

Goosebumps rash down Dane's neck and arms. He hasn't been frankly caressed like this in many moons. *Tight* dangles in the air like an invitation.

"Thanks," he says.

Nando licks his lips. "You want to get out of here?"

"What, go to another party?"

"No, to my place."

His eyes hold Dane's gaze.

An infinite silence.

"Oh fuck," Nando says slowly. "Did I read the wrong room?"

"I'm sorry."

"No no no no..." Nando is laughing again, waving a hand. "Shit, man, I pride myself on my superb gaydar and it just wenteth before a spectacular fall."

"I didn't mean to—"

Nando turns down an invisible volume dial. "Zzzt. Not your fault. Now excuse me, I like to be mortified in private."

"Wait," Dane says. "Look—"

"It's all right, you don't have to make me feel better."

"I just want to be honest. Your gaydar is fine. It's the right room. The right *house,* rather. But I'm way out of the game. It's been a while since…" He almost says *since I was propositioned,* but he bites that off and lets the sentence just die.

"I got it," Nando says gently. "So, you want to get out of here?"

"No, but thank you for asking."

"Anytime." Smooth as fuck, Nando passes a business card, and bumps Dane's side as he walks away.

Embarrassed and bewildered, Nando's touch loitering on his head, Dane makes his way back to Saskia. She's tethered herself to Maisie and while they're talking animatedly, Dane can see Saskia is tired.

All at once, Dane is tired, too. As the New Year approaches and the energy in the house ratchets up, he finds himself near tears. People start to gather around the television, flipping between Ryan Seacrest and Anderson Cooper. Dane finds his jacket and heads upstairs, down the hall to the door leading to the attic stairs. The attic is already lit up by a single lightbulb, but Dane thinks nothing of it as he climbs the ladder which goes up to the widow's walk. He pulls on his wool watch cap and steps out into the night, thinking he'll let the New Year wash over him and have himself a good, private cry.

A waft of pot smoke hits him first. Then Dane sees a man is sitting in one of the Adirondack chairs, staring at the skies over Nyack.

Not just any man, but the fox with the ridiculous purple eyes and the slight British accent.

"Hi," Dane says. "Sorry, didn't know someone was already here."

"No worries. I'm just seeking enlightenment."

Dane tries to recall if he and the man were introduced at any point. They weren't. The man's name of course is Liko Greenman, but Dane won't learn that tonight.

"I'm sorry, your name went out of my head," Dane says, he hopes graciously.

Liko smiles. "It'll come back. Sit down."

Dane likes this maneuver, and sits. Liko passes the vape. Dane takes two hits and passes it back, bracing himself for awful icebreakers.

So what do you do?

You live around here?

How do you know Huff and Maisie?

You follow football? How about them…

Nothing. Just uncomplicated, companionable silence. Fingers occasionally touching as they pass the peace pipe.

The mission of the Danelaw was peace, Dane thinks.

"Any resolutions?" Liko asks.

"No," Dane says, tongue thick in his mouth. "Well. Maybe."

"Ah. You resolve to be more decisive."

Dane laughs.

"Tell me," Liko says. "What do you resolve?"

"To live."

"Did that not become an option recently?"

"Kind of. My wife died."

Liko's head flicks toward him. "When?"

"A year in February. She died the day after her birthday."

"Accident?"

"Stroke."

"Instantaneous?"

"No. I mean, she didn't regain consciousness but she hung on a while."

"Until her birthday, you think?"

"Until after. I'm sure of it. It was such a Nomi thing to do."

"Nomi," Liko says. "Beautiful name. Short for something?"

"No. Just Nomi."

"What made it a *her* thing to do?"

"She never knew her real birthday," Dane said. "She was abandoned as a newborn. She might've been born anywhere in the last week of January or the first week in February, nobody could say for sure. Authorities put February first on her birth certificate. One of a dozen things people in power wrote down and she just had to accept. She had no ties to anything. No conviction in any of her vital stats. Not her name. Not her birthday. If she was going to die, it would be on the day *she* chose. So she hung on and died February second. Because fuck them."

Dane waits for Liko to say *I'm sorry.* But he doesn't. The night has been quiet but now an energy starts to build. People spilling out of houses and gathering along River Road. The New Year is approaching.

"Anyway," Dane says slowly. "That's what I tell myself."

Liko nods. "And you resolve to live. Keep living."

"Yeah."

"You have kids?"

"A daughter. Saskia. She's here. Downstairs, I mean."

"What if she weren't?"

This guy doesn't pussyfoot around, Dane thinks.

"What if she weren't at this party or what if she didn't exist?" he says aloud.

"Didn't exist."

"Then I wouldn't either."

"You sure about that?"

Dane exhales. "It's complicated."

"Use short words."

"I was in a…" Dane trails off laughing. "Man, I loathe the word *throuple* but for the life of me, I cannot come up with another word on the fly."

"Throuple does sound like something I'd order back home," Liko says, and his slight accent now thickens: "I'll do the throuple and mash and pull us a pint, love?"

"Whatever you want to call it, I refer to Nomi as my wife but she wasn't my legal spouse. She was married to another man, Ethan. I was their partner. That's how it was on paper but in practice, we were all spouses. The three of us were…"

"Together," Liko said.

"Yes."

"For how long?"

"Twenty-two years."

A low whistle. "How much of that time were they legally married?"

"Twenty-one years."

Liko's eyebrows raise. "You were always together then."

"Always."

"Not an open marriage that invited you in as a third."

"No, it was just us. Always us."

"Why did Nomi and Ethan get married?"

"Because she had cancer and he had the health insurance."

Liko lifts palms to the sky. "God bless America."

"Right?"

"And then Nomi died. But not of cancer."

"Yes."

"Where is Ethan?"

"Gone."

Liko looks at him hard. "Literally or poetically? Use short words."

Dane smiles. "He left me."

"Ouch."

"Yeah. Twenty-two years and turns out, I really was just the third in the marriage."

"What, did he ghost out on you? Or was there a proper breakup?"

"It ended. We said goodbye. Really soon after Nomi died, I sensed him drifting away. I fought like hell to hold on but after a while… Every day, it was like being widowed all over again."

"Well, shit. I won't say *I'm sorry*, because you're probably sick of it. I'll say I'm honestly astounded you're still here."

"Because, my daughter."

"Still."

"You married?" Dane asks.

"Divorced. She left me, so I feel you on that Groundhog Day onslaught. Every morning getting clobbered with the loss."

"Does it get easier?"

"No. It just gets different."

"You got kids?"

"A son. Kyle. He's sixteen. God help me." Liko passes the vape. "What time is it? How much longer we got to suffer this year?"

"Are you suffering?"

"Right now I am feeling no pain."

Dane checks his watch. "About thirty seconds left."

They both get up and lean elbows on the railing. Fireworks are starting to go off over the Hudson. Dane starts to ask his companion's name, then decides he doesn't want to know. Not yet. This is, all at once, a beautifully paranormal moment. Dreamy and surreal. Liko might not even be human. He's a divine messenger or otherworldly guide, come down from the stars to commune with Dane. Ask personal questions and be astounded at their answers. Be astounded by Dane, who is still here. And a charming person.

A roar of celebration two floors below heralds the arrival of 2016. The neighborhood erupts in cries, hoots, sound makers and more fireworks bloom in the sky.

"My daughter's downstairs," Dane says. "I should go find her."

"Yes, you should."

"Happy New Year."

"To you as well."

Dane turns to go but Liko puts a hand on his arm. Then he leans and kisses Dane's cheek.

A beat, and then they hug. Liko's a good hugger. Not a dissatisfying A-frame ladder but a full-frontal embrace with quads and stomachs and chests pressed tight.

Really tight.

"Hey," Liko whispers.

"What?" Dane whispers, thinking he's about to be properly kissed.

"I promise it gets different."

"What's your name?" Dane says, now wondering if the rail of this widow's walk is strong enough to hold the weight of two men.

Liko breaks the hug and steps back. "Go find your daughter. And stay alive. One more year." He points to the roof of the house beneath their feet. "Next year. Right here. Ten to midnight. We'll meet again, I'll ask nosy questions and we'll resolve further."

"Then exchange names?"

"Then exchange names." Now Liko points at Dane's face, stern but playful. "Don't cheat and ask Huff and Maisie. You'll ruin it."

"All right."

"I mean it."

"So do I. Next year. If I can't be here, I'll leave a note."

Dane goes back downstairs to the party, pausing once on a tread to touch his fingertips to his cheek. He passes a mirror and hopes he sees the faint trace of silver lip marks. The kiss of an angel marking him for life.

Only his face stares back. Thin. A little haggard. Lines deeper. Blue eyes shadowed.

No magic. Just a tired, double-screwed widower.

U P ON THE ROOF, Liko Greenman rubs a palm in slow circles on his thumping heart. His lips thrum a little. He'd kissed the blue-eyed man impulsively, and with a pure motive of compassion. But it had been the smoothest male cheek he'd ever kissed. As he drew back, a thought flickered behind his teeth: *That's…odd.*

The widow's walk feels lonely and bereft under the stars of the New Year, and Liko suddenly wants to follow Dane. He doesn't. He's always counseling his son to put twenty-four hours between his impulses and his actions. Liko's put a year between him and the blue-eyed, nameless man. Maybe overkill, but you should always have something to look forward to.

And he *is* looking forward to it.

That guy, he thinks through a sparkling, dreamy haze. *We will meet again. That guy will come back to meet me, and he will be someone in my life.*

B UT FIFTEEN MONTHS will pass until the two men meet again, and it will be Liko who comes to Dane. Bruised and smarting. Savaged and screwed. Not remembering they've met before.

In the skies above the Hudson River, the Universe—who herself has been widowed and screwed innumerable times—sighs in delight. She clutches her toes, clenches her butthole, and waits.

PART ONE
SARIS

"They say that the hare of the nobler sex (i.e. the male) bears the little hares in its womb. Can it be that a bizarre nature has made him a hermaphrodite? They also say that in the mother's womb, along with the tiny little hares, larger babies, previously conceived are carried; in this one can perceive an affront to the law of her inferior nature. Effeminate men who violate that law of nature are thus said to imitate hares, offending against the highest majesty of nature."
—Alexander Neckam, encyclopedist and abbot

THE NAOMI ROAD 1

Ceiling of Cave 407 at Mogao, Lanzhou, China.

WHERE YOU GO

June 2016
Schoenfeld's Farm
Birch Island, New York

Danelaw Strong's hands were in the dirt while his mind was on his wife.

He had let Nomi's magnificent vegetable garden lie fallow last year. In the wake of her sudden death, he had neither the energy nor the heart to prepare, plant, cultivate and tend the ten raised beds. He was still so bitter and angry. His Persephone had been cruelly disappeared into the underworld, and the advent of spring wouldn't bring her back. He'd play the role of Demeter and let it all wither and die.

He missed having the bounty outside his kitchen door, but it took everything he had that first season just to get out of bed, make coffee, manage the day-to-day business of the farm, remember to stick some food in his mouth, and go to bed again. His soul was a city under siege, and the flower beds and vegetable garden were unnecessary mouths. He threw them over the battlements and refused to feel guilty, figuring if Nomi was displeased with his decision, she'd give him a sign. When the wildflowers re-seeded themselves, and the roses put out flush after flush of blooms, and a few rogue tomato plants produced some respectable clusters of fruit, Dane felt Nomi was not just signaling, but rewarding him. The earth was still on his side, and maybe even grateful for the sabbatical.

Thanks for the time off, it said. *I miss her, too. Got your back. We'll try next year.*

Dane felt stronger this spring, ready to give it a go, and he called on his friend Fred to help him.

Fred Pierce didn't put a toe outside their house unless dressed completely in black, and they managed to retain an air of impeccable chic even when shoveling manure.

"Look at you giving immaculate horseshit vibes," Dane said. "How do you do it?"

Fred smiled behind their aviator shades, which were unnecessary on this cloudy day, but an integral accessory to their black cargo pants and form-fitting black T-shirt. Any dirt on them was fashionable and intentional.

"Promise me," they said. "If it gets to be too much, you let it go to weeds and try again next year."

"I promise." Dane's garden plan was nothing close to what it would've been in Nomi's hands. She started everything from seed and mapped out every square inch on graph paper. The raised beds would be crammed with vegetables, flowers and herbs planted in symbiotic combinations and carefully rotated every year. Her treasured rosebushes grew between the beds, spoiled by layers of compost and whole bananas buried by their roots. By July, the garden would be a riot of color, bursting with blooms and produce, stalks and stems and foliage wrestling, dancing, tangling, vying for the best of the sun. Pollinators of all kinds made the garden buzz with activity. Birds swooped through, along with the farm's chickens and ducks, looking for worms and bugs and snails. After a rainstorm, everything sagged and drooped, which made a simple task like gathering lettuce into a rainforest trek.

Dane could never do what Nomi did.

"You're sighing again," Fred said. "You don't have to start perfect, you just have to start. And this is a great start."

Being conservative on his first solo flight, Dane had prepped just four of the beds. He planted only what he'd enjoy picking and eating on a daily basis, and what wouldn't break his heart if he killed it. Lettuce, peas, scallions, parsley, lemon balm, basil, a few cucumber plants, two cherry tomato plants, and two big squares of green beans. Maybe later he'd add some flowers in between. Maybe.

"That it?" Fred said, dusting off their thighs.

"All done." Dane stood up and stretched against the crick in his lower back. "And perfect timing," he said, glancing at the skies. "Looks like rain coming through."

"Nomi's doing."

Dane smiled, gathering up the empty pots and seed packets. "Want a drink?"

"Hell yeah. I expect payment for manual labor."

"Go on in, pour and nosh whatever you want. I just need to grab the mail."

Dane walked down the driveway of Schoenfeld's, worrying at a miniscule barb stuck in the pad of his thumb. The farm looked soft and cool under the darkening skies. He could hear the hum of tractors growing louder as the crew came in from the fields to take shelter. The din of chickens and ducks rose up as if answering a challenge. One of the barn cats was coming up the road, an old tom who had to be on his seventh life. He made no eye contact, but did a neat sashay to slide his ribs against Dane's legs before moving on.

A stone wall divided the property from its adjacent roadways, with two pillars on each side of the driveway opening. One was adorned with a carved medallion of the Green Man: a foliate face of pagan origin. He was the beloved sigil of Schoenfeld's, the wise man and guardian angel of the farm. "Go ask the Green Man" was a thing sighed often at Schoenfeld's, when a problem couldn't be easily sorted.

A mailbox was built into the other stone pillar, and Dane collected the day's junk. It was an election year, so a waterfall of campaign fliers and envelopes spilled out, along with catalogs, the weekly circular from ShopRite, and the cable bill.

And a postcard.

Dane almost flipped past it. Then a fleeting thought, *Wait, that looked legit,* and he doubled back with a flattered curiosity. An actual piece of mail, addressed to him, *Danelaw Strong, c/o Schoenfeld's, 1543 Oak Hill Road, Birch Island, NY.*

The message side read: *"But Ruth replied to Naomi, 'Don't urge me to leave you or to turn back from you. Where you go I will go, and where you stay I will stay.'"*

Later, Dane would insist it took him a minute to figure it out. "I thought the Jehovah's Witnesses were getting creative," he joked. But really, he knew right away. The verse went over his head but he recognized the handwriting instantly. His mouth grew dry. Inside his chest, his heart groped for a chair and sat down. He turned the card over, then he backed up two steps and sat down on the stone wall next to the Green Man.

Never mind the handwriting. He'd recognize the artwork even if he were blind. The finished style of Ethan Hasen's paintings could only be described as hyper-realism. Or as he called it, pathological perfectionism. When he sketched, however, whether with pencil, or pen and ink, he was more relaxed, which lent these drawings a rustic, charming air, reminiscent of Ethan's early career as a children's book illustrator.

Sketched on the postcard was a stylized lotus flower, its inner petals white, the outer petals cross-hatched to black. Within the center circle ran three black hares, their shared ears making a triangle.

Dane flipped the card over, even though he knew no caption was there, describing the drawing. Front and back, this was a bespoke piece of art. The drawing was the ceiling of Mogao Cave 407 in Dunghua, China.

Where you go, I will go.

Dane looked up at the Green Man, as if the carved foliate face had been reading over his shoulder all this time.

Go ask the Green Man.

"He's really doing it, huh?" Dane asked.

The pagan bastard refused to give an answer or even make eye contact.

Dane reached for his phone and called his daughter.

"Deddy," she said grandly.

"Saskia Helen Mary Ruta Hasen-Strong von Schoenfeld."

"Pardon your French."

"Guess what I just found in my mailbox?"

She sighed. "My student loan remittance?"

"No, a postcard from China."

"From Ethan?" A long silence, followed by another sigh. "What's it say?"

He described it to her. "And I just noticed, underneath the quote is a fingerprint."

"Of course," she said. "Ain't no romantic like Ethan Hasen romantic. Well, we knew he was planning this pilgrimage. A blog isn't his style, he wouldn't be caught dead on social media, so this is his way of giving us a status."

"Us? You got a postcard, too?"

"No. Why would I? Dad, he's been texting or emailing between every point A and B. I know where he is. I think he's letting you know."

"Why?"

"Because he's doing this for Mammu."

"Right," Dane said, starting up the drive toward the house.

"And," Saskia said slowly, "if more cards are coming? If he's going to send one from each location? Well, those could be worth a lot of money someday."

"Christ," Dane said, rubbing his eyes.

"How many locations along the route?"

"Fifty-two."

"Fifty-two postcards of every location in the *Three Hares* game. Hand-drawn by Ethan Hasen. That's some serious bank, Dad. I suggest you curb the desire to chuck it in the compost."

"I would do no such thing."

"You were thinking about it. Put it in a safe place for now. If no more arrive, then do what you want with it. Promise?"

"I promise."

"What else are you up to?"

"Me and Fred started the veggie garden. They're in the kitchen, pouring us a drink."

"Perfectly pressed cargos and an Armani T-shirt?"

"With designer work boots."

She laughed. "Give them a hug for me. I gotta run, Deddy. I love you. Keep me…posted."

"Love you, smartass."

He jammed his phone in his pocket and went inside. Fred had poured two glasses of chardonnay and put out some cheese and crackers.

"I thought you wandered off," they said.

"No, I was talking to Saskia."

"How's my babygirl?"

"Good. She says hi." Dane's dog, Salma, put paws on his leg and stretched up to sniff him. "Hello, you." He put down the bundle of mail and slid onto a chair, sighing heavily.

"Jesus," Fred said. "AmEx bill that bad?"

Dane tried to laugh but it came out a shrill yelp.

"Dude, what's going on?"

Dane's friendship with Fred had only one rule: no bullshit. Without a word, he handed over the postcard and watched Fred examine the front, the back, then the front again.

"This looks like Ethan's work," they finally said.

"It is."

"He's in China?"

Dane nodded and drank some wine. "He's making a pilgrimage."

Fred narrowed their eyes. "Don't people usually do that in Spain? Or Canterbury or Mecca?"

"He's following the route of the *Three Hares* game. Sprinkling some of Nomi's ashes in each location."

"How do you know?"

"He told Saskia."

"Oh." Fred ate some cheese, flipping the card over and back.

"Don't get smudges on it," Dane said. "Sask said if more are coming, they could be worth something."

"Like you don't own enough Ethan Hasen originals." They put the card down far from the food and drinks and looked at Dane closely. "You all right?"

"Yeah."

"In my humble opinion, the Bible verse is kind of cringe."

"What else could he have written?"

"Oh, I don't know. How about, *I love you. I miss you. Having a wonderful time, wish you were here. I'm doing this to process my grief and when I get home, maybe we can talk?*"

"Maybe all that is in the fingerprint," Dane said, touching the back of his neck where that same print was tattooed.

Fred nodded. "I'll be quiet now. No bullshit."

"No bullshit."

When the wine was gone, Fred hugged and kissed Dane, then left. Dane went on sitting at the kitchen table, listening to the rain. He poured another drink. He looked at the postcard another twenty times. He sighed a lot. He contemplated throwing his glass against the wall but didn't want to clean up afterward. Instead, glass in hand, he wandered along the walls of the kitchen, which were still hung with Ethan's artwork. Oil paintings, watercolors, pencil sketches. Most of them depicting rabbits or hares.

Dane sat back down and drew his laptop toward him. He'd never deleted the *Three Hares* game off his hard drive, but he'd taken its icon out of the dock at the bottom of the screen. He had to open applications and search for it. His index finger dithered over the tracking pad. Then he clicked.

To the strains of haunting, ominous music, the opening sequence began. First the stylized letters of the Jonathan Henshe Games logo, and the tagline beneath: *Greater Understanding Through Play.*

The logo dissolved and a map of Eurasia took its place. Bounding out of the United Kingdom, a hare jumped the English Channel and began running east. It was joined by a second hare who materialized from the Black Sea and joined its mate's journey, now heading for the Ural mountains. At the same time, a third hare sprang from China and began running west.

"Along the old Silk Road they traveled," a voiceover narrated. "Leaving their mark in art and architecture. Who were they chasing? Or were they themselves being hunted? What secrets did their three shared ears hear? What stories are contained in their eternal circle?"

The music swelled as the hares converged, their separate paths wheeling into a circle. Nose to tail, they chased one another. Until their six separate ears melded to become three, forming a perfect triangle. A threefold rotating symmetry known as a triskelion or a triskele.

The title materialized over the motif: *Three Hares. A Jonathan Henshe Production.*

The screen faded to black again, then a blinding sun burst over the horizon. The player was treated to a breathless, sweeping vista along the Great Wall of China before being taken west, across the Gobi Desert, following the ancient route of the Silk Road. The aerial perspective zoomed in on a city. Subtitles named it *Dunhuang, Gansu Province.*

The player touched down in front of a tall pagoda, built into the face of a rock outcropping. *Mogao,* the subtitles informed. *The Caves of the Thousand Buddhas.*

Dane went inside the pagoda and was faced with a warren of passageways, with numbered cave openings on either side. New players could get lost for hours in this phase of the game, but Dane knew to go straight to cave 407. A panorama around the beautifully decorated space, then a zoom up to the caisson ceiling. And there was the full, technicolor version of the sketched postcard on Dane's kitchen table.

Dane drew a deep breath and slowly exhaled. He moved the cursor to the ceiling and clicked the motif of the Three Hares. They began to spin, making the triangle of their three shared ears rotate.

"Welcome, young explorer," a voice boomed. The player perspective came down from the ceiling and rotated to see the Green Man lounging against the door to the cave. The same foliate face that hung on Schoenfeld's driveway pillar evolved, expanded and transformed into a living god. Leaves grew all over his muscle-packed body, which was robed in flowing shades of pine, leaf, and moss.

"So," he said. "Are you ready to begin?"

Dane dragged fingertips from forehead to chin and blinked at the screen.

"I thought I was done," he said.

THE NAOMI ROAD 2

Ceiling of Cave 139 at Mogao, Lanzhou, China.

A MINOR HULLABALOO

December 31, 2016
Grandview-on-Hudson, New York

A POP OF THE CORK and champagne foamed into two flutes.

"Cheers, motherfucker," Maisie Jensen said. "Welcome to my small, select hootenanny."

"Quite the cordial kerfuffle tonight," Dane said.

"Eh. Just a minor hullabaloo."

Dane clinked his glass to hers. "Wouldn't miss it."

Most of the lights were off in the Jensens' beautiful house on the Hudson. No party. No fabulous pipple. And for Dane, no rooftop reunion with the violet-eyed Brit. Just him and Maisie, a box of spanakopita triangles, and a bottle of Veuve Cliquot to make it classy. Upstairs, Huff was asleep, having retired at 9:30 and floated away on his preferred cocktail of pain meds and sleep aids. 2016 could kiss his ass. He wouldn't even do it the courtesy of seeing it to the door.

"Punch it in the face and give it my regards," he called down. "Stern email to follow."

So Dane and Maisie had their little supper, then went for a swim. When the Jensens bought this house outside Nyack, they regarded the atrium with its small indoor pool as something of an embarrassment. They'd worked hard to achieve their individual successes, and this riverfront house was a shared dream, but the pool was just a *little* much. It remained empty and closed the first two years, almost like a dirty family secret, Huff and Maisie giving the stink eye to anyone who said the word *pool*.

All that changed last October, when Huff had his accident. Now his life revolved around physical therapy, especially swimming. Shame was thrown out and the men were called in. The atrium was renovated, the pool filled and the heater turned on.

"Next year, *inshallah*, New Year's Eve will include swimming," Maisie said. She popped the last bit of spanakopita into her mouth, then checked her phone, which was pinging. "Be right back. He needs some help."

"Everything okay?" Dane said, half out of his seat.

"It's fine, sit down. He has a complicated system of pillows and wedges. One cushion slides out of place and the whole house of bones comes down. I'll just be a minute."

She left the kitchen and Dane closed his eyes, following the sound of her footsteps upstairs and down the hall. He willed everything to be all right. Prayed all would be fixed with the adjustment of a pillow. Pillows, after all, had helped save Huff's life.

Last October, Huff came out of his office on an ordinary Wednesday night and began walking home as usual, absently scanning his phone like any working yahoo at the end of a long day. As he stood still on Broadway, returning an email, a cabbie suffered a seizure, slumped on the wheel and drove his SUV onto the sidewalk. Huff took the hit of the front grille, which broke his pelvis and sent him flying through the window of Pier One Imports. Doctors were sure if Huff had landed on the sidewalk or been crushed against the building's unyielding facade, he'd be dead. Two things saved his life: the cabbie's foot sliding off the gas prior to impact, so he wasn't accelerating, and Huff landing on a sumptuously-made display bed sporting a down comforter, two throw blankets and eight pillows. The bedframe collapsed, the display went to pieces, a few dozen imported tchotchkes shattered, but the memory foam mattress and its luxurious linens closed around Huff like a nonchalant palm catching a tossed set of keys. His injuries were critical, but he would live.

Maisie called Dane from the hospital. "Huff was hit by a car."

"Holy fuck," Dane said, on his feet. "Where is he? Where are you?"

"Lenox Hill."

"Oh my God, Maze."

"Please, Dane. Please, can you come?"

He'd never heard her like this. He didn't know anyone with their shit more together than Maisie. She was the rock. The fortress. The flame that never flickered. Dane took problems to Maisie. Dane called her for assurance, for sympathy, for backup. He never considered himself her mainstay. Maisie cherished him but she didn't *need* him.

"I need you," she cried. "Please can you come?"

He went without a thought, making the ninety-minute drive to midtown Manhattan, which normally tied his stomach in knots. Now he laid on the horn, ran yellow lights, wove in and out of traffic and glared at jaywalkers, willing the city to get the fuck out of his way. Yelling at the windshield the whole time.

"No," he said, pointing a finger at the Universe like it was a disobedient dog. "No. Absolutely not. I lost Nomi, I lost Ethan. Maisie does not lose Huff. Period. Full stop. This is non-negotiable. Get your hands out of our lives and start turning these lights green. I am *not* playing with you…"

For the six hours Huff was in surgery, Dane stayed by Maisie, who was a wild-eyed and desperate tiger, either pacing the perimeter of the waiting room or hunched in a chair with her hands laced behind her neck. She abruptly declared she wanted to go to the hospital's chapel. Dane walked her there. One step inside its cool, quiet interior and Maisie shook her head. No, she didn't want this place. She wanted a cup of coffee. Dane walked her to the hospital's satellite Starbucks, where Maisie shook her head again. She didn't want this either. She stood in the lobby, stunned and bewildered. She looked like she'd dropped five pounds in an hour, like she was lost inside her clothes.

Running on pure intuition, Dane drew Maisie into a restroom and flipped the lock. He hit the light switch, pulled her into his arms and told her to let it go.

Maisie let go. She cried and cried, her voice ricocheting off the tiled walls. The sound of her uncontrolled terror was horrible, made even more so by the pitch dark. But Maisie needed to cry it out and not be seen. So Dane set his teeth, locked his knees, hung on tight and let the tsunami crash down and do its worst. When the tide retreated and Maisie quieted, Dane turned on the light. Maisie looked like her own accident scene, but she didn't look lost anymore. She blew her nose, splashed her face and combed her hair. She went back to the chapel and lit a candle, then to Starbucks and got a coffee. Back on the waiting room couch, she slouched, rested her temple on Dane's shoulder, relaxed the vigil and took a twenty-minute power nap.

"Thank you," she said when she woke.

"Anything," Dane said. "Anything. Anytime. Anywhere."

"You're the first person I thought of. Isn't that funny?"

He understood her perfectly. "It is."

She laced her fingers with his and raised the clump to her mouth. "You're my pipple," she said.

He tucked loose hair behind her ears and kissed her forehead. "We're the best pipple."

"ALL GOOD," MAISIE SAID, coming back into the kitchen. "So what's on the party agenda? I think I got enough in the tank to watch…maybe a quarter of a movie?"

"Actually," Dane said, "I wanted to show you something."

"What?"

He thought about how to phrase it and decided on, "A small art installation."

She raised her eyebrows. "How small?"

"About the size of a dining room table."

She gestured with her hand. "By all means. Are these your creations?"

"I wish." Dane went upstairs to get the bundle of postcards from his backpack. As he dealt them out on the table, Maisie's expression went from confused to expert. Worried wife morphed to shrewd art dealer as she put on her glasses and took professional inventory. She turned each card over, examined it thoroughly, placed it back in the grid, proceeded to the next one.

Dane had received nineteen postcards since June. Six were postmarked from China. One from Russia. Three from Ukraine. Five from Dubai. One from Cairo. One from Seville. And the latest two from the United Kingdom. Each had a different drawing of the Three Hares on the front. The back of every card was the same: the quote from the Book of Ruth, and Ethan's fingerprint.

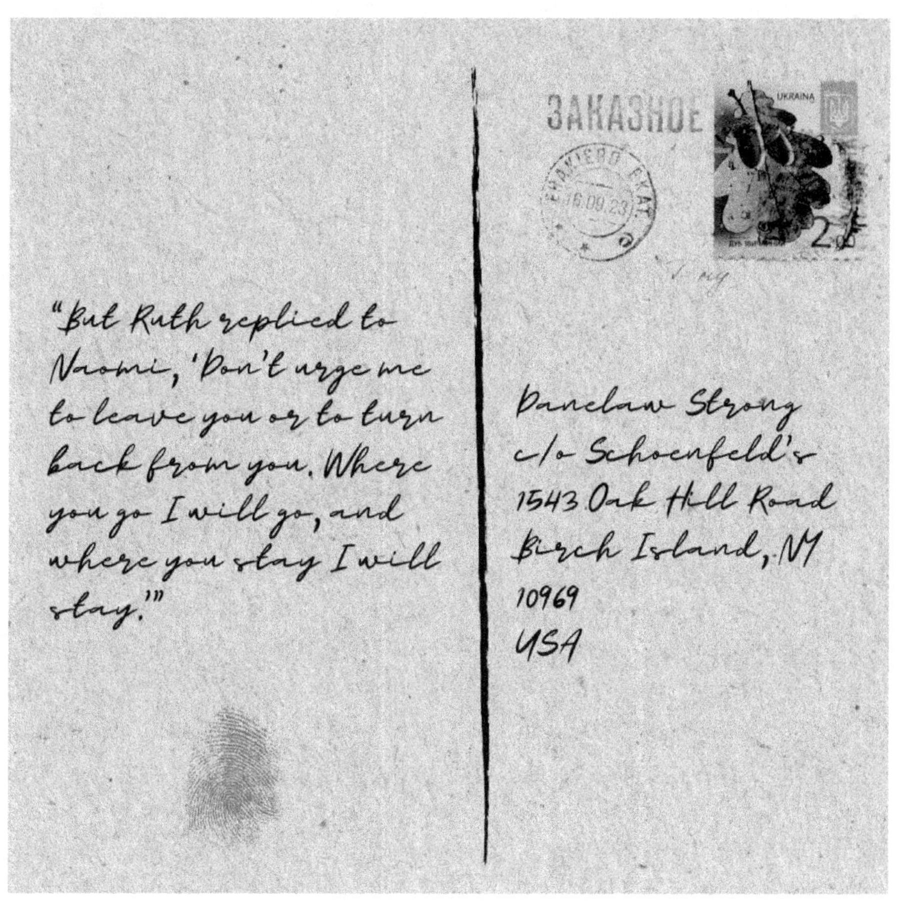

Maisie reached the end, then went back to the top row and started again. "You've been getting these since June."

"Yes."

"And they're exactly following the progression of the *Three Hares* game?"

"Yes. China to Europe, along the old Silk Road."

"Jesus, that goes through all kinds of sketchy places."

"He skipped Central Asia entirely. I brushed up on my Three Hares lore and remembered all the Iranian pieces aren't actually housed in Iran. One's in a museum in Texas. Couple others in Kuwait. I think that's why this batch of five are all postmarked Dubai. He drew them from there before going to Cairo."

"Is he sending duplicates to Saskia?"

"No, just me."

She took a sip of champagne and chewed it thoughtfully. "Do you want my professional or sisterly assessment?"

"Both, please."

"Keep these in a safe, humidity-free place and if I see you put a rubber band around them again, I will disown you."

"What's the professional assessment?"

She pointed toward the front door. "Leave this house."

He took his own smug sip of champagne.

"Anyway, I'm afraid the sisterhood is at a loss. Do we just take these cards at face value, or is Ethan trying to tell you something? Is this a pilgrimage or an apology tour? Or both? I don't know."

"What am I going to do?"

"Do you have to do anything?"

"Eventually." He gestured toward the table. "China to Europe along the Silk Road. He's in the UK already. If he's following the route of the game, he'll finish in Devon, then go back to the continent. France, Switzerland, Germany. The game ends in Paderborn Cathedral. At the Drei-Hasen-Fenster. Then what?"

Maisie slowly shook her head.

"When I get a postcard from Paderborn, the game and the pilgrimage are over."

"You think he'll come home?"

Dane nodded.

"How do you feel about that?"

His nodding head now swiveled side to side.

"I'll support you no matter what," she said. "On one hand, you do not have to give him a nanosecond of your time and energy. On the other…"

The sentence went nowhere. Dane heard the kitchen cuckoo clock whir to life and its doors fly open. The wooden bird within sprang out with a two-tone chirp. Twelve times in all.

"Happy New Year," Maisie said.

Dane leaned and put his head against hers. "This was a real swell hootenanny."

She sighed beneath his temple. "It was not the plan."

No, Dane thought. *No, it wasn't. I'm supposed to be on the roof with a violet-eyed man. Getting asked nosy questions. Resolving further. Exchanging names.*

Maybe getting kissed. I literally counted the days until tonight. I looked forward to this party like a girl plans her wedding. I was picking out what to wear months ago. I banked so much emotional capital in this vault. I was supposed to see him again. Who was he? What's his name?

He almost asked. Why not? The dream was over, it was a year Dane would never get back. Why not just ask Maisie: *Hey, last year I met a guy at your party. British. Total fox. Amazing eyes. Know who I'm talking about?*

But Danelaw Strong was a compassionate and attentive man, and he saw Maisie was exhausted, and occupied with far more important matters.

"On second thought, fuck everything," he said, scraping up a smile from the bottom of his soul's barrel. "More bubbly?"

"I can barely finish this," she said, twirling the stem of her flute.

"Forget it. Go to bed, I'll finish it myself. There's two more bottles we can open tomorrow. For mimosas."

"Visiting nurse is coming at eight," Maisie said absently. "Ugh, drawing the short straw to work on New Year's Day. I feel terrible."

"Then we'll gift both bottles to the nurse."

"You're brilliant."

They hugged and kissed, said goodnight. With a last reminder to turn off lights, Maisie went upstairs.

Dane put on his jacket, hat and gloves and went up to the widow's walk. There he finished the champagne, but didn't even get buzzed. He sat in one of the Adirondack chairs and laced his fingers behind his head. Staring over the Hudson and waiting for a rendezvous he knew wouldn't come. The day was over. The year was over. The waiting was over. All of it was over.

He's not coming, said a voice in his head. *Let's just go to bed. Enough torture. We'll get up tomorrow and find something else to look forward to.*

Dane had learned recently that some people didn't have inner monologues. No little voice narrating them through the day, making observations, rationalizing, asking and answering questions. Those people looked blankly at the concept, asking, "What voice in your head? What are you talking about?" While Dane looked back at them, stunned, because he couldn't imagine life without the voice that lived in his head in general, but spent most of its time behind his left eye. His blue eye. The voice was both a part of him and apart from him, and the voice was female.

Some people had inner monologues. Danelaw Strong had Diane.

I'm so sorry, Diane said. *These things happen. Life happens. You missed your second date with that guy. But Huff is alive. He's safe downstairs, sleeping, and it's all that matters.*

Still Dane sat. Patient and disappointed. Checking his watch through the year's first hours and hoping.

Diane sat with him. Patient and attentive. Checking on him.

And she hoped, too.

A GRANDER VOICE

1993
Schoenfeld's Farm
Birch Island, New York

"WHEN YOU TALK to yourself," Dane asks his friends, "when you think things through in your mind, is it a female or male voice?"

"Male," Ethan says.

"Are you sure?"

Ethan goes still and quiet. A little smile around his mouth. "God, it's weird when you pay attention to your inner monologue."

Nomi tilts her chin as if listening to faraway music. "My everyday inner blather sounds like me," she finally says. "But if I'm calming or reassuring myself, it's kind of a different me. It's an older voice. Like a *grander* voice."

"A wise, witchy voice," Dane says, and Nomi points at him with raised, approving eyebrows.

"Weird my mind never shuts up but I never really think about how it sounds inside my head," Ethan says. "But it's definitely male. What's yours, Dane?"

"If I'm just going about business, making a to-do list or doing a math problem, it's male. If I'm reading, it's male. If I'm talking myself off a ledge, it's definitely female. My male voice worries, my female voice reassures. If I'm framing out a conversation in my head—you know how you mentally prepare a script? That's always female."

"Your phone voice," Nomi says. "I hate making phone calls to anyone I don't know personally. Someone once said to me, *Be your own secretary.* So now I have this whole other voice for the phone."

"Exactly," Dane says. "The voice that rehearses a conversation in my head is female. But the voice that rehashes the conversation later and agonizes over stupid things I said is male."

"Huh," Ethan says. "That's so cool."

Dane loves him.

"I'm going to be so self-conscious next time I make a phone call," Nomi says.

"Does your secretary have a name?" Dane asks.

"You mean, do I dial and say, *This is Katherine Jones calling to make an appointment for Ms. Misteria. M as in Mary…*"

Dane laughs. "Just in your head. Does your phone voice or your wise witch voice have a name?"

"Katherine Jones."

"Really?"

"No." Nomi's quiet a moment. She's sitting on the pool steps, arms wrapped around her knees. Her hair slicked back from her face. She looks at Dane as if measuring him.

He looks back and loves her.

"Laugh at me and I will bury you," she says.

Dane, who is the last person to laugh at anyone's inner monologue, draws an X over his heart.

"So my witch voice," Nomi says. "Her name is Ruta Skadi. It's a character from a b—"

"*His Dark Materials*," Dane says. "Philip Pullman."

Nomi smiles in a way Dane's never seen before. "You know that series?"

"Who doesn't?" Ethan says.

"Hey, you'd be surprised, the number of people wandering around the earth, unaware those books exist." She tilts her chin at Ethan, gaze skeptical. "Who's Ruta Skadi?"

"Queen of the Latvian witch clan," Ethan says.

Dane makes a buzzer noise. "So sorry, she was actually Queen of the Lake Lubana clan. Good try. Thanks for playing."

Ethan gives a moan of defeat and sinks under the water, flailing.

"Holy shit," Nomi says. "You guys are my pipple. Most times when I say the name Ruta Skadi, people think it's some kind of potato casserole."

Dane laughs as Ethan surfaces, flipping his hair out of his face.

Fuck, he's gorgeous, Diane says.

Dane silently agrees, trying not to stare. Ethan's so sleek and shiny. Droplets in his eyebrows, lashes separated in spikes. Wet all over, even his teeth. They gleam in a soaked smile as he says, "Well, Nome, in terms of inner monologues, you could do worse."

"Hers is the voice that talks you off a ledge?" Dane asks.

"Ruta Skadi adopted me," Nomi says. "We did a family tree unit in school, which of course put me in a weird spot. I didn't want to trace my foster family's ancestors, I didn't want to do nothing, so I made myself into Ruta Skadi's granddaughter and invented a whole family history."

"Shut up."

"I fucking love you," Ethan says, floating on his back.

"I got an A," Nomi says. She pushes off the steps and glides toward Ethan, rolling on her back as well, until the crowns of their heads touch. "Come over here, Strong."

Dane does, floating on his back and putting his head with theirs.

"See, now we're three hares," Ethan says.

"Three is a magic number," Nomi says.

Dane is quiet, floating on a raft of love, listening as the water ripples against his ears. He drifts and bumps into Ethan. Then bobs the other way and nestles against Nomi. Back and forth, one is volleyed against the other two.

"Dane?" Nomi says.

"Mm."

Her hand finds his under the water. "Does your voice have a name?"

He squeezes his eyes shut. Squeezes her hand tight.

"Diane," he says softly.

She takes in a little quick breath. "Oh wow."

Ethan flips over and treads water. "Holy shit," he breathes. "Diane. Of course. It's Dane with an I."

Dane and Nomi roll and tread too, three heads bobbing in the pool.

"No," Ethan says. "Wait. Not Dane with an I. Dane with a…"

He moves closer and touches a finger to Dane's left cheekbone.

"Dane with an *eye.*"

Dane laughs, tackles Ethan and they sink under the water. Nomi dives down into the bubbling tangle of limbs too. They come up gasping, splashing, grabbing, roaring with laughter. Not yet in love, but well on their way.

THE NAOMI ROAD 3-26

Postcards sent between July 2016 and September 2016

Ceiling of Cave 205 at Mogao,
Lanzhou, China

Ceiling of Cave 237 at Mogao,
Lanzhou, China.

Ceiling of Cave 397 at Mogao,
Lanzhou, China.

Ceiling of Cave 406 at Mogao,
Lanzhou, China.

*Silver vase, State Hermitage
Museum, St. Petersburg, Russia.*

*Gravestone carving, Jewish
Cemetery, Sataniv, Ukraine.*

*Painted ceiling, Gwozdziec
Synagogue, Ukraine.*

*Painted ceiling, Chodorow
Synagogue, Ukraine.*

Postcards mailed October-December 2016. All postmarked from Dubai, United Arab Emirates, and depict the Three Hares in Central Asian and Middle Eastern art. With the exception of the Cairo ceramic shard, it's unlikely the artist sketched these cards on site. For example, the brass tray is of Iranian origin but is currently housed in the Dallas Museum of Art in Texas.

Terracotta plaque, Swat Archeological Museum, Baricot, Pakistan.

Copper coin of Iranian origin, private collection.

Brass tray of Iranian origin, Keir Collection, Dallas Museum of Art

Lead and brass tray, Al-Sabah Collection, Dar al-Athar al-Islamiyah, Kuwait.

Silver bowl, Al-Sabah Collection, Dar al-Athar al-Islamiyah, Kuwait.

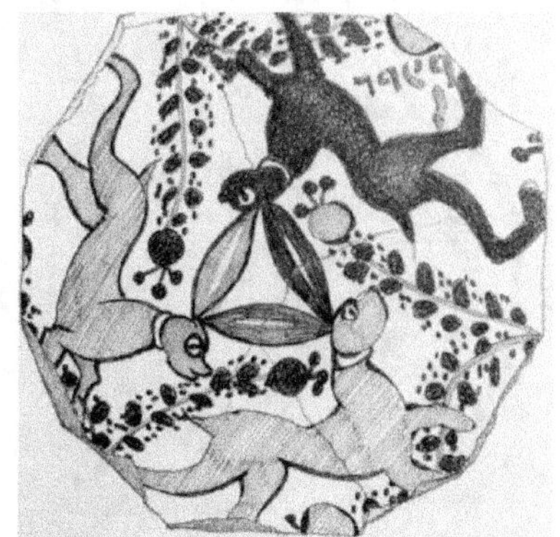

Ceramic shard, Museum of Islamic Art, Cairo, Egypt.

Postcards sent between December 2016 and March 2017

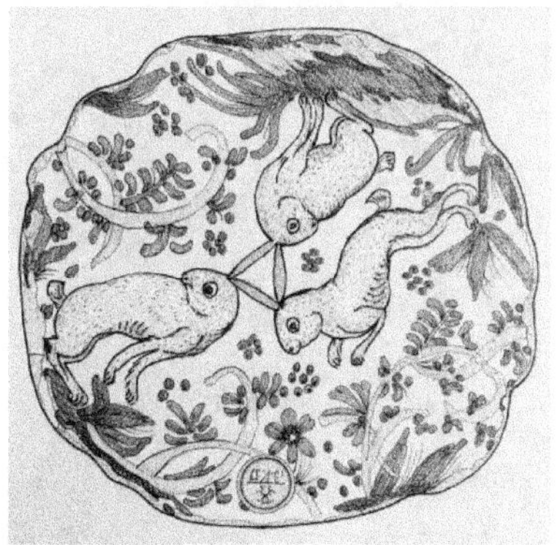

Bottom of a ceramic water bottle, private collection, Seville, Spain.

Stained glass window, Holy Trinity Church, Long Melford, Suffolk, UK.

Nave tile, St. Mary's church, Long Crendon, Buckinghamshire, UK.

Roof boss, Selby Abbey, Selby, Yorkshire, UK.

Nave tile, Chester Cathedral, Chester, Cheshire, UK.

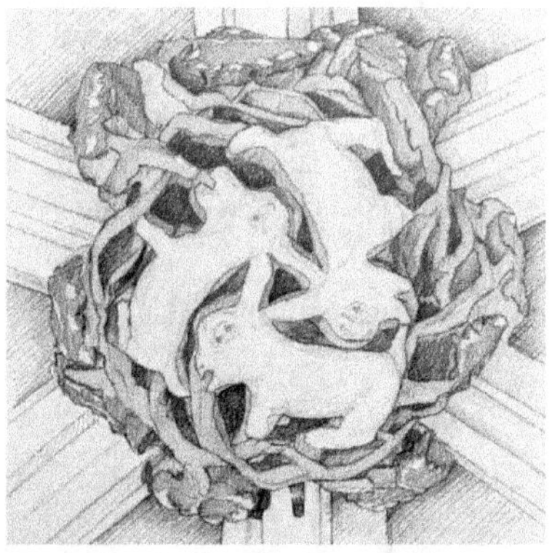

Roof boss, Lady Chapel at St. David's church, Pembrokeshire, Wales, UK.

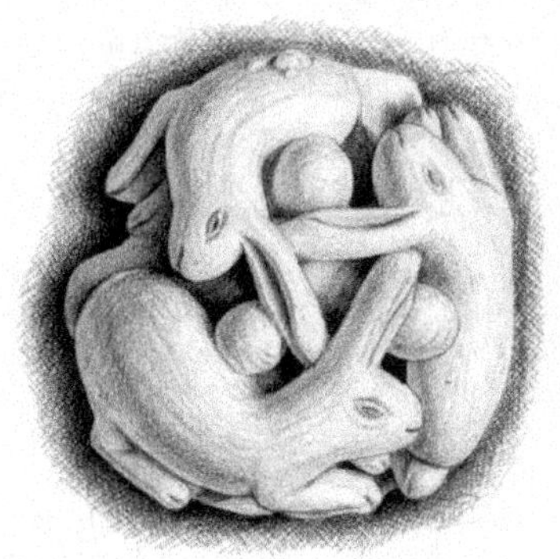

Stone boss, St. Aidan's church, Llawhaden,
Pembrokeshire, Wales, UK.

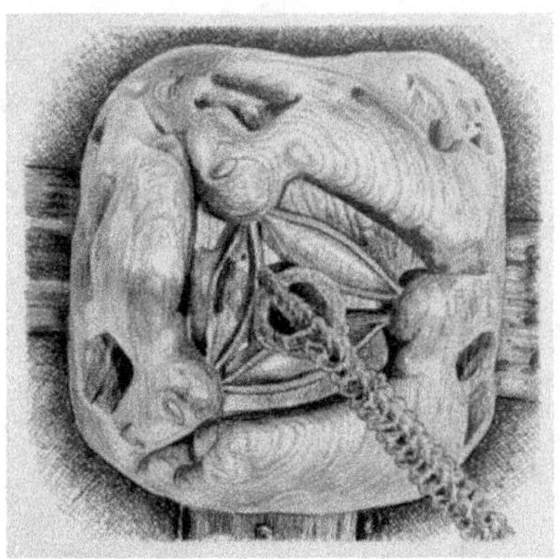

Roof boss, Cotehele Chapel, Church
of St. Katherine and St. Anne,
Calstock, Cornwall, UK.

Roof boss, St. Pancras' Church,
Widecombe-in-the-Moor, Devon, UK.

Roof boss, St. James' Church,
Ashreigney, Devon, UK.

A REASON TO LIVE

March 2017
Birch Island, New York

Liko Greenman stood at the crossroads, looking not for the Devil, but himself.

In one week, he'd learned how many roads a rural town like Birch Island could have, and he'd just about walked them all. From every charming street in the town proper, to the clusters of residential roads, to two-lane highways along the outskirts. From sidewalk to gravel shoulder, he'd walked up one side and down the other, checking off each trek on his map. He'd combed the town thoroughly with no success. He'd either have to give everything a second look, or go home and admit he'd been had.

The crossroads lay soft in the chill of a mid-winter afternoon. The intersection was best friends with the cardinal points, with Route 34 running north and south, and Oak Hill Road chasing the sun. One quadrant had a large pond studded with ducks, with a single, enormous pine tree at its far end. Across the road from the pond was a little pub. The third quadrant had an old barn surrounded by dead grasses and scrub. The fourth was a farm enclosed by a stone wall, one of a half-dozen Liko had noted during his explorations, all packed away neatly for the season. This one's road sign read *Schoenfeld's: Farm to Market.*

He felt in his pocket for the letter which had sent him on this so far fruitless journey.

JHG
Jonathan Henshe Games
"Greater Understanding Through Play"

Dear Mr. Greenman,
Your recent post on Reddit was brought to our attention. We extend our deepest condolences on the tragic loss of your son and applaud your desire

to solve the mystery of the Three Hares *game in his memory. No words can make things better, but a perhaps a clue to start you on a journey would make things different.*

Go to Birch Island, New York, and look for yourself along the roadside.
With our sympathy in this time of great sadness,
Jonathan Henshe Games

When the letter arrived, Liko was reminded of the apathetic Milo in *The Phantom Tollbooth,* coming home to find the mysterious gateway to Lands Beyond and deciding there wasn't anything better to do. It was probably a cruel hoax, and Liko didn't post about the letter on Reddit or any of the gaming forums. Still, coming up on a year after Kyle's death, Liko was running out of ways to pass, waste and kill time. Maybe mid-winter wasn't conducive to a tramp around unknown Lands Beyond—he opened Google maps and learned Birch Island wasn't on a coastline or in a body of water, just a dot in landlocked Orange County. But he had to do something. It was a drive to New York, not a flight to Mongolia. After years of saying he could work from anywhere, he should put it into practice. Take a week, have a change of scene, go on a little quest. What the hell, even if the letter were a hoax, it had a bit of intrigue and magic that made Liko's soul lift its head in curiosity. He hadn't felt curious about anything in a long, long time.

He booked an Airbnb, packed a bag and went. He opened his mind, suspended his disbelief and followed instructions.

Go to Birch Island, New York, and look for yourself along the roadside.
After a week of walking and searching, he suspected he'd been conned.
He didn't want to be conned.
It was just too cruel.
"Don't do this to me," he murmured to the crossroads.
Was it all some Zen exercise? Walking up and down these byways, he found nothing *but* himself. He glanced around, ascertaining he was alone, then shut his eyes and whispered, "Self, show thyself."
He opened his eyes.
Nothing. Except himself.
He closed his eyes again. "What, I'm all I have left? I still have me? Is that the metaphor? I know already. Having only me is my problem. I don't want to be out here searching for myself. I'm sick of myself…"

The blare of a car horn startled him out of the lament and moved him onto the shoulder. "Find myself dead by the roadside. Funny."

He sat on the stacked stone wall by the sign reading *Schoenfeld's* and exhaled a cloud of steam. Let the record show he moved out of the way. He didn't stand still and let the car mow him down. He had a reason to live.

Dear Mr. Greenman, your recent post on Reddit was brought to our attention.

Liko reached for his phone and opened the Reddit app. He had 132 new messages, all of them comment notifications on his famous post.

> *r/Three Hares Mystery*
> *RIP Kyle Dalusio Greenman (@kgr33n) •Jan 14 2017•*
> *Lkgr33n*

Hey gang. This is Liko Greenman, Kyle's dad, and you can see I've made my own account instead of using Kyle's old one. I wanted to come on this forum and thank you from the bottom of my heart for all your love and compassion and support. I was astounded how many of you messaged after he died, telling how much you loved and missed him. I didn't have the strength or bandwidth to respond but I promise I read every single one and I go back often to read them again. They keep him alive, especially on the days when it's just so hard to take in he's gone. On the really bad days, I come to this community and I always find a recent post or two that mentions him. So I know he's not forgotten. I don't have words to say how it comforts me.

I'm not a gamer, but from the perspective of a tragically unhip dad keeping tabs on what his teenage son was doing online, even I knew Three Hares *was something special. I told Kyle if I had time, it was a game I could easily learn to love. Usually I told him as I was shutting him down for the night. By the way, what time is it? Shouldn't you be in bed?*

Anyway, it seems now I have nothing but time, and sleep isn't a friend of mine, so I've joined the community as a player. Last night I finally finished the game and arrived at the Chamber of the Green Man and its yet-unsolvable mysteries. Needless to say, as a Greenman myself (ha ha), I've become really invested, and I've been lurking this sub to read all the latest harebrained theories.

Sorry. Children may die, but Dad jokes never do.

Yikes. Anyway. The point of this post is my son died and I'm just wandering around lost. Everything is awful. I need a job. Well, I have a job. I mean I need a purpose. I'm not good company and I don't want people. I need a single-player obsession. A quest. I need to finish something Kyle started. He loved this damn game and died without knowing all its secrets. I need to find them. I need to solve this mystery. I'm going to crack this chamber if it's the last thing I ever do.

You read it here first. Now get off the computer and go to bed, all of you.

Love from your new dad,

Liko

The post had over 65,000 comments. Sixty. Five. *Thousand.*

His thumb scrolled down the thread. Comments about Kyle. Tributes to Kyle. Memories of Kyle.

God, that kid was so loved.

Liko was weeping now. It ceased to surprise him anymore. Crying was part of his daily routine and he'd reached an almost casual treatment of the jags. Every day at some point, he'd take a piss, brush his teeth, eat something and cry. He was reminded of Kyle's mother, Janelle, who suffered morning sickness for seven out of nine months and came to regard vomiting as part of her daily commute to work. She'd pull her car to the shoulder, nonchalantly puke, pop a piece of gum and proceed on her way.

Come to think of it, she'd divorced Liko in much the same manner, bringing the marriage to a gentle rolling stop on the road of life. She cracked the door, hurled him out and drove off, folding a minty-fresh new start into her mouth.

The sun was slanting toward the western fields. It was colder and Liko's eyes and nose were clogged. He almost mopped both with the Henshe letter, then went for his sleeve instead, just as a car came along Oak Hill Road and slowed by the wall. The passenger window slipped down and the driver leaned across the console to speak.

"You all right?"

"Yeah," Liko said, too embarrassed to make eye contact. "Yeah, just feeling some shit."

"I see."

"I'm okay."

"You sure?"

"Yeah. Thanks."

"Well…" The man sat back, then leaned on the console again. "Don't stay out too long. No need to freeze on top of feeling shitty."

Liko managed a weak laugh. "I won't."

"All right then." The man did his little dance again, sitting back, then canting sideways toward the window. This time he pointed at the farm within the stone wall. "Listen, I live there. When you're done feeling your shit and you need a drink of water, knock on the door."

"That's cool of you. Thanks. I'm all right. Just…out here looking for myself along the roadside."

What the hell, he thought. *Maybe it's a code phrase only people in Birch Island understand.*

No such luck. The man just gave a puzzled smile. "Well, be careful."

"I will."

"Take care."

Liko watched the taillights as the car drove another fifty yards, then turned through an opening in the stone wall, flanked by two pillars. The car stopped. The driver got out and went to the mailbox built into one of the pillars. He got back in and the car headed up to the farmhouse and parked. In the thin, crisp air, Liko could hear the muffled *ker-thunk* when he shut the door.

He raised his chin, almost certain the driver was holding still, fingers on the door handle, looking back toward the stone wall.

Liko raised a hopeful palm.

I'm right here.

Along the roadside.

Can you help me?

His eyes and face were freezing. His nose was still running. His ass was numb. Crying was thirsty work.

He got up.

Snow had fallen recently in Birch Island. The roads were clear but icy drifts ringed the fields and dirty, salt-encrusted hills remained at all four corners of the intersection, still showing teeth-marks from the plow. Schoenfeld's driveway pillars were half-buried in snow. Liko walked by them, his eyes bleary from crying. He almost didn't see it. He shouldn't have seen it. He had no reason to see it.

Except maybe he was supposed to see it.

Emerging from the pile of dirty snow against one of the pillars was the top of a circular, carved decoration. A plaque attached to the stacked stones.

Liko stopped.

The carvings were leaves.

He reached his ungloved fingers and dug at the icy mound, breaking it off in flakes and chunks.

A foliate face emerged, leaves arranged around the eyes, nose and mouth.

Just the way it looked in the *Three Hares* game.

Liko was shaking now, but not from the cold.

"You," he whispered.

The Green Man smiled back.

And you, he said. *Along the roadside.*

Liko's frozen hands scraped at the snow, digging it out of the carved crevices. It was a beautiful piece, a good foot in diameter. The Green Man: ancient pagan symbol of nature, fertility, and mysteries older than God. The motif adorned thousands of churches and cathedrals, a tenacious reminder of all that came before. It reigned in the chamber at the end of Kyle's favorite video game, guarding tantalizing secrets of what might be in the future.

Along the roadside in Birch Island, New York, a Greenman stared at the Green Man. Suffused with relief, gratitude and some old, forgotten emotion that might have been joy. The letter wasn't a cruel hoax. This was real. It was real. The Green Man was here, and it was magic. Liko had solved the riddle, completed the quest, achieved his objective, completed the mission. He'd found himself along the roadside.

He hesitated, then put a palm on either side of the plaque and kissed the Green Man smack between the leafy eyebrows. Then he thrust his icy hands in his pockets and walked up the driveway.

He rang the front door's bell. A dog barked from within. The porch light went on. A man in a backward ball cap appeared, looked through the thin side window, and opened the door, smiling broadly.

"We meet again."

AMONG THE RECIPIENTS

Dane meant it as a welcoming line, but the moment "We meet again" formed a word bubble in the air, he realized it was true.

Diane gasped, *Oh my God, it's him.*

Holy shit, it's you, Dane thought.

The rooftop angel seemed half of what he'd been on that New Year's Eve. Definitely grayer. Alarmingly thinner. With a silver-threaded beard that barely hid the gauntness in his face.

But the eyes.

Those amazing, absurd, who-gave-you-permission purple eyes. Dane would've known them anywhere.

What happened next couldn't have taken more than two seconds, but Dane felt time slow down as a melee of thoughts collided, fought, and rationalized their way to a decision.

He was first suffused with a euphoric delight that was almost triumphant. *You found me,* his atoms sang. This man had clearly gone all over the world looking for his lost, nameless companion. Finally arriving here, worn down to a thread, but intent on claiming Dane as his own. Because it was meant. It was all meant to be.

You found m— Wait, do you even remember me?

The joy gave way to consternation because this dude was looking straight through Dane without a shred of recognition. His beautiful eyes red-rimmed and bleary, he looked more than tired. Something in his demeanor was utterly broken. And blank. A soldier returning from a war that had not been won. He didn't recognize Dane. Hell, if Gene Simmons in full makeup had opened the door, this guy might not recognize him either.

But then Dane remembered.

Oh shit…

The night of the party, Dane had been covering up his brown eye. He needed Diane's blue eyes to do brave things, like go be social, reinvent himself as an expert listener, and gracefully decline an unexpected proposition from… Wow, what was that guy's name again?

Nando, Diane said absently. *Short for Hernando. As in…*

Jesus Hernando Christ, Dane thought, blinking his eyes as if trying to signal this wayfaring stranger by Morse code. No use. He'd been at a board meeting with Orange County Agriculture and Farmland Protection and while he didn't need bravery among any strangers who'd be present, he noticed people tended to stare at his two different eyes more than they listened to his words. So he covered up the blue and went all brown. It was easier.

Brown-eyed and unrecognizable, he looked at his former crony and grasped it might be for the best. The way this guy was barely holding it together, it might be necessary to keep the conditions and circumstances just as they were on that New Year's Eve. Nameless and otherworldly.

Which sucked, frankly. All that long mourning year, Dane had kept the encounter tucked in a pocket of his mind like a worry stone. When things got especially tough, he'd close mental fingers around the pact he made with a mysterious man and squeeze it tight. Thinking, *I have to make it to New Year's Eve. I have a date with a violet-eyed fox. I promised him. Stay alive for Saskia. I just gotta get through the next five minutes. The next hour. This month. Five more months. One more month…*

The discipline of not cheating and asking Huff and Maisie who that guy was. The often toe-curling anticipation of it all. Trudging across a desert of grief, stalwartly putting one foot in front of another because the New Year's Eve date loomed ahead like an oasis. But then Huff Jensen had his accident and the party was kiboshed. Dane went over to the house anyway, just to keep company and help Maisie out. He'd sat on the roof, hoping against hope, even though he himself had sent the mass cancelation email to everyone in the Jensens' address book. No doubt the violet-eyed man was among the recipients.

But now here he was, standing on Dane's porch, looking destroyed. The roles had thoroughly reversed. Time had not been good to this man and it was Dane's turn to serve a purpose. Be nothing more than a gentle, anonymous safe space for this traveler to rest a little while.

Diane was making Dane's blue eye twitch at corner as she whispered, *Be careful here.*

As if to emphasize, a little high-pitched whine buzzed in Dane's left ear. A warning bell. A finger pointing to counsel extreme caution.

Be really, really careful with him.

All this time, Dane had been clutching the postcard from today's mail. The twenty-seventh of his growing collection, postmarked from an English village called Bridford. His hand relaxed and he set the card down on the hall table, opening the door a little wider.

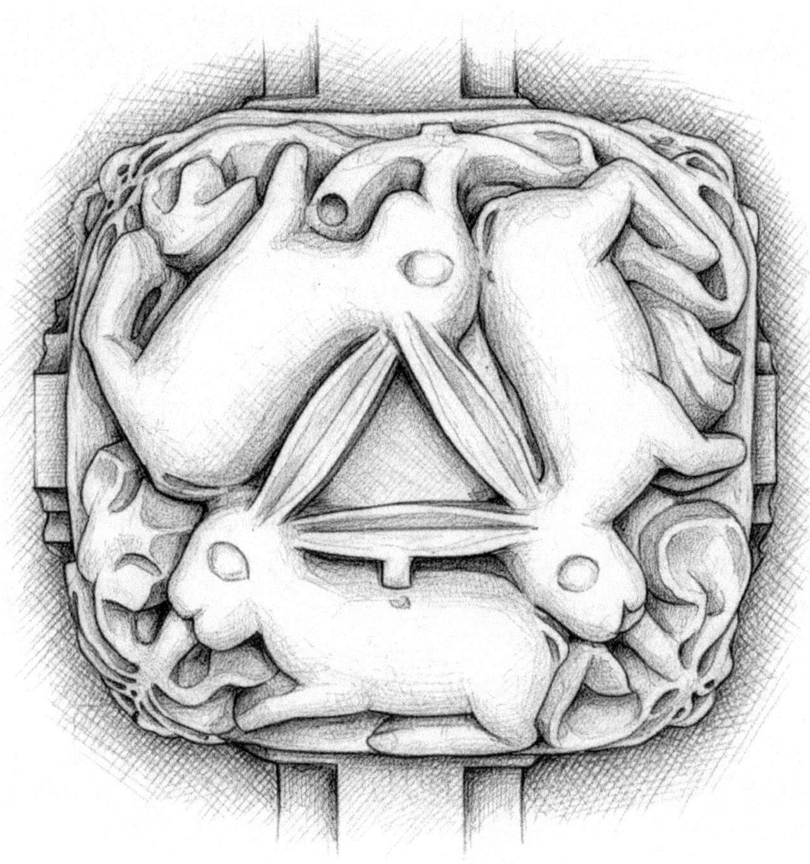

I'M HOME NOW

Feeling weirdly shy, Liko smiled at this good Samaritan. "I'll, uh…take that drink of water?" The dog put paws on Liko's hip and stretched up high, first looking for attention, then jumping for it. "Hey, you," Liko said, rubbing her head.

The man took hold of the dog's collar. "Salma, no. Down. Sorry, she's not usually a jumper. Woman, what's wrong with you? Get." He shooed the dog behind him and beckoned to Liko. "Come in, come in."

Liko wiped his feet and followed the man through a darkened living room into a kitchen you could play touch football in.

Oh, a little voice piped up in his mind. *We're home.*

If Heaven had a kitchen, this would be it. Or maybe it was better described as a kitchen with an attached sitting room, for at one end, a couch and a pair of mismatched easy chairs were grouped around a fireplace.

A fireplace in the kitchen. *Brilliant,* Liko thought, an immediate and extremely cozy vista unfolding before him. A long winter's day with nothing to do but lounge on the couch and read. Look up to watch the snow falling, look down to doze off mid-chapter. Sip coffee until noon, then nurse a good whiskey while something cooked on the stove. Watch as the snow piled deeper outside but alas, nothing for it, nothing to do but go on sitting in front of the kitchen fire.

Maybe it would start snowing right now. Maybe a freak ice storm would bring a tree down across power lines, closing off Oak Hill Road, and Liko would be stuck here tonight.

"Water?" the man asked. "Or something else?"

Whiskey neat, by the fire, Liko thought, and aloud said, "Water's fine."

He turned to take in the rest of the immense space. This was no staged, showroom kitchen but the busy heart of the house trying to keep two steps ahead of the chaos. The dishwasher was open, towels hung askew, pots stacked in the sink. A basket of paper recycling on the verge of avalanche. A laptop open at one end of the long table, surrounded by papers and envelopes, a cluster of bright orange Post-its stuck across the screen's edge.

Liko drew fingers along the tabletop, impressed. Five chairs on either side, two at each end, and surely it could squeeze in more on Thanksgiving. He took in a sturdy hutch laden with china and serving pieces. A credenza with a good assortment of booze and glassware. Over it hung a replica of the Green Man plaque from the driveway pillar. Artwork was displayed on all the walls, and a lot of it depicted hares and rabbits. Little rabbit figurines were tucked in the hutch, too, peeking between stacks of plates and cups.

Liko was definitely in the right place but unsure what to do. Kyle always said to click on everything in sight, but that was fine for video games, not when you were in a stranger's house.

Liko studied the man as he poured from a Brita. He looked in his late thirties, maybe. On the short side, but lean and fit in jeans and a fleece. He'd turned his cap forward and pulled it low, but what Liko could see of his face was…

A long-atrophied part of Liko's brain stirred to life and remarked, *Huh. He's a bit of all right.*

The dog bumped at Liko's legs and he bent to pet her. Her face was bisected cleanly in half from crown to muzzle, with one side pure white, the other side brown.

"Is this a border collie?" Liko asked.

"Australian Shepherd. Here you go."

"Thanks." Liko chugged the water in a few thirsty gulps. He looked up, running a hand on his mouth. "That's better."

The man said nothing. He'd backed up to the sink and was staring hard at Liko. His eyes were deep brown and they looked confused. Maybe even a little scared.

"Something wrong?" Liko said.

The man shook his head. "No. Sorry. I was just remembering something. Anyway. You need a ride into town?"

"Nah, I'm good." Liko motioned toward the kitchen door. "Go out that way or the front?"

"Either is fine but you don't have to go."

Liko set the glass on the table. "Thanks for the kindness. I'm Liko."

"Dane."

"Dane Schoenfeld?"

"What? Oh. No. That's just the name of the farm."

"Thanks again." Liko turned the knob, then stopped. "I need to ask you a question."

"All right."

"Will you be home tomorrow?"

"Is that the question?"

"No. I mean will you be home tomorrow so I can ask you something."

"I'm home now. Why not ask me now?"

"I'm not sure what the question is." An awkward beat, then he added, "My last name is Greenman."

Dane's gaze flicked to the foliate face on the wall and back to Liko. Then he crossed his arms but only breathed, "Huh."

"I also have a personal rule of putting twenty-four hours between my impulses and my actions."

Now Dane's eyes crinkled. "Good rule."

Goosebumps waterfalled down Liko's skin. The twenty-four-hour rule was one of many fatherly adages he hammered into Kyle's head, but the déjà vu shiver in his bones wasn't about Kyle. It was from something else.

Slowly, Liko felt his face morph into the same expression of confusion that had wreathed Dane's gaze a few minutes ago. When he'd been remembering something.

Liko was remembering, too. Remembering something he forgot. Or forgetting what he remembered.

This has happened before, he thought.

Dane put up a palm. "I'll be home tomorrow, Liko Greenman."

"All right."

They held gazes one more beat.

Then Liko left. He walked down the driveway and toward the road. Right by the Green Man pillar, the thought came to him, simple and tantalizing: *I know that guy.*

BLACKTHORNE

Dane stood on the porch, watching his visitor walk down Oak Hill Road. Even after Liko dissolved out of sight, Dane stayed where he was and gazed at the empty road. Thinking of the year he, Ethan and Nomi were obsessed with James Clavell's *Sho-Gun*, taking turns reading aloud. The copy in the living room was fat with dog-eared pages and colorful with highlights and notes. One passage branded in Dane's heart was the courtesan Kiku escorting John Blackthorne, the Anjin-san, to the pleasure house gate, the morning after their glorious, paid night together. Blackthorne bowed correctly and walked away with a proper show of arrogant carelessness. Kiku stayed where she was and did the Anjin-san the great honor of watching him until he was completely out of sight. And everyone in the square knew he must be much man for her to wait like that.

The three lovers adopted the gesture. Whenever one left the farm to do something brave or difficult or dreaded, two watched from the porch. Or even in the everyday, banal comings and goings, they'd text each other: *Watched until I couldn't see you anymore. Because you are much woman.* Or, *Did you a Kiku-san, because you are much man.*

"Liko-san," Dane said, staring at the empty road. He didn't bow, but his eyes closed and his chin dropped a bit. Whatever had brought Liko here, it deserved honor.

He opened his eyes, no longer sixteenth-century samurai but modern schmuck.

If he doesn't remember me, then what is he doing here?

He went back inside. Changed his mind and went out again. Decided he should get a jacket and went back in. Glared at the bewildered Salma. "May I help you?"

He bundled up, got a flashlight and opened the door, this time waiting for Salma to go first. Only a little streak of lemon yellow lit the western skies, and a single star had emerged over the Pub. Dane headed through the pergola walkway and up the farm road. He passed a low-slung stone outbuilding and its sign: *The Spa at Schoenfeld's.* Two cars were parked in its small gravel lot and the upstairs windows glowed with a dim, peachy light. Dahlia Bridges was obviously with her last massage appointment.

They walked on together, the Australian Shepherd and the Great Dane, past the big barn, the greenhouses, the chicken coop. Taking the trail that split off and meandered through the woods—a path beat into the earth from all the years Ethan, Dane and Nomi walked to their most sacred place on the Schoenfeld's property.

When Dane emerged into the clearing, a crescent moon was rising above the treetops. The space was about two hundred yards across and almost perfectly round. In its center was a block of rough granite. Weirdly solitary, as if placed by aliens, or a massive stone wall had been meticulously dismantled rock by rock until only this monolith was left. No one knew how it had gotten here. John and Mary Schoenfeld said it was always here and Mary's parents confirmed. The rock was part of the farm, a favorite picnic and play spot for generations. It remained unadorned until Ethan took a chisel to it, because whenever an artistic medium threw down a gauntlet, Ethan couldn't *not* take it up.

He experimented on a natural depression in the top of the stone, enlarging it into a shallow bowl, perfect for little ceremonial fires. Next he wanted to carve a Green Man on one short end of the block, and a Three Hares motif on the opposite end. Because how hard could it be?

"Fuck a duck, this is hard," he grunted, sweating and swearing over his labors. He only managed a pair of crude eyes and a couple of leaves before walking away in frustrated disgust. It was one of the few times Dane and Nomi saw him start something he couldn't finish.

Ethan was Ethan though, and when an artistic endeavor was thwarting him, he threw information at it. The man was a genius, but he had no need to be the smartest person in a room. He made some calls, read some books, talked to experts and gathered intel.

"What the hell are you thinking," a friendly but gruff stonemason said. "No experience whatsoever, you just leap right into intricate, freehand bas relief? Good lord, even Michelangelo drew out a plan before he started cutting."

"Yeah, I'm definitely out of my league here," Ethan said.

"Take my advice: It's way easier to chisel into the stone than chisel out of it. Don't be Michelangelo. Be Hammurabi. Keep it simple and draw a guide, for crying out loud."

Ethan came back to the block with a better set of chisels and his humility. He drew a simplistic version of his beloved Three Hares sigil. He gritted his teeth and made it even simpler. Almost a pictograph. He worked on it a month, but his expression was far from pleased when he showed the finished triskele to Dane and Nomi.

"Dude, it's fantastic," Nomi said.

"It's okay," Ethan grumbled.

"It's perfect," Dane insisted.

"Meh. The triangle of the ears is all skewed."

"What, by like a millimeter?" Dane said. "I think it's amazing."

"Yeah, well…" Ethan sighed, running a finger along the ear that made the top of the triangle. "This bugs me. Doesn't line up right."

"I love it," Nomi said. "The rabbit with the weird ear is me. Dibs on imperfection."

Dane turned off the flashlight and approached the stone. The three friends called this clearing the Hare Ring, and this granite chunk was their altar. The umbilicus of Schoenfeld's. The fulcrum of Ethan, Dane and Nomi.

Dane brushed out the bowl depression, clearing bits of twigs and dead leaves. He crouched and ran his gloved fingers along the long end of the granite block, where Ethan, after gaining confidence, had chiseled a line of respectable block letters:

YE THEN DEIGN TO KNOW ME

Dane traced the words, feeling he was visiting a grave. But in a way, he was. Nomi was gone from existence. Ethan was gone for good. Leaving what he started unfinished.

Only I am left. One hare chasing itself.

We are left, Diane reminded him. She put arms around his mind and squeezed. *I'm always here.*

Dane sat on the block. The Hare Ring was in near total darkness now, but he could make out the edges of the woods, ringing him like a panorama. The pines scratching the skies. The winter skeletons of deciduous trees like lace. Invisible to the eye was the thick layer of naturalized wisteria that crawled, wended, wove and twined its way through the undergrowth, seizing anything it could coil around in the journey to the treetops. Come spring, the woods would explode with the long, dripping, purple blossoms, wreathing the Hare Ring with their beauty and scent.

Wisteria time. The best time to be a hare.

The best time to be three.

The cold stone was working its way through Dane's jeans and chilling his butt. He couldn't stay much longer.

Why was he even out here?

This was stupid. He got up and almost walked away, but looked back at the short end where the unfinished Green Man was carved. Ethan had diligently tried to course correct his first efforts. He fixed the eyes and roughed out the shape of the face, but the leaves were tedious, difficult and painstaking work. He managed only one or two a year, so only half the poor fellow's face was complete. But in a way, it was part of his charm. A half-faced pagan nature spirit emerging from the rock.

Just as Liko Greenman emerged from nowhere. Half the man he used to be.

DEIGN TO KNOW ME

Liko's Airbnb was a tiny house: 225 square feet of minimalist joy. Rather than claustrophobic, he found it cozy. Everything he needed literally within arms' reach. The house had an audience of one and he was it.

He sat on his bed in the loft, which felt even cozier with the low ceiling. He'd brought work with him, but was playing *Three Hares* on his laptop instead, looking for new clues and insights. A fresh way of approaching the game after he'd found himself along the roadside by Schoenfeld's.

When it came to fan lists of the most beautiful games ever played, those created by Jonathan Henshe were always present, and *Three Hares* always near the top. It was a single-player, non-linear adventure that took the player from Asia to Europe, visiting locales where the Three Hares motif was depicted in art or architecture. Puzzles had to be solved before each motif could be unlocked and collected by the player. These ranged from easy hidden-object games to challenging puzzles to maddening anagrams. The player faced no adversity. The only enemy in the game was your own frustration.

As the player moved west along the old Silk Road, the Green Man acted as a narrator and guide. Hinting here, directing there, and, as the fans liked to say, whipping a shit-ton of knowledge on you without you realizing it.

"It's a nerd's wet dream," Kyle Greenman said once, and his father didn't quite know how to react. It was a weird day of parenthood when your kid started getting innuendo. Even weirder when they started to make their own jokes.

But a nerd's wet dream it was, and as the fandom grew, so did cheat codes and walkthroughs. Players divided snobbishly among those who got through the game on their own smarts, and those who caved to the guides. Threads splintered off to delve into the meaning and symbolism of the Green Man and the Three Hares. Reading lists were curated, and some of the picks were keeping Liko company on the bed. Mostly used paperbacks but at the last minute, he threw in the coffee table tome titled *Harefoot,* which contained works by the artist Ethan Hasen. Another definitive work was *Journey of the Green Man* by John Schoenfeld.

Liko looked up from the screen.

John who?

He paused the game, set the laptop aside and slid apart the stack of paperbacks until he found *Journey of the Green Man.*

A foliate face stared back at him, in between the title and the author name: John Schoenfeld.

"Huh," Liko said to the walls of his tiny house.

He reached for the notebook, turned to a clean page, clicked the end of a pen and wrote:

> *Go to Birch Island, NY and look for <u>yourself</u> along the roadside.*
> *Myself➔ Greenman➔ Green Man motif on the stone wall along Oak Hill Road.*
> *Farm is called <u>Schoenfeld's</u>*
> *John <u>Schoenfeld</u> is author of Journey of the Green Man.*
> *Man living there now named Dane, but last name isn't Schoenfeld.*

Liko almost added *I swear I know that guy* to the list, but didn't. He chewed the end of the pen, then flipped to the back of *Journey of the Green Man* in search of a biography.

John Schoenfeld is an historian specializing in British folklore, pre-Christian religion, and modern paganism. He earned a PhD in Comparative Cultural Studies and Folklore from New York University before joining Vassar's Folklore & Mythology program, where he taught until his retirement in 2005. A longtime resident of Orange County, New York, he and his wife now live in France.

Liko sighed, unsatisfied with the information. He flipped back to the notebook's start and re-read his research on the Green Man and Three Hares motifs. Unfortunately, both had dozens of possible meanings, and no satisfying proof to boost one interpretation over another.

As a Brit, he felt a little sheepish about his lack of knowledge of the Green Man. Growing up outside London, he'd easily passed twenty pubs called The Green Man, nearly all with the foliate head on their signage. No doubt he'd noticed the symbol as part of his country's folklore, he'd just never given it any consideration. It was no more interesting than a red phone booth on a London street.

Yet the Green Man was a motif found in nearly every gothic and Romanesque cathedral, not just in Britain but in continental Europe. Despite the varying interpretations, all the sources agreed the Green Man predated Christianity. Why was this unabashedly pagan symbol hanging out in churches, adorning bosses, archways, pew ends, pediments and altars? Coyly whispering, *Psst, look over here. Fertility. Nature. Vegetation. You want rebirth and resurrection? Honey, I got it spilling out my eyes, ears, mouth and nose.*

Liko had jotted down, *The Green Man is a ghostwriter of Christianity—the guy who took the outline and made it into a masterpiece.*

He'd scribbled over the words, thinking he had it bass-ackward. He next wrote, *The Green Man is the developmental editor of Christianity. In teasing out the union of human and nature, he became the observer of human nature. And…*

That idea died on the vine. But a few lines down, in different ink, he'd tried again:

The Green Man watches. And remembers. He says, "I'm still here. Nature is older than man, older than God. Nature is truth. I spew the truth from my eyes, nose, mouth and ears. I vomit time and eat your folly. Am I ingesting or regurgitating? Am I god or man? Male or female? Secular or divine? Venal or mortal? Does it matter?"

The Three Hares also lacked a single, satisfying explanation. The motif originated in Asia and moved west to Europe along the Silk Road, picking up an interfaith appeal along the way. As fans of the video game discovered, the hares were found in Christian, Jewish, Buddhist and Islamic culture, but the largest concentration was in Devon, in southern England. Liko's mother was from Exeter, and could've visited no less than seventeen Devonian churches where the triskelion was found. Among the locals, the hares were known as Tinner's Hares.

Triskelion, Liko had written in his notes. *Or triskele. Both mean a triple spiral motif, threefold rotational symmetry. As the* Schoolhouse Rock *song says, "Three is a magic number." Easy for Christians to adopt the Three Hares as a symbol of the Trinity. One in three and three in one. Why not—the Church borrowed so much else from pagan traditions. Kind of funny, though, that rabbits are best known for being procreative little fuckers.*

But that wasn't quite true. Between the gaming forums, his books, and the internet, Liko learned the hare was a lesson in contradiction. It was simultaneously a symbol of fertility and chastity. During the Middle Ages it was widely believed the hare was hermaphrodite—male one month and female the next—and could reproduce without loss of virginity.

Ah, said a maternal deity named Mary. *Now you're talking my language. I'll take those as my own, thank you very much.*

Liko pulled his laptop toward him and resumed the game.

Three Hares ended at Paderborn Cathedral. The Chamber of the Green Man was an invention, but it brought so much tourism to the German city that the cathedral made a page for the game on its website. A video clip showed a nattily-dressed tour guide standing beneath the *Drei-Hasen-Fenster,* the window of the Three Hares. He pointed to the stone buttress next to the window, explaining how in the game, a loose brick contained a switch that opened a stairway. The guide cheerfully assured the public there was no such hidden mechanism and please to leave their sledgehammers and crowbars at home.

"The game takes beautiful artistic license," the guide gushed. "I'm a fan myself. Paderborn is thrilled with the increased interest and visitation, but I promise you, everyone, there's no hidden stairway inside this pillar. It would be architecturally impossible, and…" The guide pointed up to the cathedral's roofline where the buttresses abruptly ended. "Where would it even *go?*"

Liko chewed a bottom lip as he moved his cursor toward the grass beneath the window of the Three Hares, where a scrap of paper seemed to be lying. When clicked, it turned out to be a photograph: a close-up shot of a stone wall, with a man's hand drawing out a loose brick. This innocuous, grainy picture was where the viral mystery started. The trick that tipped rabbits out of a top hat. The subtle arrow pointing to the loose stone in the cathedral buttress. Liko pulled it free, flipped the revealed switch, and ascended the impossible, illogical stairs to the hidden chamber.

The artwork in this magical hall humbled the rest of the game, going from breathtaking to divine. The circular space had open, arched windows, through which wound thick vines of wisteria, the long purple clusters swaying against the stone walls. Opposite the door, upon a raised pedestal, lounged the Green Man himself. Sitting like a happy Buddha, one hand composed in a gesture of benefaction, the other cradling a golden hare. No round belly to rub and make wishes, but a sensational, fit physique. His emerald eyes blinked as the user approached, and the hare's nose wriggled nervously.

On the face of the pedestal were chiseled words:

And ye then deign to know me
O wisteria hares turning

A second hare crouched at the base of the altar, where burned a little fire in a circular depression. A third hare hid in the wisteria blossoms. Beneath one window, a large dog lay sleeping. Beneath another, a duck nestled in a heap of straw. If you clicked the cursor up, you saw the famous Three Hares motif carved into the domed ceiling.

Thus the player beheld the Chamber of the Green Man, home to one of the greatest unsolved mysteries in gaming history. Some devotees declared it was just decoration and served no purpose. Most, including Kyle Greenman, insisted if eyes blinked, noses wriggled, blossoms swayed, dogs and ducks slumbered and fires burned, then the space was waiting for you. The chamber was suffused with anticipation. The game wasn't over. More was here. Someone just had to find a way to get the hares in the ceiling spinning.

Small cracks had been made in the code. Quickly it was discovered you could click on two of the hares—the one hiding in the flowers and the one at the base of the altar, hold them by the ears and move them up to the ceiling motif, where they each melded into the carving. The third hare, the one being held by the Green Man, wasn't having it. You could click on him, move him, but when you tried to drop him into the ceiling motif, he bounded out of the cursor's trap and back to the safety of the Green Man's lap.

Clicking on the dog did nothing interesting. He just yawned, shifted positions or scratched, and went back to sleep. Likewise the duck wasn't interested in playing.

Clicking on the windows did nothing. Clicking on the wisteria blossoms did nothing, or so everyone thought until one intrepid fan discovered if you clicked on one particular blossom *enough,* it grew older. The purple petals withered and died with each click, leaving the user with three seeds that went into their cache. But what to do with them? People tried feeding them to the dog, throwing them into the fire. They looked around for dirt to plant them in. They took the seeds back through the entire game looking for where they could be sown. So far, no dice.

Fans tore the place apart, researching the Green Man, the Three Hares, the significance of wisteria, the breed of dog and duck. Some fixated on the full moon in one of the windows, arguing you could determine latitude by its position. But none were so crazed as the anagram fanatics, who spent hours, days, months rearranging the letters of the Green Man's throne:

And ye then deign to know me
O wisteria hares turning

Liko closed his eyes, remembering Kyle's shoulders hunched over the dining room table, where he and his friend Mark had composed the words with Scrabble tiles, bickering and brainstorming as they moved letters around and tried to find the message within.

Tears squeezed through the tiny space between upper and lower lids, warmed with a burning pride because the night he died, Kyle had discovered something about the Green Man Chamber no one else had. He woke Liko up, which he rarely did, insisting he had to show Liko something, which he *never* did.

"I have to show you because you don't care about the game and you won't tell anyone else. You have no one to tell. Get up. Come here. Dad, *please,* you have to see this."

Stumbling and yawning, Liko followed the boy into his bedroom and leaned over the back of his chair.

Kyle had already moved the two willing hares into their positions in the ceiling motif. He demonstrated again how the third hare could be picked up and moved toward the ceiling, but no farther.

"It doesn't go in," Kyle said. "Right?"

"Right."

"As soon as you hover over the motif, the hare jumps out of your hands and goes back to the Green Man. Okay?"

"I'm with you."

"But if you move it toward the ceiling, don't let go, and then move it *back* to the Green Man's lap yourself… There, see how the flames of the fire pit shoot up just a little as you pass it. Right? And the hare kind of draws up its back feet and you see some sparks?"

"I see it."

Kyle swiveled in his chair, looking up at his father with an almost fevered expression. "It says, *deign to know me.* What does *deign* mean?"

"To base yourself. To do something beneath your dignity."

Kyle's eyes widened and he pointed a finger. "Exactly."

He swiveled back to the screen, clicked the cursor on the hare in the Green Man's lap, picked it up and moved it over the fire. Sparks belched and the creature drew its feet up.

"Check it out." Kyle released his finger from the mouse and the hare dropped into the flames.

"Dude," Liko said, appalled and impressed.

Kyle sat back, arms crossed and teeth closed on the tip of his tongue, watching as the fire leaped up tall and angry, consuming the hare. Out of the conflagration emerged a cloud of rabbit-shaped smoke that moved toward the ceiling, its four strong legs extending and crossing as it ran through the air to join its mates in the carved motif. Once in place, the three hares surged with a blinding white light, then calmed into gold.

And they began to run.

The bowl of the ceiling turned, powered by the running hares. Round and round they went, the triangle made by their three shared ears rotating.

It was the rule of the game: If the hares were running, you were on to something.

"Holy shit," Liko said, dropping a hand on his son's head. "You just figured this out now? Tonight?"

Kyle crowed a "Yeah" with undisguised relish and glee.

"Does anyone else know?"

"Not yet."

"You're literally the first and only person to figure this out?"

"Yep. And you're the only other person who knows."

"Dude, we're famous."

"I *know.*"

"You going to announce this?"

"Not yet." He glanced up and over his shoulder and in that moment, he looked more man than boy. "You always say I should put twenty-four hours between my impulses and my actions."

Liko took his hand off Kyle's head, raised both palms and took an incredulous stop back. "What, you're actually taking my advice? Hold on, let me look outside and see if the world is ending."

He made a show of flinging open the bedroom window and peering around. "My son is listening to me," he called to the streets.

"Dude, I got a *secret,*" Kyle said, and right then, Liko could've taken his son's joy, loaded it into a syringe and plunged it into his veins. He could make a career out of the expression on Kyle's face. He wanted to paint it, sculpt it, cast it in bronze, make a masterpiece of this night. He shut the window and came back to the desk to offer an exuberant high five.

"My man, you're incredible."

"I am, aren't I?"

Liko knuckled his son's mop of dark blond hair and kissed the knobby skull that enclosed that bright, beautiful mind. He moved to the door and Kyle called after him, "Hey, don't tell anyone about this, all right?"

"Who would I even tell? My dentist?"

"Don't tell *anyone.*"

"Not a word, I promise. Now shut down and get some sleep. You got a big day ahead."

Kyle grinned. "Tomorrow's gonna be lit."

But tomorrow never came.

Liko had kissed that head, not knowing a time bomb was ticking within, and gone back to his bed. Kyle went to shower and brush his teeth, had a massive brain aneurysm, collapsed and died.

Fate deigned to reach into Liko Greenman's lap, pluck the beautiful tawny hare that was his only child, and sacrifice him.

Ensconced in his tiny Airbnb, Liko threw the game's third hare into the fire, watched the smoke cloud ascend and bound toward the ceiling. He watched the three hares begin to turn and turn and turn.

The secret had died with Kyle. Liko never told a soul. He combed the gaming forums not only to validate his son's existence and confirm its continued memorialization, but to see if anyone else had figured out how to *deign* to know the Green Man a little better.

So far, nobody.

Liko hoarded the knowledge with a vicious, vindictive greed. He made his famous post on Reddit with that secret sitting in his lap. He'd never give it up. Ever. He'd kill anyone and anything that tried to click and carry it away.

Come and get it, fuckers. Just try.

Give me back my son and I'll reveal what I know.

Maybe.

Maybe I'll just let you all die without ever knowing. I'll never deign *to share my secrets.*

He reached to slam the laptop shut, then stopped.

He stared. His mouth fell open and cool air filled the back of his throat as he inhaled. And remembered.

His heart pounded as he clicked the cursor and moved closer to the inscription on the Green Man's throne.

And ye then deign to know me.

"Deign to know me," he whispered. "It's a…"

His mind fumbled for the term describing two words that sounded the same but had different meanings. A homonym? No, a homophone.

The verb *deign* was a homophone of the name *Dane*.

Dane and deign.

"Holy *shit.*" Liko grabbed his phone, laughing aloud. He had to tell Kyle. He had to—

His teeth clicked shut.

He swallowed hard.

Then, with a roar of frustrated grief, he lobbed the phone across the room. Now he did slam the laptop shut and shove it away. He attacked the bed like an enraged gorilla. His fists punched the mattress, his feet kicked at the sheets and blankets. He rolled and screamed his rage into the pillows, elbows and knees digging desperate furrows as he opened his throat and wailed, wishing he could bury himself alive. It wouldn't stop. It just never stopped. Kyle's death ought to have felled him with a stroke. Instead, it kept coming back to kill him, over and over again. A thousand deadly cuts to bleed dry the spontaneous impulses. Not giving him twenty-four seconds, let alone hours, between desire and action but no, stabbing him in the heart right in the middle of a natural thought.

Wow, I need to show this to Kyle he w—
Ugh, I should think about what Kyle wants for din—
Hm, should I give away this blazer or save it for Ky—
I need to tell Kyle th—
Did that little shit take my—
Oh my God, Kyle would love th—
Kyle woul—
Kyle—
Ky—...

THE NAOMI ROAD 27

Roof boss, St. Thomas à Becket church, Bridford, Devon, UK.

LOOK AT IT FROM BOTH SIDES

AT SCHOENFELD'S, LIFE HAPPENED in the kitchen. They had a dining room table, but it was only used on momentous occasions. Since Nomi died and Ethan left, Dane had no momentous occasions. He'd been using the dining room table as a second junk drawer, making doom piles of random stuff to deal with later.

Tonight, he moved all the piles under the table and arranged Ethan's postcards in order. He had left the continent and arrived in England, where the greatest concentration of churches with the Three Hares motif was found. The majority in Devon, where they were known as Tinner's Hares.

As his collection grew, Dane discovered he possessed enough magnanimity to honor the pilgrimage at face value. It was a grand, romantic gesture of the kind only Ethan could deliver. Still...

He sighed and rubbed at his left eye. Within, Diane was floating in and out of a mental closet, trying on outfits. Brushing her hair. Getting ready because girl, it was *on*.

"Liko," Dane said over the postcards. "Liko Greenman."

Liko fucking Greenman, Diane said. *Can you believe it? Can you* believe *this shit? Dude, screw the postcards. It's him. He's back. He found you. And his* name? *Come on.*

"He doesn't remember me."

Not now but believe me, he will.

"Maybe he's gotten remarried. If not, he's definitely with someone."

Diane put down her eyeliner and cast him the most withering of big-sister looks. *That wreck of a man is not with anyone right now.*

"Well, maybe I don't want to be with a wrecked man."

She laughed and turned back to the mirror. Dane rolled his eyes and pointedly rearranged his cards into straighter lines.

"Think he likes men?" he finally asked.

She folded her hands on the dressing table. *He kissed you on New Year's Eve.*

True. Just on the cheek, but still.

"Maybe he's South American," he said.

Diane smiled. *He also gave you a full-frontal hug.*

Also true. A hug Dane had recreated with pillows many times. Sometimes with a load of warm towels pulled out of the dryer. Or the two terrycloth robes hanging on a hook in his bathroom. A full-frontal hug was a pretty big hint of…

"What, exactly?" he asked.

Diane shrugged. *That he doesn't subscribe to toxic masculinity?*

"He's probably straight."

I want to meet him tomorrow.

"You?"

He doesn't remember you, so it's the perfect time for me.

"Shut up."

He'll remember my eyes. Let me try.

"You don't even like being in the world."

I do when it's on my terms.

"It's been years."

I hear it's like riding a bicycle.

"You have nothing to wear."

We both know that's a lie.

It was. In the attic's cedar closet were stored some of Nomi's clothes that Saskia was saving. Also a small zipped suitcase which hadn't been opened in years, but had everything Diane needed.

"You're nuts."

Diane put arms around him from behind. *I know.*

"What purpose would it serve? The poor guy looks like hell. I'm going to play head games with him?"

He didn't recognize you. You had the wrong eyes. If you answer the door tomorrow with my eyes, that's a head game too.

"He's seen tons of blue eyes in his life, he's not going to specifically remember yours."

In your face, he might.

"Your face or our face?"

She snuggled her cheek against the left side of his face and spoke through his blue eye: *You've been thinking about this guy for over a year. Just when you made peace with him being a once-in-a-lifetime encounter, he shows up at your house? Totally random? Not even recognizing you?*

"Or pretending not to."

Dude, if he was looking for you, he would've said so. This is a bizarre, once-in-a-lifetime coincidence. Don't you think you should look at it from both sides?

Dane sighed in the circle of her arms. "Maybe."

She squeezed him. *It'll be fun.*

"I'm in the middle of a T cycle. I'm not going to get your voice right. It works better when I'm at the end."

He won't know that. I'll help you. We'll Kathleen Turner the shit out of it. She kissed his cheek, exactly where Liko had on that long-ago night.

Dane shook his head. "This is a terrible idea. What time?"

DIANE

LIKO HAD VIEWS ON arriving somewhere empty handed, so after buying a new phone to replace the one he destroyed last night, he came back to Schoenfeld's with a box of doughnuts. He rang the doorbell and waited. No bark of the dog from within and no answer.

It was another cold day, but the sun shone strong and Liko was wisely layered up. He sat in one of the Adirondack chairs and put the doughnuts down on a small table. He laced his fingers, closed his eyes. Took a few deep breaths. Opened his eyes and reached for the pastry box. The doughnuts were still warm, sparkling with granulated sugar and cinnamon. He took a bite.

His throat seized, his stomach and chest hit the panic button. He spit the sodden, sweet bite into a napkin, balled it up, stuffed it in his fist and pressed the fist to his mouth.

"God fucking *dammit*," he whispered.

It wouldn't ever stop. A doughnut couldn't be a doughnut anymore. No. It was an IED along the roadside of his life, reminding him of all that had been lost.

"Doughnuts on dicks," Liko muttered, rubbing knuckles into his damp eyes like he was punching himself in the face. His tongue flicked the last granules of sugar off his teeth as he sat miserably and remembered.

KYLE WAS SIX AND in his naked phase, meaning it was twenty-two degrees out and you couldn't keep clothes on the punk. After days of battle, the Greenmans reached an impasse where Kyle was allowed to breakfast in the nude in return for uncomplaining cooperation in getting dressed afterward. He sat at the table, nary a goosebump on his skin, while Liko and Janelle were fleeced up and huddled over their coffee cups for warmth.

"What are you up to, kiddo?" Janelle asked.

"I'm seeing how many doughnuts I can stack on my penis," Kyle said.

Nobody warned you about these things when you became a parent.

It was a trademarked look that passed between mother and father: a quick reckoning to see whose turn it was to run interference.

Not it, Liko thought, and then all his coffee came out his nose. Coughing and choking, sinuses burning, he stumbled toward the kitchen sink.

"Amateur," Janelle yelled after him. "All right. Ky, my love, I adore your quest for knowledge but now nobody can eat those doughnuts because they've been on your penis. Take them off, please."

"It's only one," Kyle said, putting it on his plate. "I could stack more if it was har—"

"I'm *sure* you could," Janelle said loudly. "Now look, you have sugar all over your junk."

"You're not supposed to call it junk."

"You're not supposed to stack doughnuts on it. Go wash off or the ants will use you for a snack. Then get dressed."

Kyle slid off his seat and walked away, his pert, bare tush affronted and misunderstood.

"Hang up the washcloth and towel," Liko managed to say.

Janelle turned in her chair. "Oh *thanks* for joining us."

Their eyes met. Their ears counted Kyle's soft footsteps up the stairs.

Then they died.

Janelle doubled over in her chair. Liko folded in half by the sink. The tears streaming down their faces. And the jokes afterward. Christ, for a week they couldn't say the word *doughnut* without leering.

"How many?" Janelle asked, with a hot side-eye over the pastry box.

Liko stretched out his waistband and contemplated therein. "Right now, I'm good for three."

"I don't know, these are awfully big holes."

"Challenge accepted."

When in a mood, they texted DODT: Doughnuts on Dicks Tonight? They couldn't drive by a Dunkin' without mumbling "Dickin'." When the last doughnut went stale in the box, Janelle brought it to bed and crammed it onto the crown of Liko's manhood. They brayed laughing—"Dude, it looks like the Seattle Space Tower"—then Janelle ate it off him, licked the bits of sugar away, climbed aboard and absolutely railed him into oblivion, her mouth full of cinnamon and giggles.

It was so *them*. Liko counted it among the top five defining moments of their marriage because certainly no one else in their circle was stacking doughnuts on dicks. He stood around at sports practice and birthday parties and school assemblies, smugly judging. He'd elbow Janelle's side, jerk his chin at an unsuspecting couple and mumble, "Think they stack?"

"Oh God no," she'd say. "Please."

Please. No other couple could fuck as good as they did while asphyxiating with laughter.

Except later Liko found out Janelle was fucking George Heritage, dying laughing in a hotel room, possibly with a dozen doughnuts at the ready.

George Heritage, for God's sake.

Their fucking *accountant*.

Granted the man was a specimen, which was another of Liko and Janelle's inside jokes. "God, he's hot," one would always muse after a meeting with George.

"I love tax season," the other would sigh.

Hell, Liko would've eaten a doughnut off George's dick, and there were a few financial sessions when some sustained eye contact made him think George might rather enjoy it.

Liko thought about it sometimes. That was all, he just *thought* about it. His bisexuality wasn't a secret. He and Janelle met because he occasionally messed around with her co-worker's brother. But you were supposed to put childish things away when you got married. You could *crush,* sure. And if you had a partner with whom you could share a mutual crush, so much the better.

God, George is hot. Right? Look at that ass…

Liko only crushed.

While Janelle was…

"Hello there."

Liko shook his head out of the past and scrambled to his feet. A woman stood at the foot of the porch steps, along with the dog Liko had met last night. The woman wore a tan down jacket over a bright red sweater. A matching red wool hat under which fell dark blonde hair with long bangs.

Round sunglasses hid her eyes. He couldn't quite tell her age but she was dressed, groomed, made up and outfitted in such a deliberate way, he wondered if she were a social media influencer.

"Hello," she said again. "You looked asleep."

"Hi. Almost." Liko picked up the still-open pastry box and came down the stairs. The dog put paws on Liko's hip and lifted its half-white, half-brown face to get a good sniff. Liko hadn't noticed last night, but the dog also had two different colored eyes: one pale blue, the other golden brown.

The woman smiled broadly. "My mother always said, *If you meet a strange man carrying doughnuts, marry him.*"

"Did she?"

"No. But I'll take one?"

"I'm Liko," he said, just as the woman took an enormous bite. She chewed and chewed, then put a concealing fist to her mouth and said, "I'm Diane."

"I'm looking for Dane."

"He's my brother," she said, and finally swallowed.

"Is he home?"

"No, he had to run out."

"Oh."

"Is he expecting you?"

"Yeah, we met last night. He said he'd be home today and I could come by."

"Well isn't he the fucking asshole?"

Liko gave a single, nervous laugh. "Do you live here?"

"I come and go," she said, a little elusively. "Well, Mr. Asshole should be back soon. Do you want to come in, have a cup of coffee and wait? Or just leave a note telling him to piss off?"

"I'll wait a bit." He felt a strange reluctance to go back into the house if Dane wasn't there. "I wouldn't mind looking at the farm. I can walk myself around."

"I'll give you the tour. Come on. Leave the doughnuts. Take the gun."

She laughed loudly at her own joke and Liko's Spidey Senses shivered down his neck. Something about Diane was forced and artificial and more than a little weird, and he kept a good two feet of distance as he followed her up the road. The dog dashed ahead, then doubled back to herd its pokey charges along.

"What's her name," Liko asked.

"Salma."

"Selma?"

"*Sal*ma. With an A."

"Who are the Schoenfelds?"

"Of late, it's John and Mary Schoenfeld. They owned all the land at this intersection," Diane said. "Well, actually, just three of the corners. They sold the parcel that has the pub."

"What's it called?"

"Officially it's The Pub at Schoenfeld's, but around these parts, just the Pub. Capital P." She turned back and pointed out across the road. "You see that flat, paved extension of the parking lot? That's where the farmer's market is. Every Saturday at the Pub, May to November."

"I see."

Her finger moved to point across the road. "The pond with the big pine tree? That gets lit up every December. Schoenfeld's has some decades-old agreement with the fire department and every other year or so, they're out here with ladders to maintenance the lights. There's a lottery and the winner gets to take a ride in the truck with Santa and throw the switch to light the tree. Big party after. Skating if it's safe, otherwise we booze it up and deck the Pub halls. Fa la la."

"Sounds fun. What's that barn in the field across the road?"

"It's where we store plans that never came to fruition."

They were walking down a long flagstone path, beneath a strong trellis of concrete-footed posts and iron bars covered with ropy, twisted, woody vines. Diane reached to lay a hand on a branch. "Doesn't look like much now," she said. "But these are wisteria vines. In May, this whole walkway is covered with blooms."

O wisteria hares turning, Liko thought, but said nothing. He wasn't going to grill this strange woman for clues about the game. He'd look, listen, and wait for Dane.

"The vines are kind of special," Diane was saying. "Mary Schoenfeld's father was a horticulture professor at Oberlin college. Somehow… I forgot the connection, anyway, Japan gifted the department wisteria vines that survived Hiroshima. When Mary's father retired, the college gave him cuttings from those vines. He planted them here. They took fifteen years to bloom."

"Is that typical? Taking fifteen years, I mean, not the gift."

"Yes. Wisteria is a lesson in patience. It won't bloom until it decides it likes the place. Here's the spa…"

Diane pointed to a stone outbuilding with a sign reading *The Spa at Schoenfeld's*. Then she walked Liko a bit further uphill to where they could see three stone cottages spaced equidistant around a small pond. "Every summer, Schoenfeld's hosts three artists in residence. *Artist* being a loose term. Anything from painters to musicians to pastry cooks to someone working on a dissertation."

"Do the Schoenfelds still live here?"

"No, John and Mary retired to France. Dane owns it all now."

"Ah."

"But everything about this place… The farm, the CSA, the market, the Pub, the spa, the tree lighting—it's all Mary's creation. John did come up with the idea for the artist residencies, but Mary executed it."

"Must be a shit ton of work running this place," Liko said.

Diane nodded, then wobbled her head side to side. "One of Mary's many talents was picking good managers. She was the empress of delegation. And she also knew when it was time to downsize—like when she sold the Pub. She has a file of people with right of first refusal for the spa and the artist cottages. She guides Dane from afar."

"What about John?"

Diane laughed. "John's basically a kept man. Lovely guy, don't get me wrong. But he's your quintessential absent-minded professor. Mary built the farm around him while he did his academic thing. Classes, lecture circuits, books."

"Sounds like you grew up here?"

"No. I just heard about it from Dane."

"He grew up here?"

"He married in."

She showed Liko the barn, the greenhouses, the fields, the chicken coop. Liko asked polite questions and took mental notes. After last night, he didn't harbor much doubt he was in the right place, but this tour seemed intent on letting him know, yes, whatever he was meant to do here, this *was* the place. Liko saw the Green Man's foliate face in all sizes, adorning walls, fixed into a paving stone, painted on the side of a wheelbarrow. Little statues of rabbits dotted the flower beds—sleeping, sitting, listening, bounding. Two stone hares were up on their hind legs, boxing with teeth bared and long ears laid back. The Three Hares motif was designed as a copper wind spinner, either turning lazily to illustrate the optical illusion of the three shared ears, or catching a gust and whirling into a blur.

Get it, the farm kept elbowing Liko's side. *See? This is the place.*

I got it, Liko thought dryly.

Diane looked back and smiled. "At the risk of sounding like a dumb American, where are you from?"

"London. My father's work transferred him to New York when I was fifteen."

Liko had worked hard to shed his accent during high school, just to fit in. By the end of his sophomore year he had it dialed way down. By the time he graduated he could turn it off and on at will. But once at college, he kept it on. Partly because he was older, wiser, less needful of fitting in. But mostly because older, wiser college students seemed to find his accent irresistible.

"Are your parents still here?"

"No, they went back when Dad retired. I stayed."

"For work?"

"For love."

"Ah," Diane said slowly. Then declared she was cold and wanted that coffee.

TWO-FACED

Liko had passed through the living room the night before but it was in darkness. Now wintery sunlight flooded the windows and revealed it was a beautiful space with built-in bookcases and a large fireplace with a stacked stone mantel. Artwork and objects crowded walls and surfaces, but this was no off-limits gallery. Rather it was a homey room conducive to prowling and exploring, then bringing a bit of treasure to a chair and settling in.

"I'll put the coffee on if you can coax the fire back to life," Diane said. "Unless you prefer tea?"

His back to her, Liko could roll his eyes. "Coffee's fine."

"Mind where you put the doughnuts. Salma will insist she hasn't been fed. She is lying."

Liko set the pastry box on a high shelf, then built up the fire. On the wall above the mantel was a large, square painting Liko immediately recognized: the iconic cover for Gideon Perfect's double album, *Two-Faced.*

He stood up and crossed his arms, puzzled. He'd seen this famous album cover a million times, could envision it behind closed eyelids, took it for granted as one piece in the mural of pop culture. But he'd always thought the cover was a collage of photography.

He peered closer. It was all a painting, even the lettering. The eponymous two-face, the abstract squares, the naked girl cowering at the bottom and the strange, flayed and mutilated man at one side. All painted by hand.

"That's not right," he murmured, reaching for his phone. He Googled the album and confidently tapped an image. Closed it and tapped another, frowning. He made sure with a third, now slightly offended.

"Huh," he said again, zooming in on the minute brushstrokes he'd never noticed. The cover was entirely a painting. He stepped back, staring from phone to wall. Stepped in again. "I'll be damned," he said admiringly.

Diane came back in with a genteel tray of coffee cups, milk and sugar. She'd shed her jacket but still wore her red hat. The sunglasses had been swapped for large, heavy framed glasses. Behind the lenses her eyes were a supernatural blue, precisely outlined in black makeup and long lashes.

Liko blinked, trying to pin down what it was about her appearance that bothered him. Some women wore makeup to enhance what was there, while others wore it to keep you from seeing what was there.

"I texted Dane and told him he was being extremely rude to his new friend," she said. "He hasn't answered."

He smiled, feeling that like the makeup, she was laying it on a little thick. He pointed to the painting over the fireplace.

"Is this the original artwork for the album? Or a copy?"

She glanced up, expression a little puzzled, as if she'd never noticed the picture before. "Probably a copy," she said slowly. "But in this museum of a house, who knows?"

She sat on the opposite side of the coffee table and later it would occur to him she kept a deliberate distance all throughout the visit. If he got up to examine something close to where she sat, she got up and moved. He chalked it up to prudence, remembering he was a strange man invited into her house when no one else was home.

"What do you do?" she said, predictably.

"I'm a ghostwriter."

"Really? What genre."

"Mostly thrillers."

"Would I know any?"

"You probably would, but I'm not at liberty to share titles."

"Why? Because of NDAs or something?"

"Exactly because."

"Oh. Is that aspect of it hard? I mean, that you can't share your accomplishments?"

"Sometimes. But the money is a very nice consolation."

The minutes ticked off, aching with small talk. Finally Diane reached for her phone, examined the screen and smiled. "Dane's on his way back. Consumed with guilt." She gathered the cups. "I have to get on a work call. Make yourself at home. Look at anything, read anything, love the dog."

"Point me toward the loo?"

"Down that hall, second door on the right."

This second door was closed. Liko had a morbid fear of busting in on strangers in the loo, or, God forbid, being busted in upon. So he rapped with a knuckle first.

No answer. His hand dropped on the doorknob.

And memory dropped on him like a boulder.

Because it just never stopped. A doughnut couldn't be a doughnut and a closed bathroom door couldn't just be a closed bathroom door.

Of all the innocuous things that ambushed him on a daily basis, this was possibly the most cruel. Walking along the upstairs hall of his lonely house, passing the shut bathroom and stopping cold, knuckles itching to knock and inquire, *Kyle? You fall in?*

Most times he just thought it. On bad days, he knocked and asked aloud. "Kyle? You fall in?"

No answer of course. But once upon a time, in those tender years of little boyhood, a singsong voice would have piped up: "Here I sit, broken-hearted…"

Liko would sing back: "Came to poop…"

A wicked giggle. "But only *farted.*"

Liko would laugh too, before doing his due diligence. "Remember those wipes aren't flushable, kiddo. They go in the bin."

Time was a thief. One day you woke up and your nudist son was shrouded in baggy jeans and hoodies, and you couldn't remember the last time you saw his bare ass. You jokingly knocked on the bathroom door and asked if he'd fallen in, but no reply because he was plugged into music, videos, social media, another world you had no access to. Or he was just flat-out ignoring you, so over those childhood rituals.

Then one night you woke up and flung yourself against a closed, locked bathroom door because water was pouring from beneath it. Screaming to 911 on the phone in your hand while you battered the door with your shoulder, finally ramming your heel above the knob and breaking the whole thing down to get to your son who was slumped in the overflowing tub. There was his bare ass, but there also were his empty, dead eyes. Either the aneurysm had felled him instantly, or he'd drowned in the rising water.

Here I lie, broken-hearted.

Came to bathe, but only parted…

Six months after Kyle died, Liko had the entire loo gutted down to the studs and redone. Out went the tub, replaced with a walk-in shower. New tiles, new fixtures, new lights, new everything. All traces of that hideous night demolished and gone.

Except for the goddamn door. It was new, too, but when closed, it was the same old pain. Still here. Because it just never stopped.

Liko ran the cold tap and splashed his face. Took a few deep breaths in the privacy of a hand towel. Then went back to the living room.

As he trawled the bookshelves, the fire crackled, a clock on a side table ticked, and Salma yawned with a little keening whine. Liko yawned too, as he placed two precise fingers on a large tome and drew it out. *Harefoot,* by Ethan J. Hasen. Twin to the copy Liko had thrown into his backpack this morning, along with his laptop and notebooks. The pack was still in his car. He thought about getting it, then yawned again and sat.

As he skimmed the familiar photographs and text, his mind tried to assemble notes taken during Diane's tour of the farm. The ubiquitous presence of the Green Man. The long pergola wrapped in thick wisteria vines, the multitude of hare statues, the copper wind spinner.

O wisteria hares turning.

Wisteria vines that survived Hiroshima. Descendants planted in the soil of New York.

Resilience, Liko thought. *Survival. Beginnings and endings. From the earth to the earth. Hares chasing hares chasing hares. The Green Man ever watchful.*

And here I sit, broken-hearted…

He fell asleep mid-thought. Socked feet stretched toward the fire, the heavy book open on his lap and Salma curled against his hip.

MANY MOONS

Diane closed and locked the bedroom door. Onto the bed she tossed her red cap and glasses, then pulled the red sweater over her head and tossed it aside. Her fingers shook as they dealt with the hooks of the padded bra. Finally she twisted the clasp to the front and yanked it apart.

In the bathroom, she took a spray bottle and wet down the lace edges of her wig. While the glue was softening, she peeled off her lashes and washed layers of paint off her face. She worked quickly, but clumsily. She hadn't done this in a long time, and never with this fast a turnaround. Diane always did the brave things but there'd been no need for this kind of courage in…

"Many moons," she said, patting the water out of her eyes.

Her scalp winced as she removed the wig and set it on its stand.

She slid off the tight skull cap: The hair beneath was shaved close around her neck and ears but the top was long and crunchy with gel. She rubbed it vigorously with her fingers, breaking up what she could, then gathered it back in an elastic. She washed her face again, picking out the dried glue along her hairline. She didn't have time to do a perfect job of it. A ball cap would cover the rest.

She looked in the mirror and met her azure gaze. She leaned and pinched out the contact lens covering her right iris. It fluttered into the sink, a thin cupped bowl tinted blue.

She blinked rapidly, turned on the water to wash the lens down the drain. Pulled the silver hoops from her ears and the rings from her fingers. Then Diane stepped back and looked in the mirror again.

One blue eye and one brown eye stared back.

A long breath in. Held for five thudding heartbeats.

A longer breath out. Soft words within.

"I'm so sorry."

A drawer opened. A brown-tinted contact lens was deftly slipped over the blue iris. Another set of rapid blinks. Another gaze into the mirror.

Now Dane looked back. Rough, scrubbed, hard and brown-eyed.

"Sorry," he said, then cleared his throat a few times. "I'm sorry," he said again. And again. Until he'd coughed and apologized his voice back to where it belonged.

The rest was easy. A fleece pulled on and zipped to his chin. The women's sneakers swapped for men's hikers. Ball cap. Heavy jacket. Phone. Wallet. Keys. Shades. He slipped down the back stairs, silently out the kitchen door, and hustled up toward the farm where he'd parked his car behind one of the greenhouses. He drove out the service road, down Rt. 34, turned onto Oak Hill, then back into the driveway of Schoenfeld's. He pulled up to the farmhouse, checked his reflection one last time and got out of the car.

Up the porch steps and he could hear Salma barking. He walked into his house, strode into the living room, calling out, "Dude, I am *so* sorry…"

PART TWO
SARIS HAMAH

"A hare is incapable of legal evaluation
because it is male one month and female the other."
—Gentian Code of Law for North Wales, ca. eleventh century

NO STRANGER TO GRIEF

"I'M SO SORRY," DANE SAID. "I think I got stuck behind every goddamn horse trailer in the county."

"I'm…" Disoriented, Liko promptly forgot what he was saying.

"I feel like an ass. Hi. How are you." Dane walked over, holding out a hand. They shook. "I'm sorry you had to wait."

"No, it's all right," Liko said, putting his feet on the floor. "I fell asleep."

"Good. That means the house likes you."

"Where's Diane?"

"She had to go do a thing. When she comes home, she'll yell at me some more."

"It's all right. This place is…comfortable."

"Are you hungry? I know you brought doughnuts but I need lunch. Come in the kitchen."

Liko followed, saying, "I don't want to take up your time. I just need to ask you a question."

"You're not taking my time. I wasted yours. Sit down. Ask away."

Liko slid onto a chair at the long table and reached in his back pocket for the letter. "By any chance, do you work for Jonathan Henshe Games?"

"No."

"But you know the company?"

"Sure."

Liko smoothed the paper open. "Do you know who might have sent this to me? And why it tells me, in so many words, to come to your farm?"

Dane looked around and located a pair of reading glasses on the windowsill. He turned his cap backward, put on the glasses and read the letter where it lay, then picked it up and read it again. He slid the readers down and looked at Liko over the rims.

"Your son died?"

"Yes."

"Oh my God. I'm so sorry. What happened?"

"Brain aneurysm."

"Oh. God, I'm sorry…"

"Thank you. He loved the *Three Hares* game. He was really invested in the mystery at the end. You know about it?"

Dane nodded, teeth closed on a corner of his lower lip.

"He was playing the night he died. He figured something new out. A piece of the chamber puzzle nobody else had solved. He was going to post about it the next day. But…"

"There was no next day."

"No. And I kind of picked up the flag. Or the sword. The mantle?"

"You're finishing what he started."

"Yeah. And they…" Liko indicated the letter. "They sent me here."

Dane skimmed the paper again, faintly shaking his head. "Not even," he said. "They just sent you to the town. *Look for yourself along the roadside.* What, did you just walk all over until you found this place?"

"Pretty much."

"Shut up. How long did it take?"

"A week."

"Jesus."

"So why am I here?" Liko asked.

Dane folded the paper and handed it back. He tucked the reading glasses into the collar of his fleece, then started opening the bag of bread and the cold cuts. "You want turkey? Ham?"

"Whatever you're having."

"There's beer in the fridge."

Liko opened two bottles, curbing his impatience, sensing if he pushed hard on this guy, he wasn't going to get anywhere.

He sat again, drank his beer and studied his host. As a writer, he treated people-watching as a professional exercise, trying to describe hair, noses and faces in an interesting way. No adjectives wanted to stick to Dane. Liko couldn't get a bead on the guy's age—one minute he looked early forties, the next early thirties. Sometimes he turned his head or looked up or over, and he appeared almost adolescent. Mature laugh lines radiated from the corners of his eyes, but his face was smooth like a boy's. Something about his body was strong, but slight. He was undeniably handsome, yet in a way he was kind of…pretty.

Dude, quit staring.

"Diane gave me the tour," Liko said. "This place is really something. And

I'm only seeing it in late winter. It must be incredible at the height of the season."

"It's carefully controlled insanity."

"How many people work here?"

"I have two workers in the greenhouses right now, starting crops. More will come for land prep and direct sowing. The three artist cottages are booked years in advance. The occupants will show up Memorial Day but they're barely any work. They mostly want to be left alone. I'm called in to change a lightbulb or plunge a toilet." Dane set a sandwich in front of Liko, then turned to rummage in a cabinet and brought out a bag of chips. When he dumped some on their plates, Liko noticed his right hand wore a number of rings and was tattooed with stars that disappeared up the cuff of his fleece. His left hand was bare of both ink and jewelry.

"Diane said you married into the Schoenfelds?"

"She robbed me of all my small talk."

"Is your wife home?"

"No." Dane's tone was curt and Liko, ever mindful of people's secret battles, let the topic drop.

Hey, if he's single, this little lunch might get interesting.

He was staring again, mentally pulling Dane's clothes off. Attraction like an avalanche from his chest into his lap, making his periphery blur a little. Desire purred through his body, warm and lush and electric.

And weirdly familiar.

This has happened before.

"So I noticed the Green Man everywhere," he said. "The hares and rabbits. The wisteria."

"Subtle as a kick in the head."

"So why am I here?"

"Why indeed." Dane sat down. "Look, here's the deal. I don't know who wrote you that letter, but I know everything else."

"Everything else about what?"

"The *Three Hares* mystery. I know how to solve it. If you want, I'll get my laptop, fire up the game and walk you through it. I'll be done before you finish your sandwich. You can post the solution tonight. Case closed. Quest finished."

"Oh," Liko managed to say.

"You'll be famous."

"I will, won't I?"

"Then what will you do with yourself?"

Liko could only stare back.

"Here's what I mean," Dane said. "Are you doing this for the journey or the destination? Do you want me to hand you the answers on a plate? Or do you want me to guide you a little here, a little there. Let you nibble your way to it." He took a pull on his beer. "Look, I'm no stranger to grief. I know how much time you spend figuring out ways to kill time."

Liko gave a weak laugh. "I feel seen."

"So I'm asking, how much time do you want to kill? Do you want to solve this mystery like buying a finished piece of artwork, or do you want it like a paint-by-number kit?"

"I see your point."

"I'll give you the answers, but I'd feel better about it if I knew you had the next thing lined up to fill the void. Do you?"

"Not really."

"What do you do?"

Liko gave his occupation for the second time that day.

"Have you written any books of your own?"

"No."

"Only ghostwritten for other people?"

"That's right."

"Why?"

"Can't think of stories to tell. I don't have that kind of imagination."

"Oh come on, how can you be any kind of writer and not have imagination?"

"I have creativity, not imagination."

"Aren't they the same thing?"

"I don't think so. People with imagination have ideas. People with creativity execute ideas."

"So it's either-or?"

"God, no. Some people have both imagination *and* creativity, and we call them geniuses."

"I like this theory." Dane ran a finger around the plate to catch little blobs of mayo and mustard, then licked them off. Or rather, *sucked* them off. Not looking at Liko, but moving in a way that conveyed he liked to take his time with such things.

It's so on, Liko thought, trying not to stare as Dane rubbed his clean fingertip against his thumb.

"What genre do you write?"

"Mostly thrillers," Liko said. "I can't think of a conspiracy plot to save my life. My brain doesn't think that way. I have a theory I'm not enough of an asshole… But I digress. The point is, if you bring me your complicated plot and spell out the twists, the spoilers, who did what and when and how, I'll make it a masterpiece."

"Good to know," Dane said.

"Do you have an idea for hire?"

Dane wiped his mouth, crumpled the napkin and tossed it on the empty plate. "The mystery in the *Three Hares* game is a love letter. Everything in that chamber is significant to only three people, two of whom are gone."

Liko's eyebrows pulled down at *gone* and Dane held up a palm. "I said I'm no stranger to grief. I'll get to that. My point is, without the context, I don't think the solution to the chamber is going to be very satisfying. Or even interesting. I mean, once you click on everything just right and rearrange the letters and make this do that, and that do this… What happens then is beautiful, but it's beautiful to *me.* Because it's my life. It's my love letter. It makes sense to me. It's important to me. But everyone else will probably think, *What the fuck? This is what we've been wondering about for years? This is stupid. It makes no sense. It was more fun not knowing.*"

"Okay," Liko said, nodding slowly. "Fair."

Dane started peeling the label off his beer bottle. "But if I tell you the story and give you the context… Who knows, maybe you'll find it just as anti-climactic, or maybe not. Maybe it'll mean more to you if you know about me. Truth be told…"

He looked up and Liko noticed one of his brown eyes was slightly darker than the other.

"Lately I'm thinking I want to tell someone my story," Dane went on. "Maybe you could assess it professionally. If it's solid, you take it and run. You walk out of here with both the solution to the Green Man Chamber, and an idea for a book."

"That's unbelievably generous. What's in it for you?"

"A way to move on to the next thing."

"Your own way to kill time."

"Well, I didn't want to be rude about it. Where do you live?"

"Connecticut."

"What's there?"

"My house."

"What else?"

"A lot of memories," Liko said. "A lot of haunted places and associations, a lot of pain. My son's empty bedroom I keep like a shrine. An ex-wife I sleep with too much. A job that isn't dependent on geography."

Dane smiled. "So come here. Bring your job and your grief. Leave your ex-wife."

"Here in general or *here?*" Liko tapped the table for emphasis.

"Either."

"What about your sister?"

"Diane? She comes and goes. She's not my keeper."

"What does she do?"

"In general, she's like a life coach. In particular, she helps me do brave things."

"I see."

"It's basically just me and the dog. The house is too big for us but a lot more people used to live here."

"Who?"

Dane didn't answer. Considering Liko, he licked his lips over the top of the beer bottle and he became, all at once, a thrillingly sexy man.

"Who else used to live here?" Liko pressed.

"Jonathan Henshe."

"When did he leave?"

"Couple years ago."

"Why?"

"Go ask the Green Man." Dane shrugged. "It's what we say around here when we don't have answers."

Their eyes held, poised above complicit smiles. Liko didn't know what they were talking about anymore, only that he was exhilarated in a way he hadn't felt in a really fucking long time.

This is good stuff, something in him said. *Don't rush it.*

Dane was right. Why have it handed to him on a plate when he could nibble a little here, a little there. Kill a whole boatload of time by taking his time.

"Is there a lake around here?" he asked.

"Not since the Pleistocene era."

"Then why is Birch Island called Birch Island?"

"The region was an effluvial plain. Before settlers irrigated it, they'd see massive flooding during storms. Everyone would flee to the highest points in the area, and those points became known as *islands* in local speak. Birch Island was one of the flood refuges. Pine Island is another. There's a bunch of them."

"I see."

"You've come to a refuge, Liko Greenman. With a little poetic license, you could say you were evacuated here after a disaster."

"Mm."

"So why not stay?"

THE DANELAW

They exchanged numbers, but made no definitive plan. "If I do my due diligence and Google you," Liko said, "am I going to find anything disturbing?"

"I don't think so. But here's a thought: What are you doing for May Day?"

In his entire life, Liko had never even acknowledged May Day. He ventured a guess. "Um, dancing around a pole?"

"I always throw a party. Come back down and observe me in my natural habitat. Meet my gang. You can tell a lot about someone from their friends. If we're too weird or your gut throws a red flag, abandon ship."

"I'll think about it."

Dane walked him to the foyer, where Liko slipped on his shoes and zipped his jacket. On the wall by the coat tree was a large framed map of the British Isles. The caption read *England 866* in beautiful calligraphy.

"Ah, it's my home turf," Liko said, stepping closer. "Back in the day."

England was hand drawn in pen and ink, with minuscule cross-hatching in the detail. Kingdoms, cities and towns labeled in precise letters. Mercia, Wessex, Northumbria. And lying between, washed in pale red, were the lands once under Norse or Danish control. A sweeping arc of letters named them: *The Danelaw.*

The house elbowed Liko in the side. *Get it?*

"I'm getting the feeling no coincidences live here," he said. "Danelaw."

Dane smiled. "That's me."

"For real?"

"Danelaw Strong. Nice to meet you."

STRATHCLYDE
NORTHUMBRIA
The Danelaw
Irish Sea
North Sea
York
DANISH MERCIA
Lichfield
Leicester
Cambridge
WALES
ENGLISH MERCIA
WESSEX
Rochester
London
Canter
Winchester
Exeter
Wareham
English Channel
N
W
E
S

ENGLAND 86

"Great name."

Dane gave a little nod, but let the compliment float away.

Liko hesitated, then said, "My real name is Henry. My mother teaches European history, with a specialty in the Victorian era. There was once a lesser prince called Henry of Battenberg, but the royal family called him Liko. Mum fancied the sound of it."

"I do too. It's midway between *likeable* and *lucky.*"

He is legit flirting with me, Liko thought.

He immediately sent the impulse to its room and grounded it for twenty-four hours.

"A clue for the road?" Dane said at the car door.

"Sure."

"Jonathan Henshe is an anagram."

"Of course it is."

Dane smiled. "Now that's a clue on a *plate.* The only one of those you'll get. The rest you gotta work for."

"Understood."

"And hopefully, ye then deign to know me."

"Dane and deign," Liko said. "I actually figured that out last night."

Dane's eyes flicked to the sky as he grinned. "Oh, you figured that out but not the rest of it?"

"What do you mean?"

"Dude…" A laughing sigh. "You seriously don't remember me."

It wasn't a question. The words were wistful almost to the point of sadness, though Dane kept smiling. A beam of sunlight broke through the clouds and hit his brown gaze. One eye dazzled topaz, full of depth and rippling gold. The other sucked the light in and gave back nothing.

And then Liko remembered.

Ye then deign to know me.

Not a boulder dropping on his head but a soft hand caressing his nape.

His mouth fell open as Dane's face shifted into place within his memory. It stayed open as the rest of the game's phrase unfolded to become names. Names Liko forgot he remembered.

"Wait," he whispered, his memory whirling like a copper wind spinner. Wisteria hares turning back the clock. Back in time. To a party. Not long ago by the calendar, but another lifetime to Liko.

"My wife died," said the man on the roof, minutes before the New Year. "Nomi."

"Beautiful name," Liko had murmured.

"She wasn't my legal wife. Nomi was married to Ethan. I was their partner."

"Wait," Liko said again, begging the world to hold still because this was too much to take in.

Ye then deign to know me.

Ethan. Dane. To Nomi.

Liko's pointed finger moved through thick air to press the center of Dane's chest. Dane reared back just the tiniest bit, but held still.

"You're the guy I met on New Year's Eve," Liko said.

Dane's smile was pure delight. "Hi."

"Holy shit."

"Right?"

"Wait. No. You can't be."

"I am," Dane said. "It's me."

"But you had blue eyes," Liko said, talking more to himself now, his finger pushing a little, trying to pin down the memory. "Didn't you? Yes. It's the first thing I noticed. I remember seeing you and thinking, *Goddamn, those eyes should be illegal.* And… Wait…"

Dane only looked at him.

"Diane has the eyes I remember," Liko said slowly. "Your eyes were in her…face?"

His mind clutched the insides of his skull, hanging on for dear life and crying, *Pump the brakes, you moron.*

Dane raised fingers to his left eye and made a pinching motion. He squeezed both lids shut, blinked a few times, then looked at Liko with one brown eye and one blue eye. In his pinched fingers was a brown-tinted contact lens.

A long staring moment passed between the men.

"Okay, this is a lot to take in," Liko said.

"I know."

Liko crossed his arms, brows pulled tight, and leaned back on his car door. "It is you, right? We met. New Year's Eve. On the roof at Huff and Maisie's house."

"Yes."

"We had a date. We were supposed to go back this year. Or last year, rather. I'd ask rude questions, we'd resolve further, then exchange names."

Dane's two-toned expression went even more gentle. "The Jensens had to cancel the party. And for obvious reasons, you wouldn't have been there anyway."

"Right. I was…losing my mind."

"Which I totally understand. Because when we met, I was just finding my lost mind."

Liko nodded, suspended in the magical moment. "Because your wife died. And your partner left you. I remember."

I remember. Yes, I remember. The party. I looked at you and you at me. I felt something so intense, I introverted. Panicked.

Memory unfolded like origami, spilling little details.

I couldn't get a bead on you. It was pissing me off. The Universe was pushing me to say hello. Instead, I went up to the roof to hide. But you found me there.

Holy shit, I remember.

"When did you realize it was me?" Liko asked.

"A few seconds after I opened the door last night. The beard threw me at first. And I think you've lost weight. I remember you bigger. And happier."

"I did," Liko said. "I was."

"But then I saw your eyes." Dane smiled. "See, I'm not the only one with an unforgettable stare."

"Why didn't you tell me right then?"

"Lots of reasons." Dane put his hands in his pockets and exhaled. "You were already reeling from puzzle pieces coming together. You'd been crying. You were overwhelmed and exhausted. I figured it was fairer to give you space and not burden you with one more coincidental revelation."

"I see."

"Also, I was shocked to see you again, at this time and in this way. So shocked that I kind of panicked. I figured I'd tell you when you came back today, but when you told me about your son… I felt horrible. And the stunt with Diane seemed so cheap. Not cheap, but… Man, I don't even know how to explain this."

"Use short words."

Dane's chin tilted. "That was one of your lines on New Year's Eve."

"I inherited it from my dad, but go on."

"I don't usually… Diane's someone who mostly lives inside me. To parade her around like that was… I keep coming back to cheap. Cheap and stupid."

"Then I'll be cheap and stupid and ask are you a drag queen?"

Dane laughed now. "No."

"Are you transitioning?"

"No. Not a drag queen. Not transitioning. I don't have a multiple personality disorder. It might be a little early to play trust games, but will you trust me anyway? I will tell you, I promise. But not today. Definitely not in the driveway."

We can take it back inside, Liko thought, feeling the air crackle between them. "Fair enough," he said aloud. "One more question?"

"One. Make it good."

"The painting over the fireplace. Is it you? I mean, were you the model for Gideon Perfect's album cover?"

"Yes," Dane said, cheerful and firm, as if pleased to finally be able to give a straight answer. "I'll tell you that story, too."

THE MEANINGLESS SCRAPHEAP

Liko was smiling as he drove away from Birch Island. It felt like getting back on the exercise wagon, it had been so long since he grinned deep into his cheeks. He skirted the George Washington Bridge and took the Palisades north, winding along 9W through pretty riverfront villages and crossing the Tappan Zee. The sunset was glorious, the view magnificent north and south, and Liko felt good.

I feel good, he thought, squeezing the steering wheel to help press the emotion into his memory.

You feel good. You're here. Right here, right now. Feeling good. Looking forward to something. Kicking an opportunity around. You can do this. You can have a life and *mourn your son.*

It's allowed.

He arrived home having made no decisions, but still smiling and full of a desire to buckle down to business. Instead of heading to his office to unload his backpack, he set up shop on the dining room table. His day job would stay in the office. Here on the table he'd work the second shift.

Laptop. Notebook. His stack of research books. He had to do a little bit of hunting around the house to find their old Scrabble game, but he ran it to earth in the basement and dumped the bag of letter tiles on the table. He had anagrams to solve.

For all his love of language, Liko had never been good at word puzzles. He was always missing the obvious. As much as he tried to look for the simplest solution first, he usually found Occam's Razor after it had slashed him in the face.

He had to admit later Dane had served him a clue on a plate, but it took an absurd amount of time before Liko's brain registered the "than" in *Jonathan.*

"Oh for fuck's sake," he muttered, drawing the T-H-A-N toward him, then adding one of the Es from *Henshe* to make *Ethan.* A head-smacking flash of clarity, and the rest of the tiles moved into place, forming *Ethan John Hasen.* Liko grabbed at his stack of books, and stared at the cover of *Harefoot* by Ethan J. Hasen.

"Yes," he growled under his breath. Then, fuck it, he lived alone. He cried it at the top of his lungs. *"Yes."*

He switched the tiles back to *Jonathan Henshe* and took a picture. Slid them around to read *Ethan John Hasen,* took another. Then took a picture of the book cover.

He texted it all to Dane. After five minutes, Dane replied with an emoji of a plate. Nothing more.

Another long minute creaked by, then Liko caved and typed: ***Don't be a cagey bitch.***

LOL, Dane replied. ***See you on May Day. Bring a pole.***

You wish.

He got nothing more. He turned to the back of the book and the inside flaps, looking for a biography.

Ethan J. Hasen is a contemporary artist and illustrator who combines folklore and cultural motifs with modern influences. He first gained attention for his collaboration with Cate Coates on her children's series Madrigal Farm, *for which they won a Caldecott medal. Hasen went on to illustrate the 25th anniversary edition of Richard Adams'* Watership Down, *and in collaboration with Philip Pullman, created the art book* Daemon, *artistic depictions of the animal soulmates in Pullman's* His Dark Materials *series.* Daemon *won both a Hugo award and a Chesley award.*

Hasen branched into the online digital art world with his designs for Leporine: The Down *collectible card game. He's also a contributing artist to many popular video games and casual game apps.*

"Many popular video games," Liko said. "Like *Three Hares?*"

Weird how Hasen's artistic credentials were so detailed yet the gaming section of his resume was a throwaway. Almost coy. *Yeah, I did some work on that.*

No picture was included with the biography. No mention of a spouse or partner. Which, if you asked Liko Greenman, was damn rude.

He Googled *liner notes for Gideon Perfect Two-Faced album.* The credit was all the way at the end, after production and before the acknowledgments:

Cover artwork and design: J. Nathan Heshone

"Son of a bitch," Liko said, moving tiles around again. Same letters, a third anagram.

Jonathan Henshe.

Ethan John Hasen.

J. Nathan Heshone.

Right there in the open, for anyone who would deign to look.

Well, and anyone who had a lucky invitation to Schoenfeld's.

His hand tapped his phone, itching to text Kyle. To crow and brag and let him know his old man was really doing it.

Kyle knows, he told himself. *You either believe he sees you right now and he knows, or you don't. Pick a side and live it. Good lord, text him if you want. Who gives a shit? Write him letters, leave a voicemail. Talk out loud to him. Do what you have to do. Just don't give up on this.*

He drew his notebook toward him, read the current list and added his latest discoveries.

Go to Birch Island, NY and look for <u>yourself</u> along the roadside.
Myself➜Greenman➜Green Man motif on the stone wall.
Farm is called <u>Schoenfeld's</u>
John <u>Schoenfeld</u> is author of Journey of the Green Man.
Man living there now named Dane, but last name isn't Schoenfeld.
His name is Danelaw Strong and I've met him before. New Year's Eve 2015 at the Jensens' house.
He was part of a threesome. His wife had died and his partner left him.
He sometimes dresses as a woman named Diane? Says he's not transitioning. This part is weird, I don't know what to make of it.

Dane/Diane has one blue eye and one brown eye. Both eyes were blue when I first met him, but when we met again this time, they were brown.

Does he do this all the time? Sometimes? Is covering one or the other just a game he plays?

His shoulders relaxed and his fingers loosened. As he wrote, his lips faintly moved around questions. Sometimes he spoke aloud, and glanced toward an invisible, adolescent presence beside him.

Dane was the model for the cover of Gideon Perfect's Two-Faced album. The artwork hangs over the fireplace. Album's artist credit is <u>J. Nathan Heshone,</u> anagram of <u>Jonathan Henshe</u>, anagram of <u>Ethan John Hasen</u>, author and artist behind Harefoot.

Three names. Three hares.

So these are all the same person? The artist Ethan Hasen created the Three Hares game and also the cover for Two-Faced?

Was Dane the inspiration just for the cover, or was his face, with its two different eyes, the inspiration for the entire album?

Is Two-Faced a clue to the game?

Liko thought about the epithet *two-faced*. It meant a host of unflattering things—cunning, conniving, double-crossing, opportunistic and dishonest. You couldn't pull anything complimentary from *two-faced*. Yet the vibe Liko was getting from Dane, while unusual, wasn't shifty. Liko definitely felt all kinds of baffled right now, but he didn't feel fucked with.

"Not yet," he muttered behind a half-smile. He scratched his head with the end of the pen, then began writing again.

I'm remembering more of the details from the party. Dane's wife died on or around her birthday, I think. He told me his partners' names. Nomi—I thought this was beautiful. And Ethan, who had left him.

"Ye then deign to know me" means ETHAN DANE TO NOMI.

It's right there if you know who you're talking about.

You need the context. Anyone can solve the mystery, but Dane said it won't be interesting or satisfying unless you have the context. The Green Man Chamber is a love letter to his life. Important only to three people, two of whom are now gone.

His train of thought stalled, Liko doodled the name *Danelaw Strong* again. "I *knew* I knew that guy," he said.

The freakin' twink-otter-construction worker-poet from the Jensens' New Year's Eve party. Liko forgot. Of course he forgot. He lost his mind when Kyle died, and his consciousness quickly divided all aspects of life into two categories: The Precious Little I Give a Fuck About, and The Meaningless Scrapheap of Everything Else.

The hair on his forearms was rising and falling. This was fucking *nuts*. Shit like this didn't happen to him. Weird coincidences that made him feel all goofy and magical and willing to suspend disbelief.

Savor it, he reminded himself. *It's a paint-by-number kit. You got all the time you want to slowly kill.*

Liko tapped his pen on the pages, then he wrote: *Why was Dane even at that party? How does he know Huff and Maisie?*

Well. Ask and ye ought to receive. He texted Dane: **How do you know the Jensens?**

He waited. Dane seemed to have a personal rule of waiting five minutes before replying. The bubbles popped up, indicating he was typing. Then they stopped. Then started. Then stopped.

"You are *edging* me," Liko said.

Finally the reply came in: **How do you know them?**

What did I tell you about being a cagey bitch, Liko typed.

LOL.

Did you ask them about me?

No. We agreed not to exchange names. You said, "Don't cheat and ask Huff and Maisie. You'll ruin it."

I did?

You did. So I didn't. Because, ways to kill time.

Liko arranged Scrabble tiles on the table to read *Huff and Maisie Jensen,* took a picture and texted it, asking **Yes or no—is anagramming this a waste of time?**

Dane deigned to answer in ten seconds: **Yes.**

Liko rearranged the tiles to read *Gideon Perfect.*

Is THIS a waste of time? he asked.

Yes. Let me clarify: Gideon, Huff and Maisie are part of the story, but their names aren't clues in the mystery.

Good, Liko typed. **I suck at anagrams.**

So do I. And I'm giving away too many clues before you've earned them. Hitting the sack. Night.

ME SPOON YOU

With Liko's presence lingering in the farmhouse, along with the scent of his aftershave, Dane was horned up to distraction. All the rest of the day, he twisted and writhed and burned with wanting. To the point where he considered the Argentinian farrier who lived in a trailer parked at Kulleseid's Orchard. The man was terrifyingly gorgeous, and he'd cut quite an impressive swathe through the single population of Warwick Township, male and female. So Dane was pretty confident if he rapped on Pao's door and said with no preamble, *Wanna fuck?* he wouldn't be turned away.

But it wasn't what he wanted. Nor how he operated. He'd never mindlessly fucked someone just to scratch an itch, though he was rabidly curious about people who did. The opportunity had knocked once or twice in the years before he met Ethan and Nomi, but Dane always chickened out.

"I declined politely for my own reasons," he clarified aloud, for absolutely no one's benefit.

God, he was horny.

Horny and lonely.

Which was a suck-ass combination.

He picked up his phone, contemplated texting Liko, then put the phone down again. His body screamed for connection. For skin-on-skin contact. For passion and release and afterglow. He lay in the big king bed, wanting to feel someone's naked touch, taste someone's open-mouthed kiss. The house contracted around him, holding him in a palm that was both cupped and close, yet empty and forlorn.

He loved this house with all his heart. He didn't want to leave. But goddamn, it just wasn't built for one person. On bad nights like this, he swore he could hear it crying. Weeping and longing for the familiar buzz of activity and not understanding where it went.

Dane had no idea how superb his domestic life was until he found himself alone in this monster of a house. Every day he was made painfully aware of the unconscious divisions of labor. So many arrangements that developed as a matter of skill or preference. Like the dusting. Dane had lived in this house blissfully unaware of dust because it was Ethan's personal nemesis. He assigned himself the task, saying he did some of his best thinking while dusting. Now a film coated every horizontal service. Tumbleweeds of gray gunk gathered in corners and Dane had no idea where they came from.

For twenty-two years, he'd handled the household bills because he was good at it. He liked data, numbers, a bottom line, reconciling accounts to the penny. He'd never been a car person—if it had four wheels and a radio and got him from here to there, he was content. Ethan and Nomi were the auto aficionados, so they handled all the auto hassle. Now that hassle was Dane's to handle.

All three hares could cook well, but Nomi was hands-down best at it. Ethan was a fantastic grocery shopper, but Nomi made him lists because only she knew what was actually in the fridge, the pantry, and the extra freezer. The same way Dane noticed when the house was down to three rolls of toilet paper and two extra lightbulbs, or how Ethan declared the horde of jackets, coats, boots and shoes in the mudroom needed to be culled.

When it came to the house, they each had something they specialized in, something they were neurotic about, and things they outright hated. Nomi put clean sheets on the beds, but only Dane noticed when mattresses needed to be flipped. Ethan was the unquestioned interior decorator, deciding when furniture needed to be replaced, a new rug bought, paintings and art rearranged, but it was Dane who scheduled delivery, met the truck, and took the old stuff to the dump. Dane who kept the tool bench organized and always knew where the tape measure was. He hated things not put back where they belonged. Nomi hated when crumbs were left on kitchen counters. Ethan hated when picture frames were askew. Dane would happily fold seven baskets of laundry, but left it in piles on the couch and dining room table because he hated putting it away. Same with vacuuming—he'd vacuum all day, every day, if someone else put the damn thing away when he was done.

"Vacuum groom is here, my liege," Ethan said, winding up the cord. "I shall stable your steed."

Now Dane's duties had tripled. Managing a big house as a sole occupant felt like battling a dragon. Making dinner for one was a pathetic task he had to face every night.

"Jesus fuck, Dane, hire a cleaning person," Maisie said. "Subscribe to a meal plan, order in, go out. Who *cares?*"

He clung to Maisie and Huff and their sage, sound advice. They invited him over often, included him, lifted him up. When Dane confessed he'd been sleeping in one of the spare bedrooms since Nomi died, but was toying with the idea of moving back to the master suite, the Jensens applauded the positive attitude and showed up to help him make it feel like a different room.

They painted one wall a handsome dark orange and hung new curtains. They moved the dresser, put the headboard against a different wall, picked new bedding. Some new lamps. Dane kept the gorgeous 4x5 portrait called *Nomi With Dusk Tiara* where it was, because he truly loved looking at it, but he switched out some of the smaller pictures. The updates didn't erase Nomi's existence, they just gave a new perspective. And Dane found that while he didn't fall asleep any easier, once he fell, he stayed asleep.

Now he lay in the center of the big mattress, rolling first to the side closest to the bathroom, where Nomi always slept. Then toward the other side, which was his. Sides were for sleeping, the center was for sex. They threw each other all over this bed, but when it was time to sleep, they separated to the edges, all business.

Ethan didn't often come in with them. He functioned on little rest and his creativity kept bizarre business hours, showing up to party at nine or ten in the evenings. When Ethan came into the master bedroom, it was usually in the darkest hours before dawn.

"Are you decent?" he whispered.

"No," Dane mumbled, even though they were.

Ethan crawled up the mattress from the foot of the bed, under the comforter. He'd showered, and his body was cool, damp and bright as it settled into the warm space between the sleeping bodies.

"Hold still," Dane muttered.

"Spoon me," Ethan said to Nomi.

"Hm?"

"Spoon."

A throat-clearing moan—"Hasenpfeffer, you're trying to kill me"—and a shuffle of bodies. Through cracked eyes, Dane saw Nomi's hand slide around Ethan's waist and against his heart. Ethan put palms on Dane's chest and pushed at him.

"Turn over. Me spoon you."

Dane groaned and grunted as he rolled away. "Stop killing me."

"Shh." Then Ethan's body was tight up against Dane's back, his hand on Dane's

heart. Soon the three hares were still and together and sleeping, and it was so sweet. Nothing sweeter than being asleep in the down of hares, chasing each other in dreams.

When Dane woke, Ethan's hand had gone from his heart to his lap, inside his pajama pants, getting him hard. Then Ethan exited at the foot of the bed, laughing.

"I fluffed him for you, Nome."

"Swine," Nomi groaned.

"Dog," Dane growled.

"I'll make coffee."

"Get out," the bedmates cried, then made love when the door closed.

Dane gave up, got up and took a Xanax. He went back to bed and thought about Liko. Wondered what he was doing. Was he awake? Working? Writing? Playing the game? Curled in a ball on the floor, crying for his son?

Dane picked up his phone, went as far as opening messages, then put the phone down again. His hand hesitated, then slipped down the front of his sweats.

If you're gonna do this, then do it.

He was such a cerebral lover, he couldn't fantasize about anything the least bit separated from reality. He didn't jerk off to celebrities or entertain pizza delivery boys. If the scenario wasn't believable in his heart, it went nowhere in his hand.

He moved over to his old side of the bed. He looked toward the bathroom, imagined a light turning off and Liko coming out. It was the man from the New Year's Eve party, but with the graying hair and beard of today. A man who harbored great sadness, but no longer looked like a shipwreck. Tall and built within soft sleep clothes, which he shed with unconscious ease. He crawled onto the bed and held still, poised on his knees, looking at Dane.

No, not looking at you, Diane said. *We're not even here. This is his bed. He's alone. He doesn't know we're watching.*

Now it clicked in. Dane's bottom lip moved a little behind his top teeth as he inhaled slow and deep, rolling on his side. Liko's eyes closed as he matched the inhale and exhale, his head bowed a little, a tiny smile lifting a corner of his mouth.

He's thinking about you, Diane said. *He forgot but he remembered. He's remembering right now. The party. The roof. The anonymity. The feel of your face under his lips. Your body against his when you hugged.*

Dane nodded, remembering all those things too. Watching as Liko's hand closed around his erection. And then Dane had it. All he ever needed was one little moment, and then it was a matter of chasing it down. This moment was Liko's hand closing into a fist. Pinky to index finger and his thumb last, moving in a little circle. Touching himself with Dane in his head. Remembering. Reliving.

Dane curled tighter around his own hand in his own lap. He had Liko now. He had him.

I have you in hand, Green Man.

Diane steepled fingers over her mouth and nose, blue eyes shining with excitement. *God he's gorgeous.*

Liko's eyes opened. "I see you over there."

Dane felt the blood in his body rise up, coursing fast and furious along his limbs, whirlpooling in his chest, hardening in his lap, and setting his face on fire. His smile broke through, tongue running along the edges of his teeth because he was fucking *blushing* here.

Liko laughed softly. "If you're gonna do *that*, then do it with me."

Dane got up and moved close, sitting on his heels, pressing his kneecaps to Liko's. Putting his blushing grin against the bearded smile. Close enough to kiss. But not yet. Time for that later. This was now. This little moment right here. Kneeling close and touching only themselves. Remembering what was forgotten. Imagining all that was yet to come.

Liko's forehead touched Dane's brow. "Don't stop thinking about me."

"I never did."

"Think about me. I need it. I need to be remembered. It keeps me alive."

"We resolved to live."

"We did."

"I never forgot," Dane said. "You've been in my head and heart for over a year, Liko Greenman. Now I have you in hand. You're right in my hands and I'll never forget…"

SHENANIGANS

Dane's last text had gotten under Liko's skin: ***I'm giving away too many clues before you've earned them. Hitting the sack.***

The words weren't even remotely sexual, but *earned* dangled like an apple ripe for picking, while *sack* was fodder for a ravenous inner teenager. Hence Liko was no longer fiddling around with wooden Scrabble tiles, but standing under the shower spray, a hand braced against ceramic tiles. Breathing hard through the steamy afterglow, having gotten spectacularly off while thinking about all the ways he could hit Dane's sack and earn more clues.

"Anagram that," he said, exhaling hard.

Despite the mind-blowing release, he couldn't sleep. He went and sat in Kyle's room a long time, staring at his boy's possessions. The window out which Liko had crowed that last night, "My son is listening to me!" The syringe of joy he'd wanted to plunge into his veins.

He went back to his bed.

"What else is in Connecticut?" Dane had asked.

A lot of memories, a lot of haunted places and associations, a lot of pain. My son's empty bedroom I keep like a shrine. An ex-wife I sleep with too much.

The day after Kyle died, Janelle stormed into Liko's house and tore Kyle's room apart. Federal agents couldn't have done a more thorough sweep. She was looking for booze, drugs, porn, something from the hinterlands of the Dark Web in Kyle's browser history, *anything* that would explain why his brain had inexplicably imploded. She found nothing to blame, so she turned on Liko and tore him apart, demanding how, why, when, what happened, over and over, looking for the reason, the explanation, the *thing*. Threatening lawsuits, death, financial ruin, castration, a suite in hell, a lifetime commitment to making Liko suffer the rest of his days.

Liko let her rage. He barely heard her anyway. Except for the death part. He got really excited when it seemed Janelle might actually kill him. He wanted nothing more than to die. He'd bare his throat and go quietly. But alas, this avenging angel left Liko curled in fetal position amid the wreckage of their son's bedroom, alive and whole. Which, under the circumstances, was the cruelest thing she could've done.

The night after Kyle's funeral, Janelle came back to the house. She rang the bell, waited politely for admission. Without a word, she set a pot of her famous chicken and rice on her old stove, put a six-pack in her old fridge. Then she took Liko's hand and led him upstairs to their old bed, where they fucked like monsters. No love or tenderness in the act, merely a desperate attempt to remake what had been unmade. They had rolled, pitched and snarled from one side of the mattress to the other. They screamed in each other's mouths, left fingerprint bruises and scratches on each other's bodies. They licked each other's tears when it was over, then went down to the kitchen, naked and silent, where they drank the beer and ate chicken and rice. They had sex again and as he fell asleep, Liko thought maybe Janelle would come back to him. Something good might come of this. But he woke in an empty bed, feeling broken-backed and raw. When he went stumbling along the upstairs hall, he found Janelle had put Kyle's room in immaculate order before leaving. It had stayed that way ever since.

Liko and Janelle still slept together. Occasionally. Randomly. With no discussion. Because it made Kyle alive for a few precious moments. When the black hole of loss became too much, he and Janelle went running for the act that had created their son, desperately trying to snatch him back from the other side, will him back into existence.

Liko's hand reached for the phone on the bedside table, considering Janelle. Then deciding, no. Not tonight. It wasn't bad enough.

He lay awake. Quiet and still, yet under constant assault from within.

Grief blew a hole in you the way Schwarzenegger fired a rifle into a T-1000 and turned his head and torso inside-out. Liko had studied this theory at length, pausing *Terminator 2* to ponder Robert Patrick's intense, chiseled expression as it was shot in half. How he kept focus on his target even as the ribbons of his mimetic polyalloy brain fluttered above his shoulders. He remained stoic—all right, maybe a *flicker* of amused curiosity—as his gleaming, ravaged structure melted back together and reassembled into perfection. Crisp and commanding in his trim, unwrinkled cop uniform, like nothing happened.

Grief was like that.

Except for the stoic, amused part.

And the "like nothing happened" part.

Maybe grief was like Schwarzenegger descending into a vat of molten steel, flashing a heroic thumbs-up. "Fine. This is fine. This is *great,* actually, I'm looking forward to oblivion. Hasta la vista, baby."

Actually it was more like the foster father deep-throating a mimetic poly-alloy machete.

Or Linda Hamilton taking a nuclear shock blast to the tits.

"How you doing?" kind friends asked Liko.

"Okay," he said, thinking, *Watch* Terminator 2 *and pause randomly. That's how I'm doing.*

LIKO'S PHONE PINGED. A slight delay between the chime and what it meant.

Who's texting me?

His eyes opened.

Someone's dead.

He shut his eyes, kept his back turned to the bedside table, pretended he hadn't heard. Not tonight, motherfuckers. The bell wasn't tolling for him. He didn't have to know what he didn't know.

The phone pinged again.

He breathed in through gritted teeth. Told himself if it were one of his parents in distress, it would be a call, not a text.

He half-rolled, reaching and fumbling for the phone, squinting against the light of the display, registering it was 3:02 in the morning and it was Dane's name in his notifications.

"You little slut," Liko muttered, grinning as he swiped and read the first text:

I'm sure you figured out Hasen is German for "hares." As in Drei-Hasen-Fenster.

The second text read, **You're welcome** with the plate emoji.

Liko put a forearm over his eyes, breathed in and exhaled to the ceiling, "I am too old to be texting guys in the middle of the night."

His inner teenager promptly opined the middle of the night was perfect for texting.

Liko thought up and rejected a few lines, then typed: **At this rate I'll have a new set of china for Christmas dinner.**

Did I wake you up?

Yes.

Sorry. I won't make a habit of it.
Yeah, I'm a little old for these shenanigans.
And that was all. Liko turned the phone face-down and rolled away, thinking he'd never fall back to sleep. But he did. He slept so soundly he never heard the ping at 5:37, when Dane texted back: ***Bullshit.***

THE NAOMI ROAD 28

Roof boss, St. John the Baptist church, Broadclyst, Devon, UK

BASIL AND BOOTSY

MARCH WENT OUT LIKE a lamb and April came in like Atilla the Hun. The one-year anniversary of Kyle's death was in the vanguard, with a celebration of life memorial service and the unveiling of his gravestone. Liko was consumed with logistics, planning and anxiety. His parents flying in for a week meant airport runs and lodging. Sticky phone calls with Janelle about the catering and music. Making sure their mothers were kept at a distance. Betty Greenman and Susan Dalusio had never liked each other in the best of circumstances and Kyle's passing had not improved relations.

"What happened there?" Dane asked. He'd called when Liko was running a multitude of errands.

"I was scrutinized pretty bad when Kyle died," Liko said. "Until the autopsy results came back. He was at my place. I saw him last. And I was asleep when…" He let the sentence trail off as he loaded the last grocery bag and slammed the trunk. "So for a few especially unpleasant days, I was a suspect."

"Oh Jesus, I'm so sorry."

"Even after they determined it was an aneurysm, Susan never let it go. Never stopped holding it over my head. It's the reason she and Mum can't be in the same room unsupervised."

"Yikes," Dane said. "I'm really sorry, man."

"Thanks. This is just rough."

"Hang in there. Reach out any time, all right?"

Between the stress of planning and the stress of psyching himself up to get through the day, Liko hadn't the wherewithal to be present and mindful and take it all in. Lying in bed that night, he found he could barely remember the ceremony. All the beautiful tributes from friends and family had blended into one giant accolade. All the hugs into one embrace. All the tears into an ocean. Only a handful of crystallized memories had imprinted in Liko's mind, among them a text Dane sent at 4:30 in the morning:

Today's gonna be hard. You don't have to do it perfectly. You just have to do it. And you can. You got this.

The text was followed by a picture of the Green Man on the stone pillar. Then one more message: ***This dude will be with you, too.***

When the Greenmans flew back to the UK, Liko went with them, into the bosom of the motherland. He did little but sleep and sit around the kitchen table with his parents, eating and talking, laughing and crying, consuming innumerable cups of tea until the sun went over the yardarm and then they poured a drink and talked some more. Four days passed before Liko thought to ask, "Mum, you know what Tinner's Hares are, yeah?"

Betty Greenman, Exeter born and bred, looked over her shoulder from the stove. "Of course," she said, as if he were witless. "Why do you ask?"

Liko got his laptop and started *Three Hares.*

"There's a whole game about them?" Betty said.

"With quite a cult following. Kyle loved it."

"My nan had a set of plates with these hares," she said. "I saw it all the time on tea towels and things."

"They're in China, too?" Basil Greenman said, peering both through and over his glasses.

"The earliest depictions of the motif are in China," Liko said. "It moved west along the Old Silk road."

He fast-forwarded to where the player arrived in Devon, at that great cluster of churches in the southwest of England where the Tinner's Hares were found.

"Broadclyst," Betty said, pointing. "That's my village. Look, St. John the Baptist. My primary school was across the street."

She clicked to go into the church and was soon busy with the hidden objects puzzle. Basil, ever ignorant that he had a world of information in his pocket, got a travel map and spread it on the kitchen table. With a red pen, he circled other locations in the game. Liko sat close by, chin on a fist, occasionally leaning an ear on his old man's shoulder.

"Bootsy," Basil said, "remember the Jack in the Green Inn, out the London Road toward Cobden?"

"Of course."

"Jack in the Green," Basil said. "It's another name for the Green Man. The leafy face was on the sign out front. Anyway, why don't we take a little trip this weekend?"

They found a bed and breakfast and made a day of driving around Devon's country roads, stopping at four of the churches. St. Michael's in Spreyton. St. Mary the Virgin in Cheriton Bishop. St. Cyriac and St. Julitta in Newton St. Cyres. Then back to St. John the Baptist in Broadclyst.

Playing a bit of the game in real life, Liko texted Dane, with pictures.

Dane replied: ***Activate face recognition, please.***

Liko took a selfie and sent it, along with a shot of his parents he'd taken earlier. ***The trees under which my apple lies. AKA, the folks tucking into lunch.***

What are their names? Dane asked.

Dad is Basil. Rhymes with razzle-dazzle. Mum is Elizabeth and most people call her Betty, but Dad calls her Bootsy.

Shut up. Your parents are Basil and Bootsy?

It's what Brits call "twee."

What do they call you?

Which seemed a strange question. He answered: ***Liko?***

LOL. I mean like darling or love or shmoopykins.

Mum calls me "ducks" sometimes. Dad's not an endearment kind of guy.

Gotcha.

You can call me shmoopykins.

Bet you say that to all the Great Danes.

"And who are you flirting with," Basil said, sliding into the pew next to Liko.

"No one," Liko said, feeling instantly thirteen.

"A man only smiles like that when he's snogging on his phone. Out with it, mate."

"Just someone I met. They're into the *Three Hares* game too."

"Oh they are?" Basil said, leaning on the pronoun.

Liko smiled, shaking his head. "*He* is into the game, too."

"And into you?"

"Possibly."

Basil patted him. "Well, that's something."

"He's cool," Liko said, "but I don't know if I'm great company right now."

"Bollocks."

Betty materialized out of nowhere and swatted the back of Basil's head. "I'll remind you we're in *church*. Move over. Now what's this boll— nonsense about not being good company?"

"Our Liko's smoldering with some bloke."

"And suddenly I'm regretting this little jaunt," Liko mumbled.

Betty looped her arm through his and gave it a squeeze. "Who is he? Tell Mums."

"It's a long story."

"Use short words," Basil said.

When Liko considered telling his parents about Dane, the pew of a church in Devon had never been one of the settings. But here they were. And right over their heads was a boss—an ornamental cap locking the ribs of the vaulted ceiling—carved with the Three Hares, exactly as it was in the game.

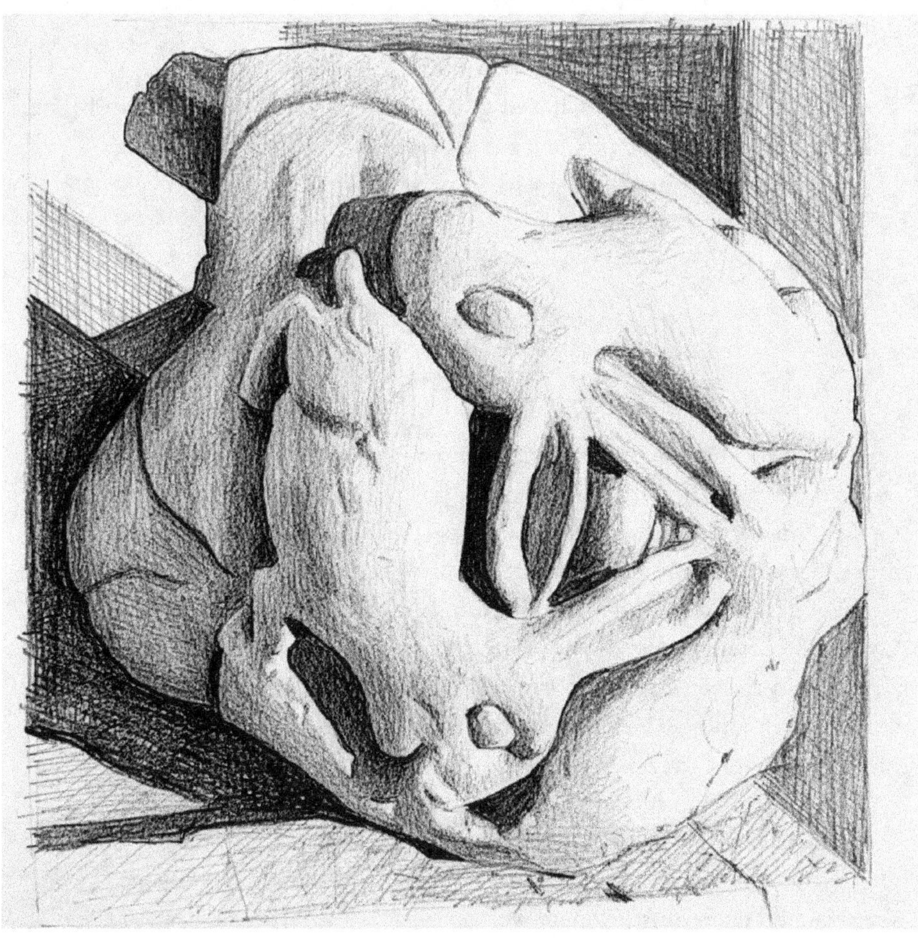

So he told them about the mystery within *Three Hares* and Kyle's fascination with it. He told them how, by an extremely weird and random set of circumstances, he'd met the former partner of the game's creator. Dane knew the secrets of the Green Man's chamber, but had proposed spoon-feeding rather than gorging. Last, Liko told about the invitation to Schoenfeld's farm for the summer.

"Why not?" Betty said. "You always say you can work from anywhere."

"It's not good for you to be alone in that little house," Basil said. "Alone with all the memories behind that bloody bathroom door. Have a change of scene. A change of company. Do it."

"It's one of the perks of owning your own business," Betty said. "Isn't it, ducks?"

"Well, I own it with two other people."

"Two good people who will tell you the same thing your Mum and I are. Take the summer. Go to this place, Schoenfeld's."

"Have an adventure," Betty said. "Then see what happens."

"I think," Liko said, "I will."

GAVIN CANTOR AND CYNTHIA MESA were indeed good people. They and Liko had met in college, lost touch, and reconnected in their thirties to discover they were all working in various fields of writing. They started CGM Creative as a freelance editing business. Over time it morphed into developmental editing and coaching, then into ghostwriting. Liko wrote thrillers and Gavin did mostly historical fiction, but they were small fry compared to Cynthia's cozy mysteries.

It was an excellent little gig which allowed Liko to work from home his entire married life and be Kyle's primary caretaker, while Janelle was the primary breadwinner at AT&T.

Liko took a month's bereavement leave after Kyle's death, stopping work on the latest Madeleine Kent book. She was his biggest client and the fees from ghostwriting her series would've easily put Kyle through state college. Luckily she was a decent, compassionate woman with seventeen ideas in the hopper at all times. She had plenty to keep her busy. She sent Liko flowers with a beautiful condolence card, and a separate email telling him not to give her a thought, just come back when he was ready.

He came back, not sure of himself. He was a changed man—would it show in his writing?

He'd done six Madeleine Kents and knew how to write her. The bigger challenge was his first new client, William Shepherd. They met, they chatted, they brainstormed, they storyboarded, they outlined. Liko went into the cave, then emerged to send the first five chapters. These were critical, for they introduced Detective Conrad O'Higgins, who would anchor the entire series.

Shepherd didn't respond for three days and Liko wondered if he'd be looking for another career. Then Shepherd emailed:

> *Wow, I wasn't expecting this much emotional depth in between the action. It moves, but it feels. A thriller with soul. It's making me plan out the rest of the series in a whole new way. Great stuff. Can't wait to read more. Really excited about this collaboration. More. Gimme.*

Shepherd released the novel with the promotional tagline *A thriller with soul* and it hit *USA Today* as a best seller. Liko's fee and the advance for the next three novels would almost pay off the rest of his mortgage. He and Janelle had taken the utterly craptastic step of withdrawing the funds in Kyle's 529. The bank decently waived the penalty fee given the beneficiary had died. Half went to charity, the bereaved parents split the rest.

Liko hated that money. He knew it was there, knew he wouldn't be a fool and not use it if he needed to, and he hated it.

Given the remote nature of the business, Liko knew he didn't have to tell Gavin and Cynthia he'd be working from New York over the summer. But he stood them lunch and let them know. He told his grief therapist, Brenda, of the plan. He would keep his standing monthly appointment with her— Norwalk was only a 90-minute drive from Schoenfeld's.

The only thing left to do was to tell Dane.

THE NAOMI ROAD 29-31

Postcards sent April 2017

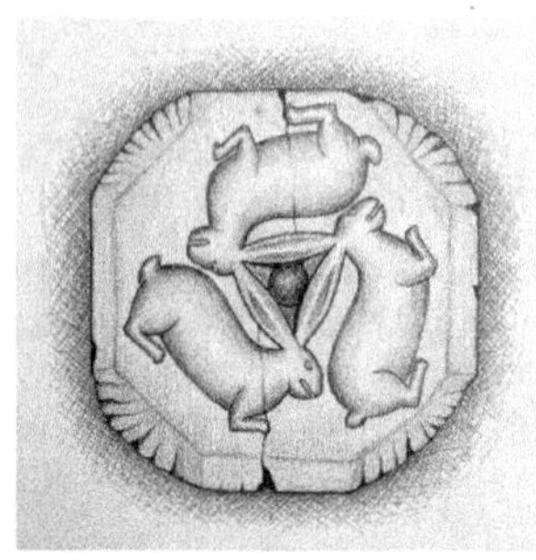 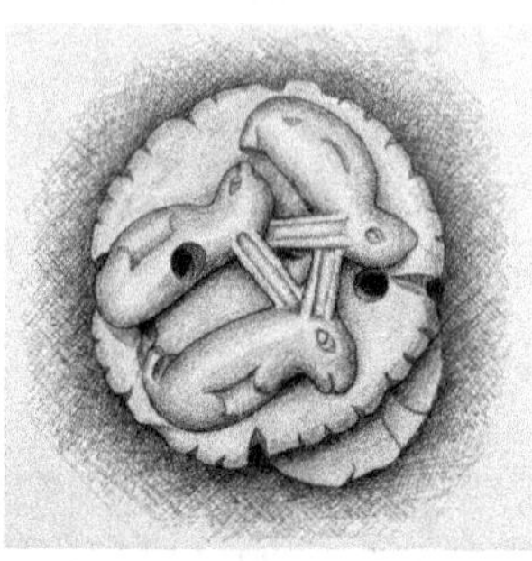 

Roof boss, St. Michael's church, Ilsington, Devon, UK.

Roof boss, St. Mary's church, Kelly, Devon, UK.

Roof boss, St. Cyriac and St. Julitta church, Newton St. Cyres, Devon, UK

ANONYMOUS CONNECTION

Given Dane's track record of delaying texts, Liko fully expected voicemail. But Dane picked up on the third ring.

"Hey."

"Hello," Liko said. "Long time listener, first time caller."

Dane laughed. "You're on the air."

"I understand there's a paint-by-number kit for sale? Along with some china?"

"The kit is free, the china you have to earn."

"I want to come," Liko said. Simply. Quietly. "This is all rather woo-woo, but I think woo-woo is what I need right now."

"I'm really glad to hear it," Dane said, just as simple and quiet.

"I found a renter for my house. My eye is on your May Day party."

"Come whenever you want. I'll be here waiting. Coincidentally, or maybe not, one of our artists had to cancel. So a cottage is waiting for you, too."

"What's the residence fee?"

"Congratulations, you're the recipient of the first Schoenfeld Scholarship for Honorary Green Men."

"Well goddamn, I never won anything in my life."

"Of course, all contributions to the farm's booze supply are welcome. And you may be occasionally commandeered for manual labor."

I can get manual with your labor, Liko thought, but aloud only said, "I am an excellent lifter of heavy stuff."

Dane laughed. "I'm really hearing your accent today."

"Two weeks in ol' Blighty does that. I talk like the company I keep. What are you up to?"

"I'm in the car with Salma. We're going to the Jensens."

"Tell them I said hi."

"How do you know them?"

Liko laughed. "You haven't earned that clue yet."

"I think you owe me a few plates by now."

"Nope. This will be your *Phantom Tollbooth.*"

"Cagey bitch."

"I learned from the best."

A bit of warm, coy silence passed from one phone to the other.

"Man, I didn't think I'd ever see you again," Dane said. "I hate that it's under these circumstances, but…"

"It's wild how a traumatic experience can just wipe parts of your memory clean. I forgot that party. Completely forgot. The memory retrieval feels so surreal."

"That night was surreal to begin with. And we were pretty high."

"That's right, we were. And we had a whole thing going. A groove of anonymous connection. Neither of us broke it with small talk or introductions."

"Maybe it was the pot but it felt like an other-worldly experience," Dane said. "Staying nameless fit the narrative I had in my head. Truth be told, I came up to the roof to have a good cry. And an angel was waiting for me."

"Angel," Liko laughed. "Bootsy would beg to differ."

"Anyway, I'm kind of an aficionado on unique eyes, so may I say, yours are bonkers?"

"Ah, you like my purple people eaters?"

"Where'd they come from?"

"My grandfather. And my uncle—my dad's brother—he has them, too."

"Did Kyle?"

"No, it skipped his generation."

"Will you tell me about him?"

Liko was quiet a long moment. "I will. Someday. Today's not that day."

"I understand. So how many awful platitudes about grief have you collected?"

"Jesus Christ, too many."

"People mean well but God *damn*…"

"There was one saying I liked, but only because it acknowledged flat-out your grief was never going to get smaller. You just build a new life around it that hopefully gets bigger. I'm paraphrasing."

"I know that one. Along with 'Grief is unexpressed love. That's why it hurts.' I'm paraphrasing."

"Yep, I've heard it."

Dane snorted. "This club sucks ass. I'm paraphrasing."

"It does. So who's Diane, what was that about?"

"Nice try, bitch."

"I learned from the best."

"Where are you in the game?"

"What game?"

"The *Three Hares* game," Dane said patiently. "What moves have you made in the chamber?"

"I know how to move the rabbits into the ceiling motif and start it spinning. And I know to click on one of the wisteria blooms until it makes three seeds. Those are in my cache. That's as far as I got."

"Hm."

"Pretend I'm standing in front of you with a plate, batting my violet eyes. Please sir? May I have some more?"

"The hares are spinning the wrong way."

The clue was served up so abruptly, Liko could only clutch the plate and reply, "Oh."

"There's a story behind that. There's a story behind almost everything in the chamber. Some long, some short."

"Gotcha."

"I can call you later tonight and tell you about the hares running the wrong way. You'll still have to figure out how to turn them around."

CUSHIE FOR THE TUSHIE

Dane pulled into Huff and Maisie's driveway and killed the engine. Immediately he heard a racket that went clear through the car. When he opened the door, it sounded like a pack of wolves being castrated. Salma barreled out of the back seat and barked up to the door, sensing puppy distress. Oscar, Huff's nephew, was here for the weekend and obviously suffering some mortal indignity.

Dane strode into the kitchen, whipped off his sunglasses and flung them aside. "I got here soon as I could. What's the status?"

Huff calmly looked up from making a sandwich, then down at his side where a sturdy four-year-old wearing nothing but a T-shirt was hiccupping back sobs.

"What manner of inequity is being inflicted upon this pantsless child and by what foul villain?" Dane said. "Tell me so I may smite them."

Silence.

"Say hi to Dane," Huff said.

"Hi," Oscar moaned, hanging on the hem of Huff's flannel shirt.

"We're having a bad day," Huff said.

"I will smite the day," Dane said. "Bring me my sword."

Usually his medieval knight routine was good for a laugh, but Oscar just went on whimpering. Salma glanced up at Dane with a look of *Can you do something helpful, please?*

"Holy moly." Dane crouched down by Oscar and thumbed away some of the tears. "My man, what's the matter?"

"I pooped really big and it hurt my heinie."

"Oh," Dane said gravely. "I hate when that happens." He glanced at Huff, who widened his eyes and held his hands a foot apart, mouthing, *It was huge.*

"It hurts to wipe," Oscar said, drifting into Dane's side.

"Oh my God, no."

"Huff put cream on it and it's *slimy.*"

"Ugh, the worst." Dane rubbed his back. "You poor kid."

"And it hurts when I walk," Oscar wailed, leaving Dane and lurching around the kitchen in a wide-legged, tortured gait.

"How did you walk before the slimy stuff?" Huff asked. "Show Dane."

Oscar sniffed and walked normally. "Like that."

"Ah," Dane said. "And how do you walk now?"

Oscar started lurching and kvetching again.

Dane glanced up at Huff. "Nice going."

"I can't do anything right."

"Look what I found…" Maisie came in, twirling an inflatable doughnut cushion on her fingers. "A cushie for the tushie. Sit down, your majesty."

"Don't mind if I do." Dane snatched the cushion, put it on a chair, and made a show of sitting. Hovering a bit, checking over his shoulder, before settling down with a little rubbery sizzle. Oscar's next sob turned into a giggle.

"Wow, this is *comfy*," Dane said, wiggling. "The support is top notch. Absolutely nothing is touching my butthole."

"Can we not say butthole," Maisie murmured, rubbing her temples.

"Let me try," Oscar said.

Maisie held out a little pair of sweatpants. "Put these on first. Otherwise you'll slime the doughnut."

When Oscar was clothed, Dane put him dramatically on the cushioned throne. Oscar squirmed around, experimenting, then looked up with a wickedly smug expression Dane wanted to eat.

"Your lunch, sir," Huff said, setting down a plate with a sandwich.

"Thank you."

Huff kissed Oscar's head. "Thank you for thank you."

"Oscar always says thank you," Maisie said.

"The best guys say thank you." Dane hugged her. "Thank you, Maisie. You're the bestest Maisie. Everyone should have a Maisie."

"She's not your Maisie," Oscar said.

"Nuh-uh," Dane said, tightening arms. "You got the tushie cushie, I get the Maisie."

"All right, cool it," Huff said. "We all know she's my Maisie."

"Ah," Dane said, "but why is she yours?"

"Because the Great Dane introduced us," Maisie said. "Thank you, Dane."

"Thank you, Dane," Huff said, with an earnest expression Dane wanted to *devour*.

"Pfft, it was nothing." Dane waved a careless hand and went to the fridge for a drink.

"It was everything," Huff said, and headed out the glass sliding door that led to the atrium.

Dane watched him go and suppressed a bittersweet sigh, rolling eyes at himself. What else could you do with unrequited love except introduce it to your sister, then sit back and pine as the mother of all love affairs unfolded before you?

Twenty years and this impossible, teenage crush on Huff Jensen showed no signs of growing up or growing out of it. If anything, Dane being suddenly single made the infatuation in vogue again. Huff having the unmitigated gall to age well had been making Dane a bit of a hot mess lately.

Which made the sudden, fantastical reappearance of Liko Greenman something of a tonic. Dane noticed that despite the sighing, he didn't feel quite so squeezed today by Huff's presence.

Maisie was busy making guacamole and marinating some chicken. Dane sat at the table and entertained Oscar into eating all of his sandwich.

"Did you bring your babing suit?" the boy asked.

"I brought my babing suit. Where are the babes?"

Oscar clambered down from his chair. "Is Salma going to swim?"

"She forgot her suit."

"She doesn't need one. Come on and see the pool." Oscar flung aside the sliding door with enough gusto to make the frame rattle.

"Easy, Godzilla," Maisie said. "You don't know your own strength."

The atrium was warm and muggy, filled with sunshine and potted plants and a thick chlorine smell. On the concrete deck, Huff was holding a plank and staring down at the iPad between his hands. He lifted one hand, pivoted to the side while holding the plank, and raised it above his head.

"Looking good, Jensen," Dane said.

"Feeling weak, Strong." Huff put a hip down, then rolled onto his butt and crossed his legs. "Are we swimming? You don't have your suit on, kid."

Oscar draped himself on Huff's back. "I want to swim nudey."

"No."

"You and Maisie swim nudey."

"Because we pay the mortgage and we don't pee in the pool. Go get suited up."

Oscar ran back toward the kitchen.

"Close the door *gently,*" Huff called after.

"Your suit's in the downstairs bathroom," Maisie added. "Pee *before* you put it on."

"And aim," Huff mumbled. "And flush. And wash your hands. And thank fucking god we don't have kids."

Dane laughed.

"We love to have him," Maisie said. "But when he leaves, we split a twelve-pack and stare into space for an hour."

"And curse nonstop," Huff said.

"I remember those days," Dane said, pulling out a chair to sit. "Except for the part where Saskia left."

"How you doing, my man?" Huff asked.

"Annoyed, because I only came for the nude swimming."

"Sorry. We try to keep the junk in the pool to a minimum." Huff crossed his ankles, planted his feet and tried to rock up to stand without using his hands. "Can he do it? Can he? Third time's the charm…? He fails. Not today, folks."

He rolled onto a knee and slowly stood, taking the hand Maisie offered.

"How you feeling?" Dane asked, unlacing his sneakers.

"Yesterday was great," Huff said, walking over and twisting his torso side to side. "Today not so much. I just have to work with what I'm given."

The sliding door gently opened and closed. Then a streak of naked boy took a lap around the pool, waving his bathing suit around his head.

"There goes the neighborhood," Maisie said, sighing.

"Is it too early to start drinking?"

"It's too late."

"I'll get some beers," Huff said. "Maze, did you make guac?"

"It's on the counter with the chips. Bring it all out."

Dane used the downstairs bathroom to change into his own suit. He brought the beers out while Huff carried the snacks.

"Take a load off," Dane said. "I'll take lifeguard duty. Will he nap later?"

"If he's tired enough."

"One tired beast, coming up. Yo, Oscar, I'm going in. Cover your butt or be left behind."

Oscar had been taking swimming lessons since he was eighteen months old, and didn't need water wings or any flotation device. So Dane went full-on Dad and threw the boy all over the pool. Splashing, swimming under water, doing funny jumps off the diving board. They constructed a raft out of every single pool noodle, save one, through which Dane blew great jet streams of water as they sailed around.

Salma took a dip, although she was a sedate and dignified swimmer, preferring to descend the stairs in the shallow end, paddle once or twice around the perimeter, then get out and shake off.

Soon Maisie and Huff joined them. Maisie cannonballed from the diving board. Huff sat on the side and slipped into the water in stages. He didn't throw Oscar or goof off on the board, but he gave whale rides and captained the noodle craft while Dane and Maisie tried to sink it. Gradually the two sea monsters retreated and left Huff to downshift Oscar into quiet mode. They floated in lazy circles, Oscar lying on top of Huff, head on Huff's shoulder, pointing up at the skylights and looking for pictures in the clouds.

Dane dried off, changed, and took the opportunity to go up to the roof. He sat in one of the Adirondack chairs, put his feet on the railing and snapped a picture. He texted it to Liko with a message: **Look familiar?**

The bubble of three dots danced up, went away, came back. **Activate face recognition, please,** Liko finally replied.

Dane got up and took a selfie with the view behind him. Then a few more before he got one that pleased him. He sent it. Waited an excruciating minute while Liko bubbled away.

"Good lord, are you writing a novel?" Dane mumbled. "Just type *I want to eat your face.*"

The reply finally came: **I'm a martinet about being outside with wet hair in cold weather. Blame Bootsy.**

I was swimming.

Lucky you. Put a hat on.

Did I mention Schoenfeld's has a pool?

LOL, I said I'm coming, you don't have to keep selling the place.

Dane smiled at the screen, then looked up at the rooftop space. Remembering how he and Liko had leaned on the railing together and resolved to stay alive another year. He typed: **Sitting here, it's kind of sinking in just how fucked up this is. Meeting and then meeting again.**

Did you ask H&M about me?

Nope.

You're a man of your word. Anyway, I'm just about to close my eyes a bit. Ass is dragging today.

It's siesta time around here too. Talk to you later.

K.

Feeling unsatisfied and dismissed, Dane sat a few more minutes, chiding himself to take his damn time and enjoy all this.

His phone pinged again. Liko wrote: **Go inside or put on a hat.**

A THOUSAND COILS

DANE CAME DOWN FROM the attic. He passed one of the bedrooms and peeked through the cracked door to see Oscar in bed, Maisie reading to him. In the kitchen, Huff was hanging onto the edges of the island, in a deep squat, rocking his hips side to side and making careful, controlled exhales.

"Between contractions?" Dane said.

"Get me an epidural, stat." Huff came to a standing position, then slowly lowered again. "Oscar asleep?"

"Almost."

"Another beer?"

"I'm good for now." Dane slid onto a stool and watched Huff stretch. He'd changed into track pants and a white thermal top and could've just stepped out of a Patagonia catalog. He was glorious. Rugged and handsome. Even creaking and groaning and struggling through his aches and pains, Dane would never tire of looking at him.

Any freshman psychology major would call Dane's mild obsession *transference*. Huff had been one of the therapists at Kingpoint Academy, an institute for troubled teens where Dane was sent to finish high school. Starved for wise, kind, older male figures, of *course* Dane fell in love with his shrink. You couldn't turn around at Kingpoint without seeing a kid who adored Huff Jensen. He was impossibly adorable, but something in Dane took it a step further. Latched on for life.

Take me. Claim me. Adopt me.

I want to belong to you.

Dane didn't possess the nerve or savvy to hint at his feelings, let alone declare them or flirt with the professional boundary. He suspected only firm rejection would result, and he'd die if he had to switch to someone else's counsel. Huff was Dane's lifeline, his savior, his shepherd into adulthood. Huff was irretrievably off limits, which allowed Dane to fall selflessly in love.

I will love you forever. Without purpose. Without an end goal. Something in me wants to adore you. Nothing will ever come of this and that's fine. Just don't ever ask me to stop.

Dane had no matchmaking intentions when he innocently introduced Huff to Maisie. But maybe his subconscious knew his two champions were meant for each other. Now they were married and Huff would be around forever for Dane to benignly adore.

A satisfying pop of a cracked back and Huff groaned deliciously. "*There* it goes. Good lord." He stood up and tilted side to side.

Or malignantly adore, Diane said archly, chin on her hand.

"How are you doing?" Dane asked.

"Me? I rotate between supernatural gratitude for being alive, followed by frustrated pissiness that recovery takes so long. I crow about the milestones, then bitch about the setbacks. I went for an innocent walk around our neighborhood and I practically crawled back home because the sound of every passing car made me freak out. A truck drove by with the gears grinding and I almost shit myself." Huff ran a hand over his face and blew out his breath. "We're slowly working through that in therapy."

"The shrinker has become the shrunk."

Huff smiled. "Telling you, man, the smell of a Pier One will straight-up make me cry. I'm not kidding. You know how those stores smell, right? I can't even walk into one. Anyway, I deal with the PTSD, then I'm back to being grateful for my life. Which is when the recurring nightmare of the cab hitting me likes to show up. I'll bolt awake and wrench my back and the circle of life continues. But hey, glad to be here."

How do you know Liko Greenman, Diane thought, and Dane was about to ask when Maisie staggered in, yawning.

"He's down. He's out." She put hands on Dane's shoulders and kissed his head. "Good work, coach."

"He's a piece of cake," Dane said.

"He makes us bicker," Huff said.

"Who?"

"Me and Maze. We never bickered. Now whenever Oscar is over, we get all snippy with each other. Things like, *not so loud, you'll wake him up. Or, don't get him all riled up before bedtime.*"

"Don't feed him chips," Maisie said. "We're about to have dinner."

"You can't run the bath water that hot. Are you trying to scald him?"

"What the hell is he wearing, did *you* pick those rags out?"

"You're not using enough expression when you read to him."

"Who taught you how to wipe someone's ass?"

"Don't say ass in front of him, you ass."

"Don't call your dick your johnson. Say penis like a normal person."

"Don't talk about my penis, you dick."

They cracked up, Maisie putting her laughing face on Huff's chest, Huff laughing into her hair. Giving Dane no choice but to laugh along and adore them.

AFTER DINNER, THEY HUNG out in the den, where Oscar had two big bins full of Thomas the Train parts. Maisie read and Huff worked on one of his steampunk bug models. The kits had a gazillion little parts: screws and washers and bolts and gears and wires. Huff worked with needle tweezers under a magnified lamp, and his desk had a set of flags he raised to signal accessibility. Green meant anyone could approach and watch him work. Yellow meant Oscar could not approach. Red meant no one could approach.

The yellow flag was up now, and Oscar stayed with Dane, building an elaborate track. Dane lay on his stomach and put his chin on his crossed arms, watching the miniature train loop around and chug past his eyes. He glanced at Maisie, brows furrowed over her book, the other hand running through her hair. He looked at Huff, engrossed in his work, tip of his tongue held in his teeth.

"Maze?"

"Speaking."

"Who's Liko Greenman?"

Maisie lowered the book and pushed her glasses up on her head. "Holy shit, I haven't heard that name in months. Huff, when was the last time we saw Liko Greenman?"

"I don't remember," Huff said.

"Maybe New Year's Eve twenty-fifteen?" Dane said.

"Where?"

"Here," Dane said patiently. "You had a party. I was there. So was Liko. We met."

"Oh," Maisie said slowly, revelation dawning in her eyes. "That's right."

"How do you know him?"

"From when we were living in Norwalk," Huff said. "He and his wife… Christ, Maze, what was her name? Jane? Janet?"

"Something like that."

"Whatever. They weren't our couple besties but just some nice, casual friends we'd go out with sometimes."

"We moved here," Maisie said, "and lost touch for a few years. Then Huff ran into him. Where was it again?"

"Totally random. I went back to Norwalk for a board meeting at Kingpoint. On the way out I stopped to get gas. There was Liko Greenman, filling up. He looked awful. Kind of beat down and exhausted. We grabbed a cup of coffee and I found out he was divorced. So I invited him over. It was our housewarming party, so that was summer of 2015."

"You met him here on New Year's Eve, Dane?" Maisie asked.

"Briefly," Dane said. "But recently, we met again."

"How?" Masie said. "Is he in New York now?"

"No, still in Norwalk. It was random."

"Did he remarry?"

"He didn't mention a wife or partner."

"Fuck," Huff cried over his work.

Maisie glared at her spouse and motioned toward Oscar.

Huff grimaced and slouched low in his chair. "Sorry."

"I cheated," Dane said to Liko on the phone.

"We haven't even kissed, we're at infidelity already?"

"I like to move at a brisk pace."

"Apparently."

"I asked Huff and Maisie how they know you."

"Ah," Liko said darkly. "So you probably know my wife cheated on me with our accountant."

"Um, no. I just heard you were casual friends with the Jensens in Norwalk."

Liko snorted. "Potato, potahto."

"Huff ran into you at a gas station. You looked like hell so he invited you to their housewarming. Wait, your accountant?"

"Let's move on at a brisk pace. Did I get a good character reference?"

"I didn't ask for one. I'm my own judge of character."

"Well, now you owe me one game clue, or your connection to the Jensens. You pick."

"Maisie is my sister."

"Oh. Didn't have that on my bingo card. Where'd you guys grow up?"

"Queens, but Maze ran away from home when she was sixteen."

"Why?"

"Because our father is a monster. Brisk pace that. We'll wander back another time."

"Okay," Liko said cautiously.

"I was only four when she left. I had no real memories of her. But when I left home, I—"

"Left home or ran away?"

"Ran."

"Because your father's a monster? Rinse, repeat, wander back another time?"

"Yes. The only other blood relative I knew anything about was this missing sister. I tracked her down, took a gamble and went to her."

"Did she remember you?"

"Well not literally. It was fourteen years later. But she took me in. Saved my life, but that's another story."

"Who is your mother?" Liko asked. "Wait, don't tell me. Mary Schoenfeld."

Dane laughed loud enough to startle Salma. "Points for creativity, but no. My mother died when I was in high school. Her name was Helen deWinter."

"Hold on, let me get my Scrabble tiles."

Dane went on laughing. God, if nothing else, he wanted to keep Liko around just for the banter.

"Hey, you're not rushing to assure me her name *isn't* an anagram," Liko said.

"Ethan anagrammed everything. He had no interest in astrological bullshit, but the hidden words in names, the meaning and power of names, legends of names—that was his thing. Also John Schoenfeld's thing."

A beat of contemplative, breathing silence passed between the men before Liko spoke. "So when I rearrange *Liko,* I only come up with *kilo.* A thousand. Don't know what to make of it."

"I can pull *oil* out of Liko," Dane said slowly. "Only thing to do with the leftover K is put it in front. Koil. A heavy metal coil?"

"A coil is any interconnected series of loops, but a kilo-koil is precisely one thousand loops."

A long silence.

I wish you were here, Diane said, as Dane ran his hand up and down a spare pillow as if it were someone's back.

"So, you called to tell me about the hares running the wrong way?" Liko prompted.

"I did. Got the game nearby?"

A bit of background noise. "I do now."

"Go to the beginning in China. Cave four-oh-seven."

Through the phone he could hear the music of the game's opening sequence and he hummed along dramatically.

"All right, I'm here," Liko said, just as the voice of the Green Man narrator boomed in the background, *Welcome, young explorer!*

"Whats-his-face is here, too."

"So sixteen caves at Mogao have the Three Hares motif," Dane said. "In all of them, the hares run clockwise. Except for four-oh-seven, where they run counter-clockwise. The wrong way. Ethan started the game here because his mother also ran the wrong way…"

THE WRONG WAY

June 1971
Mogao Caves, Dunhuang, Gansu Province, China

IN A CAVE IN CHINA, three people gaze upward at three hares.

The cave is one of over a thousand carved into the cliffs above the Daquan River, at a site called Mogao, 25 kilometers from the oasis town of Dunhuang, at the western end of the Great Wall of China. Dunhuang began as a military outpost, but over time, became a key oasis on the Silk Road. As Dunhuang tended to the logistical needs of travelers and merchants, Mogao nourished needs of the soul.

Over a thousand years, these Caves of the Thousand Buddhas were carved out of the rock. Some were living spaces, but over half were decorated with hanging silks and sculptures, the walls and ceilings painted with mineral pigments, all depicting the Buddha in one manifestation or another.

The three people—an American couple and their Chinese guide—stand in a loose triangle, heads tipped back. The American man is tall, moving consistently at a crouch through these sacred spaces, although here in Cave 407, he can stand comfortably beneath the caisson ceiling. Decorative borders in reds and blues, repetitive patterns of triangles and petals that gradually draw in on a central square. Within is a celestial procession of divine figures, floating around an eight-petaled lotus flower. Within the lotus flower are painted three black hares on a green circle. They run nose to tail, their three shared ears making a triangle.

"The lotus is highly significant in Buddhism," says Fan Jinshi, a researcher at Dunhuang Academy and their guide for the day. "It roots in the mud of river beds, and blooms above the water. This signifies the transcendence of Buddha and how he moved beyond the world."

The American man, who is named John Schoenfeld, makes an attentive sound but says nothing. The lotus doesn't interest him right now. He's been drawn into the circle of the hares. And he's thinking about the boy.

John's wife, Mary, is captivated by the ceiling's border at the moment, lost in the mineral reds and blues that blend to eggplant and tobacco. She does register the beautiful lotus flower, thinking of the beauty of their blooms but how their dried seed pods give her the creeps. *Trypophobia,* John labeled the reaction: a fear or aversion to holes.

She presses a hand to the base of her throat, tilting her face further toward the ceiling. Then a little gasp rises from Mary's open mouth when she sees the three hares.

"John," she whispers, now thinking about the boy.

"I know," he says, taking her free hand. "I know."

Jinshi moves closer to his guests, pointing up at the Three Hares as he speaks. "Sixteen of Mogul's caves have this motif of the Three Hares. Here, cave four-oh-seven, is the only depiction where the hares run counter-clockwise. Most unusual. Movement in Buddhist art is always clockwise, mirroring the movement of the heavens. We believe the painter simply made a mistake, as you will see the procession of divine bodies around the lotus is also moving counter-clockwise."

If not for the boy, perhaps John and Mary Schoenfeld would reflect deeper on the mistaken motion of the painted ceiling. Perhaps monks and pilgrims sat in this space and meditated on the divinity within human error. The beauty that arises in going the wrong way. The wisdom of trying another direction. The courage to run against the tide.

But they are only thinking of the boy. The infant abandoned at a Goshen firehouse, dressed in tan brown pajamas emblazoned with running rabbits, and swaddled in a blanket. Tucked against his chest was an antique-looking stuffed toy: three cloth rabbits sewn together in a circle, their bodies stretched long, nose to tails. Tucked in the blanket was a note:

I tried. I swear I tried, I tried harder than any time in my life. But I'm just no good at anything. I always go the wrong way. I fucked this baby up already and if he stays with me, I'll just fuck him up more.

Please help him find a good home, not some shitty place like I came from. I was going to name him Ethan, after my grandpa, but forget it, let him start over fresh with a new name.

Please be kind. He cries a lot but that's my fault. Any problems he has are my fault, not his. He likes music. And he loves his rabbits, please don't lose them. They were mine when I was a kid. The only thing I wanted to keep from that life. Now they're the only thing I have to give my own kid.

I'm such a fuck-up. I'm really sorry.
Please help him find a nice place to live. You're all heroes.
Thank you.

John and Mary had fostered the baby a month, which was all the time they had before this long-planned, complicated trip to China. They gleaned the plea in the mother's note, and continued to call him Ethan. He was in heroin withdrawal and cried non-stop. He required all of their time and resources. He turned the house upside-down. He was beautiful and brave and didn't ask for any of this. And by the time they started to love him, they had to leave him. It broke their hearts to put him back into the system, and feeling selfish and loathsome, they flew to China. They did what they came to do, and they worried. They fretted. They sighed often. When John's work was finished and two days remained in their trip, an excursion to Mogao was suggested and the Schoenfelds gratefully accepted the diversion.

Now John and Mary stand in Cave 407, looking up at three hares who ran the wrong way about the heavens.

I tried harder than any time in my life. But I'm just no good at anything. I always go the wrong way...

Fan Jinshi asks, "In America, who lives on the moon?"

Finally the Schoenfelds' eyes come down from the ceiling. "Who lives... What?"

"When you look at the moon, what do you see? What is the story?"

"Just a man," Mary says. "The man in the moon. He doesn't have a name."

At any other time, in any other place, this would be John's cue to clear his throat. Mary even sees his lips purse slightly, moving into position to form the W of the dreaded "Well, *actually...*" And then launch into a brief (to his mind) lecture on various men in the moon traditions. Jewish lore declares the face of Jacob is etched on the moon. Another legend names him as the transgressor from the Book of Numbers, who dared to gather sticks on the Sabbath and so God ordered him stoned to death. Yet another tradition declares it is Cain on the moon, his cursed, eternal wandering not limited to the circle of the Earth. An obscure Roman tale brands the man a sheep-thief.

Thank you, John. Most interesting. Oh, there's more?

Thus warmed up, John would quote Dante and Lyly, cite the Old Norse myth of Máni and draw parallels to J.R.R. Tolkien's Middle Earth, reminding his now catatonic audience of the old elf, Uole Kuvion, who hid on the Ship of the Moon "and has been living there ever since." He'd wrap it up with the Latvian legend of the maiden who dared to state her figure was more attractive than that of Dievs, the moon goddess. As punishment, the maid was banished to the moon and it's not her face etched there but her ass.

Ass. Moon. Get it?

But not a word from John Schoenfeld, professor of world mythology, specialist of signs and symbols, the endearingly bombastic nut.

"Buddha was born on a day of the full moon and reached enlightenment on a full moon," Jinshi says. "Rabbits also have lunar connotations. In Chinese folklore we have the Jade Hare. The Moon Rabbit. He pounds herbs with a mortar and pestle to make the elixir of life for the moon goddess Chang'e."

John's Adam's apple gives a tremendous bob as he swallows. "You said there are more caves with the hares?"

"Sixteen all together, yes. Come…"

They follow Fan Jinshi to Cave 205, the caisson of its ceiling painted in turquoise, lapis, gold and black. At the center of a four-petaled lotus, three black hares run clockwise.

The canopy of cave 237 is stunning, despite smoke damage that occurred when White Russians used the dwelling as a hideout in the 1920s. Its intricate patterned borders in soft blues, greens and pinks, grow progressively smaller until they surround three brown hares running.

The party must take turns viewing Cave 139, as it only fits one person. A Tang dynasty isolation tank. Green and white lotus motifs on an earth red background. The three hares are white, their black inked outlines crisp.

At the end of the tour, the Schoenfelds ask to see Cave 407 one more time, where the hares run counter-clockwise.

"Before we left for China," Mary tells their guide, "we fostered a baby boy. A foundling left at a firehouse. He was dressed in pajamas with rabbits on them, and he carried a stuffed toy. Three rabbits sewn together in a circle. The mother left a note, saying she always went the wrong way."

Fan Jinshi asks, "You said a firehouse?"

"Yes."

The Chinese man tells them a story from the Jakata Tales, a collection of legends about the previous lives of Buddha in human and animal forms. In one such life, he was a hare. One holy day, the lord of devas, Sakra, decided to test the animals' compassion by disguising himself as a hungry beggar. If virtuous of heart, the animals would offer the food they meant to eat themselves.

When Sakra asked the hare for charity, the hare had none to give. He told the beggar to build a fire, then said, "All I have to feed you is myself." And he jumped into the fire.

Immediately Sakra extinguished the flames and revealed himself. Astounded and touched, the lord of devas declared the selfless hare's act of compassion would never be forgotten, and so he painted the hare's likeness on the moon.

"In legend, we have a hare who jumps into the fire to feed a god," Jinshi says. "In real life, we have a desperate mother who leaves a baby at a fire station, gifting him the only thing she kept of her childhood. Interesting coincidence. If you believe in them. I think the real point is that there's no true faith without sacrifice. Or maybe the wrong way is sometimes the most compassionate way?"

"We need to go home," John says.

Mary says nothing. She is weeping into her hands.

Above them, the hares run and run and run…

GOOD GUYS

"So it's hard to say if the hares picked Ethan or if Ethan picked the hares," Dane said. "But rabbits were always special to him, and the Three Hares motif was an obsession."

"I see," Liko said. "They never found his mother?"

"No. Or father. His whole life, the only things Ethan ever knew for sure were he was named after a great-grandfather and the toy rabbits belonged to his mother. They were the one possession he guarded with his life. Anything else—clothes, books, music, the car keys, art supplies, the food on his plate… What was his was yours, but no one could touch or move or fiddle with those rabbits. They were his soul."

"He picked the surname Hasen himself?"

"He took John as his middle name, and the Schoenfelds were German, so *Hasen* fulfilled all his familial and symbolic needs. He felt strongly it was meant to be his name."

"Is your daughter called Hasen?"

"Hasen-Strong."

"I have a rude question."

Dane laughed. "She's my biological daughter. Mine and Nomi's."

"But Nomi was married to Ethan."

"Nomi was also a foundling who knew nothing about her parents. I had parents. One a monster, the other almost a complete unknown, but I had names. I had vital statistics. I had a sister. I could draw a family tree. I had medical history and strictly from that perspective, we felt we couldn't saddle our own kid with a blank slate. Especially after Nomi had breast cancer."

"No, no, that makes sense. I'm sorry, I didn't mean to sound like I was judging her. Or any of you."

"You're good. I didn't take it that way."

A long silence.

"Tired?" Dane asked carefully.

"Yeah. I'm gonna try to sleep."

"Okay. I'll talk to you at some point."

"'Night, man."

Dane plugged the charger into the phone and clicked out the lamp. He lay on his side, drowsily stroking the pillow a little while before falling under. He slept dreamlessly, waking when Diane stirred behind his blue eye and asked, *Is someone breathing on us?*

He opened his eyes with a sharp inhale. Oscar stared back at him, the tips of their noses touching.

"Hey, kiddo," Dane whispered.

"Where's that dog?"

Dane patted the mattress behind him where Salma was sleeping. "Right here."

"I want to come in with you, too."

"Okay."

Oscar looked around the dark bedroom. "We need a nightlight."

"I'll get yours. You need to pee first?"

"No."

"I do. You should try, too."

Dane got the nightlight from Oscar's bedside table, then checked progress in the bathroom, praising the dry pull-up and the vigorous, fifteen-second pee. "Wow, you really did need to go."

"I did a long one," Oscar said.

"Great job."

They settled back in bed, Dane switching sides so the nightlight wouldn't shine in his eyes. Which meant the light shone on him. He slept in just a pair of shorts, with all his tattoos, scars and piercings on full display. Oscar reached toward Dane's chest, but Dane gently stopped his hand. "Good guys don't touch without asking first. Right?"

"Can I touch?"

"If I say no, what does it mean?"

"No, don't touch."

"Does it mean no, I don't like you, Oscar?"

"No. You like me. You just don't want touching."

"I love you understand that. Ask me again."

"Can I touch?"

"Yes. But don't tickle me."

Oscar drew one finger along the long scar running beneath Dane's left pectoral muscle, then his right. "Did you hurt your chest?"

"Yes."

"You had to get stitches?"

"Lots of them."

"What happened?"

"I don't want to talk about it just yet. One day I will."

"Is it a secret?"

"It's private. Like not wanting to be touched without asking."

Oscar's finger had been wandering toward the gold hoop in Dane's right nipple. It stopped. "Can I touch this?"

"Yes, but don't pull."

"Why is it here?"

"I wanted it."

Oscar examined the silver hoop in Dane's left nipple without touching.

"Why are they different?"

"I like how it looks. They're like my eyes."

"Why are your eyes different?"

"That's how I was born."

Oscar turned over, putting his back to Dane. "Do scritches?"

Dane scratched his back until he nodded off. Then Dane lay awake, his fingers drawing along his scars. His hand spread wide across the plain of his left pectoral, remembering once upon a time when the plain was a hill, curving into his palm with a soft, warm weight.

I will not lie to anyone about my body or be bullied into telling lies. I was lied to all my life.

Huff said so.

"It matters," Dr. Michael Hough Jensen said to an eighteen-year-old Dane. "Things were done to you without your consent. You were abused by your father. In the clinic, you were medically and sexually assaulted. These things happened. They're on the record and they matter. You are allowed to feel any damn way you want about it. Starting with rage."

Dane's hands curved around something that wasn't there anymore. His fingers closed around a little hoop and pulled. Twisted. Did all the things Oscar wasn't allowed. Nothing. No pain, no sensation. The reconstruction of his chest had been delayed far too long. The nerves were gone and there was nothing for it. The plastic surgeon did a phenomenal job and the NAC tattooist was a fucking genius. Dane and Nomi used to stand in front of the bathroom mirror and either compete about who had the better set, or brag that they both had the best goddamn nipples on the planet.

They did look terrific. Too bad Dane's didn't feel like anything. When he curled his mouth around Nomi's nipples, she felt genuine pleasure. Not as much as before the mastectomy, but something. When she touched or licked or squeezed Dane's, he felt nothing. Sometimes he didn't give it a thought. Other times it enraged him that he'd been so ruthlessly and cruelly robbed. Assaulted. Abused. *Mutilated.*

They cut me without my consent.

They carved me up and left nothing.

My own father did this to me. Then he dangled reconstruction like a fucking prize I had to earn.

He took a deep breath in. Let it out slow so as not to wake up Oscar. He tried some silver lining humor. "At least it wasn't your dick," he mouthed soundlessly.

"There's no at least," Dr. Jensen said. "Yeah, it could've been worse. There's always a worse. But so what? What happened to you was still terrible. You don't have to downplay it or be grateful it wasn't worse. You're allowed to sit and acknowledge how bad it was until you're ready to feel something else about it."

Dane's pulling, twisting fingers went gentle, curved again around that remembered shape.

Maybe in the end I didn't want them. But it should've been my choice to make. I should've been told what was wrong with me.

"Nothing is wrong with you," Dr. Jensen said. He'd be Dr. Jensen until Dane graduated, at which time all Kingpoint alumni were invited to call him Huff.

"Nothing was ever wrong with you, Dane," he said. "Nothing is wrong with you." He leaned forward, finding Dane's two different eyes and staring hard. "Nothing is wrong with you."

Dane cried and cried. Behind his blue eye, Diane put arms around and rocked him, singing softly. I'm here, *she said.* I'm here, I'll always be here. You survived and escaped. You kept me safe. They can never get to me here. I'm here. I'm always here.

"You're safe here, Dane," Dr. Jensen said, and Dane wanted to believe him so badly.

"I don't know who I am," he cried. "I don't even know what words to use. I didn't know words existed to describe someone like me."

"You don't have to identify today," Jensen said. "Or in a week. Or a year or decade. You can take all the time you need to explore all this information. Maybe you'll eliminate some ideas straight off the bat and narrow it down. Or not. You take your time. You were never given time and safety to learn who you were. Now you have it. For as long as it takes. With whatever words you want."

Dane cried harder, demolishing a box of tissues. It was profoundly cathartic, yet every sob was followed by a flinch, as if his skin were braced for the searing strikes of a weightlifting belt. His mouth poised around the obligatory words:

Thank you, Sir.

I'm sorry, Sir.

You're right to correct me, Sir.

When Dane had quieted, Jensen spoke again. "I only have one rule in this office: truth or silence. If you're not ready to speak the truth in your heart, you don't have to speak at all. Do you understand?"

Dane could barely see through his soaked eyes but he nodded, his heart's hands closing around the simple law and repeating it back to Jensen: "Truth or silence, Sir."

It took months to stop calling Dr. Jensen Sir.

"MORNING," HUFF SAID, when Dane shuffled into the kitchen. It was perfumed with bacon and coffee. Huff stood over the grill, studding pancakes with blueberries. Maple syrup simmered in a small pot on the stove with a scrap of orange peel.

"Sleep okay?" Huff asked.

"Eh."

"Same. Coffee's made, help yourself."

Dane got a mug. "I can fall asleep but I can't stay asleep. I'm always up before dawn, worrying about Saskia."

"What kind of worry?"

"Like being useless at helping her plan a wedding. That's a popular wake-up call. I know it's trivial and I know when the time comes, everything will be fine. She has amazing friends, her wedding will be lit. All I'll have to do is show up. I know this, but I'm still awake at four in the morning, convinced I'm going to fail her."

"Are you still doing grief counseling?"

"Yeah."

"Good. Really it's your only job right now. Although…"

Dane slid onto a stool with his coffee. "What?"

"It has to be hard living in that house."

"I was just thinking about it the other night. The house is like a living entity to me. Nomi and Ethan are still everywhere and it's just really hard to endure. Sometimes it feels like even the house is crying for them."

"I'm sorry," Huff said miserably.

"I don't know what I'm going to do," Dane said.

Huff reached across the island and put the spatula under Dane's chin. "Look at me. You're going to do the next thing. Okay? Saskia's wedding isn't next. It's not even a thing. So it's not for you to stress about. Your job is to just do the next thing. Which, right now, is drinking your coffee. Next I'll put some breakfast in front of you and you will eat it."

"Okay."

"That's how you're going to handle shit for the immediate future. You ask yourself, *Is this a thing? And if it's a thing, is it next?* If it's not a thing or the next thing, then let it go." His penetrating gaze wobbled a little and he added hesitantly, "Okay?"

Dane would've hated the guy if he weren't so lovable. "Okay."

THE VEST

May 2017
Schoenfeld's Farm
Birch Island, New York

THE TWO STONE PILLARS WERE crowned with big planters of flowers and trailing vines. They dripped onto the medallion of the Green Man, fluttering in the breeze as Liko pulled into the driveway. Every available space to park was occupied, but following Dane's texted directions, Liko drove past the farmhouse, up toward the spa, toward a plywood sign spray-painted with drippy letters: *This spot reserved for Liko. Usurpers will be fed to Pao.*

Wondering who—or what—Pao was, Liko left his suitcase and boxes and took only his backpack for now. Walking down to the house, he passed a tall hunk of dude in a cowboy hat sitting on the hood of a pickup truck, hand rolling a cigarette.

"Buenas noches," he said from under the brim, giving Liko a thorough look up and down.

"Hi." Liko extended a hand and introduced himself.

"You're the owner of the coveted parking spot." He gripped Liko's handshake an extra beat, then let go and resumed rolling. "I'm Pao."

"You're the consequence to taking my spot."

"I am." Pao stared unblinking as he ran his tongue along the edge of the rolling paper.

"Eat anyone tonight?"

"Not yet."

Liko felt his face redden. The gaucho was all kinds of smoking, but a little more force than Liko could reckon with. He smiled with a vague exit line and continued toward the house.

A smile cracked his face as he approached the long pergola, the structure barely visible under an explosion of purple wisteria blossoms. They dripped from the rafters and Liko put up a hand to trail along them.

The porch was crowded with chattering, laughing people, all with drinks in hand. They called a hello or hi or welcome, and a woman opened the door for Liko with a "Climb aboard."

In the front hall Liko was greeted by a terrific-looking dog. "Hey," he said happily, sinking to a knee. "What's *up?*"

The mutt put a paw on Liko's leg and raised its muzzle high to be admired. Liko took its face in his hands and rubbed its jowls. "Were you waiting just for me? Hm? Sorry, I hit traffic on the bridge."

A slim man dressed rather smartly in black reached the foyer and held out a hand. "Hello, I'm Fred. I use they/them."

"I'm Liko." He tried to add his pronouns but now the dog was intent on French kissing him.

"Bupkis, sit," Fred said.

"Bupkis," Liko said. "That's great."

"My ex and I divided the dogs when we split up. My ex got Shpilkis. I got Bupkis."

Always appreciative of a good divorce joke, Liko laughed harder. "Not sure if that's win-win or lose-lose."

"Hey, you got here," Dane called, coming into the front hall. He wore a white butcher apron over his clothes and had a wooden spoon in one hand. The other palm slapped against Liko's, hauled him up into a hard hug. "You met Fred? Fred, Liko."

"We met," Fred said. "Finally. And we— Hey, where do you think you're going…" They lunged toward the front door and followed Bupkis outside.

Dane smiled. "You find your parking spot?"

"I did," Liko said. "Pao almost ate me until I showed ID."

"Yeah, he takes his watchdog duties a little too seriously. C'mon, I'll show you where to drop your stuff." With the spoon, Dane motioned for Liko to head upstairs. "I figure you can stay in the house tonight and move into one of the cottages tomorrow. At your own pace."

"Sounds good."

"You're right along here. Bath is across the hall. I put some towels out. Our Wi-Fi password is a mess of numbers and letters, so I wrote it down for you."

"You're quite the host."

"I try. So… Unpack, chill, don your party dress. Whatever. I'll be in the kitchen."

"Wait," Liko called.

Dane glanced back, meeting Liko's gaze with one blue eye and one brown eye.

"You're looking yourself tonight," Liko said.

"Clev-er," Dane said.

"Do you go all brown or all blue on certain occasions?"

Dane nodded. "Usually when I'm unsure of who I'm going to meet. Or what I need from the occasion. But in my house, among my people, I can just…" He made a general circle around his face with his wooden spoon, smiled a shy smile, and ducked away.

The room was simple and neat, the bed made with a white pebbled spread and lots of pillows, a stack of towels on one corner. Liko didn't have much to unpack, but he took a few minutes to set clothes in a pile, hang his shaving kit in the bathroom, and plug in his laptop. Recalling that the guests on the porch looked rather festive, he put on a nicer shirt—burgundy red with a raised textured pattern which, he'd been told, gave him a glow. Whatever that was.

He turned in front of the mirror over the dresser, tucking the shirt tails in before deciding to leave them out. He couldn't quite *see* himself in a mirror lately. He'd lost thirty pounds after Kyle's death. The gym was a good place to kill time, but the utter lack of appetite left his overworked, unrecovered body no choice but to eat itself. Neglecting rest days, he had no idea what damage he was doing until he got blood drawn for his upcoming physical and Dr. Acevedo called him immediately.

"You have an alarming amount of myoglobin and creatine kinase in your blood," she said.

"What does that mean?"

"It means I need to see you in my office. Today. And pack a toothbrush."

Am I dying, Liko wanted to ask, but didn't because he didn't want to sound too excited about it. The nurse squeezed him into the last evening appointment, where Acevedo grilled him like a burger before handing over a specimen cup.

"Go pee in that," she ordered, and then shook her head at Liko's efforts. "How long has your urine been this dark?"

Liko could only reply with "Um…?"

"Are you hydrating properly?"

"I think so."

"I don't. Ever hear of rhabdomyolysis?"

"No."

"You're overworking and underfeeding your body. Instead of building muscle, you're actively breaking it down and releasing myoglobin and other harmful things into your blood. Things that damage your kidneys while they try to filter it all out. That's why your urine looks like this. Are you in pain?"

Liko gave a bitter little laugh and Acevedo's expression softened.

"Your heart is in pain. I know, Liko. But is your body in pain? Is all this exercise making you feel stronger? Do you feel good physically?"

Liko shook his head, teeth pressed tight. "I feel pretty terrible," he said, barely trusting his throat to let the words out.

"You're on the edge of some big medical trouble." Acevedo hitched forward on her rolling stool and looked hard at her patient. "Are you trying to slowly kill yourself? Tell me the truth."

Liko closed his eyes and repeated the question to himself.

Are you trying to slowly kill yourself?

Do you want to die?

Really. Truly. Do you want to die and be no more? Leave it all? Just go forever because there's nothing left to live for?

Tell the truth.

He thought of things to do. Places to go. People to meet. TV shows to binge. Music to discover. Books to read and books to write.

He thought about what Kyle would want him to do.

And he told the truth.

"No," Liko whispered, the tears falling warm down his gaunt face. "I'm just trying to kill time."

Acevedo nodded. "Have you been seeing a grief counselor?"

"I was."

She plucked a tissue and handed it to him. "It's time to go back."

"All right."

Acevedo took him in hand, firm but compassionate. She admitted him to the hospital for kidney scans and intravenous treatment to flush him out. He was indeed close to some big renal trouble, but they caught it in time. He stayed three days, which was probably overkill, but Acevedo wanted him observed and supervised. He was banned from the gym until he gained ten pounds, and only allowed to resume with a personal trainer and nutritionist. And he was to get his bony ass back into therapy. Pronto.

Now, almost a year later from that emergency, he looked pretty good. Well, not too bad. All the lost weight gained and then some. He couldn't reverse the gauntness in his face, but the beard filled out the hollows. The seat of his pants wasn't flapping in the breeze anymore and he gave a little vain smile at the line of his shoulders in the dark red shirt. Unfortunately, being fifty-five, his waistline was a haunt for sugar and carbs. "I have washboard abs," he'd always quipped to Kyle. "There's just a lot of laundry on them."

God, it sucked how dad jokes lost their edge when you weren't a dad anymore.

"You'll always be a father," his therapist said, which wasn't much consolation.

A burst of loud laughter from downstairs snapped him out of it. Enough brooding. This was a party. And the start of an adventure. He ran hands through his hair, rehearsed a friendly smile, imagined Kyle backhanding his ass and telling him to go for it.

He turned off the dresser lamp and went for it.

As WITH ALL GOOD parties, the best energy was in the kitchen. One end of the long table was set up as a bar. The rest crammed with appetizers, chips and nibbles. The sofa and chairs in front of the fireplace were occupied, including the armrests. Dane was at the far end, back to the sink with ankles and arms crossed as he looked over and up at Pao, who was sitting on the counter like a vulture.

Liko made his way through the crush. Saying hello here. A quick nod and smile there. Taking a paper plate and making himself a nosh. Covertly watching as Dane smiled, tipped his head back to laugh first at the ceiling, then at his shoes. He was being attentive to the leering cowboy, but those arms and legs stayed crossed tight, protecting guts and jewels.

"What's up, my man," he called when he saw Liko, freeing one hand and waving. His two-toned gaze widened theatrically, then went cross-eyed a split second. Clearly signaling, *I need backup.*

"Great party," Liko said, then nodded at Pao. "Señor. Eat anyone yet?"

"Not yet," Pao said, looking at Dane.

Dane moved a little closer to Liko. "Pao's a farrier. All the horse farms around here use him."

Pao gave his hat brim a little flick, managing to be both arrogant and modest. "His Instagram has like half a million followers."

"Twenty-five thousand."

"Whatever."

Pao smiled. "People like watching me bent over, working between my legs."

"Oh my God," said a woman passing by. "You're the farrier guy? I love your reels. Hey Liz. *Liz.* Come here. It's that farrier guy."

The women started chatting up Pao, which let Liko eat his snacks, people watch in general, and study Dane in particular. He was, Liko had to admit, one of the most interesting-looking people he'd ever encountered. It wasn't just the two different eyes, although they were hard not to fixate on. The mismatched gaze was unsettling, as if the brown eye noticed your appearance and the blue one examined your soul. Dane's hair had a dozen colors in it: blond and copper and sable and gray and a couple streaks of pure white. His body seemed unable to decide on one thing, so it chose everything. Likewise nothing about Dane's appearance tonight matched up with Liko's impressions from two months ago. *That* Dane had been just a guy. Your basic dude in sweats and sneakers and ball cap.

Tonight Dane wore a black leather vest over jeans and a white linen shirt. He had a gold hoop in one ear and a silver hoop in the other. As he talked, Liko caught the flash of a tongue stud.

Pretentious, Liko scoffed, except Dane was anything but. He didn't pose or preen, didn't offer any explanation about his look. These clothes were the ones he'd thrown on, and he wore them for his own enjoyment.

Pao and his two fawning devotees left the kitchen. Liko assumed it was for a quick threesome and chuckled as he assembled his last cheese and cracker. "Dallying with the farrier. How very D.H. Lawrence."

"Better them than me," Dane said. "Jesus, I can barely put two words together when he's around."

"Any history?"

"Hell, no. Gorgeous to look at but his ego barely fits under the hat."

"Reputation precedes him and he knows it."

"He probably fucks like he's shoeing a horse."

"He'll bend you right over the anvil and start hammering away."

Laughing, Dane drained the last of his beer and set the bottle in the sink. He pushed off the counter and turned to open the fridge. His vest was laced up the back, neat tight criss-crossings pulling the leather snug to his torso, ending in a tied bow at his nape. The cords hung down and Liko thought about pulling one.

He sighed.

"Wow, that was gale force," Dane said. "What's on your mind?"

I dig your look, Liko thought. "Nothing," he said aloud.

Dane raised skeptical eyebrows, then looked around for the bottle opener. "You're so full of shit."

"I was just checking out your vest."

Dane's smile jumped sideways, full of pleasure. "You like?"

"The back was a surprise."

"The lacings? They keep me in place."

"What do you mean?"

"I have a little trouble defining the edges of my life. I always feel ever so slightly…not here."

"I see."

"I have to work really hard on grounding myself. Mentally and physically. And one of those ways is with clothing that binds me a little." Dane smoothed a hand down his vest. "I like how it feels when I draw the laces up. Not so tight that I can't breathe or it's uncomfortable. Just enough to let me feel my edges."

"Do you wear something like that all the time?"

"When I'm in a new or unsettling situation. And almost always at a party. This sounds corny but I feel braver in it. It's a little like armor. I have such an empathetic nature, I suck up everyone's emotions. The vest reminds me to keep healthy boundaries."

Liko started to speak. Stopped. Started again. And stopped.

"Go ahead," Dane said.

"Can I try it on?"

"Holy shit, yes." The pleased smile Dane had given before paled in comparison to the grin he flashed now. He set his beer bottle down so enthusiastically it foamed up. Liko mopped the puddle while Dane unbuttoned the vest, took it off, and loosened the back laces. He held it out and Liko shrugged it onto his shoulders. It was heavy, but buttery soft, and still warm from Dane's body.

"Button it first," Dane said. "Right. Now this is tailored for me so even when I pull the laces, it's not going to fit perfect. But you'll get the idea."

Liko felt the cords draw up his spine and the leather garment contracted gently, pressing his sides and lower back.

"How's that feel?"

"Like being hugged."

"Right? It's way too short on you but you get the idea. Turn around, let me see."

Liko turned in a slow circle, running a palm down the front panel, then up to where the first button came under his sternum. If he'd been shirtless, his nipples would be hanging over the edge.

"You look good," Dane said. "But more importantly, how's it feel?"

"I feel like…"

"What?"

"Like I wish it came up higher. What you said before about armor…" Liko rubbed a slow circle over his heart. "I want this covered. Know what I mean?"

"For sure. Of course."

"But I see what you mean about how it helps you feel your edges."

"Wow," Fred said, coming over to get in the fridge. "Liko, that's a sweet look on you."

"Isn't it?" Dane said.

"You wear it for fashion or binding?"

"Little of both."

Fred nodded seriously. "I have a friend who cured severe agoraphobia by corseting." They walked off, Bupkis following.

Dane's hand closed warm and strong around Liko's forearm. "I don't mean this to sound dirty, but take my clothes off."

"You totally meant it dirty," Liko said, unbuttoning the vest. He missed its warm hug as soon as it slid from his shoulders.

"You can get your own."

"Not sure if I like leather that much."

"You can get it made in suede," Dane said. "Buckskin. Broadcloth. Flannel. Come on, get in the game here."

"The whole reason I came is getting in the game."

Dane reached behind his neck and pulled the laces, drawing the vest tight to his body. "By the way, my social tank is going to dump its fuel in another hour or so. My parties always have a hard stop and most everyone will move across the street to the Pub. A few will stay. You make yourself at home, all right? You want to pub crawl, you want to sit on the porch, you want to hit the sack, you want to take a bite of Pao…"

Liko laughed. "You'd have to file a missing person report in the morning."

LIKO ENJOYED HIMSELF THOROUGHLY the next hour, especially when a good portion of guests made their way to the Pub and it was down to a more intimate handful in the kitchen. Liko. Dane. Fred. Bupkis leaning on Liko's leg. Three women—Anna, Jackie and Meg. Meg had a great smile and smelled delicious. She was not quite leaning on Liko's other leg, but close. They were all playing one of those conversational card games, drawing from a plexiglass cube.

"Do you have an irrational fear of anything?" Anna read from her card. Then gave a little shudder. "Slamming my fingers in the car door."

"Garage door," Fred said. "My fear of garage doors can only be described in psychological terms. What about you, Dane?"

"Doctors," Dane said.

"I'd literally rather throw up than go to the dentist," Meg said.

"Jackie?"

"Snakes in the toilet."

"Oh my God, *same*," Anna cried.

"Not enough people take this seriously," Jackie said. "They are in there and they *will* bite you in the coochie."

"Well thank you, I am never sitting down to pee again," Fred said.

Meg took a card. "Give a piece of non-philosophical advice."

"Non-philosophical?"

"I guess practical," Meg said. "Like…always keep extra toothbrushes in the house."

"Don't propose in public," Jackie said.

"Righty-tighty, lefty-loosy," Fred said.

"Stash extra meds in the car," Liko said

"Don't fry bacon in the nude," Dane said.

Liko took a card. "Share a weird fact or quirk about yourself."

"I can't sleep on the left side of any bed," Anna said. "No matter where I am, where I go, any bed. I have to be on the right side. Always."

"I'm afraid of snakes in the toilet," Jackie said.

Dane made a buzzer sound. "No repeats."

She thought. "I can't *not* watch any video of a haka."

"I'm addicted to videos of ingrown toenail repair," Fred said.

"Ew."

"Hear me out. It's the perfect story. The beginning hooks you with a dire situation. The middle is suspenseful. You can't look away. And the ending is always happy."

"I have to support this," Liko said. "I watch *Dr. Pimple Popper* for the same reason."

"My idea of a great date," Meg said, "is getting high and watching *Dr. Pimple Popper*."

"You free tomorrow?" Liko asked.

She winked and called, "Dane? Your quirk?"

"My eyes are different colors."

The group gave a collective gasp. "No."

"Shut up."

"Really?"

"I was wondering if you'd ever notice," Dane said.

"What causes that?" Anna asked.

"It's probably genetic, right?" Fred said.

"Usually inherited," Meg said. "But sometimes it's from mosaicism. Or even chimerism."

Liko looked at her, impressed. She smiled and said, "I'm a vet. You see it a lot in animals. Actually—"

"Oh, *ackshyually,*" Jackie said. "Here comes the vetsplain."

"Interestingly," Meg said patiently, "you see heterochromia most often with Huskies. And the Australian Shepherd. All hail the queen." She motioned toward Salma.

"Quick," Fred said to Liko, "ask me my sexual orientation."

"What's your sexual orientation?"

"Heterochromic."

"Fabulous."

"What about cats, Dr. Dolittle?"

"Most commonly in white cats." Meg delicately adjusted the frames of her glasses and went for uber-pretentious. "You see, either the epistatic white gene or the white spotting gene prevents melanin granules from reaching one eye during fetal development."

"You make it sound so dirty," Liko said. Meg bumped his hip once, settled against his side a minute, then moved away.

It was Dane's turn, and he drew a purple wild card: *You and the person on your right may ask each other anything.*

Liko stood on Dane's right. They exchanged glances.

"Who sent me the letter?" Liko asked.

"I honestly have no idea."

"What letter?" Meg said.

"Inside joke," Dane said. Then asked Liko, "How long did it take for you to stop wearing your wedding ring?"

"Wow." Liko looked at his left hand, turned it palm up, then closed it into a fist. "Wow, I don't remember. I mean, I remember taking it off but I don't recall when it was. How long after she moved out..." His eyebrows furrowed hard and he was quiet a beat. "Weird how memories blur."

They looked at each other, the stare only broken when someone cleared a throat. Then both men snapped out of it and looked around the table.

"Well, *that* got personal," Liko said heartily. He chugged the rest of his drink and slammed the can down. "Who do I gotta fuck to get another beer? And I mean it to sound dirty."

THE NAOMI ROAD 32

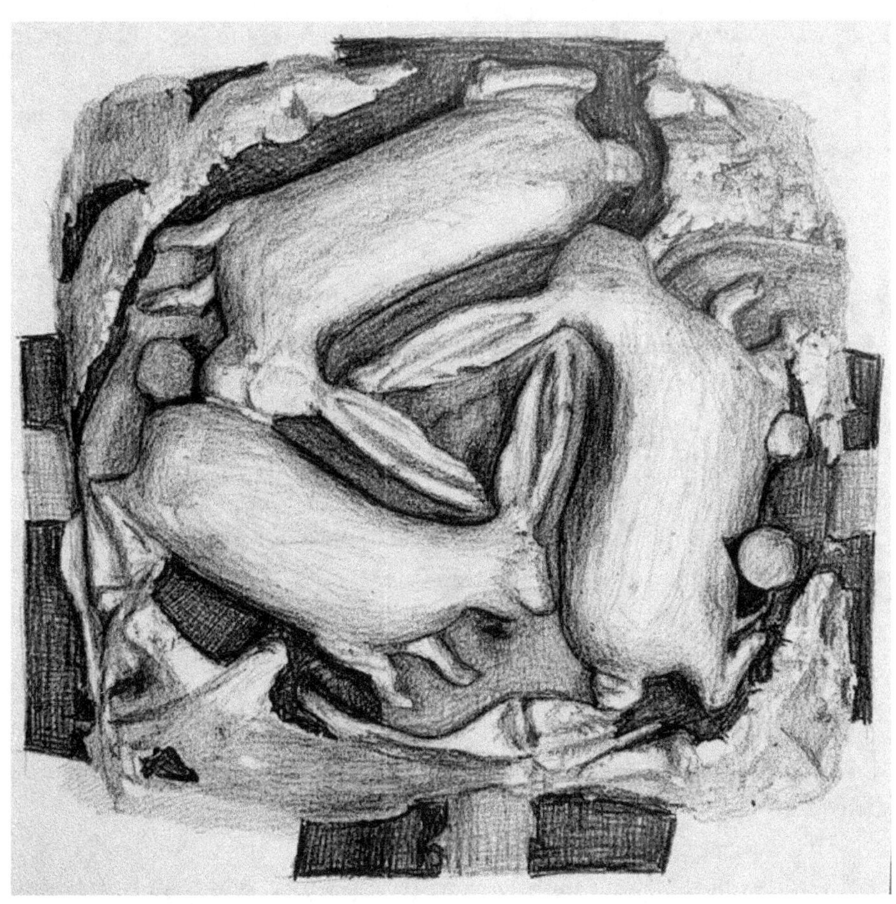

Roof boss at St. John the Baptist church, North Bovey, Devon, UK.

TELL ME A STORY

Liko was hammered. It hit him as he was walking Meg to her car. When he asked for her number, she hesitated.

"I had a good time tonight," she said slowly. "I hope you won't be offended when I say I'd like to just keep it tonight." She held up her left hand. "I've only recently taken it off."

"Gotcha."

"I'm not ready to date. But it was nice to put on a new dress, go to a party, and flirt with a handsome man. Know that I still got it. Then say, *That was enough, thank you very much,* get in my car and go home. Because I can."

"I totally understand," Liko said. "Wait, go back to the handsome part?"

She laughed and patted his cheek. "It was a good night for topping up the ol' ego tank. For real, though, this shirt? Great color on you. Wear it to all parties. I insist."

Liko smoothed down the front and smiled, pleased beyond words and not wanting to slur any words he could think up.

Meg leaned and kissed his cheek quick. "Thank you for a great time."

"You good to drive?"

"I'm perfect."

He opened her door. "You are. Don't change a thing." He waited until she was settled and buckled, then shut her door. Feeling chivalric, he guided her as she backed the car up, and waved as she drove away.

"That was enough," he said, not slurring too badly. "Thank you very much."

He took another walk under the wisteria pergola, both hands brushing the profusion of purple blooms. When he reached the porch, Dane was sitting in one of the Adirondack chairs, feet up on the railing. Salma sat beside, her head and one paw in Dane's lap. His hand ran in long, loving strokes along her neck.

"Well well," he said. "I didn't expect to see you back."

Liko put a foot on the step, a hand on the railing, and swayed a bit, grinning through numb lips. "That was the most piss-elegant rejection of my life."

Dane laughed. "Meggy's a sweetheart."

"She is. And this is a damn good party."

"Party's over, big guy."

"This was a damn good party."

"I know some good pipple."

"I love your pipple. Thank you."

"My pleasure. Go drink some water."

Liko obeyed, pounding a big glass in the kitchen and carrying a second back out to the porch. He eased into another Adirondack chair and the two men sat quietly, listening to the din of spring peepers and the faint hum of the last revelers at the Pub. Liko could see some of the outdoor fire pits were lit, and the smoke occasionally wafted up to the farm.

He set his glass down on the side table and noticed a postcard there. Innocently, he went to pick it up, but Dane's fingertips dropped on the card and swept it away.

"Sorry," Liko said, just as Dane said, "Sorry."

They blinked at each other a bewildered second.

Dane gave a wobbly smile. "It's just…"

"Love note?"

He laughed now. "No. Just personal." He tucked the postcard into his jacket pocket. "Story for another day."

"Tell me a story tonight."

"You're drunk."

"I'm a quiet drunk. Which makes me a great listener."

Dane was quiet a long time. "I don't know if I want to tell the story in order, or just tell it as I walk you through the chamber mystery."

"You gotta start somewhere."

"We'll start in the morning."

"Start now."

Dane exhaled. "You're drunk, you're also quite bossy, and I'm a terrible storyteller."

"You can break every story down into one basic formula. *Once upon a time. And then. And then. Until finally. And then.*"

"That easy, huh?"

"I'll go first. Once upon a time, a man had a son. And then the son died. And then the man wanted to die. Until finally the man decided to keep living. And then he looked for a reason why. Now you go."

"Once upon a time," Dane said slowly. He rolled his lips in tight and gazed up at the porch ceiling, blinking rapidly. "Once upon a time, there was a Great Dane. And then he met Ethan and Nomi. And then they fell in love. And then…" Dane shook his head, laughing. "This is torture. Go get your laptop."

"Yeah, baby, let's do this," Liko got up.

"Drink some more water."

"Now who's being bossy?"

"You love it," Dane called after him.

THEY SET UP IN the den, where Liko could connect his laptop to the big TV screen. He opened his saved game, which was paused outside Paderborn Cathedral, in front of the Drei-Hasen-Fenster—the window of the Three Hares. "Can we start here or do we need to play from the start?"

"Go from here."

Liko first picked up the photograph lying on the grass under the window, which showed a man's hand sliding a loose stone from a wall. The loose brick in the buttress wouldn't come free unless the photo was in the player's cache.

"Pause," Dane said.

"Bossy."

"This is a story." He reached toward the coffee table where he'd set some photographs. He handed one to Liko. It was taken in the woods and showed a broken-down stone chimney and the remains of a house foundation, all choked with weeds and vines.

The hair on the back of Liko's neck began to lift as Dane passed another picture, taken closer to the chimney. Then another shot, even closer, with a hand pulling at a loose brick. It was identical to the photo in the game.

"Shut up," Liko said under his breath. He clicked his cached picture and compared it to the one Dane held out. Exactly the same.

"This is Ethan's hand," Dane said. "I took the pictures."

He passed one last photo. Now the brick was all the way free of the chimney and Ethan was drawing out a small metal box.

"The buttress in the game isn't architecturally accurate," Dane said, pointing to the TV where *Three Hares* was paused. "Ethan modeled it to look like the old chimney in these pictures. You can see how the colors and stone shapes are the same. The real buttress at Paderborn doesn't look like this."

"My gast is flabbered," Liko said, looking from the screen to the photograph and back.

"Anyway, these are the woods where Nomi played when she was a little girl. She and a friend found the loose brick. They put treasures in a card file box and hid it inside."

Dane went quiet a minute, thinking. Then gave a sideways smile. "Told you I was a terrible storyteller."

"You're doing fine."

"Nomi was in and out of foster care until she was seventeen. When she played in these woods, she was living with a family named Silver. She was called Naomi then. Naomi Silver. She said they were the happiest years of her childhood."

He sighed. "I'll never be able to tell her stories perfectly. Not the way she would. I'll leave something out. I'll embellish or exaggerate. I'll make something up to fill in a gap. Or I just don't know some crucial detail, some feeling or insight she kept in her heart. I'll inevitably get it wrong."

"You loved her," Liko said. "You were with her twenty-two years. You saw her through cancer. You had a child together. You knew her best. Who else but you to tell her stories? You're the only one who can even try."

"True," Dane said.

"You're all she's got."

Dane looked at him. "Thanks for present tense."

"You can pry present tense from my cold, dead hands."

"All right then." Dane settled back and put his feet on the coffee table. "Once upon a time…"

PART THREE
SARIS ADAM

"The hares are but a feeble folk, yet they make their houses in the rocks."
—Proverbs 30:26

SILVER FOR SILVER

1971

ON A FRIGID FEBRUARY night, two kitchen workers at a Spanish restaurant in Newburgh, New York insist to the chef they can hear a baby crying outside. The three men retrieve a lumpy canvas tote bag from one of the dumpsters. Inside is a newborn infant girl, the stump of her umbilical cord still attached. The bag has no clothing, no diapers, no bottle, no note. Just the pathetic scrap of a baby and, inside a piece of many-times-folded paper, a thin silver chain.

Someone at child services puts *Naomi Misteria* on her birth certificate. God only knows why. Maybe they're up to the Ns in arbitrary name picks. As for the surname, ostensibly they mean *mystery*, but *misteria* isn't a word in any language. The closest is the Spanish word, *misterio*. And perhaps they, whoever they are, change the O to an A because this is a girl.

She remains Naomi Misteria as she's shuffled through four foster families, none of whom work out for one reason or another. She stays long enough with the fifth family to gain a new surname, Silver, and it's as Naomi Silver that she attends kindergarten and first grade.

The Silvers live in Rhinebeck, in an old farmhouse on a quarter-acre of rambling land that Judy Silver made into stunning flower gardens surrounding a huge vegetable patch. Judy not only grows produce but cans and preserves it. She takes jars of pickles, jams and relish to county fairs where she wins blue ribbons.

Jerry Silver, who clocks long, hard hours as a chemical engineer and recharges his batteries in amateur woodwork, builds a colony of birdhouses for the garden, painted in vivid colors and mounted on trees and posts.

At the Silvers, Naomi not only has a garden, she has a grandpa. Andy Silver, who lost an arm in the Korean War, is a quiet man with a somewhat haunted air, forever suspicious of the world and its uncertainties. In this way, he and Naomi suit each other, for already at four years old, Naomi is slow to put eggs of love and loyalty into any one basket. She's small for her age, although she hits all her developmental milestones, and teaches herself to read simply as a means of reliable companionship.

She and Andy feel each other out a few months, taking each other's measure. Andy eventually allows Naomi to look at the stump of his arm without its prosthetic, and Naomi reveals to the old man that she's taught herself to read at an astonishing level. Andy gives Naomi a very solemn, very grownup gift: a personalized embossing stamp so she can mark her books.

"Ex libris," he says, demonstrating the press on a piece of scrap paper. "It means, *From the library of.* You write your name and address on these lines here."

In return, Naomi tries to give Andy the silver chain that was found with her in the dirty tote bag. Silver for Silver.

"Oh no, honey," Andy says, crouching down and closing Naomi's fingers around the necklace, then closing the little fist in his one strong hand. "Lord in Heaven, you're such a darling girl, but this isn't a thing to give away. Not to me, not to anyone. This was your mother's necklace, understand? It's treasure. Family treasure. Don't ever give it away. Promise me."

With the exchange of these tokens of trust, Andy and Naomi become friends. Then soulmates.

Andy is haunted by war, both injured and insulted. He seeks comfort and solace in the ground, in the reliability of the changing seasons and predictable life cycles. Whether he plants these values in Naomi or whether she plants them herself is hard to say. But the first time a child attaches emotion to an event, memory is born, and Naomi's memory blooms on the day Andy takes her to a local garden center. He waits patiently as she picks out a dozen seed packets. Daisies because they're familiar. Zinnias because they're irresistible. Sunflowers because they're tall. She picks corn, because she likes corn. And pumpkins, because what little kid doesn't want to grow their own pumpkin? Other packets she picks simply for the color of blossoms or the curl of leaves or a name she can sound out herself.

Back at home, in the four raised beds Jerry builds especially for the child, Naomi follows Andy's terse, simple directions in preparing the soil, scratching furrows and dropping the seeds into the rich dirt. She lugs her little watering can back and forth, then spreads a layer of hay over the beds.

Her next lessons are more philosophical. She learns patience from her daily, anxious trips to the beds, searching for signs of life. When the first sprouts and their tiny nursery leaves push through the soil, she's inducted into the most simple and elemental acts of life. Thinning out the dense mat of seedlings teaches her about survival of the fittest. Battling weeds and pests is a lesson in competition. Even the failures serve a purpose: Some seeds don't sprout, or die despite the tender loving care. And this happens sometimes. Life isn't always fair. The chopped up stems and foliage of dead plants are worked into the soil, along with the tin of vegetable scraps, coffee grounds and eggshells that Judy keeps on the kitchen counter. Little is wasted at the Silvers. Everything has a purpose. Everything begins in the dirt and ends in the dirt.

This last lesson is driven home when Andy Silver dies at the end of Naomi's second summer with the family. She cuts a dazzling bouquet of zinnias to put on his gravesite. She's devastated when her nine cornstalks produce only a single inedible ear, and a little comforted when her pumpkin patch yields three respectable jack-o-lanterns. Two are displayed on the porch steps and the third made into a pie, which Naomi desolately picks at, crying over the seed catalogs she and Andy won't order from.

To COMFORT HER FOSTER daughter, Judy buys a book called *Mud Pies and Other Recipes: A Cookbook for Dolls*. It quickly becomes the girl's favorite and she embosses the first page with her treasured stamp:

EX LIBRIS
Naomi Silver
560 Violet Hill Road
Rhinebeck, New York

The Silvers' property is bordered by woodlands. Once a little house stood among the trees, but it's fallen to rubble, leaving only the stone chimney, the remains of a fireplace, and mossy slabs of the broken foundation. For Naomi and her next-door playmate Katie, it's a palace. They spend hours playing in the woods, dragging long logs to make walls, short stumps to make tables and chairs. Begging cast-off pots and pans so they can make all the things in *Mud Pies and Other Recipes*.

In her spare time, Judy makes little dolls with acorn hats, bead heads and pipe cleaner bodies. They're dressed in felt clothing, embroidered with tiny patterns, or in puffy skirts made from silk flower petals. Naomi is given a dozen dolls of her own. She and Katie pose them around their playhouse and work them into their imaginary games.

One day, the girls discover a loose brick in the chimney. Behind it is a tantalizing space begging for hidden treasure. Katie finds an old file card box with a hinged lid and they each comb their rooms for suitable tribute. Katie puts in a little ring with a red stone, and a beautiful geode polished smooth on its open side, the cavity sparkling with crystals. Naomi puts in three of the acorn-cap dolls and her silver chain. The girls parade the box through the woods and around the house foundation, making up ceremony as they go. They put their reliquary in the secret space in the chimney, sprinkle it with rose petals from Judy's garden, and replace the loose brick.

They visit the box frequently. Then less so. And little by little, as young girls often do, they forget about it.

Not long after, Jerry Silver receives a plum promotion at work which unfortunately comes with relocation. Naomi finds herself back in the system with her suitcase, her small library of books, an embossing stamp and a basket of smashed eggs. Hurt beyond her capacity to express. Dying of longing for her garden beds, the birdhouses, the jars of preserves, the woods and her playhouse. She's been kicked out of Eden, yanked from the earth like a weed and discarded, not good enough even for compost.

Most of all Naomi feels robbed. Robbed of a mother and father to name her something significant. Robbed of a surname with history. Robbed of security. Robbed of consistency. Robbed of love. She knows love and consistency and security are things to give as well as receive, but then and there she vows not to give them until she is *Somewhere,* with a capital S. And Somewhere will not be a place chosen *for* her, but a place she chooses for herself.

She vows the same for her name. She returns to being Naomi Misteria, but not forever. One day, when she is Somewhere, she'll rename herself. She'll know the name when it's time. Or maybe someone else will know. This hardened little girl isn't entirely without a sense of romance, and all the books she's read include a Someone in a Somewhere. Someone to love. Someone who might look at her and call her what she is and who she is. Someone who might both claim and name her.

But all that is for Someday, with a capital S. Right now, Naomi Misteria retaliates against the system by never again giving a foster family a fair chance. She resolves to plant no more seeds in dirt that isn't her own, and assigns little emotion to anything that happens to her. So becomes her mission to prepare herself as a gardener prepares soil. To enrich herself with a compost of knowledge and self-sufficiency, building a barrier against pests. To develop eggs that might be put in baskets, and to weave a basket into which one day she might receive eggs.

THE PATH TO THE HARE RING

DANE LEFT THE DEN and came back with a small metal box.

"Is that it?" Liko asked.

"This is it." One by one, Dane set the treasures on the coffee table: the ring with the red stone, the geode, and three little dolls with acorn caps.

"Saskia has the silver necklace," Dane said. "But here's everything else. Because once upon a time, a girl hid treasures behind a loose brick in an old chimney. And then she had to leave the woods, but the box stayed behind. And then time passed. And then Naomi became Nomi."

"Until finally?"

Dane smiled. "Until finally, the girl's best friends went looking for the box. Because they loved her."

IN A WAY ONLY Ethan Hasen can, he listens to the story and looks at Nomi's lost box as a game to play. A puzzle to solve. A literal treasure hunt.

"Road trip," he says, showing Dane the battered, beloved copy of *Mud Pies and Other Recipes*. The first page embossed *EX LIBRIS* with childish handwriting beneath: *Naomi Silver, 560 Violet Hill Road, Rhinebeck, New York.*

"All we have to do is go there and get it," he says, eyes lit up with adventure.

"Dude, it's private property," Dane says.

"So? We knock on the door, say who we are and what we need."

"They hid that box seventeen years ago. There's probably a new house built there now."

"If there is, we turn around and come back. What's the big deal?"

"It's just…not a good idea. You go yourself."

"It's a great idea and you're coming with me."

Dane wants none of it—the idea of knocking on a stranger's door and asking to take a walk in their woods is terrifying. But Ethan has both tremendous patience and tremendous persuasion when he's latched onto an idea. Ethan never struggles on the path from concept to execution. If he can envision it in his mind, he can make it manifest. He sees no reason why a method that works for his art won't work for everything else. He never visualizes potential obstacles, forks or detours. The path is simple: *Me see thing. Me want thing. Me create thing.*

He does encounter one small hitch, which is an excuse for him and Dane to go driving off without Nomi. "Hardest part about being three and being always together," he mumbles. "Two go off and it's immediately suspect."

"Always keep a lie simple," Dane says. Something he learned during his painful childhood. And in the end, it's he who comes up with the cover story.

"Ethan and I want to go see a Renegades game on Saturday," he says.

"A what?" Nomi says.

"The new minor league baseball team that plays in Fishkill. Want to go?"

"Fuck, no."

And that's all it takes.

The Silvers' place on Violet Hill Road is still there. An old farmhouse much like Schoenfeld's, but smaller and painted red. Judy Silver's legendary garden beds are crammed with flowers, tall grasses and thick mats of spiky iris foliage. Dane is crammed with anxious dread when Ethan rings the doorbell, but Ethan's ready with a missionary's polite smile and a simple story: He used to live here and loved to play in those woods. Could he go look?

The story goes untold because nobody answers the bell.

"Well, we tried," Ethan says, the congenial smile morphing to a shit-eating grin. And the two of them simply stroll into the woods.

Nomi described a forest to the boys, but this glade isn't even fifty yards across. Just a little woodland buffer between property lots. But Nomi was young at the time, and nature is always magnified in the eyes of children. Slopes are mountains, lawns are meadows, groves are forests and puddles are oceans.

The chimney has taken a hit in recent years: The top third is broken clear off and lies in mossy chunks on the ground. Ethan and Dane go over the rest carefully. Once. Twice. The third pass, they find the loose brick. Ethan crows in triumph and Dane takes pictures as the box is pulled out with a shower of dead, dried petals. It's rusty, and the hinges squeal as Ethan raises the lid.

"Oh my God, it's all here," he breathes. "We found it. Look. Dane. It's here."

The ring. The geode. The three dolls. And the silver chain.

It's all there.

Dane puts arms around Ethan. "I was wrong. It's a really good idea."

He's all for giving it to Nomi straight away but Ethan disagrees. This has to be an experience. A *journey* to take Nomi back to childhood.

He designs a treasure hunt and heeds Dane's advice to keep it simple: "You're springing a big emotional surprise on her at the end. You don't need to make the journey bigger than the destination."

So Ethan makes the dozen notes left around the farm simple and direct:

Look on the back of the wind spinner.

Visit the Green Man on the side of the chicken coop.

Something is hiding in the towel basket by the pool.

Take the path to the Hare Ring.

Nomi follows the clues, occasionally smiling or grimacing at Ethan and Dane, who are following at a distance. "Hasenpfeffer, if I get to the end and the prize isn't Richard Gere, it's going to be unpleasant."

"Lower your expectations," Ethan says.

"You'll be so underwhelmed," Dane adds, although his heart starts to kick up as they follow Nomi along the path through the woods and emerge into the Hare Ring. It's wisteria time, and the perimeter is bursting with blossoms. In the center of the clearing, the stone block waits, patient and majestic. And to Dane, always a little eerie.

"Now what?" Nomi says, and Ethan points toward the block.

As they follow her, Ethan takes Dane's hand tight. Dane looks at him, heart absolutely hammering through his chest wall now. He lifts their clenched fingers to his mouth and kisses them. Ethan widens his eyes, mouths *Holy shit* over their knuckles. He lets go and puts his arm around Dane's shoulders. He's just a bit taller, and Dane fits perfectly beneath its drape as his own arm slides around Ethan's waist.

Nomi approaches the block, on top of which is the file card box. She regards it, hands on hips. "What is…"

Then her hands fly to her mouth. Her shoulders hunch up to her ears and her whole body curls forward. She folds in on herself, shaking her head. She looks at the boys, eyes enormous over the steeple of her fingers and whispers, "No."

Ethan and Dane hold perfectly still and silent.

"No," Nomi says. "No. No. You didn't… How did you… No. Oh my God…"

"Open it," Dane says, unable to bear it any longer.

Her hands come off her mouth and rest on the box. "How did you get this? Where did you get this? What did you *do*…"

The boys come to her now, one on either side. "Open it," Ethan says softly.

"I can't." She seems almost afraid of the box. "No. You didn't."

"We did," Dane says. "Open it."

She does. One glance inside and her face is back in her hands. She's weeping in great shuddering sobs, fingers sliding up to dig in her hair. "Oh my God. Oh my God, how… How did you…?"

"You inscribed all your childhood books," Ethan says. "560 Violet Hill Road in Rhinebeck. We just got a map and went looking."

"We told you we were going to the Renegades game," Dane says.

"I don't believe it," Nomi says, dragging the backs of her hands over her eyes. Those hands shake as she reaches inside the box. She takes out the ring first, with its little red stone. "This was Katie's," she says tightly, sliding it onto her pinky. "And oh my God, she put in this crystal. And…" She begins crying again as she takes out the little acorn dolls and clutches them to her heart. "I can't believe you did this. I can't believe you *did* this for me."

Last is the silver chain, which rips Nomi in two, releasing a magnificent avalanche of sobbing laughter, interspersed with feverish words that sound like both celebration and confession. "Oh God, this was my mother's. Andy said not to give it away, it was treasure, I had to keep it always. But the box was for treasure so I put it inside and we hid it and…" She sways a little, and sinks onto her knees by the great stone. "I promised him I wouldn't ever give it away, but I did."

"No, you didn't," Ethan says, kneeling behind her. "You didn't give it away, you just *put* it away. For a really long time."

Dane has unclasped the chain. He kneels in front of Nomi and holds it out by the ends. "Your silver, my liege," he whispers.

She wipes her eyes again and leans toward him. He fastens the necklace at her nape. Her fingertips caress its length along her collarbones.

"Thank you," she says. "I love you. I love both of you so much."

She cants forward against Dane's chest. He holds her, while Ethan drapes over her back, his hands in Dane's hair.

"That," Liko said, "is a tremendous story." He had the geode on his palm and was staring into its cavern of sparkly points.

"And I'm all told out," Dane said, slapping his knees and getting up. "I'm going to bed. We can continue this tomorrow." He checked his watch. "Or later today."

Liko clicked off the TV and shut his laptop. "Would you say that was the moment you three fell in love?"

"I don't know about *the* moment," Dane said. "But if were unaware or pretending up until then, we weren't anymore."

KISS ME LIKE THAT

In the dark of his bedroom, Dane lay on his stomach, gazing at the little heap of silver on the mattress by his head. He stirred a finger in the coils—*It's a kilo-koil*, Diane said—picked out an end and stretched the chain long. Then gathered it all in his fist.

He'd lied downstairs, of course. Saskia didn't have Nomi's necklace. She would one day, but not yet. Dane still needed it. It was one of a dozen little psychological arrangements a mourning father and daughter had made. Another one being Dane would wait a year before he started dating.

He rolled on his back and put the bunched necklace into the hollow at the base of his throat.

Was that the moment you three fell in love?

They'd long been in love. The moment Nomi, clothed in her silver again, fell onto Dane's chest and Ethan fell on her back, love went from abstract to actual. From spiritual to physical.

Dane closed his eyes and his hands reached into the past. Time threw a veil over memories, softening and blurring recollections, but not this one. Dane remembered everything. He could recreate every detail. How Nomi's spine rolled up, vertebra on vertebra, her chin lifting last as she fell back onto Ethan.

Ethan took her. Got her cradled in the crook of one arm while the other hand spread wide across her throat in a way that made Dane's breath cease. Ethan was holding her like a lover. Strong and sure. That wide palm moving up to the side of her face, thumb stroking a cheekbone. He was going to kiss her. You couldn't hold someone's face like that and not kiss them.

Kiss me like that, *Diane said.* Kiss me. Please hold and kiss me like that. I want to look like him and feel like her…

Then Ethan did kiss Nomi, but not her mouth. His head bowed and he pressed his lips between her eyebrows, his hand in her hair now, thumb stroking her temple. "I love you," he whispered.

"I love you." She kissed his face all over, saying I love you. He wiped the tears from under her eyes, brought her body up, then gently pushed it over into Dane's arms.

Her hands went to his face. "Oh my God, I love you."

His hands went to her head. "Nomi…" And he could say no more.

Dane drew a pillow toward him. He took a corner in his hands and kissed it.

He could feel her heartbeat in his mouth. He could taste her pulse and her tongue was on his and her crying mouth was on him, in him, for him. Her hands dropped from Dane's face and her arms wrapped around his neck. He could feel her bound chest against his broken chest as his fingers traced the silver at her neck and then he reached around her and took hold of Ethan's shirt, pulling him against Nomi's back, pulling him through Nomi.

Nomi was crying again, but she was smiling, too, the apples of her cheeks curled into Dane's palms. Her mouth left his and she put her face in the curve of his neck. Over her shoulder, Dane and Ethan now looked at each other.

Ethan took Dane's face and drew it close. While Dane had seized and devoured Nomi's kiss, now he instinctively held his desire in check and let Ethan come to him, feel him out. This kiss was slower, softer, a little uncertain. More like putting their shyest smiles together and breathing. Still Dane could feel Ethan's pulse pumping hard and fast, and in just his lips Dane could taste an intense vulnerability.

So Dane said it first: "I love you."

"I'm scared how much I love you," Ethan said.

"No, don't be afraid," Dane whispered against his pillowed lover, just as he whispered into Ethan's mouth while Nomi held Dane tight and breathed against his neck.

"Don't be afraid."

They held each other tight, rocking on their knees in the soft grass.

"Don't be afraid."

The past and the present and the future.

"Don't be afraid."

Hearts and brains and bodies. A threefold energy taking turns to come in from the side and cross over the center, weaving them into a braid of silver.

"Don't be afraid."

Three pairs of hands and each had something to hold. Three mouths and each had tasted abandonment. Three hares who had been left at firehouses, thrown in the garbage and put in the cruel hands of strangers. But one at a time, immediately or eventually, they'd made their way to Schoenfeld's. Now they were binding themselves into a cord, bonding their lives. Putting their heads together, each turning an ear into the wind of the others' stories, until it was not three stories but one. And in the clearing ringed by wisteria, at the base of a stone that had no business being there, the three hares claimed each other.

Unafraid, they began to spin.

JEFFREY

THE NEXT DAY DAWNED picture perfect and Liko took his cup of coffee for a little meander around the farm. His mind meandered as well, to his first tour of Schoenfeld's, back in March, with Diane as his guide. Odd how little thought he'd given to her since. Occasionally the incident wandered through the transom of his mind—*Oh yeah, there was the time Dane was dressed as a woman*—and always he filed it under OK, Whatever, which was a crowded sub-folder within The Meaningless Scrapheap of Everything Else.

"Why should I care," Liko said aloud, then sheepishly looked around to see if anyone was in earshot. *He's not a drag queen,* he thought. *He's not transitioning. But so what if he were? He said Diane's a private thing he usually keeps inside.*

Liko smiled, remembering Dane describing Diane as a life coach, saying, *She helps me do brave things.*

He'd also used the word *sister.* And Diane had used *brother.*

Maybe Dane and Maisie had another sister who died tragically.

Liko shrugged at the beautiful day. *Diane's an alter ego. So what, we all have them.*

Fake screen names. Sock puppet accounts. A British adolescent dialing down his accent to fit in with his American friends. Even Janelle had suits and stilettos she specifically wore when she was making presentations at work.

"Uh-oh, you've got the power heels on," Liko would say.

Janelle would smirk and donkey-kick the fridge door shut. "I'm going into this meeting beav first."

The memory made him sigh as he turned down the path beneath the wisteria pergola. Dane was coming the other way, his hands cupped against his chest. "Morning," he called. "Got something for you."

"For me?"

"Put your coffee down."

Liko did and into his palms Dane gently set a duckling.

"Stop," Liko said.

"I thought maybe you'd be amenable to adopting a little creature while you're on retreat."

"Absolutely not. I've got writing to do, a mystery to solve, and I have no room in my schedule for cre— Hello, little fellow, who's the most handsome baby duck ever?"

"He's the runt of the flock."

Liko half turned away, affronted. "Sir, how dare you."

"He has eleven siblings who don't share nicely. He keeps getting pushed out at feeding time and he's not growing."

"Look at you," Liko said, holding the duckling at eye level. The little bird started nuzzling all over his face, then nibbling on his earlobes. "Yes. Yes, you're so fluffy. Oh my God, you're so floofy."

Dane smiled. "He needs a champion. How about it?"

"This is my creature," Liko said, running an index finger along the duckling's back. "I shall love him and hold him and call him…"

"George?"

"Unfortunately, George is the name of the creature who shtupped my wife."

"Oh shit," Dane said.

"I shall call him Floofy."

"Please don't."

"Actually, no, this is Jeffrey," Liko said. "Named for the runty duckling in *Charlotte's Web.*"

"Well, in the movie, not the book."

"Dane's being a purist twat," Liko said to Jeffrey's downy face. "Isn't he, Jeffrey? Yes he is."

Dane took Liko to see the duck brooder, which was a big galvanized tub with a wire cave clamped over the top. The bottom was lined with wood shavings and outfitted with feeders and water, a padded box for sleeping, and a heat lamp hooked overhead.

"No pool?" Liko asked. "My duck must have a pool."

Dane pointed to a child's wading pool against the far wall. "They splash around there until Mama takes them for swimming lessons."

A farm worker was devising a new brooder out of a large plastic tub. She'd cut out the center of the lid and was fixing wire mesh over the opening.

"Maya, this is Liko," Dane said. "Liko, Maya. She's making a separate brooder for Jeffrey and just one or two of his siblings. He'll still have company, but he won't have to work so hard to get food."

"You'll find I am an excellent brooder," Liko said to Jeffrey, scratching him around the bill. "I brood all day every day. We're gonna be such good mates."

Dane had a look of unadulterated pleasure on his face. A mix of *Whew, my idea worked* and *Look how cute you are with your duck.*

Liko smiled back a goofy moment before asking, "Will you feed him anything different?"

"Probiotics work well to help the small ones thrive," Maya said. "He'll get a little yogurt stirred into his feed. We do extra monitoring at mealtimes to make sure he gets enough."

Dane nudged Liko's side. "We meaning you. Report back at, what, noon?"

"Noon," Maya said. "Looks like he's imprinting already so he'll be waiting for you, Liko. Don't be late."

Liko felt more than a little reluctance to surrender his charge. He lowered Jeffrey into the pool, watched him paddle a bit, then backed toward the door clutching his heart. "Farewell, web-footed friend," he said, laughing. "Damn, this is like *His Dark Materials.* I'm separating from my daemon."

Now Dane was staring at him with unadulterated surprise.

"His Dark Materials," Liko said again. "Philip Pullman. It's a fantasy ser—"

"I know what it is," Dane said. "Only one of my favorite series in the world."

"Really?"

"Really." Dane headed outside. "I don't meet many others who know it."

"Does this get me promoted from people to pipple?"

"If you like Philip Pullman, you are officially pipple."

"God what a day," Liko said, looking around.

"Got plans?"

"I feel like a walk. If I take Salma, is there a good trail to follow?" At the magic word *walk,* Salma started running circles around Liko's legs.

"Sure. I'll show you the path through the woods to the Hare Ring. From there you can pick up a couple trails that loop around the property. One will take you back into town and you can walk home along Oak Hill Road. If you want a longer hike, it's two miles to pick up Liberty Loop, three to Winding Waters. Or you can drive to either and park at the trailhead."

Liko looked down at his beat-up sneakers. "I'll start small."

"Good call. You have to be back in time to feed your duck."

He and Liko walked up the farm road and onto a path that cut through the woods. Almost instantly, the humming buzz of birdsong and insects was halved, as was the din of machinery and caterwauling of roosters. A calm, hallowed quiet closed around the two men as they followed the meandering trail around trees and boulders, ducking under branches and hopping over fallen logs.

"Reminds me of when I was young," Liko said. "Summer holidays when I'd run wild in the woods with my mates. Playing knights, pirates, cops and robbers. Secret Agents. We would— *Wow…*"

The path abruptly emerged into a large grassy clearing, almost perfectly round.

"Holy hell," Liko said, stopping short with hands on hips. The ring of trees was engulfed in a purple veil. Every trunk and branch coiled in wisteria vines, dripping purple flowers like great clusters of grapes.

"Welcome to the Hare Ring," Dane said. "At its peak of purple perfection. Another reason I wanted you to come here in early May."

"This is amazing. Did you guys plant these vines?"

"No, it's all naturalized. Look out, there she goes…"

Salma had darted into the clearing at a run. Dozens of small, brown rabbits exploded out of her path and fled for the safety of the woods. Two raced toward Liko and Dane, did a mid-air flip turn and bounded the other way.

"O wisteria hares turning," Liko said.

Dane started walking toward the middle of the clearing, toward a large, square stone in its center. It was about two feet high by three feet long, rough and weathered.

And weirdly familiar.

"Where'd this come from?" Liko asked.

"Nobody knows. Maybe thrown up by the earth over eons. Maybe dragged here by glaciers. Maybe part of a fence that was dismantled but this baby couldn't be budged. So here it stayed. And Ethan being Ethan, he took it as a challenge."

The short end facing them was carved with an unfinished Green Man, only the eyes and half his face completed. The other short end had a simple carving of the Three Hares motif. Across one of the long ends were chiseled letters.

"Oh, no way," Liko said, crouching down to examine the line of words: *Ye then deign to know me.*

"It's off-center," Dane said. "Which drove Ethan *batshit*. The triangle of the hare ears is off by like a tenth of a degree or something. Also drove him batshit."

"This is the altar in the Green Man Chamber," Liko said.

"Correct."

"Which came first? I mean, did he carve the words before or after the game was released?"

"Before," Dane said, sitting on the rock. "Long before."

Liko sat on the grass, leaning back on his hands, listening to Dane tell how this clearing was where he, Ethan and Nomi came to be together. To talk about hard things. To make promises. To reach decisions. Or just be. It was most beautiful in springtime when the wisteria bloomed. Coldly magnificent in winter, under a full moon, when they'd build little fires in the stone's depression.

"Not every full moon religiously," Dane said, "but when we felt like it. Always on the winter solstice though. We had a thing about it." He glanced at Liko. "Which I can tell you, or I can point you toward the trails and let you get on with your day."

Liko lay down, laced hands behind his head and put his feet up on the rock. "I'm listening."

"So I was the only one of the three who knew their mother's name," Dane said. "The only one who had memories of a biological mother. Helen deWinter kind of went from being my mother to our mother. *The* mother. The woo-woo earth mother. Helen means *light,* so we'd come out to the Hare Ring on the winter solstice and celebrate the light coming back. Celebrate Helen deWinter, Light of Winter returning."

"I think Swedes have a saint," Liko said. "I forget her name but they have a solstice celebration in her honor, and children wear crowns with candles on their head."

"It was dumb," Dane said. "But at the same time, it was just fun as fuck to make up these rituals together and be unabashedly into them. To find meaning and magic in names and flowers and everything we saw in front of our faces on a daily basis. To treat a weird rock in the middle of nowhere as an altar. To look at the moon and not see a man there, but a rabbit."

Liko sat up and gazed around the ring. "Damn, all I'd have to do is take one wide-angle picture of this place, with the stone and the wisteria, and the gaming forums would lose their bloody minds."

"Wait, let me get out of the shot." Dane got off the block and moved a few feet away. "Go for it."

"You'd let me?"

"Haven't you been?"

"What?"

"Sharing what you've learned online."

"No."

"Why not?"

"Because it… All of this… It's yours. I don't know what it means yet, and I don't want to post something that'll result in a stampede of people showing up at this farm and clipping wisteria blossoms as souvenirs. Stealing the Green Man medallions or the hare statues. Disturbing your peace."

"The mission of the Danelaw is peace."

"What?"

"Never mind." Dane came and sat again. "Thank you," he said. "I'm protective of my peace, so I really appreciate it."

"Well, don't go thinking I'm an entirely noble fellow. Most of the not telling is selfishness. Greedy selfishness. Hoarding the secrets makes me feel I have a little power in a world where I feel so fucking helpless."

"I get it." Dane reached and pushed a little of Liko's hair back. It was a frank, unhesitating caress. The first of its kind between the men. Wasn't it? Liko's memory backtracked through the party and the late-night session in front of the laptop.

No, Dane hadn't touched him before. Not like this.

"Anyway," Dane said, in a cheerful, subject-changing tone, "the significance of wisteria in the game is it's Nomi's birth name Misteria with the M turned upside-down. Outside the game, strictly within Schoenfeld lore, it's how in nineteen ninety-one, the wisteria pergola was fifteen years old and still hadn't bloomed. Then one day, a stranger came to the farm. Naomi Misteria. She'd read about Schoenfeld's in a newspaper feature. It sounded like everything she'd ever wanted and maybe she could get a job. She came, she met John and Mary, and on her way out, she met Ethan. They had a conversation at the end of the driveway, right by the Green Man pillar. Ethan misheard her first name, Naomi, and thought it was *Nomi*."

"Really?"

Dane nodded. "She didn't correct him. She left the farm with a new name. The next day, walking under the pergola, Mary saw buds on one of the vines. The wisteria was blooming. That was all it took for Ethan to believe Nomi belonged here. She'd come and turned the world upside-down in the best of ways. He got in his car, drove two hours to where she was living, and brought her back."

He was quiet a moment and Liko stared. The sun was higher in the sky, and its rays hit Dane's head, glinting and shining on the blonds and coppers and silvers. His right profile was facing Liko, the brown eye gazing out at nothing. Then it flicked toward Liko and he smiled. "What?"

"I don't know why you gave me bollocks about being a terrible storyteller."

"Sometimes I manage to tell a concise one."

"How'd you end up at Schoenfeld's?"

Dane didn't answer.

"Story for another day?"

"The long version, yes. Concise version for now. Maisie hosted Ethan's first big art show at her gallery. She brought me along. Ethan was there, obviously. So were Nomi, and John and Mary. That's how I met them all and how I got invited back to Schoenfeld's. Parallel plot, Gideon Perfect commissioned Ethan for the artwork on *Two-Faced,* and Ethan wanted to use me as the model. So you can say that like Nomi, I first came here to make some money. Then I just…stayed."

"How old were you?"

"Twenty." Dane got up. "And now I've got work to do."

He walked Liko to the far side of the clearing, pointing out where the trail continued through the woods and the options to come back. Then he bent and took Salma's head in his hands, rubbing her neck. "You're in charge on this walk. Don't lose my friend, okay? Bring him back to the brooder at noon."

SIR, I'M THE LANDLORD

Liko supervised Jeffrey's lunch, gently nudging greedy siblings away from the feeder to make sure the littlest duck got his share. He lifeguarded pool time, then dried Jeffrey off and gave him some cuddles.

"Look at you besties," Maya said, skimming wood chips and debris out of the pool.

Liko only smiled, perfectly content in the simple moment. As the duckling nodded off between his cupped palms, he remembered newborn days when Kyle would nap on his chest. But the memory didn't bludgeon him today. It just sat quiet. Cuddling a little.

In the farmhouse kitchen, Dane was making a sandwich. "I killed the last of the cold cuts," he said. "And the bread. Sorry. You should go over to the Pub—they have a great Sunday lunch with a cider tasting. How's your buddy?"

"He's awesome," Liko said. "Thanks for introducing us."

"Everyone needs a creature." Dane took his plate over to the couch by the fireplace. "If you want, we can do a little more of the game while I'm eating."

Liko got his computer and resumed the game outside Paderborn Cathedral. Knowing what it meant now, he clicked the loose brick in the buttress next to the Drei-Hasen-Fenster, and flipped the switch that revealed the stairs to the Green Man Chamber.

"It's really beautiful," Liko said. "I know Ethan's not your favorite person in the world right now, but the artwork of this game is just stunning."

"It is," Dane said. "Objectively, outside my personal beef with him, he was an amazing artist. Show me what you know."

Liko went toward the wisteria vine first, and clicked the specific flower that grew older with each touch, until it produced its three seeds.

"Three is a magic number," he said, "and wisteria is Misteria with the M turned upside-down."

"Nomi and I would play as a team against Ethan in Scrabble," Dane said. "He'd murder us. The guy read the dictionary for fun, and the score would end up being two thousand to sixteen. So me and Nome made up all these cheaty rules to get an advantage. One of them was we could turn Ms upside down to make Ws. Or vice versa."

"I need that rule." Liko clicked the hare hiding in the wisteria vines and carried it to the ceiling motif. Then the second hare at the base of the altar. "So," he said, drawing a deep breath. "As far as I know, this is as far as the gaming community has gotten. And I told you that the night before he died, Kyle discovered something new. A piece of the puzzle no one else had solved yet."

"That's right." Eyes on the screen, Dane touched Liko's arm. "Show me."

Liko clicked the third hare in the Green Man's lap, took it to the fire and dropped it into the flames. They roared up high, releasing a hare-shaped cloud of smoke. The cloud ran up to the ceiling and melded into the motif, starting it spinning.

"Way to go, Kyle," Dane murmured.

"He figured it out from the word *deign*. Debasing yourself. Doing something beneath your dignity. I don't know if Ethan meant it that way."

"He didn't," Dane said, sounding genuinely impressed. "I swear, man, it has nothing to do with the word *deign*. It's from the Jakata Tales. The story of Buddha when he was incarnated as a hare, and he threw himself into the fire as an act of compassion, to fulfil his divine duty and feed a beggar."

"But also, from the word *deign,*" Liko said, feeling stubborn about his son's accomplishment.

"Absolutely," Dane said. "And now, officially. Anyway, like I told you, the ceiling motif is spinning the wrong way. The hares need to be running counter-clockwise."

"Why?"

"The best things happen when you're out of your comfort zone and running against the order."

Liko sighed. "Is this where the anagram comes in? *And ye then deign to know me, o what the fuck does this turn into?*"

Dane laughed. "Not yet. You have to use what's at hand."

"The wisteria seeds?"

"Bingo." He got up. "Go get lunch at the Pub. Trust me, you won't regret it."

They left the house together. At the bottom of the porch stairs, Liko paused. "If you don't mind me asking, who exactly owns the farm?"

"Now that Nomi is dead, Saskia. I own the house. It's zoned separately from the farm. I own the house and the lot it's on because you should marry for love, but keep the real estate in your name." He gave a wry smile. "That's Maisie's line. Buying the house was her idea. She said we could do commitment ceremonies every day the rest of our lives, but Nomi and Ethan being legally married was a practical disadvantage for me, should we split up. Naturally I didn't want to hear it, but she stayed on my ass. Not that she disapproved of our relationship, but because I'd walked out of my father's house with nothing, and worked my ass off to amass something. Maisie wanted me to have security, and real estate was a sure thing. She said, *If they get the marriage, you get the house.*

"When John and Mary retired, I bought the house from them. To keep it scrupulous, Ethan and Nomi paid me rent." Again his mouth twisted in an ironic smile. "Which is a snappy comeback I sometimes used when nosy people asked who I was in the arrangement. *Ah, here are Mr. and Mrs. Hasen. And who are you?* I'd say, *Sir, I'm the landlord.*"

"Brilliant," Liko said. "I confess I've been nosily wondering about the financial aspects of your relationship."

"The farm became Nomi's," Dane said. "Ethan joked it was his dowry. Nomi was pulled out of a dumpster. While she was being kicked around the system, all she dreamed about was a place of her own. A little farm where she could build a family and grow things. Ethan could give her precisely that. Security for her and Saskia. No matter what happened to me or Ethan or the three of us, nobody could ever be thrown back into the system."

"What a gift," Liko murmured.

"It was Ethan's way. Same with the cover art for *Two-Faced.* Gideon Perfect commissioned it from Ethan. Ethan used me as the model. Gideon paid ten thousand dollars and Ethan signed it over to me. As a nest egg."

"The cash or the painting?"

"Both."

Liko hesitated, then said as gently as he could, "He really loved you." He let the *you* be open to interpretation and held back his next exhale, hoping he hadn't stepped in it.

"Yeah," Dane said. "Yeah. He was… Yeah."

THE NAOMI ROAD 33

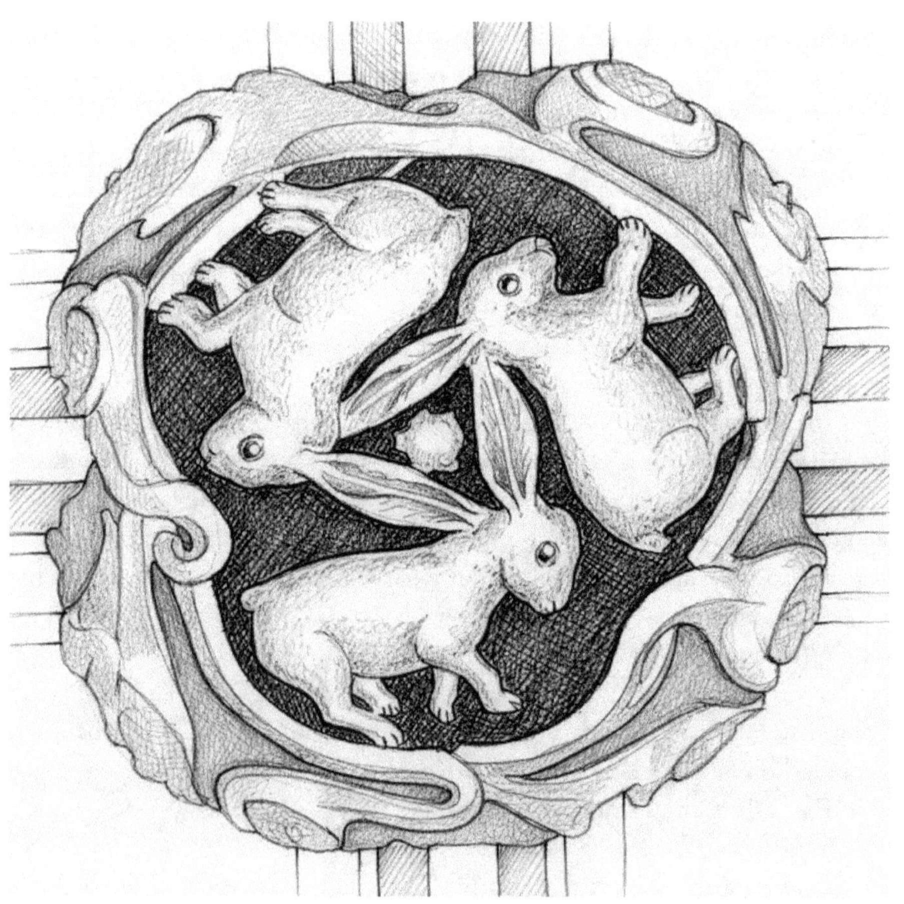

Roof boss at St. John the Baptist church, Paignton, Devon, UK

THE WORST THING YOU TASTE TODAY

The sign at the bar read, *LET ME TEMPT YOU WITH FIBER: Cider flight and Cora's choice of fibrous nom-noms: $30.*

Liko slid onto a stool, sat straight and laced his fingers like a teacher's pet.

"Well, hello," the bartender said.

"Are you Cora?"

"I am."

He raised a hand grandly. "Tempt me with fiber."

"Are you picky?"

"Not at all."

She pulled him a shot of the beetroot cider. "Practically nobody likes this," she said. "But I start newcomers off with it because things can only get better."

The brew was a beautiful ruby red, but Liko took a sip and shook his head.

"Yeah, it's dirt," Cora said.

"Carbonated dirt."

"Filthy. And not in a good way."

"People like this?"

"It has a little fan base, which is why we keep it on tap." She took the glass away and dashed it down the sink. "That'll be the worst thing you taste today."

Cora set up a flight and pulled Liko five samples. "This is the house dry. This is the house bone dry."

"Local apples?"

"All from Kulleseid's Orchard. This is a blackberry lemon shandy—look at the color on that, huh? Dudes dismiss it as a chick's drink but they order it all the time. This is our citrus hopping mad. And this is the lemon ginger. It's got a nice kick. All of these make superb slushies, by the way."

Cora set a small bowl of crispy roasted kale leaves on the bar, then went to put the order in. Liko scrolled his phone and crunched away, discreetly licking his fingertips. Cora came back and set a thick stack of napkins down with a wink.

"Like those?"

"Mmhm," Liko grunted behind a fist. "They taste coconutty."

She nodded. "This batch was made with coconut oil. I'm a purist—I like plain olive oil. But the real trick is to oversalt them *just* a hair."

Liko would've eaten them with no salt at all. He tried to be suave as he ran a finger around the edge of the bowl, catching the last fragments. Next Cora brought out a ramekin of roasted cabbage Caesar salad. "Cabbage is so good for you, it almost doesn't matter what you smother it with."

Every bite exploded with parmesan, lemon and some kind of umami magic bass note. "Nom," Liko said, scooping the tangy squares out with a bit of toasted bread. "All the nom."

"Try a sip of the lemon-ginger cider between bites," Cora said, sounding like a delighted grandmother. "It's a great pairing."

Next was a half-dozen truffled Brussel sprouts. "Again, doesn't matter how you eat your sprouts as long as you eat them."

An oblong dish with roasted asparagus spears. A little salad of arugula and blueberries, dressed with balsamic. Cora kept the bread coming because Liko needed it to mop up everything in sight. A splash of cider fell on the bar and he mopped that up too.

A thought flitted in and out between bites: *I'm so happy right now.*

"*And* the pièce de résistance," Cora said, setting down another oval dish. "Roasted carrots with thyme, lemon zest, burrata, balsamic drizzle and pine nuts. I can eat this all day, every day."

It was out of this world. Everything fresh, local, simply and beautifully prepared. Delicious as fuck but not overly filling. Liko shamelessly stuffed his face but when every crumb was gone and the plates glistened, he felt light and keen. If he'd skipped the ciders, he could've gone straight to the gym and set a couple PRs.

"I faced down temptation and lost," he said. "But I won."

"How'd you like the flight? Any favorites?"

They were all good, but the bone dry was his top pick, followed by the lemon ginger. Cora made him a slushy for the road with the blackberry-lemon shandy. He paid the bill with pleasure and left a generous tip for his temptress.

"See you again soon," she said.

"Oh, you will." He shook her hand. Growing up, he'd often seen his father shake hands with bartenders, waiters and restaurant hosts upon leaving. It impressed him as a cool, classy thing to do and he adopted the custom. Around the time he turned fifteen, Kyle started doing it too, which touched Liko to the paternal bone.

The thought held the door as Liko left the Pub. He pulled on his sunglasses. He paused for a moment of mindful gratitude, sipping his slushy. What luxury, a place like this with food like that, all a mere walk across the street.

SCHOENFELD'S FIELD CREW WAS off on Sunday and the spa was closed. Only the cluck and crow of poultry and the quacking of ducks accompanied Liko back up the driveway. The house was empty, so Liko wandered around looking for Dane. Past the pool, which Dane said would be opened on Memorial Day weekend. The impressive kitchen garden with ten raised beds. Dane had only planted four this year, saying he was keeping it simple. A miniature orchard boasted three apple trees, two peaches and a pear. Some jokester had hung a sign on the pear tree reading, *Help Wanted: Partridge. Inquire Within.*

Liko continued up to the fields, where he found Dane working on a sort of prone trolley. A skinny piece of plywood attached to a crude axle on wheels, which were spaced to fit in the dirt between rows of plants. Dane lay on his stomach, fiddling at the ground immediately beneath him, then rolling forward, bit by bit. Three ducks waddled alongside, eating what he tossed away.

"Well here's a rather ingenious contraption," Liko said.

"Like it?" Dane said, taking out one of his earbuds. "We stole it from the Dutch. It's how they manage giant fields of tulips. Saves your back a ton of grief."

"What are you managing here?"

"Carrots. They get sown direct into the soil but you have to thin them out. Everyone hates this job but I love it."

"I love the organic cleanup crew."

"Ducks are superb pest control," Dane said. "They get hired out to Kulleseid's Orchard, just to eat snails. Right, babydoll?" He smoothed the head of one of the ducks and she ate from his fingers.

Liko watched, fascinated. He knew next to nothing about growing things. He lived in a gated community and the HOA had strict rules about landscaping. Which was fine by him. He could just about handle a few ornamental shrubs and trees. He had a whiskey barrel at the base of his front steps. If it occurred to him, he stuck pansies in it in spring, impatiens in summer, and mums in autumn. Sometimes he wrapped his yard's small pine tree in lights but since Kyle died, why should he bother?

Yet after the spectacular lunch he'd just ingested, he looked around the farm with appreciative eyes, thinking he should bother.

"Can I try?" he asked.

Dane got him his own trolley and showed him how he wanted the carrot seedlings thinned. The two men worked prone, side by side, chatting easily. When one of the ducks hopped on Liko's trolley, nestled by his hip and put her head on his back, he felt slightly anointed.

"I think I'm officially Duck Dad," he said.

Dane laughed. "It's a good look on you."

Liko pulled a seedling that had put down quite a respectable root. "I legit have never seen a carrot pulled straight from the ground."

"Dude, when I first came to this place, I knew nothing about carrots. I knew nothing about *food…*"

TRUTH OR SILENCE

1993

Birch Island is a hamlet of the town of Warwick, and lies smack in the Black Dirt Region. This 26,000-acre expanse sprawls over the border of New York and New Jersey and used to be a glacial lake. Until the 1880s it was called the Drowned Lands. Then settlers drained the Wallkill River, revealing the largest concentration of muck outside the Florida Everglades.

"Yes," John Schoenfeld says to Dane, "*muck* is a scientific term."

Muck is deep, dark, rich soil, perfect for farming. The black-dirt onion was the region's prize crop until the late 20th century, when changing tastes and economic realities made many farmers diversify and embrace agro-tourism.

Schoenfeld's grows farm-to-table crops and raises chickens. Together with Kulleseid's Orchard and Voorhees & Sons, they operate as a collective called SKV, and nearly everyone in a 50-mile radius subscribes to their harvests.

The work is hard but the tasks are simple. Every job has a clear, set goal and all goals are oriented to the ultimate need to produce food. Mary Schoenfeld prowls the fields and greenhouses and determines what is ready to harvest for the 200 CSA members. The crew bring in the bounty while Dane, Nomi and Ethan are tasked with distribution.

The heavy cardboard boxes are laid out in a ten-by-twenty grid on the barn floor, with space enough between rows to pull a giant dolly loaded with produce.

Dane shakes his head at the staggering harvest, realizing he has no complex relationship with food whatsoever. He grew up with cooks in his father's house, and every morsel of food he consumed was strictly regulated. He never snacked in his life, not even secretly—one candy wrapper or empty bag of chips found in his room, one ounce off his mandated weight, and his father would beat him up. Dane found it was easier to eat what was put in front of him when it was put there, and ignore hunger.

When he escaped his father and went to Maisie's house, she declared her kitchen was his kitchen, but he didn't trust the overture. When he grew to trust it, he didn't know the first thing about feeding himself. All his life, food was procured and prepared out of his sight and brought to him. Food appeared and he ate it. Lettuce was lettuce. It went into a sandwich or on top of a burger. It was served at restaurants and Dane ate it nicely with no thought past it being green, crunchy, and a course to get through. It was a task, not a meal.

Now he looks at the different mounds of lettuce heads and the rubber-banded bundles of greenery. He looks at the guide to what each CSA subscriber is allotted and he doesn't know what anything on the list *is*.

He doesn't know which bundles are spinach and which are dandelion. The latter is something he'd only see growing between cracks in the sidewalk. "Wait, you can eat dandelions?"

He knows what arugula is on a menu, but not when it's staring him in the face. He recognizes red globes as radishes, but doesn't know the long, pink cylinders are also radishes. He picks up a mass of leafy greens with astonishing, colored stems—yellow, orange, magenta and red—and looks at Nomi, helpless.

"Swiss chard," she says, and Ethan half turns away, putting a finger down his throat. "Ignore him. Prepared correctly, it's delicious."

"I can't make friends with chard," Ethan says. "I've tried, but we have nothing in common. Kale, though. Kale is the shit." He holds up a bundle of leaves, delicately ruffled at the edges.

"Kale is the new cocaine," Nomi says.

Dane picks up a net bag of weird green coils. "What are these?"

"Garlic scapes," Nomi says. "We'll make pesto with them tonight. You'll lose your mind."

"Where do they come from?"

Ethan and Nomi stare. "From garlic."

He stares back. "How do you grow garlic?"

"In the ground?"

Dane isn't such an idiot that he can't recognize garlic. It's a dry, bulbous looking thing with white, papery layers of skin. Like an onion, but you can break it into cloves.

"So… Wait. The bulb part. The cloves. That goes in the ground?"

"Yes."

"And these things, the scapes, they grow out of it?"

"Exactly," Nomi says. "Like scallions." She trawls the bins and holds up an amethyst onion bulb that elongates into a white stem and long green tubes.

"See, you cut this part off and that's your scallion. You can cut them when the bulb is still in the ground and it'll just keep sending up more."

"What's the difference between scallions and chives?"

"Size."

Ethan puts a hand on the back of Dane's neck. "Dude, were you raised by wolves?"

"Sort of," Dane says.

Ethan laughs and gives Dane a little shake. "Nomi, the kid needs help."

He needs a lot of help. Dane knows what a carrot is but he's never seen one pulled out of the earth an hour ago, dirt clinging to its roots and the feathery tops still attached.

"Don't soak the carrots," Nomi says one day when they are watering all the crops.

"Why not?"

"Keep the ground saturated at the surface and they'll just hang around there. You want them to grow long, so you deprive them a little. Make them extend down to where the water is."

Later, Dane realizes Nomi is treating him like a carrot: depriving him of things he takes for granted, things that keep him loitering around the surface where it's easy. She makes him put down long, long roots in that ancient, magical black dirt of Birch Island.

JOHN SCHOENFELD, LIKE ETHAN and Nomi, is a foundling. As John Smith, he spent sixteen years bouncing around various foster homes in New Jersey. His family tree lopped off at the roots, he planted a new one in Mary's soil and when they married, he took her name as his own.

Mary Schoenfeld is a quiet, reserved woman with frightening business savvy, and phenomenal instincts for raising crops, animals and troubled children. At the time Ethan came to live permanently at the farm, Mary was in the middle of two projects: opening the spa, and renovating the three little cottages to host artists-in-residence. She put her ambitions aside to care for this addicted baby. To get him settled in the rich dirt. To tend and cultivate and nourish him.

As their Chinese guide said when touring them in the Mogao Caves: *There's no true faith without sacrifice.*

Soon it became apparent Ethan was an extraordinarily intelligent and gifted child, whose instincts and ambitions outpaced even Mary's. Still, abandonment lingered in his soul. His ego always feared the world didn't think he was good enough to keep. He had to prove he was good. Better. The best. His hyper-realistic painting style developed from a need to capture the beautiful moments of his life and make them *stay.* Forever. He was always happiest in his own company, but whomever Ethan chose to love would be loved until he died.

A farm is the perfect place for such a child. Or such a young man as Danelaw Strong, in whom Mary senses a vast, aching gulf of loneliness and a desperate need to be cherished. To build confidence, she assigns Dane tasks he can easily master. To help curb his perfectionism and embrace *good enough,* she gives him jobs at which he's mediocre.

Her nurturing doesn't manifest as physical or verbal affection, rather she practices a stoic kindness that Dane, also by instinct, gravitates toward. He's becoming more comfortable in his skin, more amenable to being touched, but still cautious with words, living by Huff Jensen's strict rule of *truth or silence.*

Parker, Ethan's mixed mutt puppy, follows Dane everywhere. Until now, Dane has only known the mean watchdogs of Malba, barking and baying at him from behind gates and walls. To him, dogs are hired mercenaries, not companions. He shies from Parker's exuberance, but little by little, they make friends. Then fall into cahoots. Soon, rare is the night Dane doesn't fall asleep without Parker curled on the floor beside his bed. Dane feels a little guilty commandeering Ethan's pet, but he'll soon learn Ethan Hasen has many flaws, but a lack of generosity isn't one. If something belongs to him, it belongs to everyone he loves.

Mary is well acquainted with Ethan's manner of imprinting on creatures—human, animal and otherwise—and claiming them as his own. Unabashedly adoring with his whole heart and soul and forgetting the imprintee might have reservations or just need some damn time to get used to his surroundings. Dane is a new puppy and Ethan the enthusiastic Golden Retriever, dying to play and wrestle with little brother. Mary wisely keeps her son crated, as it were, and keeps Dane with her for most of his day.

She assigns him simple tasks in the kitchen garden and teaches him basics of cooking. Narrating in her capable, matter-of-fact way, she shows him how the household runs, how the farm operates. Above all, she stresses that he is a guest here. An intern of sorts. Obviously Ethan already adores Dane, and Nomi loves anyone who takes an interest in the things she does, but Mary regularly counsels Dane that he is here for educational healing. He is, in the truest, noblest sense of the word, being *fostered.*

Mary is quiet. She's kind. She's consistent. "Truth or silence," she says thoughtfully. "I rather like that myself."

She theorizes, and is eventually proven correct, that Dane will take more interest in food he's grown or harvested or prepared himself, and that he'll come to enjoy eating by being in the company of those who do. All that's asked of him is to sit at the table. Once seated, he is left in peace, with no pressure to start eating, finish eating, eat more, eat less, explain every mouthful. No longer is he weighed, measured, examined, critiqued and scrutinized. Nobody gives a good goddamn how he looks.

Soon Dane's morning routine is whittled down to a pee, brushing teeth and picking a ball cap. The clothes he brought with him to Schoenfeld's are completely useless, so he wears Ethan's clothes. Getting dressed takes thirty seconds, the most of which is devoted to good socks so he doesn't get blisters. He barely glances at the mirror. There's no need.

Little by little, he takes to the work and takes pride in his part. His roots start to dig into the soil. His body grows hungry and food becomes interesting. His palate begins to learn.

"I can taste the basil," he'll tentatively say over some homemade marinara sauce. And on another night, with a little more confidence, "You used more oregano this time."

Oh yes, the family agrees, and then they talk about herbs for half an hour, John and Ethan expounding on herbal folklore and mythology, while Mary and Nomi debate companion planting and how it's best to grow together whatever tasted good together.

The world of salad is Nomi's domain. She plans and grows all the greens and packs the CSA boxes with her signature mesclun blends. *Don't make boring salads,* counsels a flyer in each box, with instructions to throw in some chopped kale, scallions, the leaves from those celery stalks, and don't be shy about fresh herbs. *Chop up a bunch, throw them in. Come on, get in the game here, people!*

Dane gets way into the game. Day by day, bite by bite, over that first growing season at Schoenfeld's, he comes to love it. He eats and works and does little else, often falling into bed by eight o'clock. He sleeps in dreamless, ten hour stretches, wakes up sore and ravenous and drags himself up and out to do it all again.

Weeks pass before it occurs to him he's eaten little to no meat since arriving at Schoenfeld's. Bacon in the mornings. Roast chicken once or twice. The rest is eggs and plant protein and tons of it. Mary taught herself to make homemade pasta, to a point. She has the knack of the dough but lacks the patience and equipment to make it into traditional shapes. She rolls the dough out, zips across it with a pizza cutter, and throws the oddball shapes into boiling water.

"Rags," she says, setting down a huge bowl of them, doused with olive oil and herbs.

"Ragaroni," Ethan elaborates.

"Raghetti," Nomi says.

Dane doesn't play along. He's too busy eating. The rags soak up sauce and salad dressing and are declared perfect. Dane, totally at home now, shovels them in, along with the greens and vegetables he's starting to identify by both sight and taste, and develop distinct preferences for. He feels simultaneously wiped out, yet light and keen.

Holy shit, I'm happy.

"I'm really happy," he says on the phone to Maisie, overcome and amazed. She and Huff, now deeply in love, come to visit and Dane burns with pride and passion as he tours them around. He makes the entire dinner, including a chocolate cake that collapses in the oven. Everyone piles whipped cream on the slumped slices and praises every bite, because Dane did his best and it's all Schoenfeld's wants from him. His best and the truth.

Truth or silence.

HONOR-BOUND

"Don't answer if it's too personal," Liko said, as they walked back to the house. "But did you fall in love with Nomi first? Ethan first? Or was it a simultaneous thing?"

"Tough one to answer," Dane said. "And not to be even more evasive, but I gotta jump in the shower before I can tell stories."

"Sure, go ahead," Liko said mildly. "I'll look in on Jeffrey."

"You are duck-whipped."

"I am."

"Fix yourself a drink when you get back. Mi casa es su casa."

Dane stripped off his work clothes, left them in a heap on the mudroom floor and went upstairs, the house blissfully cool on his grimy skin. His neck and shoulders were demanding to see the manager, and he itched all over. Normally he'd quickly shower and then soak in the tub for an hour with a drink. But he felt honor-bound to be a proper host. At least for a few more days.

It wasn't a sacrifice.

He smiled as he thought about Liko checking in on Jeffrey.

Holy hell, Diane teased. *Find a man who looks at you the way a Green Man looks at a duckling.*

"No shit," Dane said, soaping and scrubbing.

I like this guy, she said.

So do I, he thought. *In fact, I can't find anything to dislike about him.*

The ease with which Liko fit in with Dane's circle of friends. How he didn't make a sloppy move on Meggy when he was shit-faced. His respect for Fred's pronouns. The raving praise of Cora's lunch. The genuine interest in the farm work and his willingness to chip in. And good grief, the look on his face when he stroked a finger along Jeffrey's downy softness.

I see you're petting a back, Diane said. *I also have a back.*

"Girl, get a grip," he said, though he was grinning like an idiot. He turned off the spray and sluiced water off his limbs.

You going to tell him about falling in love?

Dane wrapped the towel around his waist and stood at the sink a moment. Steam had clouded up the mirror. He reached and ran his palm in an arc, clearing a swathe.

He looked at himself a long time, touching the scars on his chest, thinking it had been Nomi first. Ethan not long after but if Dane had to put it in order, then of course it was Nomi because of how they revealed themselves.

1993

NOMI TURNS HER BACK and shows Dane how bra straps dig painful red divots into her flesh. Shows him the bruises and atrophied spots, made from years of binding herself with Ace bandages because she can't find a sports bra to fit her properly. She lets him feel the tight, bunched muscles in her neck and back, the constant strain from being so top-heavy. She hides the mass of her immense bust with both her hands and her shirt so she can show Dane the irritated, chafed skin on the underside of her breasts and along her ribs.

"I hate them," she says, trembling beneath the cross of her arms. Voice shaking inside the chest that's the bane of her existence. "I hate them so much. People say I can just get breast reduction but they don't understand. I don't want them smaller. I want them *gone*."

Dane is torn in two. One half feels honor-bound, soul-bound, to simply attend and witness with no comment. The other half is terrified, crazed, adamant that what happened to him not happen to her.

"Hating my breasts doesn't mean I don't like being a woman," Nomi says, in tears now. "It doesn't mean I'm gay. I know who I am but nobody believes me. Nobody's believed me since I was eleven. All my fucking life, the things people said about me and the names they called. First it was *tomboy* in kindergarten. By fifth grade it was *butch, dyke, lesbo*. Then *Mister*. Then when these fucking boobs started to grow, it was *slut, whore, easy lay, trash*. You don't know, Dane. You just don't know what it was like…"

"Tell me," Dane says. "Tell me everything."

"Strangers staring on the street. Male teachers leering at me in class. Boys making a game of snapping my bra straps. Some senior jock got his girlfriend to steal one of my bras out of my gym locker. He tied it to his car antenna and drove laps around the school."

"Oh Jesus Christ," Dane says, hands going to fists.

"I slashed his tires and got suspended," Nomi says.

"Good for you."

"Two foster fathers each took a swipe at my tits. The last one? His wife took his side and threw me out. Nobody believes me. Nobody sees me. They only see *these…*"

Her hand slices the air and she almost hits her breasts. Dane catches her wrist, keeping his eyes above her collarbones, barely blinking. He feels sick and furious and so afraid, but he doesn't let go her soaked gaze.

"They got to decide my narrative," Nomi cries. "They preyed on me because I *confused* them. They couldn't sort me into a convenient box. I wore my hair short, I didn't wear makeup, I liked wearing boys' clothes. I had a body that frustrated men and threatened women. Everyone treated me like a suspect. If I had a close girlfriend, they said I wanted to fuck her and all of a sudden she didn't want to be friends anymore. If I had a guy friend, then either I was in denial, or he was in my pants. Nobody asked me. Nobody ever bothered listening to me. Nobody ever believed me…"

"I believe you," Dane says, knowing it isn't enough to say it to this extraordinary girl. This tough-as-nails survivor, fiercely protective of her spiritual basket and slow to place eggs within, has literally bared herself to him, letting him look in secret, painful places. Letting him see how the world has injured her while refusing to believe where it hurts or how badly. Dane has to let her know just who she's talking to. Prove he knows how cruel people can be and he's her ally.

"I believe you," he says, reaching a hand behind his neck. He takes the back of his shirt collar and draws it over his head, gathering it to his chest. Creating the same barrier Nomi has. "I'll show you," he says. "I'll show you what was done to me. I don't want this to happen to you. All right? I'm showing you because I trust you."

His heart is an enraged gorilla shaking the cage of his ribs, as he lowers the balled-up T-shirt and shows her.

Nomi claps a hand over her mouth, backing away. The other hand piles onto the first, and she shakes her head above them, eyes flooding tears.

"I don't want this to happen to you," Dane says.

"Oh my God," she says, voice thick behind her fingers.

"I'm not trying to one-up you, I swear. I'm showing because I'm really scared for you. I don't want someone to just…carve you up and leave you with nothing."

"Dane, what happened? Who did this?"

"I…" He looks at the floor, shaking his head. "I can't tell you yet. I trust you, but I'm not ready to tell."

Nomi drops her face into her hands and weeps. Dane pulls his shirt on, comes to her and they fall into each other's arms.

"I'm sorry about what happened," he whispers into her hair.

"I'm so sorry too," she cries.

"I didn't show you for me. I did it for you. Because I know. I know what it's like to look in the mirror and be confused or angry at what you see. It's been that way my entire life."

She hangs on him, nodding, a hand at the back of his head. She was pruning the herb garden today and her fingers smell of thyme.

"Promise me," he whispers into her hair. "You do it right. You find someone, you find a doctor, you find the right person who will listen and take care of you. You find the best, you understand? No matter how long it takes, you wait until you find people who will do what you want and do it right. They're out there. I know they are. I have to find them too, see?"

"Yes," she says. "You promise me, too."

"I will," Dane says, holding her tight. "You and me. And Ethan, too. He doesn't know yet. He hasn't seen me. But he will."

Dane goes into the bathroom and wets a washcloth icy cold. Nomi wipes her flushed face and manages a little laugh.

"It's nothing a hot shower or a cold washcloth can't fix," she says.

"You don't need fixing." Dane tenderly pushes her bangs back and blurts, "I think you're beautiful. I mean it. I think you're one of the most beautiful women I've ever met."

He can see the effort it takes for her to stand still next to the compliment. Her eyes close and she breathes it in, her tight shoulders softening a little as she whispers, "Thank you."

"Listen. I'm just going to put this out there. Whenever I have a problem with…" He awkwardly motions between them. "With how I look, or how I feel about how I look, or sex or bodies or anything personal or embarrassing…

When I need someone to talk to, I go to Huff Jensen. He's always helped me. At school, he gave me a lot of language and a lot of words and a lot of resources to help me figure shit out. He helped a lot of girls, too, with all kinds of things. I trust him with my life. Okay?"

Nomi nods faintly. A little warily.

"I swear, Nome, I'm only saying this because I don't want you to be in pain. If there's a better way for you to bind your chest, a way that won't hurt you so much, I think Huff would know. Or he'll know somebody who knows. He'd help you and I give you my word, he'll be kind."

"All right," she says.

"I'll give you his number. If you want me to call, I will. We can call together. Or go see him in person. Or I'll shut all the way up and let you do it. You or whats-her-name. Your phone assistant. Katherine Jones."

Nomi laughs then, puts her hands on his face and draws their foreheads together. When she speaks, it's in a velvety, professional tone. "This is Katherine Jones calling for Ms. Misteria, with a message for Mr. Strong?"

"Speaking."

"The message is, I love you."

ADAM

"Bad news and good news," Dane said, when Liko came downstairs Monday morning. "Bad news is the cottage I was going to let you use for the summer just got rented out from under you. I'm afraid money trumps hospitality."

"You're dead to me," Liko said.

"Good news is…" Dane motioned for Liko to follow and they went into the front hallway, where Dane opened a set of curtained French doors. "Your scholarship has an inner sanctum clause. Welcome to the holy of holies. AKA, your new office."

"This is terrible," Liko said, walking into the handsome space.

"A real dive, right?" Dane watched him take in the big desk and chair, the large picture window behind, the floor-to-ceiling shelves, the beat-up leather chair and ottoman.

Liko sighed darkly. "No, I'm afraid this is out of the question. Won't suit my needs at all."

"Thought you'd like it." Dane ran a finger along one of the shelves and wrinkled his nose. The dust in this house was going to kill him. "Believe it or not, the books left here are a fraction of John Schoenfeld's library. He took all the good stuff to France. This is just the riffraff."

"Excellent. I'm easily distracted and I'll get no writing done if interesting books are about."

Liko perused the walls, hung with their share of Ethan's artwork. He paused, staring at a locked gun case with three rifles. "Great," he said over his shoulder. "Now that I've seen these, one will have to be fired in the third act."

"Also left behind by John. Can you shoot?"

"No. You?"

"I'm no marksman but I know what to do with a rifle and not shoot myself by accident."

"You ever have to?"

"No, but for a short time after I came to live in Schoenfeld's, I had a lot of anxiety about my father coming to find me. Knowing John had guns and knowing he wouldn't tolerate my father on his land… It helped me sleep at night."

"Not your average, absent-minded professor."

"Not at all." Dane sat in the leather chair and put his feet up. "The things I learned in this room. If all the therapy I'd done up to that point had roughed me out as a person, John came in and polished up so many details. Just by telling me stories and giving me books and talking about… God, so much shit." Dane pointed back toward the front hall. "He gave me the map of the Danelaw. He was obsessed with my name."

"As am I."

"I come from a family of lawyers and nearly every Strong boy has *law* in his name. Morelaw. Renlaw. My father is Ivelaw. Don't get your Scrabble tiles because he has no place in the game. Or in my life. Suffice it to say, you can pull the word *revolting* out of Ivelaw Strong."

"You told me he's a monster," Liko said, sitting at the desk. "I didn't forget."

"John, though, he zeroed in on the literal meaning of my name. The historical Danelaw, which were the lands in Britain under Norse control. Forgive me preaching to the choir."

Liko waved a dismissive hand. "You're already on my list for dumping me in this horrific home office, so go ahead, make things worse."

"John said, *At its essence, the mission of the Danelaw was peace.* Which kind of stopped me cold. Then he added, *Only you can write the laws that keep your peace.*"

Dane laced hands behind his head. "I'm sure it wasn't anything I hadn't heard in therapy already. Yeah, yeah, I'm in control of my emotions. I can't control what happens, I can only control how I react to what happens. I can set boundaries, blah blah blah. It's all good stuff and I know I heard it. But something about standing in front of a map that had my name emblazoned across a swathe of land, and hearing John say, *The mission of the Danelaw was peace. Only you can write the laws that keep your peace.*" Dane touched fingers to his forehead and blew them out.

"You finally *heard* it."

"And finally believed it. John did that shit all the time. He was something else. Impractical and abstracted and ever so slightly out-to-lunch when it came to everyday life. But he gave me so many spiritual gifts that were rooted in history and literature, folklore and mythology. He had a way of simultaneously letting you know you were unique, but your story had all been written before. He loved to help people find their purpose. Find their destiny."

Dane got up and stretched. "Anywho. I'm off to toil in the land and you have your own toiling. But for real, man, work wherever you want. That's partly the point of being here, right?"

"Right."

"Other than Saskia's bedroom, no place in the house is off-limits."

"What about your bedroom?"

Dane stared.

Diane stared, too, then quietly tiptoed out of the room, shaking her head.

Liko laughed softly, touching his mouth. "Did I say that out loud?"

Dane laughed, too, wishing he didn't blush so easily. "You did. And for the moment, my room is off-limits."

"Dude, I was joking."

"No, you weren't."

They stared some more, Liko slowly nodding. "No, not entirely."

Dane was getting a hard-on. "All right then," he said. "I'll just…be on my way."

"Excellent." Liko put hands behind his head and feet on the desk. "I'm easily distracted and I'll get no writing done with you around."

Blushing and bothered, Dane went out the front door. Diane tapped his left shoulder and whispered, *What are we going to do with him?*

1993

"So what are we going to do with you, Danelaw Strong?"

Dane looks at John and has no answer.

"Let me think…"

Dane comes to Schoenfeld's right after John's study has suffered the inequity of being gutted and redone. He was forced to clear the shelves and make a ruthless inventory of books, papers and academic clutter. He's still milking the offense, but the new shelves and the new, bigger windows with their beautiful view of the farm are a joy to behold.

On rainy days or weekends, Dane joins John in reshelving the volumes. It's quality time, just like Ethan had growing up, and Nomi when she came to Schoenfeld's. Each learned something profound in John Schoenfeld's study, something that helped them forge purpose and latch onto their identity. Ethan Hasen learned about the Three Hares motif from his father. Nomi Misteria turned her M upside-down and studied the taxonomy of Tribe Wisterieae, learning its legends and lore.

Dane will learn a lot of things within the walls of the inner sanctum, but John starts by gifting the beautiful map of the Danelaw, which will hang in the boy's room ten years before being moved to the front hall. Next is the story of how the philosopher Jean-Jacques Rousseau was once run down by a Great Dane.

"*Reveries of a Solitary Walker,*" John says, taking a book from one of the unpacked boxes. "Forgive me, I only have the French version."

"Unacceptable," Dane says.

John sits in the leather chair and Dane sits on the ottoman. Sometimes Ethan and Nomi are present, but they keep mostly silent, respecting Dane's time at the professor's knee. This is especially touching from Ethan, because Dane now knows he's a brilliant auto-didact, speed reads in between artistic endeavors, possesses a mind that never shuts off, and knowledge is his religion. The fact that he knows when to shut up and listen makes him lovable.

While being read to was as intrinsic a part of Ethan's childhood as being vaccinated, and Nomi orchestrated her own story times by frequent trips to the library, Dane has never known such cultivated, personal attention. Never known anything like this room full of books and dust and maps and papers, rain streaming down the windows and the gun case on the wall standing guard.

"The date is October the twenty-fourth," John says. "Seventeen seventy-six. Jean-Jacques Rousseau is walking in his village of Ménilmontant, outside Paris. Coming in the opposite direction is a great carriage, and loping alongside the carriage is a Great Dane. Seeing the massive dog rushing toward him, Rousseau comes up with what he later calls a 'lightning plan of action.'"

"Get out of the way?" Dane says.

"You'd think a sixty-four-year-old man would go for the simplest solution first. No, his plan was to, and I quote, 'leap into the air at precisely the right moment to allow the dog to pass under me.'" John looks at Dane over the rims of his glasses. "Terrible plan. Rousseau had barely flexed his knees when the Great Dane ran him down. He was knocked to the ground, hitting his head on the cobblestones. Let that be a lesson to all old men."

"Get out of the way when a Great Dane is coming," Nomi says.

"I disagree," Ethan says, looking at Dane intently.

"But why did our esteemed philosopher even contemplate jumping over the dog?" John says. "Did he *want* to get knocked over?"

"Probably," Nomi says. "I've seen boys do a lot of stupid shit just for the experience."

John points a finger at her. "Punto. Rousseau was often presented as seeking out trouble."

"What experience did he gain from being clobbered by a dog?" Dane asks.

"Well, after the fall, he couldn't remember what happened, where he was, or even his own name. Which he thought was fantastic." John opens the book. "*I felt throughout my whole being such a wonderful calm, that whenever I recall this feeling I can find nothing to compare with it in all the pleasures that stir our lives.*"

He closes the book and looks at Dane, who looks back.

"Sorry, I don't get it," he finally says. "Sounds like he had a concussion and just got a little woozy."

"He was quite seriously injured," John says. "His health declined after the incident, and possibly he developed epilepsy. The point is…" He smiles broadly, a little sheepishly. "Nothing, really. It's just a story, and I confess I don't find any deeper meaning in it. Except to note the irony in Rousseau, lauded as the precursor of all modern autobiographers, being happiest when he forgot who and where he was."

"Read the part again where he describes the feeling," Ethan says.

"*I felt throughout my whole being such a wonderful calm, that whenever I recall this feeling I can find nothing to compare with it in all the pleasures that stir our lives.*"

"Peace," Dane says. "He means peace."

John raises eyebrows, pleased. "And what is peace?"

"The mission of the Danelaw."

By now, Nomi has laid her head on her crossed forearms and dozed off. Ethan, though, is looking at Dane. His gaze goes far away, then comes back to stare hard.

"What?" Dane says, not wanting Ethan to stop looking at him like that, but morbidly curious why.

"Nothing, I was just thinking."

Not too long after the Rousseau lesson, Dane finds a note on his pillow:

Do you remember the night we met? At the Montresor Gallery? Your sister introduced me to Gideon Perfect and on the spot, he commissioned me to do the cover for his next album. I don't ever remember being terrified by a commission. I'd never been the least bit nervous at making bespoke art for someone. But this was Gideon Perfect. The chance of a lifetime. I felt sick at the thought of screwing it up. I was almost in full-on panic mode, considering changing my mind and telling him no, I wasn't the one he wanted. Then you walked out of the bathroom and straight into me.

Do you remember?

I was knocked over by a Great Dane, just like JJ Rousseau. Just like him, I felt this wonderful calm. It was instantaneous. I looked at your face and your eyes and all my panic and doubt and fear vanished. It was you. Not just inspiration for the cover but you. It was the Great Dane and the peace of the Danelaw. It barreled into me and I forgot where and who I was. I was knocked down, but I only knew peace. I've known nothing to compare with it in all the pleasure that stirs my life.

The mission of the Danelaw is peace.

And I will go to war for your peace.

It is not lost on Danelaw Strong that the very first love letter of his life is sent by a boy.

WHEN REALLY FIRED UP on a topic, John will pull out his massive whiteboard. He paces to the bookshelves to browse, to the window to think, then back to the board to scribble. Dane follows the circuitous path, sometimes writing things down, but mostly listening as John explores gender roles and identities in different cultures. They discuss the Polynesians first, then Native American traditions. The world's indigenous peoples seem to have no trouble whatsoever eschewing a binary. But Judaism, too, has some surprising game. Six identities in all. John reads them out and Dane writes them on the board:

Saris: male at birth but develops female characteristics at puberty. Can be broken down into:

> *—Saris hamah, female characteristics develop naturally.*
> *—Saris adam, female characteristics through human intervention.*

"Human intervention, meaning what?" Dane asks.

John grimaces. "It's a nice way of saying castration."

"There's no nice way to say that," Ethan murmurs.

> *Ay'lout: female at birth but develops male characteristics at puberty.*
> *—Ay'lout hamah, male characteristics naturally develop.*
> *—Ay'lout adam, male characteristics through human intervention.*

"So I'm saris hamah," Dane says. "Born male and the female characteristics developed naturally. But then my father intervened and forced me back to male. Wait, does that make me a saris adam? Or an ay'lout adam?"

"Or an *androgynos* adam," John says, jumping up for a book.

He finds the commentary of Rabbi Yirmeya ben Elazar: "Adam was first created with two faces, one male and the other female. These the Lord set back to back, as we read in Psalm 139:5—*You have formed me behind and before, and laid your hand on me.*"

"Adam was created androgynous," Dane says slowly.

"Genesis 1:27," John says. "*So God created mankind in his image; in the image of God he created them; male and female he created them.*"

"Them," Ethan says. "Adam's pronouns were they/them."

"God is they/them," John says. "Elohim. Plural. Many gods. Genesis 1:26—*God said, Let us make man in our image.*"

Our image, Diane says, a little smugly. *See? I told you.*

"The first beings were hermaphrodites?" Dane asks, exhilarated and confused.

John's eyes light up. "Now, *that* word has a backstory everyone gets wrong."

He goes after another book, a beat-up tome of Greek myths. He tells his young charges that Hermaphroditus was the offspring of Hermes and Aphrodite. Salmacis, the water nymph, fell in love with Hermaphroditus. Wanting to be helpful, the gods made them into one androgynous male/female being.

"Many people think Hermaphroditus was the intersex being," John says. "No. Salmacis and Hermaphroditus were *merged* into an intersex being. But notice the female name Salmacis disappears and ever after, this new person is known only as Hermaphroditus? Or a hermaphrodite? The feminine name is completely absorbed."

Like you and me, Diane says breathlessly. *The gods made us, Dane. We were merged into one. I'm Salmacis—the absorbed female name.*

Her awe fills the space behind Dane's blue eye, then his brown one. His mind fills with understanding. He feels seen. Recognized, ordained and anointed. He feels *historical.* He cries and cries, because it's all starting to make sense.

John has no idea what he's done or how he's just changed Dane's life, but he hugs the boy tight, knowing an epiphany when he sees one.

"You are not outside the bounds of God's image," he says, rocking Dane against his chest. "Far from it. You are closest to God's original creation. Adam androgynos. You were made in their image and they adore you."

"You think…" Dane swallows a sob and tries again. "You think God loves me?"

John holds Dane away, a thumb roughly wiping tears away. "By whatever number and whatever name, God in their multitudes loves you."

One day, many decades later, Dane will rescue an Australian Shepherd with one brown eye and one blue eye. He will name her Salmacis. Salma for short.

THE DUSK TIARA

Liko quickly established a routine at Schoenfeld's. Dane was always up and about at seven, leaving the coffee made. Liko got up at eight-thirty, had a cup, a bite of something, then he took Salma on a long walk. No earbuds, no music or podcasts. Just silence and nature and his thoughts tumbling into place for the day. Untangling plot twists, filling holes in the story, wearily analyzing why the usually brilliant Detective O'Higgins would do a dumb thing like *that*.

Back at the farmhouse, he showered, made more coffee and ate a more substantial breakfast, answering emails or returning calls. Then it was ass in chair for a solid three hours, with his phone left in the kitchen and the Wi-Fi turned off on his laptop. If he got stuck, or bored, or antsy, he went outside. Sometimes a few deep breaths on the porch could put him back on track. Sometimes he needed to walk to the duck pond and commune a bit with his creature. He hit the kitchen garden first to gather peapods and lettuce, because he'd been told bread wasn't good for ducks.

Jeffrey would eat salad from Liko's hand, patient and attentive as Liko bitched about the manuscript. Sooner or later, one of the crew would notice him and yell through cupped hands, "Liko, quit fucking around and write."

He'd wave back with a grimace, or a flipped bird if his mood was particularly sour. After all, he had invited the farm's workers to use the line whenever they saw him goofing off.

Basil Greenman would call this being hoisted with your own petard.

A break for lunch at noon, then derrière back in chair for another three hours. Then a nap, and when he woke up, Dane was usually coming in.

Today, Liko had caught the edge of a creative comet and rode its tail long past his customary quitting time. He barely grunted a hello when Dane walked by the office doors. He pounded the keyboard with gleeful relish, his mind one exquisitely timed word ahead of his fingers. High on the sick thrill of having scattered a half-dozen themes throughout the story, but now pulling them together and *nailing* their asses to the page with one, perfect, concise closing sentence.

"*That's* how you do it, motherfuckers," he growled, slapping palms on the desk. He read it over. Yes. This was indeed how it was done. He saved the document, emailed it to William Shepherd, and refrained from typing *You're welcome* in the subject line.

"Don't anticipate a compliment," Betty Greenman always said. "Because lord, you feel a bit shit when it doesn't come."

He went into the kitchen and mixed a gin and tonic. He remembered Dane saying contributions to the farm's booze supply would be accepted in lieu of rent, and made a mental note to hit the liquor store. He should buy more coffee while he was at it.

Dane came in, wet-haired and chipper. "What's going on, what are we doing, what's to eat, are we drinking?"

"A drink is the thing. What can I do you?"

"I'll have what you're having. And I'm dying for a burger. That do you?"

"Done."

They put together massive burgers with melted cheddar and fried onions, and Dane picked lettuce from the garden to layer on top. No fries, but Dane ripped open a new bag of Lays potato chips and they gobbled and crunched.

"I'll probably hit the sack early," Dane said, "but want to play a little more of the game?"

"Sure."

Dane got up, wiping his mouth. "Quick seminar. Hopefully not the John Schoenfeld definition of quick."

He took a picture down from the wall and set it on the table. A long frame enclosed three pencil sketches of Green Man motifs.

"So when I came to Schoenfeld's," Dane said, "John was writing *The Journey of the Green Man.* I wasn't anything close to a research assistant, but I knew how to type and I was good at transcribing his scribblings and making sure he backed things up. Keeping piles of paper from avalanching off the desk, bringing in a sandwich. He'd share bits of this and that, all the theories about the origin of the Green Man. Between listening to him and typing up chapters, I learned a lot, and one of my favorite stories comes from the Legend of the Rood."

"What's a rood?"

"A cross." Dane drew the framed picture closer. "Sidebar, because I'm a terrible storyteller. The Green Man has three variations. The Foliate Head, which is completely covered in green leaves. The Disgorging Head, which has leaves coming only out of his mouth. And here, the Bloodsucker Head, which has leaves coming out mouth and nose, or mouth and eyes:

"The Foliate Head is nicest to look at," Dane said, "in my opinion. But Mr. Disgorging and Mr. Bloodsucker align best with the Legend of the Rood. It's a compilation of medieval tales loosely derived from the Old Testament, and one tale is about Seth."

"My Old Testament is rusty," Liko said "Who's Seth?"

"Adam and Eve's lesser-known son. Basically the replacement kid after Cain slew Abel."

"You're going to hell."

"Come on, Seth's the ancestor of Noah so he's the real father of mankind. Anyway, when Adam is dying, he sends Seth back to Eden to find an elixir of immortality. An angel is guarding the gates and won't let Seth in. Instead, the angel gives Seth three seeds from the infamous Tree of Knowledge. Seth returns home and finds Adam has died. He puts the three seeds under Adam's tongue before burying him. Hence…" Dane's finger tapped the three Bloodsucker Heads.

"Ah," Liko said. "This is the deceased Adam. The seeds from the Tree of Knowledge are growing from his face."

"It's kind of gnarly," Dane said. "But satisfying in a literary way. What Adam stole from the tree in his life is given back in his death. Threefold, because three trees grew from his face."

"And three is a magic number."

"The wood from the trees shows up in other Old Testament tales, but ultimately, it makes the cross that Jesus is crucified on."

"Well, that comes together neatly."

"New leaves mean new life for humankind," Dane said, "growing from the mouth, nose and eyes of the First Man. New chances for redemption from the resulting tree which will bear the fruit of a new savior and… I forgot where I was going with this."

"Something, something, let's play *Three Hares?*"

"Yes," Dane said, picking up plates and silverware. "Go set up in the den."

Liko hooked up his laptop to the TV and had the game open when Dane came in. The screen was focused on the ceiling, where the hares were still running the wrong way.

"You got three wisteria seeds in your cache and the tale of Seth," Dane said. "Figure out what to do yet?"

"I think so." Liko clicked on one of the seeds and brought it toward the Green Man's mouth.

Then all at once, the scene was blurred by his tears. He let go the mouse and pressed his forehead into his hands.

"You all right?" Dane asked.

"Yeah. Yeah, I…"

Dane's palm rubbed slow circles on Liko's back. "Tell me."

"Up until now, I only knew what Kyle showed me. I'm going on without him. It's not his game anymore."

Dane made a soft hum, his hand warm and strong between Liko's shoulder blades.

"Shit, this got emotional."

"For sure."

"Fuck my life," Liko said, knuckling his eyes. "All right, I'm doing this."

"You're doing it for him."

"My heart's pounding," he mumbled. "This is ridiculous." Liko carried the seed to the Green Man's mouth and let go the cursor. "Down the hatch…"

The eyes in the foliate face closed as the leafy jaws chewed and swallowed.

The pagan god belched. A real frat house special. A glut of leaves spewed from his mouth with such unexpected violence, Liko sat back a little. "What the fuck?"

"Disgorging Head," Dane said.

The leaves whirled in a circle around the Green Man, turning metallic shades of silver, bronze and copper. Gradually they joined, melding into a crown, which slowly lowered onto the altar.

A long beat of silence.

"Okay," Liko said. "That happened."

"Seems a good time to remind everyone this entire chamber is a private joke between three people."

"Hey, don't harsh my vibe," Liko said. "I'm the only gamer who's seen this crown."

"It's called the Dusk Tiara," Dane said, standing up. "Come on, I'll show you something. Shut down because I'm going to bed after."

He took Liko upstairs and along the hall to his bedroom.

"Gosh, I get to enter the holy of holies," Liko said.

"Don't get ideas."

"You wish."

He took in a king-sized bed, a dresser, an open door to an adjoining bath. A large rug over hardwood floors. One wall was painted a deep, smoky orange, but the rest of the room was minimalist and neutral, which made the large canvas between the windows the focal point.

"Wow," Liko said. "Is that Nomi?"

"The queen," Dane said.

Queen, hell. This was a bloody empress. She was turned away from the viewer, looking over her shoulder, which rose from a purple froth of wisteria blossoms. Ethan had painted the vines into a garment that wove, coiled and twisted around Nomi's body, the blossoms spilling in cascades and ruffles and flounces. Every petal painted so meticulously, so realistically, Liko glanced at the floor beneath the painting, half expecting to see strays scattered. Memory flicked the edge of his mind: his mother's signature compliment for a friend's smart dress.

"Nice frock," he said softly.

"Isn't it something?" Dane said. "I swear Ethan could've made an equally successful career in fashion. The talented son of a bitch."

Hares peeked from in between the wisteria flowers, and a golden duck was cradled in Nomi's arm, also looking at the viewer. On Nomi's head was the crown of leaves Liko had just discovered in the Green Man Chamber. It was bejeweled with smoky pearls and tiny jewels in twilight colors. Down low in a corner of the painting, Ethan had painted the caption in precise letters: *Nomi with Dusk Tiara.*

"This is stunning," Liko said.

"I know," Dane said. "That's why it hangs on my bedroom wall."

"Dusk Tiara," Liko said. "Annoying anagram, or just another inside joke?"

"Both. But also a real thing." Dane was opening a dresser drawer and taking out a small drawstring bag. He drew from it the Dusk Tiara.

Liko hardly dared to take it, but he did. He turned it this way and that, admiring the construction of filigree elm leaves along the base. Two gingko leaves in beaten gold framed a beautiful gray pearl at the center. A single delicate oak leaf at the tiara's apex, and two tinier clusters of oak leaves and acorns at the ends.

"I assume the talented son of a bitch designed this, too," Liko said.

"In his spare time. In between painting and designing digital art and reading six books a day and teaching himself Japanese. He just threw it together."

Liko carefully handed it back. "A bit of paste, as Mum would say."

"Saskia wants it for her wedding day."

"Of course. It's an heirloom."

"And an anagram."

"Thanks for showing me."

"You're welcome." Dane tilted the tiara back and forth, making the lamplight reflect off the surfaces. "Now get out of my room."

GLITTERBOX

Dane had, it couldn't be denied, the mother of all bathrooms. It was once the adjoining bedroom's walk-in closet. The corner bathtub was immense and could easily fit three people. It had a separate glassed-in shower stall, and a long vanity with two sinks.

"What's the secret to open marriage?" the Hasens and their Great Dane were often asked.

"Separate bedrooms," Dane said.

"Separate sinks," Nomi said.

"Communal socks," Ethan said.

The bathroom walls were marigold yellow, the fixtures creamy white. Ethan painted the ceiling in trompe l'oeil as a cloudy blue sky. And, luxurious oddities of oddities, one short wall was floor to ceiling bookshelves. Because reading was the second greatest thing you could do in the bathtub.

Nomi had always kept a small vase of fresh flowers on the vanity and Dane tried not to be remiss in keeping it filled. Today he'd cut the tips from a few wisteria blossoms, along with some tiny ferns. Next to the vase was his favorite picture of Nomi, taken at Saskia's graduation. Not by the talented son of a bitch, but by Dane himself. He caught Nomi standing alone, staring proudly at her daughter, who was off camera. Nomi in her fabulous white pantsuit, wide trousers and a double-breasted jacket. To those not in the know, it looked as if the suit were worn over a purple lacy top of some kind. To those in the know, Nomi wasn't wearing a damn thing under the jacket.

She'd kept her promise to Dane: that she would find a doctor who would do what she wanted and do it right. The search started frustrating and became enraging. No plastic surgeon seemed sympathetic to a woman who didn't want merely smaller breasts, but *no* breasts. She pleaded her case with surgeons, psychologists and social workers. She brought her journals, detailing the years of teasing, bullying, body dysmorphia, suicidal and self-harm ideations, unwanted advances from one end of the violence spectrum to the other, ending with assault in her own foster homes.

"I don't want breasts," she said. "I don't need them to feel like a woman.

They never made me feel like a woman. Or beautiful. Or feminine. They are the bane of my existence and I'll be happy to see them go."

"But if you have children…"

This horror at not being able to nourish her hypothetical future children seemed at the root of every doctor's reluctance to help Nomi go electively flat. Consultation after consultation went nowhere, until even the Universe got annoyed with the pokey pace. Ever abundant and generous, but often really stupid, the divine power thought giving Nomi stage III breast cancer would be *super* helpful in achieving the desired goal.

"Okay," Nomi said slowly, as she processed the diagnosis. The cancer was already in her lymph nodes and given her utter lack of family history, the recommended treatment was aggressive. Radical mastectomy and reconstruction, followed by chemo and radiation.

"Okay," Nomi said again. "This is not what I *meant*. But… I guess it's a teachable moment for everyone? When you petition the Universe for something, be *specific*."

It was a teachable moment for all three hares, who grew up in a hurry during the year of Nomi's ordeal. Cancer forged friendship into forever, love into loyalty, three into one. Nomi was alternately amused and disgusted that she had to be deathly ill to get plastic surgeons to finally listen to her, but in the end, after two surgeries, chemo, and disciplined time in the gym, Nomi Hasen had a clean bill of health and the body of her dreams. Her physique was lithe, muscular and flat, with a magnificent profusion of wisteria blossoms tattooed across her entire chest. It was these flowers that made Nomi look like she was wearing some fabulous lingerie beneath her white pantsuit.

Dane put the picture down and stared through his reflection, absently drawing fingertips on his chest. He'd had his reconstruction a year after Nomi, with the same plastic surgeon. He wisely scheduled the procedure at the end of the growing season, so he could heal over the winter. Even then it took another year before he could really pull his weight on the farm.

The journey sucked, but holy hell, the destination… Dane found himself loitering in front of the bathroom mirror, often moved to tears by the sight of his own body. After all the years of pain and confusion and shame, he finally looked at his shirtless reflection and liked what he saw.

And the people he loved seemed to like it, too.

Damn, Diane said, peeking over his left shoulder.

"Damn, lover," Nomi said, dragging him upstairs.

"Damn, woman," Dane said, unable to keep his hands off her.

"Dammit, you two," Ethan mumbled on the other side of the bedroom door, his muse impatient, his hands itching to paint his two mates. But every now and again, he'd sidle up to Dane, suffused with a different impatience, his elusive desire now honed on a target. Looking for love. Looking to get Dane in bed and afterward, run hands all over Dane's heart and whisper, "Damn…"

Dane's phone pinged. Liko had texted: ***I got it. The anagram of Dusk Tiara is Kadi Sutra. It's the updated version of the Kama Sutra.***

Dane smiled over the keyboard. ***Did you pack your own Scrabble tiles?***

No, I'm cheating with an app. How about Kasai Turd. It's the specialized manure from Japan that gives Schoenfeld crops their unique deliciousness.

Points for creativity, but no.

Isaak Turd? Usaak Dirt?

No.

Kaia Turds and that's my final offer.

Goodnight.

Liko replied with the poop emoji.

Dane tapped his fingers on the side of the phone, then put it down on the vanity. He went out to the dresser and opened one of its top drawers. Most of Nomi's clothes had been donated or thrifted. Things Saskia couldn't bear to part with were stored in the attic. But Dane kept something for himself: a camisole top in bronzy-green charmeuse. No lace or frills, just a simple silhouette that used to cling to Nomi's hard curves and slide like liquid over Dane's palms. He loved when she wore it and got on top of him, especially when one strap fell down around her bicep, and one nipple fell over the edge.

He stripped off his hoodie and T-shirt and put the camisole on, then took the Dusk Tiara into the bathroom. He shook and brushed all his hair over to the left side of his face and settled the leafy crown in place. He swiveled his head so only his blue eye was showing, leaned palms on the vanity.

And stared.

I miss her so much, Diane said softly.

Dane turned his brown eye toward the mirror and whispered, "I do, too."

Will you make me up?

"You bet."

Dane took off the tiara and lit a couple candles. Dimmed the overhead lights and put some music on his phone. He got his makeup bag out of a bottom drawer and hitched a thigh onto the vanity, humming under his breath. He was a little out of practice but his grip on the brush soon stopped trembling. The pencils drew with more precision. He got his small scissors and trimmed one false eyelash into sections, the way he'd been taught…

1990

"Now TAKE ONE OF these and trim the length down a little," Charmaine says. "Good, now you glue it to the middle of the lash line. That's right, hold it by the tips and settle it right… No, closer. There, that's right. Now the longer section goes on the outside. It's easier to work with lashes if you cut them up this way."

She and Dane huddle around her dressing room mirror, bordered with tiny lightbulbs and layered with photos and notes and dried flowers. The table shimmers and sparkles with cosmetics. Bouquets of brushes stand up in jars or are laid out like a surgeon's tools.

Dane meets Charmaine DuJour at one of Maisie's art shows. Or rather, he meets Charles Durant, handsome and flamboyant in a well-cut suit and big glasses, then finds out Charles is one of New York's top drag queens. Dane feels instantly comfortable in Charles' loving, joyful presence. He shares a bit of his story, asks a few shy questions. Turns his head this way and that to show Charles the blue eye, then the brown eye. Charles passes him a business card.

"Why don't you come to the Glitterbox tomorrow around three? We'll have some fun."

Dane goes, and Charmaine is waiting for him, gliding through the club in a scarlet kimono. Her wig cap taped in place but her face not yet made up. She gives Dane a backstage tour, making blithe introductions to her fellow queens and the crew. She sits Dane at her dressing table and pulls a second chair up close. She studies his reflection. Asks her own questions. She teaches him some basics, and queens coming in and out offer advice, make recommendations. Every one of them leans over Dane's shoulder or looks in his face, and calls him beautiful. Gorgeous. Stunning. A few lean further into his personal space and Charmaine whacks them away.

"He's my pupil, not trade. Hands off, ladies."

Charmaine puts him in full drag, wig to heels, and watches as Dane turns in front of a three-way mirror.

"How do you look?" she asks.

"Pretty," he says.

"How do you feel?"

Invoking truth or silence, Dane contemplates his reflection a long time. "I like feeling this way," he finally says. He puts fingertips on the mirror and turns his blue eye toward the glass. "I like the way I feel and I want to learn to feel this way on the inside, while looking like Dane on the outside." He looks back at Charmaine. "I'm not a performer. I don't want to be one. This is something I just like to do for myself." He sets the edge of his hand vertically on the tip of his nose. "And only for one side. If that makes sense."

Charmaine gives an appreciative hum and opens a jar of cold cream. She gestures for Dane to sit again, and she meticulously cleans off the right side of his face. The wig is removed, and Charmaine fusses with Dane's natural hair, pulling and teasing it to the left. She spins Dane toward the mirror and together they study the new look.

"Like that?" Charmaine asks.

Dane turns his brown-eyed side toward the glass. "That's Boy-me," he says softly, secretly. Then he turns the other way and whispers, "And that's Girl-me."

He puts arms around Charmaine, burying his face in her stomach. She holds him tight, murmuring, "You're beautiful. You're perfect. You are beautiful and perfect and you can be anything, look like anything, feel like anything, whether it's made up on the outside or just something you imagine on the inside."

Dane insists he's no performer, but when Glitterbox hosts an Amateur Night, he decides to make sure. He invites nobody, tells no one of his plan. With Charmaine's help, he devises a costume to go with his half-man, half-woman look. Ten minutes before his set, he slams two shots of tequila. He tells the emcee to introduce him simply as Two-Faced.

Terrified and buzzing, Dane lip syncs to "Can't We Try"—the duet by Dan Hill and Vonda Shepard.

And the house goes apeshit.

People are screaming as Dane turns from side to side with each lyric. Man, then woman. Dan, then Vonda. Dane, then Diane. At the end, he faces dead forward and bows his head for the standing ovation. At a front table, Charmaine is on her feet, yelling her head off, tears streaming down her face.

Whoa, Diane says. *This is a lot.*

Holy shit, Dane agrees, the adrenaline dumping out both sides of his body and the tequila shots clobbering his thoughts.

I'm glad we did this, Diane says. *But it's a lot.*

It's enough, Dane assures her. *This is one night only. I've learned what I need to know.*

DANE LEANED BACK FROM the mirror and scrutinized his efforts. He smiled, pushed his hair around a little more, then settled the Dusk Tiara on his head.

Diane smiled back at him. Beautiful, and she knew it.

"You are a lot," Dane said.

She winked.

Dane took a couple selfies and his teeth closed on a corner of his bottom lip as he contemplated sending one to Liko.

Do it, Diane said.

"Not yet," he said. "It's a paint-by-number kit. And I still don't know him all that well."

He looked at Diane again, shimmering gold-green, jeweled leaves in her hair.

Thanks, she said.

"Anytime, girl."

He put the camisole and tiara away and washed his face. He searched the bookshelves and took down his worn copy of *The Subtle Knife,* second in Philip Pullman's *His Dark Materials* trilogy. He snapped a picture of the text he wanted, then texted Liko: **You awake?**

Unfortunately, Liko replied.

No, seriously. Did I wake you up?

No, seriously. I was awake. Watching videos of ingrown toenail repair. Thanks, Fred.

Dane sent the text from *The Subtle Knife:*

...she had killed the tigers herself in order to punish the Tartar tribe who worshipped them, because the tribesmen had failed to do her honour when she had visited their territory. Without their tiger-gods the tribe declined into fear and melancholy, and begged her to allow them to worship her instead, only to be rejected with contempt; for what good would their worship do her, she asked? It had done nothing for the tigers. Such was Ruta Skadi: beautiful, proud and pitiless.

Liko's reply bubbled, went away. Stayed away a minute. Bubbled again. Then he answered: **Dusk Tiara = Ruta Skadi??**

Dane sent the plate emoji.

RUTA SKADI

1981

By MIDDLE SCHOOL, Naomi Misteria has eschewed friendships and takes refuge in the library. School librarians and public librarians become her mothers. Bastions of information and safety. Get on a librarian's good side and the world is yours.

"How old do I have to be to get a job?" she asks one.

You can ask a librarian anything and they always take it seriously.

"Where do you want to work, dear?"

"Here. Or a farm. But here is easier to walk to."

"Why a farm? Do you like animals?"

"I want to grow things."

"I see."

Naomi shyly pushes up her sleeve and shows the quote she's written on her arm with a permanent marker: "Might I have a bit of earth?" from *The Secret Garden*.

The librarian smiles. "I can let you water the plants?"

Naomi reads and reads and reads and reads. She's devouring John Irving novels at far too young an age but she finds her heroines in nearly all of them. She's the sexual suspect of Jennie Fields. The angry loner of Melony. The bear in Susie—oh how she longs for that bear suit.

She reads *The Thorn Birds* and sinks her teeth into the indomitable Justine O'Neill, who has no use for childhood, doesn't smile or play or joke or let anything bother her. Her one weakness is her beautiful younger brother, Dane.

One day, Naomi will meet a Great Dane, and allow him to be her one weakness.

When she devours Philip Pullman's *Dark Materials* trilogy, she falls in love with Serafina Pekkala, but falls into obeisance when the character Ruta Skadi comes on the scene. The Latvian witch is beyond beautiful, vivid and passionate. Proud and pitiless.

Proud and pitiless, Naomi writes on her arm.

Her class does a family tree unit. The teacher says Naomi can trace her adoptive parents' lineage.

"I'm not adopted," Naomi says, proud and pitiless.

Mrs. Weintraub does an unexpected thing: She apologizes. "I'm so sorry, dear. It was thoughtless of me. What would you like to do for the unit instead?"

But already the girl has learned an interesting lesson—being offered agency can move her deeply. "I'll think of something," she says, and slips away before the tears come.

Over the next two weeks, Naomi Misteria invents a family out of whole cloth. She leaves the maternal branch barren—her mother threw Naomi away so her life wasn't even worthy of imagination. Instead, Naomi creates a paternal grandmother named Ruta Skadi and from her, a Latvian heritage. She puts in the work, researching history and places. Crafting occupations and migratory routes. Hunting down a Latvian-English dictionary to create names out of the nouns important to her: *mystery, garden, flowers, earth.* She translates *proud and pitiless* to *Lepni un Nežēlīgi* and makes it the family motto. She designs a heraldic banner from when Latvia was a crusader state called Terra Mariana, and fills it with flowers, books and witches.

Her bound family history project comes back with a circled A and a note to see the teacher after class. Naomi stands before Mrs. Weintraub's desk, proud and pitiless.

"*His Dark Materials?*" the teacher asks.

Naomi nods and rolls one of her shoulders. "Ever love a book so much you want to live in it?"

Mrs. Weintraub smiles. "It's a beautiful series. I'm offended daemons aren't a real thing."

She reaches in her desk drawer and takes out a little sprig of pine needles. Naomi knows at once it's meant to be cloud pine, which is ridden by witches in Pullman's world. She takes it and presses it between the pages of *The Subtle Knife.*

Years later, Naomi will meet a man who mishears her first name, and calls her Nomi. She keeps it. Adopts it. Builds her family tree on it. The man, Ethan Hasen, will become her husband. He loves anagrams, and instead of a wedding ring, he takes Ruta Skadi and rearranges it into *Dusk Tiara.* He designs the headpiece and commissions a jeweler to execute it. Standing before a justice of the peace, Nomi wears this gorgeous coronet of leaves in her short, thick black hair. Hair that will soon fall out from chemo, then grow back silver.

When saying their vows, Nomi and Ethan join hands and rest them on the open palms of a third man, a Great Dane who is Nomi's weakness.

LIKO AND DANE TOOK their coffee and breakfast into the den. Liko connected his laptop to the big TV and opened his saved game.

He tried feeding another wisteria seed to the Green Man but the foliate face kept its mouth shut. He tried with the duck, who wasn't interested, then with the dog, who went on snoring.

"I'll show you something funny," Dane said. "Nothing to do with the mystery, just an Easter egg. See the vase of flowers by the dog? Those are lotus blossoms. Click one. Any one."

Liko did, and like the wisteria bloom, the blossom aged with every click, until the petals fell away, leaving the many-holed seed pod. The dog raised its head. Sniffed.

Then it threw up.

"Yikes," Liko said, as a loud, ripping hurl came from somewhere else in the chamber. Dane started laughing. Liko clicked back toward the altar. The Green Man had gone utterly, stonily white, his eyes bulging, a hand over his mouth, stifling gags.

"What is going on?" Liko said.

"Trypophobia," Dane said. "Fear of holes. Both Nomi and Mary Schoenfeld had it bad, and dried lotus seed heads could make both of them sick." He gave a few last chuckles, shaking his head. "It's just one big inside joke. Anyway, the wisteria seed. No one wants to eat it. You have to grind it up."

"With?"

"A mortar and pestle. You borrow it from a rabbit."

"The ones in the ceiling?"

Dane shrugged. Liko clicked on the ceiling motif but nothing happened. He hunted all over the chamber, looking for another rabbit while Dane just watched. Frustrated, Liko picked up his empty plate and held it out. "Please?"

Dane crossed his arms and raised his eyebrows. He looked at the plate. At Liko. Back at the plate.

"Kiss me first."

"What?"

"You heard me."

They stared a beat. The air roaring in his ears, Liko leaned toward Dane, a hand lifting to take his face because screw the game, he was going to kiss this guy into next week.

Dane drew back. "Dude, put the plate down."

"Sorry." Liko set it down. At least he thought he set it down. It hit the floor and smashed rather spectacularly.

"Smooth," Dane said.

Liko sunk his face into his hands. "I hate everything."

Dane thumped his back. "It's okay. Pick up the bigger pieces. I'll get a garbage bag." He scrambled over the back of the couch and went toward the kitchen.

"Fuck," Liko hissed, pushing back the coffee table and gathering the larger shards into his palm. He was sweating and his heart hiccupped like a drunk as he replayed the moment, cursing his asinine impulse control. Who the fuck cared about a broken plate? He should've grabbed the back of Dane's shirt and hauled him back down onto the couch. Kiss first. Clean up later. The hell was wrong with him?

"Quit brooding," Dane said, wheeling the vacuum cleaner in. "The moment came once, it'll come again."

"No, it's gone forever," Liko said moodily. "I killed it."

After damage control, Dane took over the cursor and backtracked out of the chamber and down the stairs. "You don't notice it on the way up, you have to be going the other way." He circled a painting hanging on the bulkhead over the treads.

"This is the Jade Rabbit," Dane said. "From Chinese tradition. He grinds herbs to make the elixir of life for Chang'e, the moon goddess. Click the mortar and pestle and take them back to the chamber."

Liko did, and dropped another wisteria seed from his cache into the mortar. As he ground it up, a little flare rose from the bowl, then the fine powder swirled toward the window and encircled the full moon.

Then nothing.

"Now what?" Liko said, thinking, *How about kissing again?*

"Remember the story from the Jakata Tales?" Dane said. "When Buddha as a hare threw himself into the fire to feed a beggar? As a reward, he was set on the face of the moon. Western civilization calls it the man in the moon. But in Asian culture, it's a rabbit. Anyway, click the moon."

The iconic surface shadows coalesced into a rabbit, which bounded out of the moon, through the window and into the chamber. Sleek and snowy white, it leaped into the Green Man's lap and put something in his hand. The foliate god then held the hand out to the player.

Liko clicked over and saw it was a pearl.

"What do I do with this?"

"A pearl is a…" Dane turned a hand over in the air.

"Stone?" Liko said. "A gem. A jewel."

"Stones, gems and jewels go in a…?"

"Necklace? A ring? A…"

Dane mimed putting something on his head.

"A crown. A *tiara.*" He turned toward the laptop. "Duh."

The tiara had two circular spaces on its front. The pearl slipped into one. Unprompted, Liko went for the third wisteria seed in his cache and slipped it into the second slot.

"Nice going, big brain," Dane said. "Now find a head to crown."

Liko took the coronet and set it on the Green Man's head. The god smiled and his emerald eyes closed. From beneath the lids, silvery tears began to stream.

"Watch," Dane murmured.

The Green Man opened his eyes. Now one was blue and the other brown.

"Look at that," Liko said. "It's you."

The mouth in the foliate face opened and this time, pine needles flew out. A cloud of them swirling in front of the altar, then dropping to the floor to form two words: *Tinner Wheeled.*

"I'm afraid it's an annoying anagram," Dane said. He exhaled and scrubbed at his face. "Still so much to tell you, but I have to get to work."

Liko checked his watch. "Same."

"We're about halfway through the clues and it's not even June. I'm going to slow us down a little." Dane glanced sideways. "And I don't mean just the game."

Liko sighed moodily, nodding.

Dane got up, collected cups and took them to the kitchen. "If you want to be my best friend," he called back, "put away the vacuum cleaner?"

"Sure." But Liko just sat alone a long time, doing nothing. Unsure what he wanted to be to Dane.

THE NAOMI ROAD 34

243

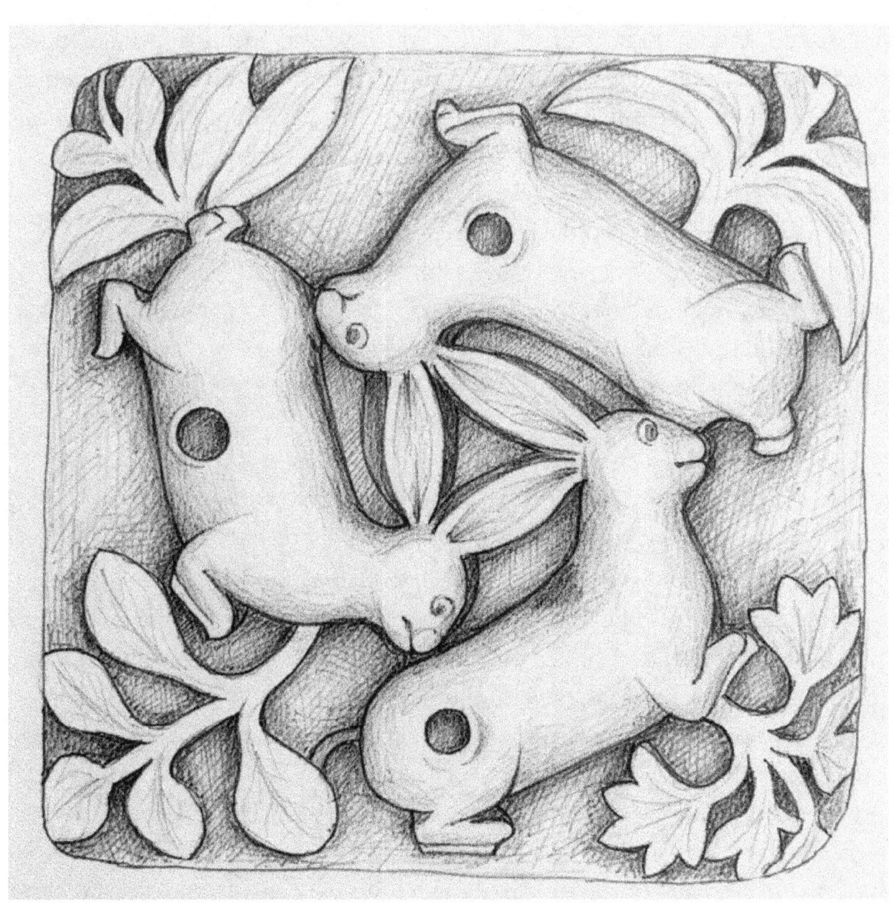

Roof boss, St. Andrew's church, Sampford Courtenay, Devon, UK

BLASCHKO'S LINES

Memorial Day weekend came and a truck arrived to fill the pool. It was blistering hot and muggy, and Liko couldn't suit up and dive in fast enough. Dane was slower to come downstairs, putting on and taking off a sunshirt four times while auditioning excuses. *I'm fanatical about sun exposure,* he could say, or, *I have new ink and I don't want the sun on it.*

"This is so fucking stupid," he muttered, taking it off.

He's a decent, gracious guy, Diane said. *Most likely he'll notice the scars and mind his own beeswax. And if he asks, treat it like you used to treat Saskia's questions: Answer only what's asked.*

"You're right," Dane said, tossing the shirt on the bed.

Fuck it.

"Fuck everything. I'm forty-six years old, what do I care what he thinks?"

And you're fucking gorgeous, remember? Hey, if he's rude or makes fun, you'll know he's not worth your time. Don't worry about it.

Dane went down to the pool shirtless, worrying anyway.

"Goddamn, this is the life," Liko said, drifting on one of the floats. His hair was all slicked back over a pair of Wayfarers, and he looked dynamite. Dane felt things stirring below the belt and quickly dove in.

"Wow, nice ink," Liko said as Dane surfaced in the shallow end. "Holy shit, let me see."

He paddled closer as Dane turned slowly around. He had the same wisteria blossoms as Nomi, but only on the right side of his body. The vines started a little below his elbow and twined up over his shoulder. One braid headed across his chest and stopped at his sternum. The other continued onto his back, coiling close to the midline of his spine but never crossing. On his shoulder blade, a circular patch made a break in the flowers, and here was tattooed the triskele of the Three Hares.

"We all had our hares right here," Dane said, patting it. "And Nomi and I had the wisteria."

Dane's artist had started to bring the vines down onto his side, but then Nomi died, and so did Dane's enthusiasm. The vine continued under the waistband of his suit and over his hip, and one unfinished blossom dripped onto his quadricep muscle, but that was nothing Liko could see right now.

"What's on the back of your neck?"

Dane floated backward toward him, chin dropped. "Their fingerprints."

"And the ink on your other shoulder—what's it mean?"

"This? It's not a tattoo."

The skin on the left side of Dane's torso was distinctly darker. As if he'd lain on his right side under a sun lamp and forgot to turn over. An even darker pigmentation gathered in patches and streaks, creating an arcing whorl across half of Dane's upper back. A coppery wave that ended in a coiled tip under his arm.

"It's just a birthmark," he said. "Actually it's called a Blaschko's line."

Liko gave a low chuckle. "Jesus, Strong, even your birthmarks are cool. I mean look at that thing. Perfect spirals."

"A kilo-koil," Dane said, grinning.

"A kilo-koil birthmark would look like a mangled Slinky. Your blah-de-blah line probably has the golden ratio. You're like a natural work of art here. Go fuck yourself."

Dane laughed. "Shut up."

"Seriously, could you give us average guys a chance?"

"You have ink?"

"Nah. I have a dozen ideas, but I'm too chicken to execute. It's a cowardly twist on the creativity-imagination thing." He'd bumped into the side of the pool and pushed off with his feet, swanning past Dane with hands behind his head. "Was tattooing just one side of your body a deliberate design choice?"

"Yeah."

"Do your eyes being different colors tie into that choice?"

"Yes."

Liko looked over the rims of his shades. "If I prove trustworthy, will you tell me about it someday?"

"Maybe." Dane planted hands on the deck and hoisted himself out, streaming water. His back to the pool, he plucked a towel from the big basket and started drying off, feeling Liko's eyes on him.

"I have another one here," he said, hitching up the left leg of his suit and showing how a second Blaschko's line rippled down his hamstring and wrapped around his calf.

"On the same side," Liko said. "What causes them?"

"Lots of things. But in my case, it's from tetragametic chimerism."

"Say again?"

"Tetragametic chimerism. I have two different sets of DNA. One male, one female."

He turned around and casually touched the front of his suit. "I present male. Out of my pants, I look the same as you."

Liko shook his head vigorously. "No, you don't."

Dane smiled. "Well, true, because like Hitler, I only have one ball."

"Hm?" Liko sat up a little too quick and fell off the float. He came up tangled with the armrest, spitting a stream out the side of his mouth and laughing. "I'm sorry, what?"

"I think you heard me. Want a beer?"

"I would love a beer."

Towel around his neck, Dane went inside and opened two local brews.

It's going well, Diane said, perched prettily on the counter.

"I think so, too."

She moved her legs aside so he could get into the drawer for the bottle opener. *I'm proud of you. Just tell a simple story.*

He winked at nothing and took the beers outside. Liko had gotten out and was drying off.

"So," Dane said, flopping onto one of the chaise loungers. "I have two sets of DNA. Draw blood from my arm or leg and it's XY. Draw it from my midline, or take tissue samples anywhere along the midline, and it's XX."

"How does that happen?"

"Usually when two zygotes are present in the womb, and one twin absorbs the other."

"Oh," Liko said slowly. "I've heard of this. I didn't know it had a name."

"Well, fetal absorption, also known as vanishing twin syndrome, is one thing. Chimerism can sometimes be a result."

"Is it common?"

"Hard to say. People can have chimerism, not present any symptoms, and go a lifetime not knowing. It's not a disease or a syndrome or a condition. Sometimes it causes problems with your immune system. Each set of DNA thinking the other is the enemy. But most of the time, it's just a flukey thing that's discovered incidentally."

"So not everyone would have outward signs like different color eyes or the lines?"

"Right. And the reverse is true: not everyone with heterochromia or Blaschko's lines is a chimera."

"Were you pulling my leg with the one ball thing?"

"No. Only one testicle descended when I was a baby so—"

"That happened with Kyle," Liko said. "He had surgery to fix it. Sorry, go on."

"I think the statistic is one percent of male babies are born undescended. Also not a big deal—a half-hour surgery and they bring it down. You know this. Anyway, when they did the surgery on me, they found the missing jewel wasn't a testicle at all. It was an ovary."

Liko pushed his sunglasses up and looked at Dane a long moment.

"Put those back on," Dane said.

"Why?"

"One, you look good in them. Two, it's a little easier to talk about this without your purple people-eaters in my face."

Liko laughed and flipped the shades down. "Better?"

"Thanks. What was I saying?"

"I think you were telling me you're intersex?"

"Right. Yes. Chimera and intersex. One didn't necessarily cause the other. Most chimeras aren't intersex. Most intersex people aren't chimeras."

"So you're, like, one in a million?"

"I don't know about a million but it's an interesting perfect storm. I'm a non-binary intersex chimera. How's that for an identity?"

"It's like a half double-decaffeinated double half-cap," Liko said.

"Everything about me just screams: *excellent decision making skills.*"

"You identify non-binary but you don't use they/them pronouns." Liko put up his palms. "Not that you're required to. If you do, you haven't corrected me. Either way, all due respect. I'm here to learn."

"This is where, to this day, it still gets tangled up in my head. I'm literally they/them, and while I appreciate and respect they/them, I don't… Sometimes I'll say my pronouns are he/they, but it never feels quite right. He/him feels like me. The outward me. I like to present male. My she/her is an extremely separate, extremely private thing."

Liko raised his glasses. "And her name is Diane."

"Yes."

Liko put the shades down and drank the rest of his beer. "Another?"

"Sure."

He went inside, his drying suit loose around his thighs but still clinging damp to his butt. His arms and shoulders defined with muscle, but blurred with age. He looked simultaneously hard and soft, and it made Dane remember when Dr. Obrera took him off the testosterone shots so she could get a baseline reading of what his body naturally produced. How Dane had felt like his muscles were collapsing. Softening around his bones. Sliding away along with his strength and energy. Coupled with the massive emotional breakdown and a lifetime of trauma bubbling to the surface, it was like getting sucked into a black hole.

"Hang in there," Obrera said. "I know it's hard, I know you feel terrible, but just hang in there a little longer, Dane. We're going to figure out who you are…"

Dane shuddered off the memory as Liko came out with another round and a bag of pretzels.

"So I had a whole conversation with myself in the kitchen," he said. "Remembering all my first encounters with you. New Year's Eve, when you had blue eyes. Ringing your doorbell, when you had brown eyes. Then meeting you as Diane, with blue eyes. How you described her as a life coach."

"She helps me do brave things."

Liko pointed a finger. "Okay, that part. When you had both eyes blue on New Year's Eve, were you being Diane or were you being brave?"

"Brave. Remember Jackie from the May Day party, with the gorgeous curly hair? She blows it out sometimes, and says she's an entirely different person when her hair is straight. A tougher, more confident person. Straight hair makes her swagger. Blue eyes kind of do the same thing for me."

"The leather jacket effect," Liko said. "I put on a leather jacket and aviators and I'm untouchable. It's all I wanted to wear to Kyle's funeral."

"It's armor, exactly."

"So something made you need a lot more armor when I came back to the farm the second day."

"Honestly, man, I don't know what the hell I was doing. I don't dress up as Diane for other people. Like ever. But when you were coming back… I don't know, it wasn't for armor. More like a dare or prank. It was weird."

"But you do dress up as her sometimes?"

"Only for myself." Dane reached for his phone and scrolled his photos. He found the ones he took in his bathroom, wearing Nomi's camisole top and the Dusk Tiara. "Sure you want to see this?"

"Yes," Liko said. Softly. Seriously.

Dane gave him the phone. Drew a long breath in and out as Liko looked at it. Looked up at Dane. Down at the phone. Up. Down.

"Two questions," he finally said. "One: do you prefer me to say *this* is beautiful, *she* is beautiful, or *you* are beautiful?"

"Any of those. And thank you." Feeling a sudden, shy need for a little more distance, Dane got up and dropped into the pool.

"Two," Liko said, "am I to understand while I was watching videos of ingrown toenail repair, this was going on?"

Dane crossed arms on the float and pushed off the bottom. "Diane likes you. Or maybe, more accurately, she doesn't fear you."

"Huh." Liko studied the picture another moment, then put the phone down.

"Diane is of the world but not in the world. In fact, instead of saying I absorbed her in the womb, I prefer to give her agency and say she decided, of her own volition, to hide inside me. Where she's always been."

"Always?"

"I can't remember a time when I didn't feel her with me. My inner monologue is in her voice. A female voice. I remember being four, five years old, sitting in front of the mirror and turning my head side to side so only one eye was showing." Dane turned his right cheek toward Liko. "Saying this is my boy side." He swiveled his head the other way. "And this is my girl side. Always in my mind, I had Boy-me and Girl-me, and a sort of over-arching Me-me. An *us* that was neither-nor. It was both. Still is both. Her and I. We. Which is me."

"Does all this circle back to your father being a monster?"

"Yes," Dane said. "But since this conversation is going a lot better than I expected, let's not ruin it by talking about him."

"Better?" Liko's brow wrinkled. "What, did you think I'd be weird about it?"

"I really didn't know what to think. I don't know you all that well, and I haven't told my story to someone new in a really long time."

Dane left the float and hitched up to sit on the deck. Liko stretched long to hand him his beer.

"Thanks. Talk about being of the world but not in it, I came to this place when I was twenty and never left. I met my soulmates, found my life's work, had a child, built a life in this… Let's face it, in this bubble. When Nomi died and Ethan left, I thought about opening my heart to someone new and was like, *Christ, I've never been* out there *in my life.* I mean, I never dated. Never played the field. I flirt like a moron and—"

"Excuse me," Liko said. "Your flirting is top notch."

"How would you know?"

Liko opened his mouth, then closed it. "I walked into that."

"I flirt like a moron but my smartass game is pretty good."

"Hey, back in March when I told you why I was named Henry and called Liko, you said *It's halfway between likable and lucky.* And I thought, *Damn, he's flirting with me.*"

"It's not that I don't flirt at all," Dane laughed. "I just do it weird."

"I think your game is better than you think it is."

They were quiet a while, finishing their beers.

"For real though," Dane finally said. "It was easier telling you than I expected. Thanks."

"You're welcome. You're interesting as fuck. I'm sorry the story has a really unpleasant underbelly, and I have a vile hunch when I hear it, the idea of you staying in a safe, rural bubble for twenty-whatever years will make perfect sense. But hey, if it doesn't make sense, so what—it's still your story. Can I ask a rude question about it?"

"As many as you want."

"Did you have top surgery?"

Dane touched his scars. "You saw these."

"I did."

Keep it simple, Diane said.

"So the ovary on my left side was attached to a fallopian tube and a little scrap of a uterus. None of them worked, but they made their presence known. I'd always been small for my age, and when I hit puberty, my voice didn't change and I wasn't growing facial hair." Dane held up a leg and turned a forearm over in the sun. "Or any hair, really. Turns out in the normal fistfight between testosterone and estrogen, estrogen was winning, and when I was thirteen, I started growing breasts."

Liko's mouth opened a little but he said nothing. Just pushed the shades up on his head and stared.

"Now you look a little horrified," Dane said carefully. "What are you thinking?"

"Knowing how mean kids can be, I'm thinking middle and high school must've been a fucking nightmare. I kind of feel sick wondering what it was like."

Diane was pulsing behind Dane's left eye. Counseling, *Keep it simple, keep it simple, keep it simple.*

"What you have to understand," he said, "is that I didn't hear the words *intersex* or *chimerism* until I left my father's house. When it came to anything about my health or my body, I was either kept in the dark or lied to. Mostly lied to. In fact, until I was seventeen, I believed I had a rare form of chronic cancer. I believed a lot of things my father told me, and he kept me far away from any truth-tellers."

"Like your mother and your sister," Liko said.

"Maisie is twelve years older than me. By the time I started to create memories, she was at boarding school and away for long stretches of time. This is so cliché but to me, she was a princess. She lived far away, busy with important princess things, and every now and then she'd make a state visit and I would just adore her."

Keep it simple, Diane warned.

"Anyway," Dane said cheerfully, "suffice it to say my father's house wasn't the best environment to be gender non-conforming and I had no idea what it even meant. Fast-forward to when I got out of there and was living with Maisie, and I finally got proper care and honest information."

"Your head must've exploded."

"Everything exploded. After a shit-ton of therapy, I learned I identify non-binary and have a very real, very significant female aspect, but I prefer to present male."

"That's when you had top surgery?"

"Yes," Dane said, lying. "And started testosterone therapy."

"And you're okay now? I mean…"

"Healthwise? I'm fine. Thank you for asking."

"How does the testosterone therapy work?"

"I'm on a twelve-week cycle. I started one in May. If you're still here in August, you'll get to see me take a shot in the ass."

"Now you're flirting with me," Liko said, getting up.

"Trying."

PART FOUR
AY'LOUT

"A hare is the most marveylous beste of the world."
—William Twiti, huntsman to King Edward II

WHEN HE FACES FORWARD

1976
Whitestone, Queens, New York City

ONCE UPON A TIME in a place called Malba, Danelaw Strong lives in a magnificent house under the Whitestone Bridge. It's an enviable place of wealth and ease, but isolated and insular. No ferry service touches that north shore of Queens, no subway station services its affluence. Only bus service and most residents wouldn't be caught dead traveling by bus. These elite people would never say they live in Queens or Whitestone or even, God forbid, Long Island. They grudgingly acknowledge being part of New York City, but it's made abundantly clear: They live in Malba.

Dane lives with his mother and father and a group of people known only as *the staff* or *the help*. Dane has a beautiful older sister with a name like music: Marie Elisavette. It's a lot of syllables for a four-year-old, and the V is especially tricky. Dane mashes it up into *Marizabet*.

Most of the time, Marizabet lives in a mysterious, elusive place called *Away at School*. Her bedroom door is shut but not locked, and Dane often sneaks into this sun-filled palace with its big windows, creamy pink walls and soft white pillows. Books and stuffed animals, makeup and perfume, and gorgeous clothes hanging in the closet.

Sometimes Marizabet comes home when Dane's father has boarded his big helicopter and gone someplace called *Away on Business*. These are wonderful times when Dane summons himself to his sister's palace, as if by royal decree: *Marizabet, I come your room. I come stay your room, Marizabet.*

His sister's room isn't just a place. It's a state of mind. It's also off-limits. If Dane's mother or the Help find him sitting at Marizabet's sparkly dressing table, napping in her empty bathtub or perusing her cavernous closet, he's quickly shooed out. If his father finds him, Dane will have to take his pants off and lie on his bed or kneel on the couch, and his father will whip him with a belt. Dane mustn't cry during these beatings. And he must never, never tell about them.

This is the law.

Dane is a child, and most of a child's brain is wired only with on-off switches, not dials of nuance. He is aware something is not quite right at home, not quite right with his mother, and something is entirely wrong with his father, who is not so much a man as a weather system. He need only walk into a room to change its barometer, wreak destruction, and displace everyone present. Often with no warning.

Dane's father is not *Dad, Daddy, Papa* or *Father*. He is *Sir*.

Yes, Sir.

No, Sir.

You're right and I'm wrong, Sir.

I'm sorry, Sir.

One forgotten *Sir* upon coming, going, asking, answering or obeying, is one stroke of the belt, which must be acknowledged with *Thank you, Sir.*

This is also the law.

Sir's first name is Ivelaw, for all the men in the Strong family have *law* in their names: Morelaw. Whitlaw. Wardlaw. Renlaw. Ivelaw. Their portraits line a long hallway which leads to Ivelaw's office.

There is no portrait of Danelaw Strong. Perhaps because he's a child. Perhaps because in his developing brain, little switches are flipping on and off in ever-adapting, sophisticated combinations, and the data output is telling him he's not a law. He's a mistake. A button flashes on indicating something is extremely wrong with himself, and it's he who is the cause of all the not-right-ness inside this beautiful house in Malba. The button has a name: *cancer.*

Dane grows up believing he's chronically ill. Cancer is a perpetual cloud cover in his life story. It's the word that explains everything. Why he feels so bad all the time. Why he looks the way he does. Why things are done to him. Cancer never moves into past tense, but always stays present.

Because you have cancer.

Dane has two different-colored eyes because of cancer. The blue one is weaker, damaged by cancer, so he has to wear a contact lens in that eye, tinted brown so it matches the other one.

Cancer causes the skin discoloration on his torso and dark, spiraling lines on his left side. His blue-eyed side.

(My girl side.)

When he discovers his own goodies and the uproariously funny words for them, he studies the birds-and-bees picture books on his shelves and demands to know why the illustrated boys have two *tessicles* but Dane only has one.

When his body is the question, *cancer* is the answer.

But it hasn't always been that way.

He has memories. Secret memories from a year he later labels 4 BC: *When I was four years old, before cancer.*

In the year 4 BC, he takes his mother's hand and pulls her into the little bathroom off the kitchen, where he clambers onto a stepstool so he can see himself in the mirror.

"This is my boy eye," he says solemnly, touching the skin beneath his brown iris. "And this is my girl eye," he says, touching beneath the blue.

"Really," Helen said. "How do you know?"

"I just do." Dane shows how he can turn his head just enough to the left so only the brown *(boy)* eye shows in the mirror. "See, that's one me."

He swivels his chin to the right, keeping his gaze on his reflection. "That's other me."

He turns his head front and looks at his blue and brown double gaze. "That's all me." He laughs. He's so funny looking when he faces forward.

"Do you want to be one or the other?" Helen asks. "Boy or girl?"

"Both."

"Boy *and* girl."

"Yes."

"A boy sometimes and a girl other times?"

Dane thinks. "No, both."

"But everyone calls you a boy," Helen says. "We use *he* and *him* when we talk about you. Is that all right?"

"Mmhm," Dane says, leaning forward until his nose touches the mirror and his two eyes merge into one. "Now I'm sy-blocks," he says.

"Cyclops," Helen says.

Still giggling, Dane tilts his head back and forth, making his eyes seesaw crazily, then settle back into one eye in the middle of his face. He loves the optical illusion of his gaze, loves the blue and brown mixed together. At preschool, other kids mix red and yellow, yellow and blue, blue and red. Dane mixes blue and brown. They're the best colors.

"I have one eye and one tessicle," he says.

"Testicle," Helen says.

"Why?"

"Sometimes funny things happen. Your body forgot to make the other one. But that's okay. The one you have is just fine."

"It's blue and brown," Dane says softly, watching his breath fog the glass, then clear.

Helen leans a hip on the sink. "Hey," she says. "You sure it's okay if people call you a boy?"

"Uh-huh," Dane says, exhaling hard to make a big foggy patch. "That's me most of the time." With a fingertip, he makes the letter D in the condensation. The best letter.

"Ah," Helen says. "You're not always both."

"Both live in the me-house," Dane says. "But boy-me likes to live outside. Girl-me likes to be inside."

"Is she afraid to come outside?"

"No. She just likes it better inside."

He jumps off the stepstool, launching himself at Helen's crossed arms. He startles her, but she catches him. She's always there. Always believing Dane means what he does and says. Dane wraps arms and legs around her body, buries his face in her hair and loves her terribly, thinking it will always be like this.

But in 5 BC, Helen goes to jail and Marizabet disappears. She's not Away at School—the *school* part also disappears and now she's simply Away. She ran to this incomprehensible place and all Dane needs to know is she will never come back. If he asks why, the answer is the belt.

From 5 BC onward, it's Dane alone in the house with a man he calls Sir. Dane is a mistake that can't be fixed. A portrait that will never be painted. A frightened boy taking refuge in a girl's space. A childish mind frantically flipping switches on and off and calculating how much pain is worth the risk of being found in Marizabet's room, where love still lives. He can no more stay out of this room than he can stop breathing. He summons himself to the pink walls as if by royal decree.

Marizabet, I come your room.

I come stay your room, Marizabet…

THE GRAYLOCK PROTOCOL

THE CSA KICKED OFF in June, which made the work level on the farm go nuclear. The produce stand at the end of the driveway spilled radishes, baby beets, heads of lettuce, asparagus and strawberries. The hens and ducks were laying like there was no tomorrow. The tops of the egg cartons flipped up to display shells in a watercolor palette of brown, green, cream and blue. The yolks dazzled bright orange and the whites barely moved as they dropped into a sizzling skillet. Liko ate two every day and said he didn't feel bad about it. Dane got a rise watching Liko lick the plates clean and didn't feel bad about it.

Dane was consumed with work, but his eyes were ever watchful for the Green Man, who moved in shifts between his writing and the farm. For the latter, he helped fill CSA boxes, manned the register, or did whatever little task Dane left in a note on the kitchen table. Whether assigned to pick peas, thin carrots, weed or prune, Liko's buddy Jeffrey was always tagging along.

Dane knew grief tagged along, too. It always would. Liko had days where he didn't write a word, didn't lift a finger. A morning walk turned into a six-mile hike, just to kill time. Dane saw him pulled away in the farm's secret spaces, crying into Jeffrey's feathers or Salma's fur. More than once, Dane watched Liko crouch on the bottom of the pool, holding his breath long past the comfort zone. Wondering if he could really take himself out this time. Dane knew because he often did it himself.

He stayed at a respectful distance from the pool, but he watched and counted seconds, scanning the surface of the water. Playing the role of the Japanese courtesan Kiku, but instead of watching until Captain Blackthorne vanished from sight, Dane did the honor of watching until the pilot reappeared. Which he always did: In a bubbling geyser, Liko would resurface, gasping, flipping water out of his hair and putting his face in his hands.

"You are much man," Dane whispered each time. "You are reborn and you are Samurai now. Liko-san, you are so much man…"

He believed Liko's soul was in agony, but it wanted to stick around. Dane hoped it was because Liko liked this place. He liked the work and the crew and his emotional support duck.

And maybe because he liked Dane.

THE PUB OPENED ITS outdoor seating area, strung new lights, and put its sand-wich-board sign close to the road, heralding each night's specialty. Wednesday was Pork Rinds & Cabernet. Thursday was Champagne & French Fries. The bubbly could span a budget from $250 bottles of Grand Cru to a six-pack of Miller High Life—champagne of beers. The fries came one way: shoestring thin, fried in duck fat, sprinkled with Himalayan pink salt.

Friday's happy hour was called Cocktails & Suspicion. Ethan Hasen had first envisioned it as Cocktails & Slander, but the Pub couldn't manifest an environment where people came to talk shit about each other. So slander was downgraded to suspicion.

"I'm suspicious because you don't drink coffee," someone would accuse over drinks.

A collective, horrified gasp.

The accused would counter, "I'm suspicious because you have no celebrity crush."

"What?"

"None?"

"Come on, nobody is *that* mentally disciplined."

All the beer, cider, wine and liquor was local. There was no set menu during the farm season: Whatever was pouring off the field and vines at Schoenfeld's was delivered to the Pub and made into flatbreads or salads. Grilled aspara-gus was tremendously popular right now, as was the sign at the door bidding departing patrons, *Goodnight, thanks for coming! Think of us later when you pee!*

Cocktails & Suspicion was followed by an open mic night. Tonight was the first of the season and Dane told Liko it wasn't to be missed. "Wear your party shirt."

Dane wore his leather vest and covered up his blue eye.

"Not a lot of your pipple at the Pub?" Liko asked kindly.

"There are. But also strangers. Strangers stare. Sometimes I don't mind, other times I just don't want to deal with it."

"I Googled famous people with heterochromia. You keep good company. Like Robert Downey, Jr."

Dane gave a purist snort. "He has partial heterochromia. Different color flecks within the iris."

"What do you have?"

"Heterochromia iridum. Also known as Fred's sexual orientation."

They took a couple gin and tonics to a high top and toasted.

"Welcome to Cocktails and Suspicion," Dane said. "You're up."

"I'm suspicious because the second, no, third time I met you, you were dressed as a woman."

"Fair." Dane smiled. "I'm suspicious because you still sleep with your ex-wife."

Liko opened his mouth. Closed it. "Fair."

"You still love her?"

"It's hard to mourn a child when you're no longer a couple," Liko said slowly. "I don't know if I still love her. I know I kind of need her right now. It's hard to explain."

"She's the last link to Kyle."

"The last human one."

"She really cheated on you with your accountant?"

"Pathetic, right?"

"Did you find out or did she confess?"

"She confessed. After she slept with him, which violated the Graylock Protocol."

"The what?"

Liko smiled. "Let me ask first: Did you, Nomi and Ethan have outside partners?"

"No."

"You had a conversation about it? Laid out rules and expectations and defined infidelity? Made it clear?"

"It was many conversations," Dane said. "Did you and Janelle?"

"When we got engaged we went camping up in the Berkshires. We brought along this book, something like, *50 Questions to Ask Your Lover.*"

"How do you define infidelity," Dane said, pretending to read. "Do you fold towels in quarters or thirds? Do you have an irrational fear of snakes in the toilet?"

"All important things to know before you tie the knot," Liko said. "So we went through the whole book, every question, talking while we hiked, or sitting around the fire. We talked a lot about fidelity. We liked the idea of it. Believed in it. We both came from really solid families and parents with good, long marriages. We wanted to emulate that. So, we set the intentions and made it clear: Crushing is allowed, crushing is human. Sleeping with anyone else is cheating. But…"

Dane tilted his chin. "But?"

"We made a deal. If either of us was feeling an attraction that was inching toward the forbidden fruit bowl, we would make space to have a conversation about that, too. Just us. Or with a counselor. However we wanted to say, *I'm feeling something more than a crush and I need to talk about it.* We even made a safe word: Graylock. It was the name of the campsite in the Berkshires."

Dane half moved out of his seat. "Hold on, let me get my Scrabble tiles."

Grinning, Liko raised an arm like he was going to backhand Dane. A slice of sun hit his face, lighting up the violet of his eyes. He was dazzling right then and the laughing rapport suddenly suffused Dane with memory. Recalling the New Year's Eve party and how, for a couple hours, he felt *on.* Astounded by himself. Realizing he was a charming person.

"I need some food to go with the cocktails and suspicion," Liko said. "Otherwise you're taking me out of here in a wheelbarrow."

Dane watched him go, liking him intensely and not knowing what to do. He bit his bottom lip, thinking how close they'd been to kissing. How weirdly relieved he was when the plate broke. How eager he was for the moment to come back.

Liko leaned on the bar, hands placed wide, a foot crossed over an ankle. He looked especially good from the back.

Desire always hit Dane in the back of his throat first. A little thick thrum, like eating too much cake frosting at once. Squeezing his breath in a rich fist, then letting go and melting down into his chest and migrating toward the rest of his body.

This is a wicked crush, Diane said. *If memory serves.*

Dane definitely remembered this heady feeling from his youth, curious excitement making his cells sit up and crane their necks at Liko. Charmed by everything he said and did. Wanting to charm in return, show off, be impressive, make him crush, make him *want.*

Physically speaking, Liko was unlike anyone Dane had ever been with. Good. He'd been forced back onto the dating scene without a warning, without consent, without even a goddamn consultation. So he was entitled to a few rules. He wanted a lover that wouldn't remind him, either in looks or body. Dane, Ethan and Nomi had absurdly similar physiques. They wore each other's clothes easily, even shoes. Lowered in water, they would all displace the exact same amount. Three hares occupying equal thirds.

Liko was taller than Dane. Broader. Ten years older. Dark-haired once, but heading toward silver. The beard couldn't mask the air of tired sadness, nor the way his expression often stopped cold, as if his son's death had freshly blindsided him. Even with a thousand-yard stare, he had a quiet sexiness that made Dane's toes curl. Liko was a wreck, but he was a confident wreck. No doubt he could throw Dane around a bed and show him things. Fuck him in a way Ethan could never…

He looked away, clenched and blindsided. He fished a pen out of his pocket and wrote *Graylock* on the placemat. His pen flicked between letters before he finally wrote *rock.* Then *Glock,* which Ethan would've discounted as a proper noun, but screw him. Oh, and *yak.* Good word, probably worth a mess of points in Scrabble.

"Here we go," Liko said, setting down a woodfired pizza, the cheese still bubbling in between asparagus spears and caramelized onions. "God, I'm starving."

Dane realized he was too, and they demolished the pie in minutes.

"So, Graylock?" Dane asked.

"Right. We had a conversation. We established the Graylock Protocol and stuck by it for seventeen years. One of the things I loved about being married to her was we were allowed to acknowledge attraction. We could be open about crushes or fantasies. And George, the famous accountant, was a shared crush. The man is gorgeous. I mean objectively stunning. He's lost a lot of his appeal and I'd put my fist in his pretty face if I saw him now, but before the shit went down, Janelle and I would be positively giddy when it was tax season. *Time to see George. I gotta go to the gym. I gotta go to the tanning salon. I'm getting a lash lift. What are you going to wear?"*

"We're due for a deep, thorough audit," Dane said. "This is the year. I can feel it."

"Right? It was fun. It was hilarious. And it was so *us.* Then she comes to me one night, sits down and speaks the safe word. *I need to talk about Graylock.* And man…" Shaking his head, Liko pinched the bridge of his nose. "I miss the obvious, but not this time. I knew. Talk about a gut feeling. Right in my stomach, I knew this was happening out of order. We were supposed to instigate the Graylock Protocol *before* we went and did something stupid."

"Like George."

"She was doing George. I mean *seriously?*"

"What's the statute of limitations on playing devil's advocate?"

Liko rolled his eyes. "What would I have done if she'd invoked the Graylock Protocol before sleeping with him?"

"If it's not too stupid a question."

"Dude, I don't know. I'm not being cagey. I really don't. Maybe I did once but when Kyle died…" He touched fingertips to his temple then exploded them out. "It changes everything. Literally everything. Your brains, your memories, your recall, your body. Your fucking priorities. Things that mattered suddenly don't. Things that never mattered are suddenly dire." His expression startled, eyes widening, and he looked up at Dane. "I'm sorry. Your wife died, you already know this."

"No, it's okay. Keep going."

Liko drew a breath in and let it go. He took a drink and chewed on a sliver of ice. "It was a betrayal," he said. "Like violating the Geneva Convention. We had the Graylock Protocol and I didn't know how important it actually was until she broke it. We'd always been so open with each other. Now she was keeping secrets. When you fuck with someone's trust like that…"

"It's a tinier death," Dane said. "Nothing's the same."

"I couldn't get past it."

"Was George married?"

Liko nodded. "Me and his wife went to lunch."

"Shut up. After you found out about George and Janelle?"

"The cuckolds go to lunch. So civilized. Two drinks in, we were like *fuck this.*"

"So much for British sangfroid."

Liko laughed and something in Dane's chest notched a mark on a post. He was beginning to love making this guy laugh.

"Janelle and I did some couples counseling," Liko was saying, "but I kept coming back to the broken trust in my mind. I hated to think of myself as an unforgiving person, but…"

"Have you forgiven her?"

"I've forgiven her for the utterly human experience of being attracted to someone else," Liko said slowly. "We've all been there." He glanced sideways and up again. "I used to love that Elton John song 'Sacrifice.' *Into the boundary of each married man sweet deceit comes calling…*"

"Right, right," Dane said quietly. Fascinated, and starting to feel the buzz of the second drink.

Liko held up his glass and shook the melting cubes. "Staying with her would've been more suspicion than cocktails. You know? And it wasn't just my heartbreak and wounded ego. There was Kyle. He was fourteen. Splitting up meant completely devastating his life. At the most rotten time in any kid's life. When he's exploding with hormones, deciding his parents are the bane of his existence and already experimenting with pushing every boundary. Really, woman, you're going to make me have *this* fucking conversation with an adolescent alien? And if I survive it, then hey, what the hell *is* next for me? I'm fifty bloody three years old. I gotta be out there again? Who's gonna want me?"

Me, Dane thought. But aloud only said, "I know the feeling."

Liko exhaled and slumped a little. "Want to get another pizza? I'm still hungry."

"Yeah, sure." He turned the placemat to show his anagram of Graylock. "So far, I got *rock, Glock* and *yak.*"

Liko peered. "Oh. It's *grey* with an E, not an A. Greylock."

"Ah." Dane fixed it, then sourly scribbled out *yak.*

"Sorry, old boy." Liko went up to order, waving off Dane's offer to pay.

Dane fiddled his pen over the letters. His hand slowed. His eyebrows drew down. Slowly, he picked out the K, Y, L and E from *Greylock.*

He looked up at Liko, back down at the name. He rearranged the remaining letters, but they only spelled nonsense. *Corg. Groc.* He could do *Orc.* Orc was great—it perfectly described an adolescent. But then he had a G left over. Like a middle initial.

Kyle G. Orc

G for Greylock?

Gruesome?

George?

"Oh my God, you're going to hell," he mumbled, scribbling over all the letters and words, then moving his plate on top.

THANK GOD
I'M A COUNTRY BOY

They killed another pizza and another round of drinks, then wandered outside. Ken Millerton—a pitch-perfect musical genius who could pick any tune out by ear—was setting up his keyboard and a small drum set. A sign leaning against his keyboard stand read: *Yeah, I can play that.*

All the tables and fire pits were occupied, so the men moved to the stone wall enclosing the outdoor patio area. Liko hitched up to sit. Dane leaned beside him.

The pub's social media manager made a little welcome, holding the clipboard with the signup sheet, then calling "First victim to the stage."

A middle-aged man with a guitar played a couple acoustic covers and one original. Applause was generous. A woman came up and spoke to Ken. They hemmed, hawed and hummed, finding the key. Then she stepped to the mic and sang "To Make You Feel My Love." The courtyard went utterly silent and transfixed, and as the last chords died away, there were loud calls for an encore. She put her palms together and shook her head.

"One and done," she said. "Next?"

A teenage boy took the mic. Tall and gangly, with a kazoo on a string around his neck, a guitar in one hand and a small cardboard box in the other. He set the box by the mic stand, spoke to Ken, then looked around the crowd and said weakly, "Gon. Na. Vom. It."

A spattering of applause and people called encouragement. Still, you could see the kid's knees trembling inside his pant legs.

"Uh, hi, I'm Brian."

"Hiiiiii Briiiiiian."

"I'm really fucking nervous. Sorry, *sorry,* are there children present?"

"Fuck it," someone called.

"I've never played or sung in front of anyone before," Brian said. "But fuck it, I'm gonna sing this. Please be nice. Don't laugh. And uh…clap along?"

He exhaled hard, then started a stomp-clamp beat that half the audience picked up. A cappella, he belted the opening verse of John Denver's "Thank God I'm a Country Boy"

Dane jumped in his shoes as Liko let out a yell worthy of Antietam. He hopped down from the wall and picked up the beat over his head, turning to get everyone else involved. They barely needed the coaxing. By the chorus, nearly every person was on their feet, clapping, stomping and singing.

> *Well I got me a fine wife, got me an old fiddle*
> *When the sun's coming up I got cakes on the griddle*

The grin on Brian's face could've powered a small island country. He went into the second verse on guitar, and Ken played under him. Someone slipped behind the drum set and laid down a two-step riff. There was no fiddle for the solo, but Ken worked magic with buttons and dials to create one. Brian's voice got stronger and his knees held still. He got a screaming, standing, sustained ovation and was practically in tears as he bowed, shook Ken's hand, shook the drummer's hand, bowed again. The crowd yelled for more.

"No no," he said. "Like the lady said, one and done. I'm gonna go throw up now."

They pleaded. A chant began to pick up: *Bry-un! Bry-un!* Someone brought a soda to the stage. Ken got up and put an arm around Brian, encouraging him as he drank. Brian handed off the glass, picked up the box by the mic stand and gave it a shake. "I brought kazoos," he said, giving it to the closest table. "Pass them around. You can all help me with this next one."

He started the iconic riff to "Tequila" and everyone picked up the saxophone melody on kazoo. People doubled over as they tried to blow and laugh at the same time. Everyone yelling *Tequila* to the skies and cracking up harder. Brian next played "Yellow Submarine," and for his closing act, he sang Benny Bell's "Shaving Cream." The patio turned into a German beer garden, people swaying with drinks held high. Warbling and kazooing.

> *I think I'll break off with my girlfriend.*
> *Her antics are queer I'll admit.*
> *Each time I say, "Darling, I love you,"*
> *She tells me that I'm full of shhhhhhaaving cream*

*Be nice and clean
Shave every day and you'll always look keen*

"This is fucking awesome," Liko said. "I mean *look* at that kid."

Dane nodded, his body trying to contain seventeen different emotions. Pride in his community. Happiness for young Brian. Content in excellent company. Yet lonesome. Wanting Nomi. Longing for Ethan. Missing Saskia. And a rich thrum in the back of his throat every time he brushed against Liko's thigh.

This is your life right now, Diane said. *It's the story being written. Once upon a time. And then. And then. You're not at the "until finally" part. This is still "and then."*

And then Liko came to your house.

And then you invited him to stay.

And then you started walking him through the chamber mystery and telling him stories.

And then you almost kissed.

And then you went to open mic.

"Are you feeling here?" Liko asked.

Dane glanced at him, puzzled. Then he understood. "Ever so slightly not here."

"C'mere," Liko said, putting a hand on the back of Dane's neck. "I double as a human vest." He guided Dane a little forward, then back between Liko's knees. He crossed his arms over Dane's collarbones, and rested his chin on Dane's crown. His feet curled a little around Dane's legs. And he squeezed.

"There," he said. "Can you feel your edges?"

"I can now. Thanks."

"It's so hard to be present sometimes," Liko said. "Lean into the happy moments without feeling guilty. Or look at a beautiful boy and let him have his moment without resentment."

"Look at loving couples in your hometown and not think of what you lost."

They gave a doubled, identical sigh, then went on being present through a few more performers. "Switch," Liko said, so Dane sat on the wall and Liko leaned back against him, vested.

A vested interest, Dane thought. *I am invested in this guy.*

"Can I tell you something?" he said by Liko's ear.

Liko turned his head and looked up. In the firelit night, he was dazzling again.

"Know what word is inside Greylock?"

"You mean what obvious thing have I missed? Go ahead, tell me."

"Kyle."

Liko's eyes flicked side to side, blinking rapidly, then closed. "Oh for fuck's sake. It is."

Dane slid his hand up the back of Liko's head and dug fingers in his hair. He tilted Liko's face up and kissed him between the eyebrows. Liko's hand ran slowly along his leg. Dane kissed his mouth. Soft lips inside a rough beard. He didn't make it long, but he made his vested interest known.

"Want to go back?" Liko said, his palm on Dane's leg spreading wider.

"I'm going to be as piss-elegant as I can about this."

"Oh shit," Liko moaned, closing his eyes again.

"Shut up. Look at me. Yes, I want to go back. Yes, I want to sleep with you. But not yet. Not tonight. I have things I need to tell you first."

"About the Green Man Chamber?"

"Yes, but also about me."

Applause filled the patio as another song finished.

"All right," Liko said. "You're not just making an old man feel better?"

"Would you— Jesus Christ, here's a dating tip, okay? If any human being snuggles you between their thighs and kisses you, then your age isn't a problem."

"Sorry," Liko said. "It feels like forever since I've done this. With any human being."

"We're doing a paint-by-number kit, remember?"

"Right."

"For the record, I'm not interested in late twenties stupidity or mid-thirties crises. You being in your fifties is an insane turn-on. Yeah, you're in an extraordinarily fucked-up, vulnerable place right now, but I *know* that place. I'm a neighbor. Your basic shit is together and you're not after me for my money."

Liko leaned back a little further, expression mercenary. "You got money?"

Dane put their brows together. "Even better," he murmured. "I got real estate."

WHALE RIDES

"Want to swim?" Dane asked.

"I'll need to get my suit."

Dane leveled a gaze at him. "Try again. Want to swim?"

"Yes," Liko said cheerfully.

Dane switched on some lights by the pool, pulled towels out of a basket and laid them on two chaise chairs.

He and Liko looked at each other.

"You first," Dane said.

They went on looking, Liko recalling the last time he took his clothes off for anyone, it was to put on a hospital gown.

"This got hard all of a sudden," he said. "And I don't mean it to sound dirty."

Dane smiled and turned around.

"Thank you," Liko said, pulling his shirt off. He kicked his jeans off an ankle and dove. The water was perfect. A cool, jolting shot that closed around him like a fist. He surfaced in the shallow end, flipped water out of his hair, dragged it back with both hands and looked around.

Dane had taken off his vest, but still wore his jeans and shirt. He sat on the deck, knees drawn up and arms wrapped around.

"You coming in?" Liko asked.

"Soon."

Liko closed his teeth on his tongue, cutting off any and all jokes. He swam underwater to the edge. He put his hands on Dane's bare feet, then slid them around Dane's ankles. He put his face against Dane's shins and just stood still. After a minute, Dane's hand started drawing through Liko's wet hair.

"Seems every time I think I'm ready to let someone new see me, I get nervous."

"If you're nervous, don't. If you're not sure, don't. I'm a grown-ass man and this is a paint-by-number kit. I can deal with delayed gratification. The moment came once. It'll come again."

Dane scooted forward a little. He dropped one foot, then the other into the pool, soaking his jeans to the knees. Liko moved between, resting his head on Dane's thigh and letting his legs float. Naked, he couldn't tell where he stopped and the water began. He closed his eyes and let himself be weightless.

"In fact don't come in," he said dreamily. "Let's just do this."

So they sat there, Dane's hands in Liko's wet hair, or drawing up and down his back, his arms, his shoulders. A faint din of music and voices floating up the hill from the pub. Ripples lapping against the pool's sides. Every now and again, one would hum the refrain from "Thank God I'm a Country Boy." Or the other would softly sing, "Shaaaaaving cream…be nice and clean…"

"You ever date a guy," Dane asked. "Like, for real. A relationship."

"No," Liko said. "I just had fuck buddies. Good buddies, some of them. But the sex was… I don't want to say a service, but… A hobby? A shared activity?"

"A way to kill time?"

Liko laughed. "It was always straightforward. *Yo. Hey. You wanna? I wanna.* And we'd do what we wanted. Then get dressed, go somewhere else and have beers or whatever. Not talk about it. Like we just…clipped each other's toenails. I don't know."

Dane laughed, then scooped up a handful of water and poured it down Liko's back.

"I've certainly never done this," Liko said, rubbing his forehead back and forth along Dane's thigh. "Just lie in a guy's arms and let him touch me. While talking. So maybe we each have something to learn from the other?"

"When I was eighteen, I made a personal credo of not going to bed with anyone I couldn't look at with both eyes. So to speak."

Liko waited a beat, then said tentatively, "Hi?"

Dane's head tipped back, laughing. He reached up and pinched out his brown contact lens, flicked it away. Blinking rapidly, he caressed Liko's head, then his face. "Dude, I love looking at you but I'm being so careful about it."

Liko was about to protest Dane didn't need to be careful, then all at once realized, yes, he did. For a moment, Liko just floated on the idea of being looked at. Looked out for. Looked after. He reflected on how Dane had, in such a short time, given Liko a haven. Not from pain—his pain was a rolling suitcase he'd always have to lug or check or stow on the journey. Maybe that was it. Schoenfeld's was a place Liko could put his suitcase. Open or shut.

Unpacked or crammed. Dane was making both intimacy and distance for Liko. Giving him both space and closeness. Giving Liko *time,* for the mindless, indulgent purpose of killing it. Knowing Liko's sole goal in life right now as putting as many minutes as possible between him and Kyle's death and hopefully, someday, enough minutes would have accumulated to make killing himself less of an option.

Because face it, dying was still a horrifyingly attractive idea. Not just attractive but seductive. Which made Schoenfeld's, among other things, a bit of a cock-block.

"Thank you," Liko said. "Whoever sent the letter… It said nothing they could do would make it better, but maybe they could do something to make it different. It's not entirely better right now. But it is different. And it's peaceful."

"The mission of the Danelaw is peace."

"Mission accomplished."

"You do whale rides?"

"Sure."

Dane pushed Liko off his legs, then dropped into the pool, clothes and all, big bubbles and foam in his wake. Liko was reminded of a time, years ago, in the foaming wake of a ripshit argument with Janelle. He couldn't even remember what about, but afterward she was in the shower, crying. And he'd stepped in with her, clothes and all. Put arms around her and said he was sorry. They stood under the spray a long time. She nude and drenched. He fully clothed and drenched. They often referenced the moment in the years after.

"I really loved you then," she said. "No regard for yourself or your clothes. Just barged right in to apologize. It was…romantic."

Dane came up, drenched, his hair plastered down to his head. Liko took his face in both hands and brought their eyebrows together. Dane held his wrists. They stood still a long time. Liko made no move. He wasn't clicking a thing in this game. If a kiss was hidden around here somewhere, he'd let it come to him. If not, it might be for the best.

Dane floated back and turned Liko around. Liko crouched and drew Dane's arms around him.

"You look good from the back," Dane said against his cheek. "At the bar, when you were waiting for drinks. Leaning on your hands, your ankles crossed. Couldn't take my eyes off you. A few chicks were checking you out, too."

Liko bit his tongue and closed his eyes, sucking on the compliment, savoring it coming from a male voice. Letting it bookend the other night when Meg stroked the front of his shirt and insisted he always wear that color to a party.

"Thanks," he said.

"Thank you," Dane said. "For being so patient."

Liko looked up at the stars. "So much sucks, that I want good things like this to last as long as they can."

"Me too." Dane squeezed him. "Let's go."

Liko pushed off. The water streamed cool along the front of his naked body, while Dane's heavy, rough clothes ran along his back. He swam into the romantic moment. Present. Unresentful. And believing he looked good from both sides.

THE NAOMI ROAD 35

Roof boss at St. Andrew's church, South Tawton, Devon, UK

THE TRAMPOLINE

If Liko's friendship with Dane had phases, June was definitely their Debauched Era. The siren call of the Pub, with its fabulous food and drink, beckoned them across the road, and the conversation there was decidedly unrefined.

"You know your relationship has gone long-term when frombé becomes the default," Dane said.

"Frombé?"

"From behind."

Liko wheeze-laughed but Dane kept a cool face. Demanding, "What, you don't know frombé?"

"I know what it *is,* I just never heard it called that."

"And now you'll never call it anything else."

"Jesus."

"Don't tell me you and Janelle didn't have private cutesy names for your repertoire."

"Buttercup."

Dane turned over a hand. "See? I don't even want to know what that is. Tell me."

"You're too young."

"Shut up. What is it?"

Liko closed teeth over his bottom lip and slid his empty plate over.

"Fuck you," Dane said, and signaled Cora for two more shots.

Liko and tequila had never had a subtle relationship, so naturally he blabbed within five minutes. "Buttercup is kind of like reverse cowboy, except you're sitting up. And instead of kneeling across your legs, she kneels between them and gets her feet under your butt. Which lets her scooch back real close so you can…" He raised eyebrows and mimed holding a pair of hips. "Frombé. Actually now the official name is Buttercup Frombé. Buttercup for short."

Buttercup, boobs or blow jobs—what was discussed at the Pub stayed at the Pub. Back at the farmhouse, whether in the pool, the den, the kitchen or on the porch, Liko and Dane's conversation always turned to tougher topics. Harder things, sadder things. They talked about grief's journey ("Fuck that word!"), told hilarious stories about their lost loved ones, or shared memories that could bring them to their knees. The moments they were grateful for the time they had, and the moments when they looked at how they'd been so unfairly, unjustifiably *cheated,* and their thoughts turned appallingly violent. Wanting to tear the world apart and make everyone hurt as much as they did.

"Check this out." Dane passed Liko his phone, with a video of the performance artist Yoann Bourgeois. The set was a trampoline next to a tall white staircase without railings. Over and over, Bourgeois attempted to climb the stairs, only to topple over the side, bounce off the tramp, and have to begin again. Sometimes he recovered where he left off, sometimes he started over from the bottom. He took a step and fell, bounced back to take the same step again, only to fall, bounce, take the step again, fall, bounce, over and over a dozen times before achieving the next step. Maybe two steps. Then crumpling over the side.

Liko held his breath, watching Bourgeois come within two steps of the top, then roll off the edge and fall. He bounced on his back, defeated, let-ting the rebounds shrink from feet to inches. Almost coming to a complete standstill, but then somehow building momentum between bounces to get himself going again, the springs growing larger. His feet ran up the smooth side of the staircase and down again. A little further each time. Gaining purchase on an edge. This time he had it. No, not yet. This time for sure. No. One more bounce. One more good one. And then he was back on the stairs. Where the journey began all over again.

"Jesus," Liko said, resonating with understanding. "This is one of the best depictions of grief I've ever seen. And I've seen too many."

"I watch it at least once a week," Dane said. "For a long time I was focused only on the stairs and the falling. The Sisyphean struggle. One step forward, nineteen steps back. Then I started thinking more about the trampoline."

"How so?"

"Well, what is it? What's mine? What's yours? What's the thing we bounce off to keep going?"

"Huh."

"I guess I just started to marvel at its existence. That the trampoline is *there.* We all have one. Soft and cushy and bouncy, but tough. We can lie still on it, but if we start moving enough, pushing on it enough, it'll push us right back. And up. And onward."

"Yeah," Liko said. "Yeah, you're right."

"Some days it's about climbing a step or two. Other days, it's just about bouncing off the tramp. Or figuring out how to start moving again."

"Like if someone else steps onto it with you," Liko said slowly. "Just their footsteps will get you to bounce a little."

They looked at each other and bumped fists.

"The first September after Kyle died was tough," Liko said, as he and Dane hiked along Liberty Loop Trail. "Back to school always meant all this running around. School supplies. New sneakers. Physicals. Sports equipment. A million forms."

"Hemorrhaging money," Dane murmured.

"Fifty bucks here. A hundred bucks there. Filling the fridge and the pantry. Just a circus of shopping and planning and organizing and nagging. I always hated it. But that first September came around and the absolute dearth of activity smacked me in the face. I had nothing to do. Nothing to buy. Nothing to sign. Nothing to supervise. No one to nag. Money to burn. The first day of school, I was stumbling around with a cup of coffee. I looked out the window and saw our school bus come down the street. I fell on the floor and…"

"Died."

"Yeah. But," Liko said, holding up a finger. "The floor was a trampoline."

Dane smiled. "You think you're lying there dead, but you're bouncing, ever so slightly. Doesn't seem like it, but you are."

"This will be my new answer when people ask *How are you?* I'll just smile and answer, *I'm bouncing.*"

They walked quietly for a long time. Liko never found the silences between them awkward. They didn't run out of conversation, rather it seemed they ran so far ahead, jawing and jabbering, they needed to pause every now and then to let the conversation catch up.

A gentle place to lay my head, Liko kept thinking.

You make a gentle place for me to lay my head.

"Do you miss being married?" Dane asked on another night.

"To Janelle or in general?"

"Either."

"I miss having a person."

"God, same," Dane said. "I remember the first time I caught a cold when I was on my own. Man, I felt lower than low. The first cold, the first flu. Being alone in the house and sick is fucking awful. It really brought the hammer of loss down."

"Yeah, I remember my first post-separation cold," Liko said. "No longer having a person who gave a damn. It was beyond lonely."

"The worst was the first stomach bug. One of those throwing up and throwing down apocalypses. All alone, sitting on the toilet, puking into the garbage can. And nobody knowing or caring. Thinking, *I'm gonna die here. This is how they'll find me.*"

"The misery of running your own cold water on your own washcloth."

"Groping for the Clorox, wiping everything down yourself, crawling back to bed and feeling… Like what word even applies? You left *lonely* a hundred miles behind. Now you feel totally forsaken."

"Wretched."

"Insignificant."

"Abjured."

"But," Dane said. "The trampoline."

"Even as you lie on the cold tile of the bathroom floor and wish you were dead, you're bouncing."

They sat in one of their long, easy silences, nursing their drinks.

"Are you ready for the thing called love?" Liko asked.

Dane smiled and set his glass down. "Saskia asked me to wait a year before I started dating."

"And it's been…two and change?"

"Two and a lot of change."

"I have so many nosy questions."

"About?"

"Being a house of three."

"Oh that. Ask me anything," Dane said.

"You sure?"

"One, it's a much more pleasant topic than grief. Two, my dude, there's nothing I haven't been asked. I'll be thrilled if you come up with something original. Fire away."

"Um…" Liko laughed, blanking out. "Now that it's time, I can't remember what I wanted to ask."

"What's your kneejerk impression of polyamory? First image your mind comes up with."

"The three of you spooning in bed."

"Bed. Okay. The three of us rarely slept together. You've probably noticed this house has no shortage of sleeping space, so we all had separate bedrooms. Where I sleep now, with the king bed and the adjoining bath, used to be John and Mary's room. Then it became Nomi's room. You're currently staying in my old room. Ethan slept on the third floor. The whole attic space was his studio before he had the freestanding one built. Got that mapped out in your head?"

"Got it."

"Nomi and I slept together the most, usually in her room. Actually it was…" Dane trailed off. "Wow, I haven't explained this to someone in a long time," he said. "I've kind of forgotten how to make it sound simple."

"Use short words."

"I love when you say that."

"Did you have a bedroom schedule?"

"God, no. It was all instinct, mood and vibes. I don't know if it was a unique thing about our threesome, or typical. We just were. We just did. It worked. No, wait, I'm making this sound too ideal. It wasn't all effortless. Not by a long shot. I'll put it this way: We had ninety-nine problems but the sleeping arrangements weren't one."

"But the three of you rarely slept together?"

"It was a chore to get Ethan to sleep anyway. He's one of those annoying people who can function on four or five hours. And his creativity was always highest at night. We'd have to go over to the studio and demand his presence. But he hated bedtime on demand, so usually it was me and Nomi going to bed in the king and we'd wake up sometimes to find Ethan had come in. Man, he was a thrasher. He'd sleep diagonally on us. Like a dog. Or a toddler. Turning and kicking and punching. Then Nomi had to pee at least twice a night. And they both said I snored but I think they were full of shit."

"Hence, your own bedrooms."

"Three in a bed sounds romantic and thrilling, but you don't get much sleep. And not for the reasons you're thinking."

"So that negates my next image which was the three of you in the bathroom."

"The three of us sharing a bathroom would've ended in murder."

"Billpaying? Finances?"

"Business finances were handled by professionals. Jonathan Henshe Games and Ethan's art dealings were handled by his people. The farm and spa had their own people. I handled the household bills and day-to-day finances. The big picture of what money was where."

"Grocery shopping?"

"Usually Ethan. He was good at it."

"Cooking?"

"Usually Nomi. She was good at it. Ethan and I had chops in the kitchen, but we were never as good as Nomi."

"I must say the ratio of three adults to one child sounds rather genius."

"You know how exhausted couples wonder, *How do single mothers do this?* We'd always wonder, *How do couples do this?*"

"Who were the school parents?"

"Ah," Dane said, pointing a finger. "Good question."

"For want of a better word, were you *out* to the community?"

"In nursery and elementary school we kept it basic: me and Nomi were ex-spouses, Saskia was our daughter, Ethan was the stepfather. We lived in the same house because we were all friends. All went smoothly until the infamous sleepover of two thousand six."

Liko raised eyebrows. "Should I get popcorn or my Scrabble tiles?"

"So Saskia's friend Page comes to sleep over. They're bedded down on the floor of the den. Nomi and I have long made a ruling that if we have a young guest in the house, it's best I sleep in my room and Nomi in hers. It just avoids middle of the night trouble or young guests asking nosy questions. Ethan's sequestered in his studio, as usual. He'll come in at his typical ungodly hour and go up to the attic. Cool. That's settled. Nothing conjugal going on while children are present. Goodnight, everyone."

"Here's where the Universe decides to make things interesting."

"First off, Ethan does come in at one o'clock. But he's feeling amorous, so he shows up in my room. Okay. Unexpected. Sort of against the rules. But we lock the door and stifle the sounds because Nomi is on call, right?"

"Wrong?"

"She's feeling…not amorous for Ethan, but needing to connect with him in her own way. So she's gone up to the attic to wait, and fallen asleep there. Meanwhile, downstairs, Miss Page has suddenly spiked a fever."

"Oh shit."

"Saskia brings her upstairs and naturally goes to Mom's room first. But Nomi's bed is empty. So logical plan B, Saskia pounds on my door, which is locked, because…" He turned a hand over in the air.

Liko pretended to dip fingers in an invisible bucket of popcorn and crunch. "Keep going."

"Saskia's yelling for me now and I can hear Page crying. I stuff myself into clothes and open the door. The poor kid is shivering so bad she can barely stand up. Teeth chattering out of her head. Pandemonium. Nomi comes downstairs. We call Page's parents, they pick her up. Crisis averted, we go back to bed, Nomi and I thinking Page, in her feverish state, couldn't possibly have noticed Ethan was in my bed."

"But she did."

"While debriefing her parents, Page innocently mentions that Saskia's parents don't sleep in the same bedroom. Mrs. Hasen wasn't even in her room. And funny, when Mr. Strong opened his door, Mr. Hasen was in his bed."

"Oh boy. What happened?"

Dane rolled his lips in tight, then exhaled. "I think any other parent would've deduced their daughter was having a fever dream and let it go. But Page's mother was *that* mother. You know the one."

"Unfortunately."

"So we get a phone call from Sandra. Starts out friendly, Page is feeling better, thank you for taking such good care of her. But Page also said something concerning?"

"Sod off," Liko sang under his breath.

"Nomi's got the call on speaker but she's motioning at me and Ethan to be quiet. Sandra relays what Page said about the sleeping arrangements. Nomi counts off five on her fingers, then says deadpan, *And?*"

"Textbook piss-elegance," Liko said.

"I never loved her more. She put the ball right back in Sandra's court, shut up and waited."

"Spot-on. You make *them* say the quiet part out loud."

"Sandra tried again and Nomi was just like, *I'm sorry, what's the concerning part?* The bitch finally got the hint, thanked us again for our kindness and hung up. But afterward, while nothing was said to our faces, Nomi and I could feel this little change in how people acted around us at school events. A lot of staring. A lot of conversations behind hands. When Saskia had friends over and parents came to pick up, they'd make polite chitchat but you could see their eyes looking around the house. Trying to sniff out the situation. Looking for… I don't even know what. Lube and sex toys left strewn about? A coffee table book, *The Modern Ménage à Trois: What your teen needs to know.*"

Liko touched his chest. "Well, that's what I'd be looking for."

"Mothers would drop baited hooks at Nomi, like, *Well, ahem, God knows I could use a second husband.* And more than one father started making real intense eye contact with me at soccer practice. One guy flat-out propositioned me: *I'd love to get with you some time.* I actually looked over my shoulder and back at him, like, *Who me?*"

Liko said nothing, only pretended to eat more popcorn.

"It was one of the few times I got bitter and resentful about my place in the relationship," Dane said. "I wanted to clap back, *Dude, thanks, but I'm married.* But I wasn't. Not in legal reality, and not in the cover story we crafted. *Dude, thanks, but I'm committed* just doesn't have the same shut-down effect. And it takes too long to explain that *they're* married but we're all spouses, we're together, and I'm the one who sleeps with both of them and I have no desire to sleep with anyone else. You can't condense all that into a one-line zinger."

"None of your goddamn business?"

Dane sighed. "I was treading carefully for Saskia's sake. Anyway, overnight it seemed like a door opened and people were either keeping their distance, or extending invitations to swing."

"Was anyone respectfully curious about it?"

"A few people approached us and earnestly asked advice about opening their marriage."

"What advice did you give?"

Dane smiled. "Separate beds, separate sinks, communal socks. We really couldn't speak to outside liaisons and openness because we didn't have either. It was us three and only us."

"And Saskia understood the situation?"

"Saskia was, is and always will be the sharpest knife in the drawer."

A HOUSE OF THREE

IT'S EASILY DECIDED DANE will father this child, for a multitude of reasons. The strongest being he has the most complete family history.

"One barren branch of a family tree is enough for any kid," Ethan says.

Nomi whole-heartedly agrees. "I don't want my child to be hit with a medical bombshell the way I was."

"Sometimes medical bombshells come direct from family," Dane says.

"Touché, lover," she says, hugging him.

"Anyway," Dane says, "let's not put all the eggs in my basket. I'm already down one ball and I have no idea if the other one works."

But it does work. When the urologist's office calls to say his sperm sample is well within normal limits, Dane first gets light-headed, then teary.

"Are you sure?" he says.

Doctor Zajac laughs. "Positive. Motility's a touch on the low side, but nothing we can't work with if need be. Try it the old-fashioned way a few months."

"I don't believe it. I really thought it wouldn't… I didn't think I…"

"You have a vas deferens and it understands the assignment," Zajac says. "Gonads gonna nad. Congratulations. Go screw."

Fathering a child validates Dane, but it dredges up old physical grief, sometimes in bizarre ways.

"Dane, you're making the curtains ripple with these sighs," Nomi says. "What's wrong?"

He leans on the back of the glider rocker, watching Nomi feed their daughter. "It's dumb."

"Oh please, you've been listening to my dumb neuroses for the past nine months." Which is true: Instead of morning sickness, Nomi spent the first trimester in her therapist's office, dealing with all her repressed abandonment issues.

Dane runs his hand through Nomi's hair and sighs again. "You know, if my old man hadn't put me under the knife, and with the right hormones, I could've breastfed this kid. Maybe. It isn't out of the realm of possibility. I am *just* saying."

Nomi looks up at him, her shadowed eyes full of love and understanding. "I bet you could have. In fact, I know you could."

The name Saskia means *knife.* Dane and Nomi pick it out together, wanting to arm her from birth. Ethan is pleased by both the meaning, and that you can pull *a kiss* out of Saskia. It leaves an extra A he doesn't know what to do with. Worrisome extra letters can ruin Ethan's sleep in a way no newborn infant can.

But then the exhausted new mother speaks: "The leftover A is from when my name went from Naomi to Nomi. It's been waiting patiently all this time for a purpose. Now it's in Saskia's name. A kiss A."

Which is so brilliant that everyone rises from the dinner table and applauds.

Taking no chances, the three parents cram her birth certificate with powerful names: Saskia Helen Mary Ruta Hasen-Strong. John suggests they drop the other shoe and use Hasen-Strong von Schoenfeld. It's too much for the form, but when calling their daughter in to dinner, it's fun to stand on the back porch and yell, "Saskia Helen Mary Ruta Hasen-Strong von Schoenfeld!"

She's dynamite because she has Nomi's best qualities with a solid foundation of love and security under it.

"Saskia is the best thing I ever did," Dane says.

"If I had Saskia's confidence," Nomi says, "I'd hold world domination."

"She's so smart," the genius Ethan says softly. "She's scary smart."

Saskia calls Ethan either by name, or by Hasenpfeffer. Sometimes he calls her Saskapfeffer. For Nomi, Saskia uses the Latvian *Mammu,* which is shortened to Mam. Dane is Dad, which becomes *Deddy* when Saskia becomes a Rhodes Scholar.

"Is this the grandest deddy of the Danelaw Deddies?" she'll inquire on phone calls from Oxford. And the Great Dane will answer, "Yes, 'tis I."

They're a family. They have their traditions, their rituals, their silly nicknames, their weird words for things. All three parents, but Dane especially, vow always to be honest with this cherished child, but understand honesty must be conveyed in an age-appropriate way.

"Keep it simple," Nomi says to her partners in the tender years. "Answer only the questions she asks. When she wants to know more, she'll ask more."

So the years pass, adoring Saskia, spoon-feeding, answering questions, waiting for the time she makes a quantum leap and realizes something is different at her household. She finally brings it up on a winter evening when she's ten. The family is gathered at the long kitchen table, cozily occupied with projects. Ethan is drawing. Dane is cutting out paper snowflakes for the windows. Saskia's working on a puzzle. Nomi is sorting her seeds. Important conversations always happen around this table and, Dane notices, they go particularly well when everyone has a bit of distraction in their hands.

"So Mam, you and Dad are my parents, right?"

"That's right," Nomi answers. And no more.

"I mean, like, you made me. Your egg, his sperm."

"Correct."

Only answer the question asked, Dane thinks.

"But you're married to Ethan."

"Yes."

"You don't sleep in the same bed."

"Sometimes we do."

"But not all the time. Usually you and Dad sleep in the big bed."

"That's right, we do."

"Why?"

"Because I stay up too late and when I do go to sleep, I fart all night," Ethan says. "Nobody wants to sleep with me. Not even the dog."

"But I don't get it," Saskia says. "Mammu, you and Dad kiss and hug and act all mushy, and you sleep in the same bed, but you're not married. Ethan's your husband but…" She trails off, more confused, realizing her mother and Ethan occasionally get kind of mushy. And sometimes sleep together. The gears are turning in her scary smart head, but math just ain't mathing.

"You probably notice," Dane says, brows furrowed around a tricky angle he's trying to cut, "that most of your friends have just two adults in their house. Which is how it usually is in families."

"But families can look all kinds of ways," Ethan says. "You know kids who have two mothers and two fathers."

"And kids whose parents divorced and then got married again to other people. So they have stepmothers or stepfathers."

"I know *that,*" Saskia says patiently. "But none of them have parents *and* a step-parent in the same house. Nobody I know has three parents, and I've never read any books where there's three."

Nomi looks up. Her face glows with love and pride, knowing her daughter measures the world by what she can find in books.

"Ethan and I are married," Nomi says, "because I got really sick and getting married helped me get the care I needed." She put her hand on Dane's arm. "I'm not married to Dad because it's against the law to be married to more than one person."

Saskia looks at Dane. "You mean, you and Mam were never married?"

"No."

"If I hadn't gotten sick," Nomi says, "I wouldn't have gotten married. To either Dad or Ethan."

"Is that allowed?"

"It's against the law to be married to more than one person," Ethan says, "but there's no law saying unmarried people can't be parents."

"It's traditional," Dane says. "It's usually what happens. But not always."

"Any two people who love each other can become parents. They don't have to get married," Nomi says.

"But wait," Saskia says. "You said if you didn't get sick, you wouldn't have married Ethan."

"Ethan carries our health insurance through his work. I was able to get the best kind of care if I was his legal wife."

Saskia looks between Nomi and Ethan. "So you're not in love?"

For a microsecond, Dane questions every choice he's made. Wondering in despair what he's done. What they've all done.

Your mission is peace, the voice of John Schoenfeld reminds him. *Only you can write the laws that keep your peace.*

He shakes off the doubt and reaches across and sideways to take the hands of his life mates.

"We," Dane says to his daughter, "are in love."

"We've always been in love," Nomi says, squeezing Dane's fingers hard.

"It's not the way in every house," Ethan says. "But it's the way in this house. Look…" He gets up and peruses the kitchen wall where hang a dozen depictions of the Three Hares. In pen and ink, watercolor, acrylic, collage. He takes one down and brings it back to the table. "You know how I'm obsessed with this motif."

"Sure."

"What's so interesting about it?"

"It's an optical illusion. It looks like each hare has two ears, but really they share three."

"Right now, tonight, knowing what you know about me, Mam and Dane, do you see it any differently?"

Saskia looks at the motif a long time. She looks at each adult, then back down. She slowly turns the picture frame to make the hares chase each other.

Then she smiles.

"It's you three."

"That's right," Ethan says. "And you know what this is?" His index finger comes down on the triangle made by the three ears. In this particular piece, it's a nighttime sky filled with stars. "This magic space right here?"

Saskia bites her bottom lip a second, then smiles wider. "Me?"

Ethan's finger comes off the glass and points at her. "You."

All four of them inhale and exhale together. A little cozy accomplishment pulls a chair up to the table, pleased. The adults gently turn their heads back to their respective puttering, leaving the girl to ponder all the things in her heart.

If she wants more information, she'll ask, Dane thinks. *If she's gathered enough, let her be.*

"So you're all together," she says after a while.

"Yes," they answer.

"Some people don't understand this," Nomi adds. "Or they don't approve. They think love only works in twos. That people are meant to live, love and parent in pairs. Most of the time, people will mind their own business and keep their opinions to themselves. But what did I tell you the other day about life—you know, when Wendy Santorelli was giving you grief?"

"You're always gonna run into jerks."

"Yep. You can fight the jerks, or you can give them nothing to work with. In other words, what happens in this house is nobody's business but ours. If you want to keep telling people that Dad and I used to be married, but we divorced and now I'm married to Ethan, and Dad lives here because we've all stayed friends, that's perfectly fine with us." She glanced around the table. "Am I right, guys?"

Ethan raises a hand. "Stepfather representing."

Dane raises one too. "Ex-husband reporting for duty."

"But it's kind of a lie," Saskia says.

Anxiety uncoils in Dane's chest, for this is what keeps him up at night. His daughter having to weave a web of dishonest stories to keep her peace. Under the table, Ethan's foot presses against Dane's calf. On top of the table,

Nomi's hand strokes his forearm as she says, "You do not have to lie. You can *choose* which parts of the story to tell and which parts to keep private. You can *choose* whom you trust with what."

"The truth is easiest," Dane says, pleased that his voice sounds so normal over the thump of his heart. "But it might end with people asking nosy questions or jerks making unkind remarks."

Saskia nods in big up and down arcs, her mouth pursed a little.

"So what's the story you want us all to tell?" Nomi says, in her best family meeting tone. "We can't have four different stories. There has to be one, and you need to help us decide."

"I think," Saskia says slowly, addressing Nomi, "I'll just keep saying what I always have. You and Dad were together once but not anymore. You're married to Ethan now. But you're still friends with Dad. You're all really good friends and we live in the same house."

"Which part of that isn't true?"

"The part where you and Dad aren't together anymore?"

"That's right."

"You're all together."

The heart of the house thumps now, as they all answer truthfully: "Yes."

"Together, like…romantic."

"Yes."

"You all have sex together?"

"Not together," Nomi says.

"One at a time," Dane says.

"And me rarely," Ethan says, surprising everyone. "This is very personal, but I actually don't like sex much. Which is my private business that I only trust to a few special people."

"Okay," Saskia says.

"I love Nomi and Dane passionately, but it's a different passion. An emotional passion. They're my best friends in the world."

"Oh," Saskia says slowly. "I didn't know you could be married but not have sex."

Nomi smooths her daughter's hair. "There are a million different ways to be married. A million ways to be romantic. A million ways to be friends."

"A million ways to be a family," Dane says.

"Maybe not a million," Ethan mumbles.

"Fine. There are four hundred and seventy-two ways to do things," Dane says. "Happy? The point is, Sask, you can decide who gets to know which is your way."

"However," Nomi says, raising a hand. "A favor? Tell us before you confide to others? Call a meeting so we can discuss. We need to know who knows, so we're not surprised when we find out they know. Is that fair?"

"That's fair," Saskia says. Her brows knit for another minute, and then she goes back to her puzzle. The three adults stare at her, then glance at each other. Ethan winks. Dane touches his forehead. Nomi mouths, *I love you.*

Then they let it be.

THE MANAGERS OF HEAVEN

"So," Liko said.

"So?"

"Sex."

Dane laughed. "About time you asked."

"See also: ways to kill time."

"Along with us spooning in blissful slumber, did you envision the three of us fucking every night?"

"Well, maybe not every night."

Dane extended a hand. "I'm sure this is shocking news but hello, I'm bisexual."

Liko shook it. "I'm positive you already knew this but hello, so am I."

"I'm bi, Ethan is gay, Nomi was straight. Nomi and Ethan didn't have sex. They'd go to bed together, but just to sleep."

"I see."

"I was intimate with both of them, but Nomi was my lover all the time while Ethan was more an occasional thing. Sex wasn't a driving force in his life."

Liko smiled. "I'm getting on in years but I do know what *asexual* means."

"I didn't know it spanned a whole spectrum of behaviors and preferences. Ethan experienced sexual attraction, but it was a solitary pleasure with no target. He enjoyed the abstract idea of sex in his head, but had no need to share it with a partner. Now, when I met him, no word existed for his specific experience. He and others like him were just thrown under the *asexual* umbrella. It wasn't until the twenty-tens that he came across the word *aegosexual*."

"Which means sexual attraction with no target?"

Dane nodded. "And while I don't want to imply I alone was able to change Ethan's basic human nature, as the years went by, I gradually did become a target. The face that would sometimes show up in his fantasies. Gradually. Sometimes."

"A partner to share pleasures of the head with," Liko said.

"Exactly. He was like some rare orchid and every now and then his flower would bloom in my sunshine. The longer we were together, the more frequent it became, but still nothing compared to my sex life with Nomi. It was point-less to compare the two anyway. Or think Ethan would ever change. I had to accept him as he was and take the sex as it came."

"Was it hard?"

"Sure. Frustrating as fuck sometimes. But marriage is a lot of compromise and life is constant multitasking. I could be totally accepting of Ethan's nature *and* still wish he were a more aggressive lover. Be a top and take my ass to church. *Yes, I actively wish this. No, I will never have it from Ethan. But I love him. And I'm sticking around. Because when he does come looking for me, it means something...*

"If I learned anything from Ethan, it's that sex and romance are two com-pletely different things. Because that guy wasn't sexual but he was romantic as fuck. This was not an undemonstrative partner. He left no doubt, zero, that we were valued. He would do anything for us and he did. If we had a dream, a plan, a wish, a desire, a need—no matter big or small, he was right there. *I'm in, let's do this, what can I do, how do I help?*

"He lived for making me and Nomi psychologically visible. He wrote love notes. Illustrated love notes. He was forever capturing the little moments of our lives on scraps of paper. He sketched the way other people take photos on their phones. He'd draw us and leave the sketch on our pillows. He'd make treasure hunts. God, he couldn't ever give a present without making a whole quest to find it. Crossword puzzles clues that were about us. Trivia about us. Private jokes. Anagrams, all the time with the anagrams because the hidden words inside names was such a *thing* with him. It was how he made love. Literally how he created it. Sex wasn't a driving force but he loved to *love*. Loved to cherish. Christ, he… Sometimes I'd walk into my bathroom and he'd have left a Post-it on the mirror: *I've known you 5,976 days.* He kept track. And I kept the Post-its. I have a whole folder of them. All those notes and games and sketches and demonstrations of love. It's all I have left of Ethan. I don't know, should I burn it? Be buried with it? Plant it in the ground with a new wisteria vine?"

"You've given this some thought," Liko said.

"Because, ways to kill time." Dane stretched and looked at his watch. "Holy shit, we've been talking for hours. You hungry?"

"Always."

"I'll throw something together."

"Need help?"

"Nah." Dane ruffled Liko's hair. "Enjoy the sunset."

Liko did, watching as the skies darkened and the first stars appeared. Thinking about everything for a long stretch of time. Followed by a longer interval of thinking about nothing. The scent of onions frying in butter wafted from the screen door. His stomach growled. His eyes drooped.

He dozed.

AT THE SOUND OF a chime, his chin came up and his eyes popped open. He glanced at the side table where his phone lay, pinging an incoming text.

It was Janelle.

I miss him so much.

Liko rested fingers on the phone but didn't pick it up. He always had to take a minute before he responded to these overtures. Decouple from Janelle Greenman, the ex-wife who hurt him so badly, and recouple with Janelle Dalusio, the mother of his son, who was the only one who truly understood the smoking crater in the middle of his soul.

When he was in place, he picked up the phone. Texted: *I do too. So much.*

Everyone's posting prom pictures and graduation pictures. I want to be happy for people but at the same time, I want to scream because it's so unfair.

Yeah. Never a good time to be on social media, but especially in June. Fucking brutal.

June followed by July and family vacations. Then comes back to school pictures. College acceptance pictures. Holiday pictures. It won't ever stop.

I know. I can't stand it.

Can I come over?

He took a breath. *I'm not at home. I'm in New York. Doing something. Something for Kyle, actually. I can tell you about it?*

Call me.

He did, and he told her. She didn't like video games and she'd always been Bad Cop in the policing of Kyle's screen time. Now she listened. Asked questions. Went online and downloaded the *Three Hares* game and said she'd give it a try.

"It's a gentle game," Liko said. "And a beautiful one. No violence, and the only adversary is your own frustration."

"All right."

"Take your time with it. And make sure you have the next thing lined up."

"If you solve this mystery, what'll be your next thing?"

"Sharing it. I don't know after that."

A long, aching pause before Janelle said, "Tell me what Kyle's doing."

Liko closed his eyes. "He's sleeping."

"Are you sure?"

"It was a long day in Heaven. All days in Heaven are jam-packed because you get to do everything you ever wanted. Learn everything. Experience everything. Talk to anyone in any moment of time. Climb every mountain chain. Step on one of the moons of Jupiter. Touch the edges of the Universe. Watch galaxies being born. Discover who killed JFK. He's learning so much. He's smarter than we are and he's glad we finally know it."

A bubble of teary laughter in his ear. "You make it easy to believe."

"He was run ragged from one end of the stars to the other," Liko said. "He had lunch with Kurt Cobain. Julia Child cooked for them. He got drunk with Hemingway. Dropped acid with Jim Morrison. Had sex with Helen of Troy. Touched the face of God. Now he's sleeping. Sprawled in the center of a giant bed like a rockstar. Head under the pillow. A foot sticking out. Best sleep he's had since he was a newborn."

Janelle sniffed. "God, I needed this."

"He's sleeping so soundly. Hidden under the covers but I can see them moving up and down. Big long breaths like ocean waves. He has no worries. No stress. No drama. Nothing bothers him. Nothing hurts him. Nothing worries him."

"I can see it," she whispered. "Keep going."

"A chair is pulled up by the bed. Loved ones who have gone before take turns coming to sit by him. Watch over him. Your father. My grandparents. Ancestors we couldn't dream of. His four thousandth cousin once removed. The ancient caveman who possessed our Y chromosome. Ultimate Alpha Grandpa, first of his name."

"Do you think he'll be reincarnated?"

"Absolutely. All children who die before their time don't stay long in Heaven. A really elite angel is assigned to their case. It's a whole process.

Heaven, Incorporated has to make a formal apology. Dress in sackcloth and kneel in the celestial courtroom to explain how they screwed this up and what they'll do to make it right. Whose head will roll in atonement. A walk of shame. Wings clipped. You know, like a military thing where they strip your epaulettes and break your sword."

"Then exile you to Devil's Island."

"Right?"

"Get me the goddamn manager."

"The managers of Heaven could not handle you. And Kyle is letting them know in no uncertain terms. *You're lucky it's me here and not my mother. She would burn this place to the ground. Hell will be the new Heaven when she gets through with you.*"

"I wish it were me."

Liko knew better than to chide her or insist she didn't mean it. "I know," he said. "Me too. We were supposed to go first. It's all out of order and no heavenly court hearing or rolled heads will ever make it right."

"When he comes back," she said, "will we know him?"

"I'm not sure."

"Pretend you are."

"Souls are eternal," he said slowly. "When we made love, we manifested a door this particular soul could walk through. We claimed it, shaped it with our genes and called it *Kyle*. You and me, we're in an elite club that has privileged access to this soul. We made one of the portals he can use. He belongs to us across space and time and dimensions and parallel Universes. He'll brush up against our lives. Maybe in an incidental way. Or a profound way. We probably won't realize it. But he *will* cross our paths." He sighed and pulled at his hair. "Or not. I don't know."

"You do know," she said. "You're the only one who does."

"Tonight's hard."

"Lee, I'm so sorry I hurt you."

"I know. I know you are and I appreciate you saying so."

"Can I stay on with you a little longer?"

"Sure."

"You're not busy?"

"No, I'm just sitting on the front porch."

"What is this place you're staying. Tell me. Describe it."

He did. She got on Google maps on her end and looked at the satellite view of the intersection of Oak Hill Road and Route 34. Liko took her on a guided tour. He wasn't sure why he lied and said he was staying in one of the cottages. But it didn't matter. Not tonight.

"And this guy, Dane. He's cool?"

"He's really cool," Liko said. "Easy to be with. No bullshit, no drama, no expectations. And he's in the club. His wife died a couple years ago." He hesitated. "They were actually in an open marriage."

"Really?"

"It's not the right term. They and a third man were a… I won't say *throuple*, he can't stand it. They were together. Always together. It didn't start out two and a third came along. They were all friends and it turned romantic."

"But then she died."

"Yes. And the other partner left him. So he gets it."

A long breath in and out. "That's good. I mean, good you've found a new friend who's sympathetic. And you're having an adventure."

"Yeah. He's friends with some good people so I'm slowly getting social again. But if I get all brooding and weepy, the farm has lots of places to disappear."

"Sounds like you're right where you're supposed to be," Janelle said.

"And you?"

"I got a little side job. At a dog groomer. I just wash dogs all day long. They're good company. They don't say a damn word, only gaze adoringly like I'm the best thing that happened since treats."

"Oh, did I mention Heaven is full of dogs?"

"You did not."

"Six are on the bed with Kyle. About fourteen more on the floor. All the dogs. The best dogs. He went to this seminar and got to watch the entire evolution of dogs from dire wolf to Labradoodle. You think IMAX 3D is cool, wait until you see the movie theaters in Heaven."

"The popcorn must be out of this world."

"It is. Perfect ratio of butter and salt. And it never gets stuck in your teeth."

They were quiet a long time, listening to each other breathe.

"Lee, I'm so sorry," she whispered.

"I know. It's behind us. It happened and it hurt me, but there's precious little I give a fuck about right now."

"I understand."

"No, wait. That came out meaner than I intended."

"It didn't."

"Let me finish. I don't ever want to talk about George. But I do want to talk about Kyle. You're the only one I *can* talk to about him. So whenever it's a hard night like this and you want to text or call and say *I miss him so much,* I'll pick up. I'm his father and I'll always answer in that context. I'll talk about Heaven and tell stories about his day. I'll use present tense. I'll believe he'll cross our paths again and help you believe it too. Because we can do this however the fuck we want, and if we say in Heaven, we're still a family, then that's how it is. Full stop. You and me are still *us* in that context. Fuck anyone who says otherwise."

She was crying now.

"We're not married anymore and Kyle is gone, but we can still be a family," Liko said, his voice raising with the conviction. "Still be the portal for his soul. Still be us. It's the only *us* that matters and we can be good to each other. All right?"

"In that context, I love you."

"I love you in that context too," he said. "I miss him so much."

"You call or text me. I'm nowhere near as good as you at creating scenes, but I'll do my inarticulate best."

"What's he doing?"

"He's sleeping. Out like a light. Big day in court tomorrow but he's not worried about it. He's not worried about anything. Well, maybe his hair. But I assume the barbers in Heaven are pretty fucking lit."

Liko smiled. "You feel a little better now?"

"Yeah. And I have a new game to play. Goodnight, Lee."

"'Night, babe."

Liko set the phone down on the side table and laced his hands over his heart. He thought about a jovial barber having a ball with Kyle's mop of tawny hair. He pictured his son in a slick suit and tie. Cufflinks and a pocket square. Shoes like mirrors. A brisk morning in celestial court followed by lunch with Nostradamus. Kyle would attempt to show off all his new knowledge and the prophet would reply dryly, "I know… I know… Kid, I *know.*"

Liko smiled, sipping a cocktail of happy sadness. Wondering why *babe* still fell so easily out of his mouth when talking to Janelle. Looking for his son in the stars. Believing that in Heaven, the three Greenmans were still a family.

"I love us," he said softly, daring anyone to believe otherwise.

THE NAOMI ROAD 36

Roof boss at St. Michael's church, Spreyton, Devon, UK

A PHANTOM MARRIAGE

"...Because we can do this however the fuck we want, and if we say in Heaven, we're still a family, then that's how it is. Full stop. You and me are still *us* in that context. Fuck anyone who says otherwise."

A hand poised to push open the screen door, Dane stopped in his tracks and froze.

"We're not married anymore and Kyle is gone, but we can still be a family," Liko said.

Oh shit, it's Janelle.

Dane slowly and carefully backtracked, making no sound.

"...Still be us," Liko was saying. "It's the only *us* that matters and we can be good to each other. All right?"

Dane crept back to the kitchen, feeling weird. Just one side of the conversation sounded so painfully intimate and vulnerable, even accidentally overhearing seemed a violation of privacy.

And I'm suspicious because you sometimes sleep with your ex-wife.

He'd made pasta with caramelized onions and peas. He put some on a plate, sprinkled parmesan cheese and ground fresh pepper on top. Then he sat and picked at it.

The pile of today's mail was rubber-banded on the table. Dane broke it apart and flipped through, not at all surprised to find another postcard from Ethan. The man was moving at a brisk clip through Devon. Today's sketch was from St. Michael's in Spreyton. Perhaps a half-dozen left in the UK before he'd go back to the continent, looping through France, Switzerland and Germany. Heading for Paderborn.

When are you going to show these to Liko? Diane asked.

"Soon," he said.

The front door opened and closed. Dane was sure Liko wasn't coming in to eat, rather to collect his car keys and drive to Norwalk. But he did come into the kitchen, looking perfectly fine.

"Smells amazing," he said, getting a plate.

Dane stopped playing with his food and took a bite. "There's white wine in the fridge. Or open a red if you want." He slid the postcard to the bottom of the mail pile and perused the L.L. Bean catalog.

"Janelle called me," Liko said, pouring wine.

"Everything okay?"

"Bad day. She was missing Kyle. Called to connect."

Dane smiled. "I was actually coming to call you in for dinner and heard a bit of it."

Liko sat. "Which bit?"

"Still being a family in Heaven and fuck anyone who says otherwise. You're still an *us*. You can be good to each other."

Liko nodded. "Think I handled it okay?"

Dane blinked. "Dude, more than okay. It was a beautiful thing to say to her."

"Right," Liko said gruffly.

"Do you believe it? In your heart?"

"Yes."

His own heart fretted, knowing it lived within a Great Dane, on a farm that had long been a haven for lost souls and grieving spirits. He gathered together every scrap of compassion and empathy, every last dreg of courage, and asked, "Do you want to go see her?"

Liko was quiet a long moment, staring straight ahead. "I just want him back."

"Yeah."

"This is nothing I expect anyone to understand, but I don't think of sex with Janelle as sex. It's…"

"Time travel?" Dane said.

Now Liko looked at him hard. "Exactly."

They ate in tired silence a while, each going back to get another helping. "I was thinking," Dane said, "about widowhood versus divorce. Not in a competitive, one-upmanship way about who suffers worse. Just the different ways a marriage can end. When it ends by death, a sudden, unexpected death, the survivor is kind of like an amputee. The spouse is gone but they still feel the marriage. A phantom marriage."

Liko chewed and swallowed. "As opposed to divorce, which is a slower uncoupling?"

"I guess."

He nodded thoughtfully. "You separate and live apart, preparing yourself for surgery."

"You know what, never mind," Dane said. "It all sucks. Can I show you something?"

Liko blinked, bewildered. "Sure."

Dane retrieved today's postcard and slid it down the table. "Start with that. Don't drip anything on it. Be right back."

He got the others and dealt them out on the kitchen table. Thirty-six cards in all.

"I don't understand," Liko said, now walking along the rows. "Are these from a fan?"

"They're from Ethan. He's been walking the route of the game, sprinkling Nomi's ashes in all the locations."

"You're kidding me. Really?"

"Yeah."

Liko gave a low whistle. "He's sending these cards to let you know where he is?"

"I guess." Dane drummed fingers on the back of a chair. "Not sure why I didn't show them to you sooner."

Liko sat down again and picked up his fork. "It's none of my business."

Which wasn't quite what Dane wanted to hear. But what did he want—a jealous rage? He rounded the table again, pushing edges square, lost in a game where he didn't know the rules.

"Dude, sit down," Liko said gently. "Your food's going cold."

Like a sullen teenager, Dane slid into his seat and took an unenthusiastic bite.

"He's in Devon and the game ends in Paderborn," Liko said. "Then what?"

"I don't know."

"Think he'll come back?"

Dane shrugged.

Liko corralled his last two peas onto the tines of his fork. "I'm an observant fellow. I like to think I'm a good listener. And a little while ago, I heard you say that whenever Ethan came looking for you, it meant something." He ate the peas and twirled the fork to point at Dane. "You also just said something interesting about the sudden end of a marriage, leaving the survivor to feel a phantom pain."

"Kind of like still being a family in Heaven."

Liko chewed his last bite reflectively, then took a sip of wine. "Two questions," he said. "When you were together, did Ethan tell you, and I mean say the words, *I'm in love with you?*"

"Yes."

"And at any point while uncoupling, did he say, *I'm not in love with you anymore?*"

"No."

Liko nodded. "Me and Janelle didn't either. Not to each other. Maybe she said it to someone else but I can't remember telling anyone. She broke my heart, she stabbed me in the back, she betrayed me, she blew up our life and our home. But I honestly can't remember telling anyone, not even my therapist, *I'm not in love with her anymore.*" He smiled and gestured between them. "I don't know what the point is. I'm just throwing it on the already crowded table."

"Maybe I'm flattering myself that there's a deeper meaning to these postcards," Dane said. "They all say the same thing on the back. Ethan never had issues telling me how he felt. More the opposite. If he had something to say to me, he'd say it. But he hasn't, so I need to just take the cards at face value. They're status updates along his journey, end of story. He's moving on. I need to get going, too."

He polished off the wine in his glass and thumped it on the table. "Sorry for the speech. Part of the moving on will be fine-tuning my sparkling conversation."

Liko shrugged. "I'm not here to be entertained."

"Why *are* you here?" Dane mumbled, shaking his head.

"Because I wanted to bed you the first time I saw you. So I forged Jonathan Henshe stationery to write myself a letter that would give me an excuse to ring your doorbell."

Dane knew he was joking, still he felt his eyebrows draw down. "Really?"

Liko sucked his teeth and pretended to throw what was in his glass at Dane's face.

"I told you I flirt like a moron."

"You also told me you were just going to focus on doing the next thing."

"That's right."

Liko's hand reached and dropped onto Dane's forearm. "Well, I'm a thing. And I'd like to be next."

His hand slid up Dane's arm, across his jaw and around the back of his head. It wasn't much of a kiss at first. Just two laughing mouths colliding.

"I also kiss like a moron," Dane said.

Liko's other hand slid on Dane's face. "Stop talking," he whispered, and now the kiss calmed down. Slowed down. Opened up and got interested. Dane's hands slid along Liko's chest, feeling muscles contract hard against his palms, then soften around a little moan. Dane curled fingers around Liko's shirt, pulling him closer. He turned into the kiss, curling his tongue so the stud dragged along Liko's tongue. Liko sighed deep in his throat, fingers tightening in Dane's hair.

"You would kiss me after I just ate fried onions," he murmured.

"Um, you kissed me," Dane said. Behind his blue eye, Diane was smoothing her hair and catching her caramelized breath.

Liko kissed him a few more times, then ran his thumb across Dane's mouth. They sat still a while, foreheads pressed together, quiet and smiling.

"I told you once," Liko said, "I was used to sex with men being an immediate thing. Fast and service-oriented. Get in, get off and get out. If you were any other man, I'd have shagged you yesterday. But you're not like any man I've ever met. You're not like any person I've ever met. So… Where was I going with this?"

"Hopefully you mean the slow pace is frustrating as fuck but you're kind of enjoying it?"

"I really am. I know the pace is slow because you have more to tell me about your life and your childhood and what your father did to you. More about your body, which you wisely keep guarded." Liko sat back and reached for his glass. "Anyway, thanks for the snog." He swirled the wine around, expression thoughtful. "Man, I miss making out. Whenever Janelle and I hook up, we're too busy crying to kiss. I don't want it from her anyway, it's too…"

"It's what people in love do," Dane said.

"Yeah. But for real, if you want someone to flirt with like a moron and occasionally snog, I'm your man."

The color was up high along his cheekbones, still he looked unfazed, easy and trustworthy. Nothing about him pushed or pressed on Dane.

It's time, Diane said, and Dane didn't question her. He reached in his back pocket for his phone and opened his maps app.

"So, when you drive to Long Island," he said, "do you take the Throggs Neck or the Whitestone?"

"Depends on traffic but usually the Whitestone."

"Ever look under it?"

"What do you mean?"

"As you're crossing the span, ever look down at the gorgeous houses fronting the East River and wonder to yourself, *Who lives there?*"

"I'm sure I have."

"I lived there."

Dane turned the map layers to satellite, pinched and moved around until he was zeroed in. "This was my house," he said, turning the screen toward Liko.

The house, mansion rather, was indeed in prime real estate position. Fronting the river on one side, abutting a small city park on the other. With what had to be speechlessly beautiful views of Manhattan, Bronx, and Little Neck Bay, and an eye-watering price tag.

"Damn," Liko said admiringly.

Dane moved west a little and pointed. "On a clear day, you could see Riker's Island." He moved back east and touched a pin down in the mansion. "This place was a different kind of prison."

"You look so good right now," Liko said quietly. Again his hand reached and his fingers moved through Dane's hair. "Give me a second to fill up on this. Then I'll listen to whatever you want to tell me."

"None of it is good."

"I'm in, but thanks for the heads up."

ALONE TOGETHER

It is the last day of the year 4 BC.

Danelaw Strong stands on a step ladder at the kitchen counter, fenced in by its safety rails. A sweet, swishing feeling around his knees because his legs are bare and he's wearing a *(skirt)*.

Helen stands behind him and her hands are soft in his hair, fingernails scratching along his scalp and sending rivers of goosebumps all over his arms. "Shh," she whispers. "This is secret."

She's scraping and drawing his hair into an elastic band, which is both secret and naughty. Helen and Sir have Little Fights about his *(hair)* and Bigger Fights when he wants to wear a *(skirt)*. But today there is no Fighting. In fact, the house in Malba hasn't heard raised voices in three months because Dane's father has been Away on Business, and in that time, Dane's hair has grown long enough to pull back in a little ponytail. Helen told all the Help to go on vacation, so it's been just her and Dane. The two of them. Or rather, in Dane's heart, the three of them: Boy-me, Girl-me, and Mom-me. Alone together in the kitchen. It's something Helen always says: "I like to be alone together."

Dane and Helen have been living in the kitchen. It's the *best* kitchen because it has a fireplace at one end and a big couch in front of the fireplace where Dane takes naps. After Marizabet's bedroom, this is his favorite room in the house. Helen lets him help with cooking, teaches him to properly use knives and chop vegetables. She sings songs. Tells stories. Listens to everything Dane tells her. Takes him seriously. Asks serious questions.

He loves her terribly.

The last day of 4 BC, Dane is in the kitchen with Helen, helping her cook. He stands on the stepladder with the safety rails, chopping vegetables with his special knife. It's plastic, but its edge can really cut things. After many knicks and scratches on his fingers, he's learned to be careful with it.

White lights line the kitchen windows. Paper snowflakes dangle on invisible black threads. Cold outside, but warm within because a fire is burning in the fireplace. Stockings hang from the mantel, which is festooned with pine branches and oranges. The air is spicy and festive. Dane's hair is pulled into a little tail and he's wearing clothes that are against the law when Sir is home. A green *(skirt)* with sequined candy canes around the waist. It swishes loose and lovely around his bare knees. His head is warm and snug inside his favorite fur hat with the rabbit ears. They're white and silky soft and the most perfect eggshell pink inside—the exact pink of the walls in Marizabet's room.

Dane and Helen are singing Christmas carols. Loud. Helen's favorite album is playing at high volume, and the two of them are singing at the top of their lungs, which is one of Dane's favorite expressions.

"I love you at the top of my lungs," he shouts in between verses.

Helen laughs and laughs. "I love you so much, I have to *scream.*"

This competitive hullabaloo is a mistake. They are screaming and singing and laughing so loud, they don't hear the sound of helicopter rotors outside.

Sir comes into the kitchen.

This is bad.

Sir is not alone.

Marizabet is with him.

This is strange, because she is supposed to be Away at School. Sir has her hair wrapped around his hand and is dragging her in a way that makes Dane's hand go to the back of his own head, horrified. His throat drops to the top of his lungs, then to the bottom of his lungs. His lungs drop into his stomach and his fingers reach to pluck at the skirt around his waist. He is wearing all the clothes that are against the law.

This is bad.

Dane has been very, very bad.

Things happen quickly, and already Dane's memory is putting hands over his eyes, telling him not to look. Not to listen. Not to remember.

But he can peek between fingers. He can remember a few things from the first day of 5 BC.

Marizabet doesn't look like a princess anymore. She's crying, her clothes are torn and her nose and mouth are bloody.

Helen turns from the counter. Dane sees her eyes go wide and narrow into slits. He will remember this all his days—how his mother's eyes turn to sideways windows of fury.

She takes the plastic cutting knife away from Dane and pushes him behind the couch. She throws herself at Sir.

The hand with the white knife comes down and Sir bellows like a lion as Helen cries, "Marie, run…"

Dane pushes his face into the cushioned couch frame. He shuts his eyes, puts hands over his ears, and bites his tongue hard, the way he does when Sir hits him with the belt.

Memory, wanting to be helpful, grabs a cloth and starts scrubbing things away in Dane's head.

No, no, this isn't important.

You're not really here.

This isn't happening.

It's just a dream.

Don't worry. Pay no attention. You'll forget this soon.

All the while, the Christmas music has played at the top of its lungs. The end of the record is reached and the kitchen goes eerily quiet.

Dane peeks around the back of the couch, one of the ears from his rabbit hat folding across his eyebrows.

Marizabet is gone.

Helen is lying down on the floor.

Sir is getting to his feet, a hand at his back. He looks at the hand, shakes his head, then he kicks Helen.

Dane's eyes narrow to slits.

A new sound fills the kitchen: helicopter rotors. Sir's chopper is taking off again.

This is strange.

Sir hauls Helen to her feet and drags her, stumbling and moaning, to the windows. He looks out, craning his neck. His hands shake Helen's body in short, sharp jerks. A hand wraps around her hair and pulls.

The sideways windows of Dane's two-colored eyes fall on the kitchen counter, where he and Helen had been chopping vegetables. He with his white plastic knife. Helen with the big silver knife Dane wasn't allowed to touch.

But Dane isn't allowed to wear a *(skirt)* either.

Or wear his hair long.

Or be in Marizabet's room.

Or not say *sir* when addressing Sir.

He looks at his mother, remembering how her arm went up high and came down.

Sir always did the hitting.

Today, Helen hit back.

Dane didn't know such a thing was possible.

Helen half-twists in Sir's grip and looks back at Dane. Her mouth shapes a word—*Run*—and her eyes roll. Toward, Dane is sure, the stepladder at the counter.

Run.

Moving at the bottom of his lungs, Dane darts across the kitchen floor. His hand closes around silver, heavy and forbidden in his young fingers. He gathers Boy-me, Girl-me and Mom-me close. He runs toward Sir at the windows, arm high.

And he hits back.

TO FEEL LIKE HER

"I'm shocked you ever made friends with Christmas again," Liko said. "If it were me, I'd hear 'Jingle Bells' and go into convulsions."

"The brains of traumatized children do really weird shit," Dane said. "I've read oh so many books about it."

"So what was going on with your sister?"

"I wouldn't find out for another twelve years, but she was pregnant. The nurse at her boarding school ratted her out to Ivelaw, who collected her in the chopper and brought her home."

"But your mother told her to run."

Dane nodded. "This part is a little white knight-ish, but it also affirms that good people are in the world. My father's chopper pilot usually dropped him and took off again, but Maisie was on this ride, getting berated and smacked around. The pilot had a bad feeling in his gut when he landed the bird. He watched my father and Maisie go across the lawn to the house, saw Ivelaw hit her again and grab her by the hair, and the guy just couldn't take off right away. He sat tight, watching the house, biting his nails. Five, ten, however many minutes later, Maisie came running outside, saw he was still there and went screaming toward the helipad. He didn't even hesitate. Just threw her in and they were outta there."

"But you were left behind."

"Right." Dane drew in a long breath. "So I was told… I'm going to be starting a lot of things with *I was told*."

"All right," Liko said.

"I was told my mother stabbed my father, and she went to jail. I was told what I remembered of that day in the kitchen was all wrong. I got it mixed up. Helen was crazy. She'd tried to kill Maisie and kill my father. He stopped her from killing me and now she was in jail."

"But none of that was true?"

"One part," Dane said. "Helen did stab my father, but with my kiddie plastic knife. I ran at him with the butcher blade."

"Oh shit," Liko said. "Where?"

"Kind of…here. Lower side back. *Just* missed his kidney. Which is bananas because I was all of four, and he was wearing his winter overcoat. But I was full of adrenaline, I got a running start, and it was a really good knife. I nailed him." Dane sighed, rubbing his face. "I also put a poetic nail in my coffin. I gave him everything he needed to manipulate me for the next decade."

"So he confirmed it was you?"

Dane nodded. "He said to protect me, Helen told police *she* did it, and they put her in jail. My father was the only one who knew the truth, and all he had to do was pick up the phone and tell. They'd come and put me in jail, too. They'd put me away for being crazy. I'd get sicker than I already was. And I'd die. I was living in that beautiful house in Malba utterly by the grace of Ivelaw Strong. I could see Riker's Island from our dock. On clear days I could see it from the living room windows. All my father had to do was point in its direction and I understood the message. *One phone call and you'll be there.*"

"Christ, and I thought Bootsy pointing toward the naughty corner was the height of cruelty."

Dane smiled. "It sounds asinine when you're an adult, but I was a kid. You believe what you're conditioned to believe."

"And he was your father."

"He was also a monster. Did you ever end up Googling him?"

"You told me not to on a full stomach. Since coming here, I've rarely been hungry. Plus my new philosophy on life dictates that I avoid things that'll spoil my appetite."

"So, despite his esteemed legal pedigree, my father didn't practice very long. He took over as CEO of Suffolk Health Solutions, a little start-up on Long Island that had twelve employees and no revenue. He transformed it into a Fortune 500 company called Paumanok Health Services."

Liko looked up and to the side, brow furrowed. "Why does that sound familiar?"

"Probably two reasons. First, a lot of their mental health facilities have been in the news for questionable practices. Second, PHS was the center of one of the biggest Medicaid fraud lawsuits in history, also for providing substandard mental health services."

Liko rubbed his temples. "Oh my God, this is gonna suck."

"Yeah. You can read up on the litigation when you're fasting for your next colonoscopy. Suffice it to say, thousands of people suffered so PHS could profit. So my father could have his mansion in Malba and commute to work by private chopper. But the main takeaway for this part of the story is my father was an insurance mobster. He knew how to disappear people within the legal system *and* the healthcare system. Sometimes a combination of both."

"Would you mind fast-forwarding to the part where he's in jail?"

"He's not in jail, but how do you feel about the word *ruined?*"

"I'll accept it on a trial basis. Continue. You are now five and living alone with a master manipulator mobster."

"When I started elementary school, my father made me start covering up my blue eye."

"Why the blue one?"

"It's easier to cover blue with brown than brown with blue."

"Right."

"He said the blue eye was weaker and couldn't tolerate strong light, so the lens was necessary. And the lens was brown because two different eyes wasn't normal. I'd be teased. Bullied. He was only looking out for my best interests. Wasn't I grateful? Say thank you to your father. If not for him, you'd be in jail with your crazy mother. Getting the picture?"

"Unfortunately, yes. Who was taking care of you all this time? I mean the day to day taking care. Meals. Bath time. Bed time. New shoes."

"A string of nannies. We always had a cook and housekeeper. My father didn't allow me into the kitchen after Helen was gone but I remember women taking care of me. And one of their jobs was putting that contact lens in my eye every day."

He was still a long time, a tiny muscle twitching in his jaw as he thought.

"My father did a lot of things to make sure I stayed a boy," he said. "Especially if he caught me in Maisie's room." He looked up. "Maisie's bedroom was a huge part of my childhood. It was kept exactly as she left it. The door was shut but never locked. I always wondered why. If my father just forgot, didn't think of it. But that wasn't like him. I think he kept it unlocked as a temptation to me. Which it was. Maisie's bedroom was my haven. Her clothes. Her shoes. Her makeup. Her…things. Girl things. I'd go in there and dress up. Lie on her bed in her clothes. Read her books. Look through her old magazines. It was a huge risk but I couldn't *not* go in there. It was the one bright place in my life and I needed it like oxygen. Needed it to the point where it was worth the beating. And the beatings were bad. My father was a

USAW weightlifting champion at the University of Michigan. He gave up the sport. He kept his belt."

"Fuck." Liko dragged his hair back from his forehead. "I'm… I'm nothing. I have no words."

"Basil ever hit you?"

"No. Once I mouthed off to Mum and he backhanded my arm. One good *pop* and the sting lasted a long time because of the shock factor. Otherwise it was the naughty corner when I was little. Lost privileges when I was older."

"And you raised Kyle the same way."

"Ugh, I hit him once," Liko groaned. "He was fucking around on my laptop and erased a whole manuscript. I was on a deadline, the author was a real bitch, I was under a ton of stress and I lost my shit. I whacked his ass and instantly regretted it. Apologized for days. He was laughing after a while, like *Dad, cool it. I screwed up, I deserved a smack.*"

"*I'm a man, I can take it,*" Dane added, then shook his head hard. "Sorry, I'm projecting my shit. My father would beat me if he saw me acting like a girl, and beat me harder if I cried about it. Crying was forbidden. Sometimes I thought he'd rather I walk down the street in lingerie than cry in public. Anyway. It was bad."

"He understated," Liko said. "Did anyone know this abuse was going on?"

"No. Because if I told…" Dane made a dramatic pointing gesture. "He just motioned to the windows and Rikers Island. He had a hold on me both physical and mental. But he was such a manipulative… I hate to use the word genius. Sociopath is more accurate. He knew just when to give a smidgen of praise. A scrap of approval. A little pearl cast before the swine and I would fall on it, gobble it down, want more. Believe the problem was me, not him."

"And all this time, you're still being told you have cancer? Nothing about being intersex?"

"Nothing."

"That's…" Liko shook his head. "I'm sorry, I'm not doubting you, but how the fuck is it even possible? How do you lie to a child about their health for so long, and for what purpose? I can't get my head around it."

"Of course not," Dane said. "Because you have a Basil and Bootsy. Not an Ivelaw."

Liko blew out his breath. "This is bad."

"It got worse around sixth grade when I wasn't displaying signs of puberty. No body hair, no facial hair, my voice wasn't changing and, my father's biggest concern, I wasn't growing. He had a thing about height. Height was power. All Strong men are *tall* and strong. No son of his was going to be a weakling.

"So he got a doctor to put me on growth hormones. They worked, but not as much as my father wanted. Five foot six was the tallest I'd ever be. He would've prefer those numbers reversed. And I was still slight and hairless, which offended him. But things got really bad when I was thirteen. When I started to grow breasts."

1985

DANE IS TOLD HE HAS CANCER, which is why he has one testicle and two different-colored eyes, and why the skin on his body is darker on one side than the other. He's sick. He has to go see Dr. Porto, who will make him better.

Dr. Porto says Dane is a boy and only a boy. A brown-eyed boy with cancer. Dr. Porto's hands poke and prod, reaching under Dane's hospital gown to touch, talking about Dane's body with words that aren't so funny anymore. Not even talking to Dane, but with other doctors who gather in a circle, hemming and hawing and heeding Dr. Porto. Dane has to take off the gown and let them look and touch and talk.

He's a child, but something within tells him this isn't right. The voice telling is a female voice. It doesn't have a lot of good words, only a deep, stretched, desperate and indignant feeling that things are being done which aren't fair. Things aren't being asked. Things aren't being explained. Reasons are missing here. Something is wrong. This isn't *right.*

Dane's memory rolls into a tight ball. He doesn't talk about anything. He does what he's told. He becomes invisible to himself as his childhood stops imprinting. He curls into the female voice deep within and asks her not to speak, only to hold him. And hide him. She's a good friend and she hides him well. But then Dane becomes a teenager and new things start happening.

At thirteen, he's small for his age, and slight. His male classmates are growing facial hair. He isn't. Their voices are changing. His isn't. They're starting to get into girls, even date. Dane…sort of is. Dane likes girls. But when he's thirteen, he starts to look like one.

His peers are growing mustaches. Dane is growing breasts.

He binds his chest with Ace bandages and learns to arrive early at the gym locker room, then leave late. He doesn't tell anyone about his breasts, because secretly he likes them. Or rather, they *interest* him. He wants some time alone with them.

He likes the feel of a breast in his hand when he masturbates. He cups his one lonely ball and thinks about burying his face in a girl's cleavage *(silky soft white and pink)* while from behind someone *(a boy)* holds Dane's breasts and believes everything Dane says.

He moves forward and back in his body, forward and back in time, part of a three again. As he moves, the lines between *she* and *he* and *him* and *her* began to blur in a swishing feeling around his bare knees because he's wearing a *(skirt)* in the kitchen with his *(Mom-me)*, in the beautiful time of twinkling Christmas lights and paper snowflakes, the soft cushioned life in the kitchen where Dane is allowed to be himself.

He learns he likes the feel of his own breasts in his hands, but not the way they look in the mirror. He wants to look like the high school guys he and his classmates idolize—fit, tight, muscular athletes who always get the girls.

On the other hand, Dane also crushes hard on fit, tight female athletes who always get the guys.

I want to look like those guys and feel like those girls.

The thought stops him cold. So rarely does he have insights that feel like his own that he takes this one to the mirror, pinches out his brown contact lens, and tells it to his face. He turns his head to the left and whispers, "I want to look like him." He turns his head to the right. "And I want to feel like her."

Locked in his sister's bedroom, Dane tries on one of her bras. It's *(silky smooth)* pink with white lace. His breasts just fill the cups. He steps back from the mirror and turns his head so only his blue eye shows.

This time, he likes how it looks, but not how it feels.

He's confused.

His thoughts are mushy, his body trying to be two things at once.

I'm not a girl. I like girls, but I don't want to be a girl.

Yet, his reflection admits, part of his being has always felt…sort-of girl. Secretly kind of girl-ish.

Something new happens when he's fourteen. Every few weeks he's wracked with stomach pains—a weird stabbing ache that makes him panic the first time, thinking it's appendicitis. Except the pain is on his left side.

(My girl side.)

He can't bind this problem down. Can't arrive ahead of it or leave before it comes. Dane has so little he can call private. And now it seems his body wants to blab his secrets to everyone.

One month the pain is so bad he faints at school and ends up in the ER. His clothes are taken off and the Ace bandages unwound.

He's discovered.

THE NAOMI ROAD 37

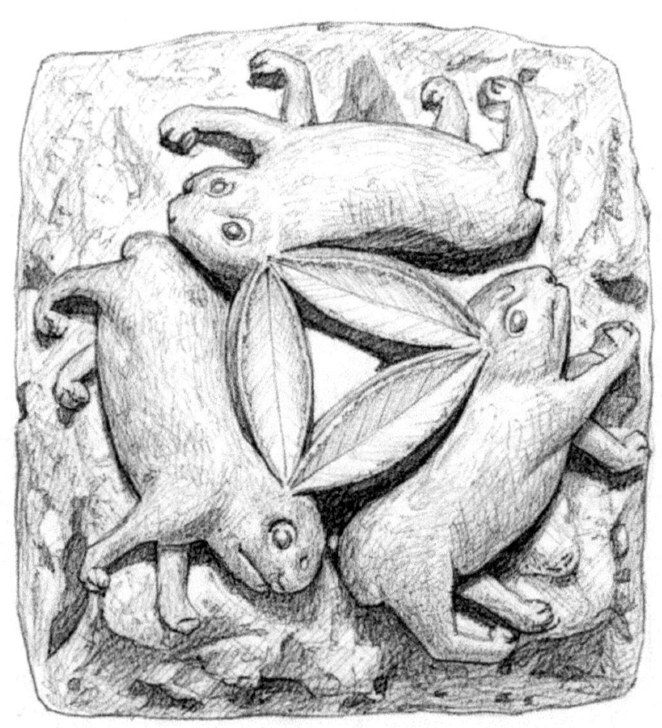

Roof boss at St. Mary the Virgin church, Throwleigh, Devon, UK

FRED

"My father sent me to a private clinic on Long Island," Dane said. "You think such places can't exist. I mean, when you read about sadistic doctors in books or watch medical thrillers. When *Law & Order SVU* episodes show medical abuse based on real-life accounts… You wonder, *How can this happen? Doesn't anyone working there know? See? Do something? Aren't people supposed to report these doctors? Aren't there rules? Laws? Who's in charge? How does this happen?*

"It happens. The medical world has an underbelly and the health insurance field has an underworld. My father and Dr. Porto were running all kinds of schemes to game the Medicaid system, most of them in PHS's mental health facilities. Like a place in Dutchess County that was falsely represented as a residential facility for Medicaid-enrolled children. Really it was a juvenile detention center with no medical doctor or licensed psychiatrist on site. That's just one of many appetite-ruining things you can research for yourself."

"Noted," Liko said, his stomach in a knot.

"Dr. Porto ran a private clinic on Long Island to 'treat' intersex children." Dane made air-quotes around *treat*. Then his hands dropped into his lap and he was quiet a long moment.

"I want to make this part of the story as concise as possible," he finally said.

"You only tell me what you can," Liko said. "You want to write it down and have me read it, that's fine too."

"Maybe some interpretive dance," Dane said absently.

Another long beat. Liko held perfectly still.

"It was like… You know how some families send their gay children to conversion therapy? This was conversion therapy for intersex kids, but with a lot of drugs and a lot of non-elective surgery. Mostly cis boys who had experienced botched circumcisions, and it was decided they'd be better off living as girls. They could be conditioned to be girls. Porto would do surgery, start pumping them full of hormones, and…"

A muscle flickered in his jaw. His hands opened wide, then curled soft on his knees again. "So I end up in this place and… You gotta understand. All my life, nobody ever explains what's going on. I'm fourteen years old and I've never heard the word *intersex*. Or *chimerism*. *Cancer* is what I hear. I've been brainwashed into believing I'm sick. Conditioned to crave approval and fear displeasing authority. I'm not a rebel. I'm a kid in a private clinic, thinking all this is happening because I have cancer. I have no agency. No information. No honesty. No other family members to appeal to. The one sister I can barely remember ran away years ago. My mother is in jail. I don't know how to reach any of the staff at my house. Or any of the teachers I like. I have no one who can help me. The only way I'm getting out of here is if I go under the knife. The only way my father will bring me home is if I be what he wants me to be. So I did."

Liko felt legitimately sick now. "Dane, my man, this is a lot."

"I know. I appreciate you hanging in to listen. You have no idea how much."

"I'm staying. I'm in. But I think I need a drink."

"Whatever you're having, bring me one."

The gin was kicked, so Liko mixed two vodka tonics and brought them over. "You all right? Don't wait for me to tap out if it's too much."

"I'm okay," Dane said, taking a long swallow. "It's actually worse if I leave off in the middle of this part. I have to see it through the storm, bring the story back into harbor, so to speak. Anyway. I wake up from the surgery and my chest is all bandaged up, which I expected. But I also have this long incision on my stomach. Porto tells me he took out a cancerous tumor, which was the thing giving me all the pain. Which, let the record state, was the one time he was minimally honest with me because it was the ovary he took out. But then the chest bandages came off and I was…"

Dane looked over, mouth slightly agape. "To this day, I can't find a good word for how I felt. The labels I use now are retroactive. The kneejerk reaction was I'd been *sterilized*. Which doesn't apply at all but the feeling of it was real. Sterilized. Neutered. Dehumanized. Mutilated. Ruined."

"I don't understand."

"Porto took off my breasts and left nothing. Just erased my chest entirely." He traced remembered lines on his T-shirt. "Two big ugly scars. They weren't even symmetrical. One went up and down this way, the other kind of skewed this way. The stitches were something out of *Frankenstein*."

"Porto didn't… He didn't do any reconstruction?"

Dane shook his head. "It looked, I shit you not, as if someone had taken a kitchen knife and sliced my chest off. You can analyze it however you want, but I think my father wanted revenge for me stabbing him. A constant reminder of what I did to him and if I wanted reconstruction to look like a boy, I had to be a good boy."

"Oh my God."

Dane gave a little laugh. "Sidebar. While I do have a massive praise kink, please don't ever call me *good boy* in bed. I will straight up puke if I hear it in that context. It'll kill the mood."

"Jesus, Dane, what the fuck…"

"Anyway. Now that my breasts were gone, I thought Diane would be gone forever, too. I really thought they'd cut her out of me. It's when I learned she was my inner monologue. I don't know if you pay attention to the voice in your head that narrates you through life, and whether you notice if it's your voice, a male voice. But mine is female. It always has been. Diane lived in my head, just behind my blue eye. She lived in the things my father couldn't change. And the trick to her staying with me was to pretend she'd gone. Pretend I was cured. Pretend I was a boy and only a boy, and had no desire to be effeminate in any way."

"And they let you out?"

"Not right away. I had to be a good boy, start testosterone therapy and go through a lot of Porto's conditioning bullshit. He was a sick nurture versus nature fuck…" Dane downed the last of his drink and waggled the glass in the air. "I'm getting another because this part is really unpleasant."

Liko wasn't sure he could take much more. He took a leak and stepped onto the porch for a few deep breaths. He prayed they were past the eye of the storm and heading out the other side. Prayed he could be a gentle harbor for the ship. Then he went back in.

"So," Dane said. "All us kids in the clinic… They made us read or watch porn, then simulate sex with each other. We were paired off. Like partners. My partner was a cis boy being forced to live as a female. We'd be brought in a room. Porto would make us take our clothes off and lie down together. I had to get on top and thrust. The other boy had to take the submissive role. Porto would make him get on all fours. I'd have to kneel behind and… You get the idea."

"What if you refused?"

"Some parents signed a release form saying physical force could be used. It wasn't my father's weightlifting belt, but it was a leather…thing. Strap. It looked kind of Victorian."

Liko drained a third of his drink. "I'm sorry. I don't know what else to… I'm so fucking sorry, man."

Dane was quiet a long time, one hand on his leg opening and closing into a fist. "That boy," he finally said. "The boy I had to pretend to fuck, while pretending he was a girl... Hold on, I can't tell the story this way anymore. I mean, I'm gonna use they/them from now on, because it's what they prefer." He trailed off again, his expression twitching. Almost wincing.

"Take your time," Liko murmured.

"They... Of all the shit I had to work out in therapy, what happened with them is the most haunting and lingering, the most unforgettable, the most resistant to resolution. Even when I was forgiven to my face, multiple times, it just doesn't want to settle in. I still feel responsible and guilty. Every time I see them, I have to bite my tongue to keep from apologizing again."

"You're in touch?"

Dane nodded. "It's Fred."

"Oh shit."

"One of my first counseling sessions, when the therapist listened to everything and said, quietly and simply, *You and Fred were sexually abused in that clinic,* I lost my mind. I erupted, completely enraged. Insisting no, no, *I* was the abuser. I sexually assaulted Fred, I practically raped him. I was a coward. Weak. I didn't stand up to Porto, didn't fight. I should've let Porto beat me rather than keep doing it, you don't understand..." Dane sighed, deflating into the chair cushions.

"You were fourteen," Liko said softly. A vision of Kyle at fourteen flickered at the edge of his mind, all big eyes and braces and gangly limbs. He squeezed his eyes shut against it.

"It took a really long time to believe I was a victim, too," Dane was saying.

"You were."

Dane glanced over. "Hey, no offense, but I need your word Fred's part in the story doesn't leave this room."

"None taken," Liko said. "And it won't."

"I think I'll stop here. I'm tired."

"You back in harbor?"

"Yeah." He reached and laid a hand on Liko's knee, jogging his leg back and forth a little. "Thanks again."

"For?"

"The trust." He leaned and kissed Liko's cheek quick. Then stayed leaning, his face against Liko's shoulder. Liko put a hand on Dane's neck and they held still as the story's ship rocked and bumped, looking for a gentle place to lay its head.

GETTING IN LOVE WITH HIM

Dane, my man, *this is a lot.*

This is a lot.

This is a lot.

"Stop," Dane whispered to his reflection in the bathroom mirror. "No more."

No more, Diane said. *Put your thoughts down.*

Round and round his mind went, hares chasing hares across the hinterlands. Another triskele of them whirled in his chest, running the opposite way. Each needing to run down what the other had.

My man, this is a lot.

This is a lot.

Dane rested hands on the vanity, dropped his chin between hunched shoulders and wept. For what, he had no idea. For himself, for Liko, for Fred, for everything. For the fucking goddamn *lot* of it.

"You know what this is," he mumbled into a hand towel. "Being intensely connected and then abruptly disconnected is upsetting. Triggering. You don't have to stand here and suffer. Go knock on his door and ask for a little more time. Or a little more contact. Or reach out to someone else. You need a hit of connection to settle you down. It's no big deal. You have community. Call on them."

He picked up his phone and texted Saskia. ***Hey, kiddo. Having some really deep conversations about parenting and fatherhood lately. Feeling mushy and just wanted to say I love you so much. Miss you rotten. XO.***

Bless that child's heart, she replied almost right away. ***Aww, Deddy! I love u2. At a party right now but your mush made my night. I'll try to come see u soon. New season of Drag Race dropped, we'll make popcorn and binge-watch. XOXOXO.***

It was a little. But it wasn't enough.

Dane, my man, this is a lot.

He texted Fred. ***Hey, my friend. Was thinking about you. Everything good?***

No reply, but no surprise. Fred had much better screen management skills and not only shut their phone off an hour before going to bed, they left it charging in the kitchen.

You're probably asleep, Dane typed. ***I was just saying hi. Catch up later.***

"I'm sorry," he whispered over the sent words. "I'm still so sorry."

Sinister memories flickered at the edges of his mind. The feel of the scratchy carpet in Dr. Porto's office, rough against his kneecaps. The smooth-skinned plane of Fred's back *(Erica's back.)* The ponytail of dark hair at their *(her)* nape because he *(her)(no, them, it's them)*, was forced to be a girl. The sound of leather striking skin. Fred *(Erica)* muffling cries into *(her)* elbow until *(they)* couldn't anymore. Dane was better at staying silent. He'd been through this too many times. Dr. Porto's Victorian-era tawse had nothing on Ivelaw Strong's weightlifting belt. The blows hurt. It was humiliating. But Dane knew how to disassociate. Fred*(erica)* had never been hit in his life. *(Their life).*

"Stop," Dane said to the bathroom mirror.

Stop, Diane echoed behind his left eye.

("Stop," FredErica cried. "Stop, please stop…")

Dane tried one more text, this time to his sister: ***If the world is my oyster, who is my pearl?***

After a minute, Maisie replied, ***Meeeeeeeeee*** with a bunch of hearts and a kissy face.

Goodnight, he wrote. ***Love you.***

Goodnight, my Great Dane. Love you more.

And a minute after that: ***Huff says goodnight, dipshit.*** With a winking face.

Sleep badly, asshole, Dane replied.

He sat down on the edge of his bed, practicing mindful gratitude. He was blessed with pipple. He was loved. Valued. Cherished.

And so fucking lonely.

Perched on Nomi's old side of the mattress, his hand stroked up and down the pillow, pretending it was her body while a catalog of delicious sexual memories fanned its pages, enticing him to choose, buy, order. Free shipping. Own it now.

Except he'd never own it again.

He leaned, curled, dropped his face into the pillow and breathed in the ghost of Nomi's scent, as if she'd left the room two seconds ago and not two years. He closed his eyes. Turning pages. Remembering. God, they'd fucked so good. Even their sloppiest, laziest, bare minimum grapple on an exhausted Tuesday night was terrific.

"Good enough?" he liked to ask after such half-ass sessions.

"Thoroughly adequate," she'd answer. And they'd laugh and laugh.

Dane sighed, remembering all the encounters with school parents and soccer fathers and even well-meaning friends. They talked around the subject, but Dane could *see* it in their eyes. The question dying to be asked:

So who fucks who?

Come on, Strong, spill the tea. Who exactly is fucking who? Who's the top? Who's the bottom? Who's in the middle? Who rides bitch on the cuddle train? Do you keep a schedule? Do you have assigned nights? A monthly orgy? Do you get jealous? And when you take a break from your exhaustive sex and constant jealousy, who does the laundry?

Sometimes, Dane had to admit, he wanted to smash the teapot and let it all spill. In detail. Tell them Ethan was neither top nor bottom, but a side.

"One day I'll write an autobiographical novel," Ethan said. *"It'll be called* The Sider House Rules. *"*

"You mean The Sider House Laws, *" Dane said, laughing and tackling him.*

The questions were casual but the answers had no middle ground between pedantic and crass. Dane's choices were *We don't penetrate each other during intercourse,* or *Sorry, no dicks in asses at Schoenfeld's. Try Kulleseid's Orchards. They get pretty wild.*

Your choices were truth or silence, Diane said. *You wrote the laws that kept peace.*

Dane gathered the pillows to his chest and stomach, spooning an invisible body, electric with memory and wanting so bad it hurt.

Nomi was the top. No question. Not just in bed but in their entire existence. If life was a pyramid, then Schoenfeld's was the base, the sides were Dane, Ethan and Saskia, and Nomi was the gold-capped pinnacle. Perched above her empire, cloud pine broom in hand, the Dusk Tiara on her head.

In bed, though… God, in bed. Tears flooded Dane's eyes as he poured tea all over his catalog. The encounters taking up a full-page spread were all from when Nomi took charge of him, took him in hand, took control. When she not only got on top but held him down. Told him what to do. To her, to himself. Told him he could come now. Told him he couldn't come yet. Or when she had him kneel on the bed, then came around from behind and jerked him off. Or in the shower—she loved to soap him up then turn him away and slide arms around his waist. As her hands stroked, she'd grind right up into his butt in a manner that left nothing to the imagination. She was topping him.

He loved it.

Ethan would never take him that way. Dane accepted it and while he had no reservations about letting Ethan know all his thoughts, his feelings, his desires, his fantasies, Dane perfectly understood Ethan's asexual nature. He knew while it would ebb, flow, spike and retract, it would never change. At the end of the day, wasn't that the essence of unconditional love? Recognizing your partner's basic human nature and not treating it as a challenge, a thing you could fix or alter or change?

The infrequency of Ethan's sex was what rendered it precious. When Ethan came to Dane, it *meant* something.

He and Ethan always made love.

He and Nomi did, too, but holy hell they could fuck. Nomi gave him the obliteration he craved. She knew him the way she knew the location of every seedling and weed on this farm, and some nights, she just *harvested* his ass.

I want you, he begged. *I want you back. I want to go back to bed with you. I want to make love so bad. I hate it here. I want what I had before. Bring it back. I want it inside me. I want…*

It was no good. It was a lot. It was too much for this room.

He went downstairs on silent feet. Through the living room and into the kitchen where Salma curled in her bed. Dane slipped past her and out the back door. He left the pool lights turned off. He slid out of his clothes and into the water.

Nomi, he thought, crouched on the bottom of the deep end, hands reaching out in all directions. *Nomi, it's so hard tonight.*

Through the cool drink, she came to him. Her short dark hair undulating. The plum and lavender wisteria tattooed all over her body. Her strong hands twining with Dane's and her green eyes looking into his.

I am Nomi.

You know me.

Speak my name to the stars.

Dane surfaced, breathing hard. "O mister anima I," he said to the sky.

O mister anima I, Nomi said from beneath, holding him up.

It was Ethan who separated the hated epithet Mister *from* Naomi Misteria, *and immediately recognized* anima *in the remaining letters.*

"Oh," he said. "It's right here. Anima. Carl Jung. The inner feminine side of men."

"The related Greek word anemos *means* wind," *John Schoenberg said. "And the Latin derivation means* soul.*"*

Nomi's eyes filled with tears and she turned away to the window in John's study. Outside, a soulful wind was blowing the copper spinner, making the three hares chase each other.

John looked up from a book. "Jung said, 'Anima is the archetype of life itself.'"

"O mister anima I," Ethan said, putting gentle hands on Nomi's shoulders. One day he'd create a love letter for the hares within his most famous video game, and he'd use wind to precipitate clues.

Hands gripping his own shoulders, Dane spoke his wife's name and anagram to the skies, then sank beneath the water again. She caught him. Cradled him to her strong, hard body.

Know me, Great Dane, she said.

I am a granddaughter of Ruta Skadi, queen of the Lake Lubana clan.

I wear the Dusk Tiara.

I am proud and pitiless.

I live in the Danelaw and I will go to war for your peace.

Dane came up. "I miss you so much," he whispered into his palms.

He thrashed about in the water, kicking and fighting the heartbreak. Sinking beneath until his lungs screamed and Nomi pushed him up again. He spoke her name to the stars. He cried for her. Begged for her back. Wanting to sink into her kiss, slide into her body, watch her grow things in the earth, feel her asleep in his arms, fall through the gap between her two front teeth and be forever inside her.

Dane, my man, this is a lot, Diane said. *I'd erase myself from your memory if it would bring her back*

His stomach seized, coiling around the terrible, Faustian lament of losing someone dear. The wild, desperate bargains offered to a cruel Universe: *Anything. I'd do anything, give anything to get them back.*

"I'd erase myself from your memory," Dane said.

And then his heart and mind bubbled up and over in a murderous wail as he sank under the water again, where it was Ethan waiting for him. Dane thrashed at him. Wanting to love him. Wanting to *kill* him. Bubbles of *I miss you* colliding with *I hate you,* tangling up with anagrams and love notes and treasure hunts and little sketches left on pillows and taped to bathroom mirrors. Ethan's triangle smile, the apples of his cheeks fitting precisely into Dane's palms. The golden glint of his eyes, like a sleepy lion. How they squinted at a canvas beneath furrowed brows. Then lit up when he stepped back from work, pleased. The feel of the hair on his chest and arms and legs, all along Dane's skin. That beautiful body asleep in Dane's arms even as his bright, beautiful mind went on spinning, spinning, spinning behind his closed eyelids.

And every so often, like a rare orchid blooming, he'd want to make love. And oddly, Nomi always picked up on it first.

"I need a night in my old cave," she'd say casually. "You guys take the king tonight."

In the huge bed, beneath the eye of *Nomi with Dusk Tiara,* Dane was the artist and Ethan the curious pupil. The nervous model baring himself, letting the most private aspects of his soul be seen. The courage and effort to take what was in his mind and put it into words for Dane. Learning to start sentences with *I want you to…* The even greater bravery to say *No, let's stop, let's try something else, can I show you something else? Can I tell you? Can I show you? I want you to…*

"I want you to come back," Dane whispered over the sloshing water of the pool, fists pressed to his salty eyes. He sank onto the concrete steps in the shallow end, furious and forlorn as an abandoned child.

"Where's Ethan?" a teary, six-year-old Saskia demanded. "I'm getting in love with him."

"What, hon?" Nomi said.

"Ethan's in the city," Dane said.

"But I want him home," the girl said. "I'm getting in love with him."

"Oh, sweetie," Nomi said, smoothing Saskia's hair. "You want to call him?"

"No." Saskia stomped to the living room windows and flung aside the curtains, peering out at the driveway. "I'm getting in love with him and I want him to come home now."

Dane looked up at the farmhouse windows, as if expecting to see a little girl's woebegone face pressed to the panes, looking out.

I'd erase you from my memory if it would bring you back for Saskia.

He slipped once more under the water and then it was Nomi on one side, Ethan on the other. Dane in the middle. Lover to both. The fulcrum on which the other two balanced.

I will go to war for your peace, Nomi said.

Great Dane, Ethan whispered, because he knew Dane had a massive praise kink but hated to be called *good boy.*

They knew him.

Know me.

Nobody could ever know him like those two.

Ye then deign to know me.

I'd erase myself.

Stop, Diane said behind Dane's blue eyes.

("Stop," FredErica begged, on their knees under Dane.)

I'm sorry.

I'm getting in love with you.

I want you to come home now.

My man, this is a lot.

My man.

I would go to war for your peace.

"Erase yourself from my memory," Dane begged. "Please…"

This is the Danelaw and its mission is peace, Diane said in Nomi's voice, a little green shining through the blue of her eyes.

Go to war for your peace, Great Dane.

You're not alone. You're loved and cherished and you can call for rescue. You have a family.

Don't erase them from memory. Remember how you called them to arms…

PART FIVE
AY'LOUT HAMAH

"There is a peculiar notion that elegant plumage and fine feathers are not proper for the male, when actually, that is the way things are in most species."
—*"My Conviction," from Hair, the American Tribal Love-Rock Musical, lyrics by Gerome Ragni and James Rado*

IF IT WOULD BRING
HER BACK

2015

I HATE TO BOTHER *you,* Dane types into his phone. ***Can you help me?***

His thumb trembles over the "send" button. Maisie told him, *ordered* him to text anytime. Any hour of any day. She will be there.

Won't she?

He grits his teeth against the doubt and sends the text.

Immediately an automated reply pops up: ***Can't talk, I'm driving!***

"Fuck," Dane says through his teeth. He's exhausted. It's been one of the worse days, and now Saskia is melting down. Dane finds her by the living room windows, sobbing into the curtains.

"I miss Mammu so much," she sobs, distraught and irrational. "And I miss Ethan."

"Come here…" Dane puts arms around her from behind, holds onto the quaking body.

"I just wish he'd come back." Her voice is both rising in anger and regressing into a childlike petulance. "I want him to come home."

"I know," Dane says, feeling his grip on the world slide free, one finger at a time. His left eye is twitching at the corner.

This is a lot, Diane says nervously. *I think we need help.*

Saskia is inconsolable now. "I'm getting in love with him and I want him to come *home.*"

"I know, sweetheart."

"It's not *fair.*"

"I know. I know…"

Dane does his best to calm her down, but her anxiety only seems to increase as the hours go by, while Dane is slowly consumed by a fog of incompetence verging on apathy. He's starting not to care. Diane is right. He needs help.

His phone pings.

Hey, it's Huff. Maze is driving. What's up?

Dane stares, at a loss. Enough time for another text to come in.

You there? What's going on?

Dane hesitates, then types. ***It's a bad day. Saskia is falling apart and I just feel like I… I don't know.***

You need backup?

I need another adult in the room. Saskia needs a rational voice that isn't mine.

Got it, Huff replies. ***We were heading home from friends. Turning around. Be there soon. Hang tight.***

Dane exhales. ***Thank you.***

No worries. Just hang on.

They walk in fifteen minutes later. Maisie gives Dane a quick hug, then asks "Where is she?"

Dane points toward the kitchen. Maisie sets off, shedding her jacket and laying it over the back of the couch. She barely disturbs the atoms as she slides onto the chair next to Saskia and takes her hands.

"Hey, baby," she says.

"Something's wrong with me," Saskia says. "I don't know what's wrong. I've been having a nonstop panic attack all day. I can't… I don't know where I am…"

"Tell me," Maisie says, putting a palm on the girl's cheek. "Tell me everything."

"My heart is racing. I can't catch my breath. I can't eat anything."

Huff puts his flat palms on her shoulder blades. "Say more."

"I feel like I'm outside myself. I'm here but I'm not here. My brain is so fuzzy. Every thought is just…outside myself. I can't explain."

"You're explaining fine. Keep going."

"I'm going around doing things but I'm not here. I hear myself talk and it's not even me."

Maisie ran a hand back along Saskia's hair, then a thumb under each of her streaming eyes.

"What's wrong with me?" Saskia cries.

"Your brain is protecting you," Huff says. "It's put up a veil between you and reality so you don't get overwhelmed."

"I think I'm going crazy."

"You're not," Maisie says.

Saskia's eyes are wild as she looks up at Huff. "Do I need to go to the hospital?"

"No," he says firmly.

"Something's wrong with me."

"It's okay. I promise," Maisie says. "Nothing is wrong with you. We're going to stay here and help you through this."

"I want my mother," Saskia says hoarsely. "I want my mother so bad."

Maisie throws a shrewd look toward Huff and Dane, and a small tilt of her head that asks, *Can you give us the room?*

"Let's get some air," Huff says. He gets two beers from the fridge and leads Dane out onto the kitchen's porch. Through a fog, Dane looks back through the screen door to see Saskia throw arms around Maisie and cry like she's coughing up a lung. Both hands in a white-knuckled clench on Maisie's shirt. Sobs like screams.

From the empty, bleeding abyss in his brain, Dane regards his daughter with no opinion, simply knowing she's flinging the ugliest of her cries onto Maisie to protect her father.

"Are you all right?" Huff says.

"I don't know. Today sucked. I got nothing in the tank. I miss my wife, I'm so angry with Ethan I can't see straight, and I can't help my daughter."

"Then you were right to call us. We'll stay as long as you need."

Dane rubs his face. "I'm so tired."

"Sit down."

"I don't know what I'm gonna do."

"You're going to sit down. Then you're going to drink your beer. In between sips, you will breathe."

Laid low, Dane chooses to sit on the porch floor, leaning against the railing. Huff sits on the steps. They drink their beers and, out of nowhere, start telling funny Nomi stories.

"Remember she made the beef tenderloin for your fortieth birthday party," Huff says. "And it bombed?"

"It was a fifty-dollar cut of meat. The recipe was supposed to be a no-brainer."

"Something like setting the oven to a million degrees, putting the roast in, turning the oven off and walking away. Right?"

"Yeah. She had a sign on the oven: *Do not open under pain of death.*"

"Everyone swore you couldn't mess it up," Huff says. "But it came out so well-done, it was unsalvageable. Nomi just laughed, took a bow, put the tray in the yard for the raccoons to eat, and we ordered Chinese food instead."

"It was one of our best dinner parties."

"She had so much grace."

"We had good times," Dane says. "Memories live forever. I always heard Jewish people say, 'May their memory be a blessing,' but I never really got it. Now I get it."

The words sound trite. Scripted. Like they come from a motivational speaker. He doesn't believe in them. Huff says nothing either and after a long, uncomfortable pause, Dane glances at him. Huff goes on gazing straight out across the pool, his beautiful face a stone.

"What?" Dane says.

"I'd erase myself from your memory if it would bring her back."

Now Dane stares, incredulous. Not sure whether to be touched or offended. Huff looks at him then. "I would."

"Oh fuck you," Dane says, and bursts into tears. The nearly empty beer bottle slips from his fingers, bounces down the stairs but doesn't break. He puts his face in his hands and weeps, coughing up his lungs. Huff slides over, puts arms around him and holds on tight.

"Fuck you," Dane keeps insisting between sobs, leaning harder against Huff with every garbled curse.

"Dane," Huff says over and over. "I'd do anything. I swear to God. I'd do anything to get you out of this."

Dane would, too. But he can do nothing but cry. So viciously, his nose starts to bleed. Huff takes him back into the kitchen. Saskia is sitting in her chair again, not crying anymore, but looking like she was pulled out of a cement truck.

"Huff, dear, we don't punch people in the face to comfort them," Maisie says mildly. "We've discussed this many times."

"It's an extremely effective technique," Huff says.

"This is how hard you can cry, ladies and gentlemen," Dane says behind the dishtowel pressed to his nose.

"Jesus, Dad," Saskia says thickly, then hiccups. She and Dane look at each other and start laughing hysterically. Maniacally.

"I miss her so bad, I'm literally bleeding," Dane brays.

"Huff, punch me in the face," she cries. "Please. I'll feel so much better."

"Hey…"

Dane took his wet head out of his hands and looked up just as the pool lights flicked on. Liko stood on the deck, wearing just a pair of gym shorts. Hands on hips and expression worried.

"You all right?" he called.

"Yeah."

"Doesn't look like it."

"I was just…feeling some shit."

Looking for myself along the poolside, Diane said miserably.

"Same." Liko stooped and picked up the pile of Dane's clothes. "Conversation tonight gave us a lot of shit to feel."

My man, this is a lot, Diane said.

"I heard talking," Liko said. "Thought someone else was with you."

"No, just me. Screaming into the abyss."

"Don't scream into the abyss, they're not insured for it. Scream into the void. The abyss is for staring."

A maniacal, hiccupped laughed came out of Dane's chest. "Green Man, sometimes I kinda love you."

"Yeah, well…" Liko crossed his arms. "You want to be left alone or bossed around?"

"I'd like to be punched in the face."

"What?"

"Nothing. Boss me around, please."

Liko snapped his fingers. "Out. Now. Free swim is over."

He took a towel out of the basket, then casually turned his back as Dane got out and dried off. The towel knotted around his waist, he followed Liko inside like a duckling.

"You're my emotional support Green Man," he said.

"It's how I pay rent around here. My bed or yours?"

"Mine."

Dane pulled on shorts while Liko got his phone and water. He shook a prescription bottle into his palm and handed Dane a pill. "Klonopin," he said. "One for you, one for me."

It was all simple and straightforward. They lay down in the king bed, their backs to the center. Turned out their lights.

"You'll be asleep real soon," Liko said. "Klonopin's the shit."

"Better living through chemistry."

"No points for style, no shame in tapping out. Whatever we couldn't feel tonight will keep until morning."

"Thanks," Dane said.

Then they were quiet in the dark. No goodnights or last words. Just two sets of long, deep breaths.

This is a lot, Diane said, still fretful.

Yes it is, Dane said, running a hand along her hair, then a thumb beneath each of her blue eyes. *It's all so much.*

Life is so much.

But I'm here.

We're here.

We're together.

"Thanks," he said again.

He heard a smooth rustle behind him. A bit of movement. A prickling energy gathering in the center of the mattress. Gingerly, he eased his bottom leg back a bit. Then a little more. His foot touched another foot, the sole warm and rough against his own.

"Green Man power activated," Liko murmured. "Great Dane locked in?"

"Locked," Dane said. Thinking, *Sole to sole.*

The soul wind activates through the soles of the feet.

Stand on your soul.

Go to war for your peace.

He yawned as the edges of his mind softened and blurred, and the night began to erase itself from memory.

THE NAOMI ROAD 38

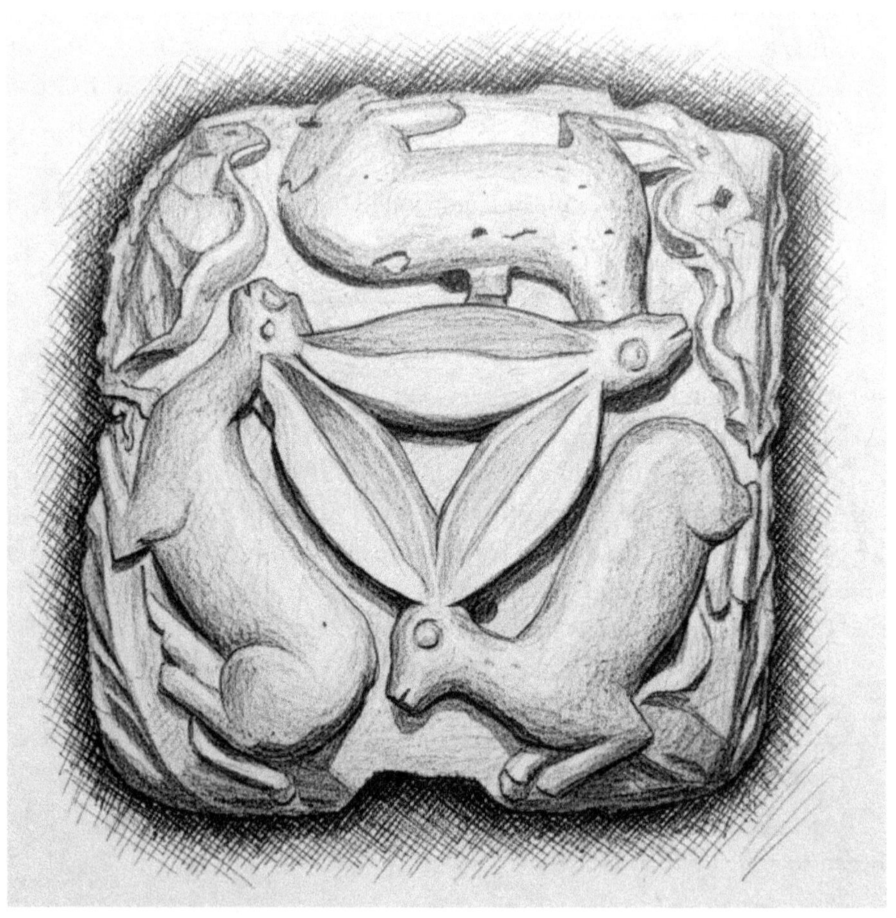

Roof boss at St. Michael's church, Chagford, Devon, UK

THE COLONY OF GRIEF

"I'm doing a Norwalk day tomorrow," Liko said, as he and Dane cleared up after dinner.

"Anything fun?" Dane asked.

Liko made a face. "Absolutely nothing. Physical with Dr. Jellyfinger, then—"

"Wait, *that's* fun," Dane insisted.

"Oh yeah. It'll be the most action I've gotten in years."

"Will you roll on your side or just put elbows on the table?"

Liko fired a dish towel at him. "One snog and a sleepover doesn't entitle you to doctor-patient privilege."

"I'll put you down for elbows."

"Fuck you."

"I would, but whatever comes after Jellyfinger is bound to disappoint." He dodged Liko's swat, laughing. "What else is on the agenda?"

"Eye doctor. Oil change at the dealership. Break for lunch with Gavin and Cynthia to discuss a really insufferable client and how we can let him go without breach of contract. Then Janelle and I have a meeting with financial advisors because we're doing a scholarship for Kyle's graduating class. Then I see my therapist."

Dane hated that he stopped listening after *Janelle and I.* Hated the frisson of suspicion in his chest, *because you still sleep with your ex-wife.*

Did one snog entitle him to make some casual rules about exclusivity? Did a sleepover on Klonopin qualify as dating?

What are we doing here anyway?

You're the one setting the slow pace, Diane reminded him.

Shut up, Dane thought, which he didn't often do with his other half.

"…So traffic willing, I should be home around three," Liko was saying. "At which time I will curl into fetal position with my emotional support duck, and you can hook me up to an intravenous G & T."

Dane uncapped the dry erase marker and wrote *Buy gin* on the whiteboard.

Liko closed the dishwasher with his foot, and rubbed at the moody wrinkle between his eyebrows. "I swear, man, a finger up the ass is going to be the best part of tomorrow."

"I'm sorry," Dane said. "You don't have to do it perfect, you just have to do it."

"If I say *fuck you* again, it means I understand and appreciate the thought, but I hate hearing it. Fuck you. Whoa, is that ice cream?"

Dane turned from the freezer with a pint in each hand. "Let's see, we got… The Colony of Grief and the Prism of Abandonment. What's your jam?"

"The what of what? Gimme that." Liko took the coffee chocolate chip, which Dane knew he would.

"You know how you have The Precious Little and The Meaningless Scrapheap? First year on my own, my two modes were The Colony of Grief or The Prism of Abandonment."

Liko ripped off the inside plastic seal with relish. "Both resonate. Find us some spoons and tell me more…"

2016

"How you doing?" Huff says.

"I'm just awful," Dane says, because he can give honest answers to Huff.

Everyone is being incredibly kind, still Dane doesn't feel like any one understands. Or rather, he's bewildered how they're being compassionate, yet going along with their lives. Everything continues to go along, as if Nomi's death and Ethan's absence don't make any difference in the machinery of the Universe. Dane wants to rent a billboard and broadcast his pain. Or stand by the side of the Palisades Parkway with a sign:

MY WIFE DIED. MY HUSBAND LEFT ME.
WHAT THE FUCK ARE YOU ALL DOING?
DON'T YOU CARE?
DOESN'T ANYONE ELSE FEEL THIS?

Of course they don't. They ask "How you doing?" and hope Dane won't give an answer that makes them feel things they'd rather avoid. They listen with empathetic expressions but behind their eyes Dane can see the there-but-for-the-grace narrative.

"How you doing?" they ask him.

"I'm okay," he says. "Bad days and worse days."

Even that makes some people wince. But sometimes blithe, black-humored quips are the only thing getting him through, so he learns to whom it is best to give the generic answer, and to whom he can give the quip.

"Okay," he says to the former. "Hanging in there. One day at a time."

To those he trusts he replies, "Not too bad, considering I'm driving around life with the *check engine* light on."

"I feel like I've gone deaf in one ear and blind in the opposite eye, but hey, I have on matching socks."

"I did not consider swan diving into a wood chipper today. Can I get an amen?"

"Honestly, I wake up wondering when I can go back to bed again. What time is it?"

"Yesterday was decent. Today, I hate everything and everyone. You included. Get out of my face. I'm kidding. No, come back. Hug me. I love you. Thanks for asking…"

Time passes. Somehow. In eternal minutes and disappearing days, it slides in and out of meaning as Dane negotiates grief, Saskia, and the farm.

He feels Nomi's loss like both a wasting disease and an empty space in his brain. He wonders if the way your spouse dies determines how you grieve them. If their death is sudden and violent, do you feel the loss like a constant surprise: an axe to the face, over and over and over again? If they die peacefully in their sleep at a satisfyingly old age, are the sharp edges of their absence padded, because their death is sad but it makes sense?

Nomi's death from a stroke breaks important blood vessels in Dane's head. He's slow and sluggish. He can't *think.* One side of his body feels paralyzed. Ethan leaving is a cancer, spreading into his bones and organs, making him ache all over.

No longer belonging to a trio means Dane no longer belongs to himself. He is being colonized by grief. He writes it down on a Post-it: *The Colony of Grief.* Then he stares a long time at the words, not knowing what he means. It's a joke with no punchline. Or an unfinished proverb.

In the Land of the Blind, the one-eyed man is king.

In the Colony of Grief, the…

He has support, but at the end of the long and lonely day, it's his pain and his burden alone. His heart might get over Ethan one day, but he'll never get over Nomi being gone. Death comes into your house and takes a giant cosmic dump in your soul. No crack team of postmortem cleaners can remove a turd of this magnitude. You have to endure it stinking up your house until it petrifies. Then maybe you can box it up in some attractive container and take it along for the rest of the miserable ride. But it'll always be with you.

"That's accurate," says Sharice, his grief counselor. "But can we rewrite the petrified part?"

"To what?"

"Biodegraded? Composted? You could grow something new in it."

Dane grunts. "If you don't mind, I'm going to sulk with my petrified turd metaphor for a while."

"You're entitled."

"I'm thinking about Huff," he blurts. "A lot. Fantasizing."

Sharice tilts her head. "Why do you think that is?"

"Because I've always been attracted to him."

"I meant why are you thinking about him more now?"

"Because the pilot of desire has taken off the *fasten seatbelt* sign and my attraction to him is free to move about the cabin."

"That's a better metaphor than the petrified turd."

"Thanks. I worked a long time on it."

"Besides the obvious, how does fantasizing about Huff make you feel?"

"Frustrated. Pissy. Angry. Resentful."

"All the colors of the abandonment rainbow."

"Pardon?"

"In the deep, primitive, binary parts of your brain, the loss of a loved one is abandonment. They left you. The circumstances are irrelevant because the switch only has two settings: *they here* and *they not here*. You don't get half-settings of nuance to explain. It's on or off."

"Interesting."

"You know the five stages of grief, with stage one being anger. I often frame that as stage one: primitive. You're angry because you're abandoned."

"Huh. How does this circle back to Huff?"

"He left you, too."

"Well, not ex—"

Sharice holds up a finger. "The circumstances are irrelevant, remember? One switch. No explanation."

"Right."

"The switch is pointing to *they here* but you're not getting the result you want. Hence you are angry and frustrated and…"

"Abandoned."

"Mm. And for the first months, maybe first year of grief, bereaved people tend to view everything through the prism of abandonment."

Dane's mind goes to the cover of Pink Floyd's *Dark Side of the Moon,* with its iconic triangle refracting a single beam of white into the rainbow spectrum. In his imagination, he picks up a glass prism and lays it on his grief, refracting the white-hot beam of his daily pain. Out shoots the red of anger, the orange of resentment, the yellow of fear, the green of envy, the blue of desolation and the purple of frustration.

"I'm going to take some time with this," Dane says to Sharice. "It's an excellent theory. I mean that sincerely. But at the end of the day, I just want my fucking people back."

"Of course."

THE LAST TIME

"This is great shit," Liko said. "The prism of abandonment, Christ, I can go for a month on that one."

"I thought for sure you were a petrified turd kind of guy."

"That'll be my kicking-around-the-house-in-sweats attitude. When I have to go out in public, it'll be with the prism of abandonment." Liko's smile slowly faded. "Who are we kidding, though. The only attitude is, *At the end of the day, I just want my fucking people back.*"

They were quiet a long time.

"In the year of whatever lord there is, twenty-thirty-four," Liko said, "I will be seventy-two."

"Why's that significant?"

"It'll be seventeen years since Kyle died. Then the time I live without him will become longer than the time I lived with him."

"Fuck," Dane murmured.

"It's the kind of shit I think about. This is who I am and what I do, my friend."

"You're the Green Man," Dane said. "A soul older than God. You watch everything. Then you write the stories."

Liko smiled. "And you're what? A single hare left running?"

"I'll always be part of a three," Dane said. "I am polyamorous. That is, I know I can love within that paradigm. I just don't know if I want to again."

"Try to find out before you sleep with me," Liko said. "Because I don't share well with others."

"With you, I can see myself getting into single-minded possession."

"Or maybe I'll just ruin you."

"Maybe."

The windows were darkening but Dane hadn't turned on the kitchen lights. He reached for the little red Bic and lit the table's candle. The wick sputtered high, then mellowed. The two men sat quietly in the softening evening, watching the flame burn. As Dane's fingers spun the lighter round and round on the table, Liko sensed a tremor of deep, repressed emotion. The vibe coming off Dane was almost shamed.

"What are you thinking?" Liko asked. "You're remembering something."

"The night before he left the farm, Ethan and I had a banger of a fight. One for the road and we left it all on the floor. I said some rotten stuff to him. Unforgivable things."

"Tell me. I'll judge what's forgivable and what isn't."

"I couldn't take hearing how I'd be free to be with a man the way I'd always wanted. His words. Like it all came down to sex and with Nomi gone, Ethan assumed he couldn't be enough for me. He was pulling the plug before I could, and nothing I said could convince him otherwise. This is what we argued about, all day long every day. But that last night, I was out of fucks to give. I wanted to kill him and I knew just how to do it. I said, *Good. I'm free. You know what I'm gonna do first? I'm gonna find some hot piece of beefcake and let him fuck the shit out of me. I'm gonna get a goddamn bear to take my ass to church, the way you never could. I'm gonna find out what it's really like to get fucked by a man. A real man. I'm getting everything I couldn't get from you. I'm going into Grindr with an agenda…*"

Liko gave a low whistle.

"I regret it," Dane said. "God, I'd do anything to go back and sew my lips shut, keep that shit in the silence of my heart."

"We all say thoughtless things when we're pissed off."

"It was worse than thoughtless. It was a cheap potshot at his identity. It was cruel. I knew it would hurt him, I knew exactly how to hurt him and I did. It felt good, too. For all of five seconds."

"He hurt you, too. Hell, I probably would've said all that, then punched him."

"I should've decked him instead of saying what I said. I should've… Fuck, I don't know."

"I hear you," Liko said, with a thunderous sigh. "*Should've* is my daily mantra. I was snoring away when Kyle died. Blissfully nodded off to the sound of the shower. Fast asleep as that shower went on and on and on and on…"

"Oh, man," Dane said, his face in a palm. "Why is life is such a cunt?"

"Why did I send him to bed that night? I should've dragged out the victory. Encouraged him. *No, don't wait until tomorrow. Forget what I said about putting twenty-four hours between impulse and action. Do it now. Fuck school, I'll call you in sick. You start writing a post, I'm gonna make popcorn…*"

"You had no idea," Dane said. "You couldn't have known."

"I know, I know. It was an aneurysm. It was gonna blow no matter what. That blood vessel still would've burst, but it would've happened right in front of me. I could've called 911 in a nanosecond. Started CPR. Done something besides sleep through it. And I can't stop obsessing about that any more than you can stop wishing to go back and shut your mouth. I don't know if it was the aneurysm that killed him, or if he drowned in the tub. All I can do is pray it was fast. Painless. Hope to God he wasn't scared. Didn't call out for me and I didn't hear and— *Christ,* would you stop me already? What kind of friend are you, letting me blather on?"

"The worst friend," Dane said.

Liko scrubbed at his face. "I'm sorry. That was a trauma-dump when you were trying to tell me something important."

"It doesn't matter."

"It does."

"Nothing matters to *them,*" Dane said. "I mean, nothing can hurt Kyle or Nomi. It's just you and me left, handling all the hurt."

"We're not even drinking," Liko groaned into his hands.

He looked up and they stared at each other a time, the pained laughter and smiles slowly fading. Then Dane got up.

"Move back," he said, pushing at one of Liko's shoulders.

Liko slid his chair back, and Dane straddled his legs and sat down in his lap. He scooted close, wrapped arms around Liko's neck and put his face in the curve of Liko's shoulder.

"This okay?" he said.

Liko could barely speak, suddenly flooded with an emotion so complex and elusive, so immense, it seemed the kitchen could barely contain it, let alone his lap.

"Just hold me a minute," Dane whispered.

Liko was shaking now, unable to understand what was happening. He sat, trembling and frozen, willing his arms to move. Finally they lifted, and he slid his palms beneath the open sides of Dane's hoodie and around to his back.

"More," Dane said.

Tears flooded Liko's eyes as his arms tightened a little, then a little more. The knot of their limbs slowly drew close and small, settling into place. Chest to chest. Heartbeat to heartbeat.

It was all in Liko's arms.

Back in his arms.

What is it? His thoughts were a wind spinner. Three thoughts chasing each other counter-clockwise:

What am I holding? What am I feeling? What is happening?

Danelaw Strong was a small man and now Liko knew the reason why. The years of forced growth hormone had barely gotten Dane past five feet six. One of his myriad failings in Ivelaw Strong's eyes. If his son couldn't be tall, Ivelaw would make him strong. So started the years of testosterone supplements, the weight training and conditioning, and the strict regulation of calories in, calories out. The grooming, the policing, the humiliating exams and inspections. All with the goal of destroying Diane and making a man out of Dane.

He had escaped that terrorized regime, left the worst of it behind and kept the better habits. He created a new body of his own, not to please anyone, but to keep Diane safe. To allow her to exist where she'd always wanted to be: inside Dane. He was a small man, but he was hard and lean. The power in his long muscles was a guarded secret he could unleash on demand, with awesome effect. And yet…

And yet in Liko's arms…

And yet…

What? Liko thought desperately. *What is… What?*

He dared to draw it closer, bury his nose in it and inhale. Fabric softener and skin. Freshness and musk. Sweet and sweat. The unique blend of elemental scent that was so…

Young? Liko thought, the tears now streaming down his face.

Insane. This was a forty-six-year-old man.

But also a man who needed a month on HRT to achieve five o'clock shadow.

Liko lifted his head off Dane's shoulder and tilted it to rub his temple along Dane's smooth jaw.

"Hey," he whispered, barely audible because what he felt teetered on the edge of forbidden. *Hey, kiddo,* he wanted to say, but didn't dare.

What was he doing?

This was a grown man.

But for one, single, beautiful, magical, impossible, belief-suspending moment…

It was a boy.

"Oh my God," Liko whispered, awash with feeling, thinking he might choke.

Time was a thief. One day your young son would sit in your lap and you had no way of knowing it would be the last time. It wasn't like he knew either, and made an announcement: "No more lap time after this, Pop." It happened gradually but the realization was painfully sudden. Like realizing you hadn't seen his bare ass in a while. One day you lifted your head with a startled "Huh," thinking how long it had been since that little boy sat in your lap. Or wrapped both arms and legs around you when you picked him up. The last time had been the *last time,* and you didn't even notice.

You still hugged, of course. You wrestled, you canoodled, you rough-housed, but never again would you feel all that boy weight limp on your legs and snuggled into your chest. Where you could wrap both arms around it and inhale the freshness of his clothes and the tinge of earthy sweat on his skin.

Liko felt himself seize, body and mind. This wasn't right. This was inappropriate. It was wrong to be holding a grown man he was sexually attracted to and be thinking of his dead son. And yet…

And yet.

Sex was the furthest thing from Liko's mind. All this evoked youth and beauty and remembrance in his arms—he didn't want to kiss it, caress it, strip it bare and fuck it.

He only wanted to hold it.

Feel it.

Remember it.

Time was a thief. But sometimes, once in a great while, it brought back what it had stolen and let you hold it one last time.

Liko's mouth shaped his son's name with no sound, arms closing tighter and tighter around this unexpected present. For this boy-man soft in his arms, heavy in his lap, was nothing less than a gift. A portal to an alternate Universe. A divine proxy. A single last chance to hug Kyle.

"It's all right," Dane whispered, his hand sliding to the back of Liko's neck. Then fingers digging up into his hair. "Don't let go."

If the stove exploded or the ceiling collapsed, Liko wouldn't have let go. He was crying now and instead of excruciating and toxic, the grief was glorious. Clean. Pure.

It was all sitting in his lap and it was magnificent.

Dane rocked on the fulcrum of Liko's legs, his hand strong on Liko's head. "It's all right," he said, over and over.

"Oh my God," Liko said, over and over.

"Hold on."

"Oh my God, you don't know."

"I do know," Dane whispered. "I know everything. This is everything. Just hold onto it."

SOULMATERY

LIKO NEVER FELT MORE of an inept ass than during the first fifteen minutes of a therapy session.

"Hello," Brenda would say as Liko sat down.

"Hi."

"How are you?"

Of course Liko would promptly reply *fine, all right, doing okay, not bad.* Or the very British *not too bad, all things considered.*

Of course, Brenda would say nothing. Continue to sit silent and receptive until Liko stopped squirming and sighing, and hit on something to talk about.

"This attraction to Dane is so odd," he said now. "It's intense and physical and…and want-y, but I feel no urgency to act on it. Always when I've had sex with men, it's been so frank and immediate. Urge there. Act on it. Urge gone. Have beers. With Dane, I'm more interested in the beers."

"I see."

"I've tried to honestly ask myself if I'm falling in love, and the honest answer seems to be *not yet.* It's not purely sexual. It's not romantic. I seem to be falling into deep friendship. Or into soulmatery. Sorry, I'm inventing a lot of words here."

Brenda smiled. "They're extremely accurate words, even if you wouldn't find them in a dictionary."

"Whatever I'm falling into, the point is I'm intensely aware of the process in the way I typically am when I'm falling in love." He smiled sheepishly. "If memory serves. It's been a while."

"I think sometimes as adults, we're surprised we can find and make new friends. Like we all carry around a weird psychological rule that all friends must be picked by the end of college. The roster is set and finalized."

"Right. Exactly."

"Ties into what we were talking about last month," she said, turning back a few pages in her notebook. "Opportunities still existing. Experiences you have yet to live. People to meet."

"Mysteries to solve."

She smiled. Silence coiled around the little room and Liko concentrated on not being intimidated by it. He was still reeling from the feel of Dane in his lap last night, and the strange, strong emotions it evoked. The memory sat in his heart like a small nuclear reactor, giving off a quiet, efficient hum of power. A rhythmic drone like spiritual white noise: *my friend, I have a friend, my friend is here, my friend did a great thing for me, I can count on my friend, soon I will see my friend.*

Liko had been drawing on it all day. He didn't want to talk about it. He felt it didn't *need* to be talked about.

"I like Dane's energy," he finally said. "He's non-binary so he has things… Traits, behaviors, mannerisms whatever. They strike me—and I admit this is my own culturally brainwashed perspective about gender—as masculine. But he's physically demonstrative and affectionate, and he has a tenderness that strikes me—again, binary-programmed me—as feminine. So on one hand, he's a typical male friend who clowns around with me. We work on the farm, we hang out having beers, talking about shit. He's become a really close mate. A new friend.

"On the other hand, he's a mate who touches me. A lot. And I like it. It's flirtatious as fuck sometimes, but it hasn't turned sexual. Yet. I'm trying not to think ahead. I like being right here."

"It sounds like a good, stable place."

"Dane has a way of letting people know where they are, what they're about, what's going on, and what he needs. It's hard to explain. I guess I'm badly communicating that his communication is really top notch. I don't think I've yet to feel that I'm not in the picture or don't know what's going on."

He went on rambling out loud, Brenda continued her smiles and precipitating comments and encouraging silences. Sometimes the ramble would crash into a deeper insight. Sometimes Liko's mouth finally admitted it was talking around the issue bothering him.

"I never came out to Kyle," he blurted. "We never got past the phase where anything linking sex and one's parents was revolting. Plus the years between fourteen and sixteen, it was all about the fallout from the divorce. All of his anger at the disruption of his life, adjusting to the routine of shuffling between houses, the holiday schedule and the possessions in two places. He got really guarded and surly, didn't want to talk about anything personal. He never shared if he was smoldering over a girl. I think we had one really good chat about consent. We were driving somewhere. And maybe a couple months before he died he told me he thought one of his buddies might be gay, but he wasn't sure…"

Liko lifted up his hands and let them fall. "I swear, it was like trying to exist in a phone booth with a cactus. Whenever he softened up and did come to me with something personal, vulnerable or private, I went into listen-only mode. I did what you do: *Oh? Huh. Wow. Tell me more. Are you worried about your friend, do you think he's safe?* It wasn't the time to make it about me. Not the immediate time, and not the time in his life."

Now his eyes stung and the back of his throat ached. "He died when so much of our interaction was butting heads. When I was still just his nagging old man and not a confidant, or even someone who actually knew a thing or two. We never got a chance to be equals."

"You were robbed," Brenda said. "No other word suffices. Not only robbed of seeing Kyle do, see, learn, experience and become so many beautiful things, but robbed of him getting to know *you* better."

"Christ," Liko whispered, as it all came pouring into his eyes.

"Teens are narcissists, no two ways about it. But you were on track to a beautiful phase of life when your adult son would stop fighting his old man, and start talking man-to-man. I know you would've gotten to that phase with Kyle because you knew how to go into listen-only mode when it mattered. You got into that booth with the cactus. You got pierced, stabbed and scratched, but you kept making a safe place for his feelings and worries. You cultivated a magnificent field of trust and compassion, and then you were robbed of everything that might have grown there. The fruits of all your parenting efforts were stolen from you. These are not things easily endured."

She didn't often go into a monologue, but when she did, it always pinned Liko to the couch. He hung on her words, impaled, nodding vigorously as the tears dripped down his face.

"He died not knowing something important about me," he said, yanking a tissue from the box. "I know he knows now, but it's no consolation because I can't *see* him knowing now. I don't get to have those man-to-man sessions over beers. I don't even get to have a fucking beer with him. They stole the *beer,* Brenda."

"Do you ever talk out loud and tell him things?" she asked. "Play both parts of the conversation?"

"I try," Liko said. "But it's hard to…" His hand turned over, fingers trying to pick his meaning out of the air. "Hard to make a man out of him. Hard to hear him engage in a truly mature way. Again, because it feels like we argued so much those last two years of his life. It's hard to imagine him saying, *Wow, tell me more. How'd that make you feel, Dad? Were you worried about how Nan and Grandpa would take it?*"

"Well, if you're amenable to an assignment," Brenda said, "maybe in the next month you can meditate on memories, however small, of when you and Kyle had good talks. The chat in the car about consent. What made it a good one?"

"All right," Liko said absently.

"You're in the shitty position of having to invent the adult version of your son," she said. "I don't want to make it sound like an artificial intelligence Kyle, crafted from your own memories, will be any kind of substitute for the experiences you were robbed of."

"But my memories are all I got," Liko said. He closed his eyes, weary to his bones, wishing for the umpteenth time he could pull a handle and eject himself from the grief jet.

The Colony of Grief, he thought, envisioning it painted on the side of gleaming fuselage.

"Use memories to create a future I was robbed of," he said. "I'll give it a shot. I'm going over to the cemetery after this anyway."

Another session was folded up and put away, another three balls of soaked Kleenex thrown in the bin. The bill would come by email. Insurance would cover a couple of bucks. And life went on.

Liko went to the cemetery, but neither meditated on memories, nor had a heart-to-heart chat with the gravestone. He managed, "Hey, kid," then crouched on his heels and hung his cheekbones over his thumbs, fingers at his hairline. He didn't weep, didn't speak, didn't move. Barely thinking, he balanced, feet wobbling in the soft dirt where grass struggled to grow, and breathed through the fire in his throat and the break in his heart.

Then he left.

He drove past his house for a quick look-see. He'd rented it to a professional couple from Manhattan and so far, they'd only called him once, when the ice maker in the fridge got jammed. The house looked trim, neat and shipshape. The whiskey barrel by the mailbox overflowed with a profusion of annuals and trailing vines. Nothing more to see or do, so he went home.

Leaving my house to go home, he thought. *My friend is waiting for me. With my duck. And my intravenous drinky-poo.*

DANE CALLED AS LIKO was approaching the Tappan Zee. "Hey, you up for Maisie and Huff coming over for dinner?"

"Why wouldn't I be?"

"Because therapy can bring a fellow to his knees, so I wanted to check the level on your social tank."

"You really are a Great Dane."

"I'm just a veteran of the couch and cemetery. Either can send you back to bed for the rest of the day."

"I do feel a little shredded," Liko said. "But I haven't seen the Jensens since the infamous New Year's Eve party, and I remember them as lovely people. I think a drink and a dip in the pool will fill up the tank."

"I can grill some steaks and get corn from Edholm's?"

"I am happy to show up whenever and eat whatever. Boss me around tonight. You have permission. Back to the company we'll be keeping, is there anything I should *not* ask Maisie? I mean, about her childhood or when she ran away?"

"Let's see, we last left our teenage heroine being dramatically evacuated by chopper from her abusive home."

"That's right," Liko said. "Yikes, I forgot this part. You said she was pregnant?"

"Yeah, and she ended up miscarrying. At least, that's what she told me, and I mind my business. It's best if I summarize what happened between the chopper and her adulthood, and then we leave it alone unless she brings it up. It's definitely an interesting story, but not something she likes to talk about herself. I can tell you about it now."

"Are you busy?"

"Nah, I'm icing my back."

"What happened?"

"Nothing, I just forgot to lift with my legs. So the boyfriend that got Maisie pregnant was a young, little-known musician who'd just signed with

A&M Records. You never miss the obvious so I'm sure you know who I'm talking about."

Liko stared at the windshield, his mind a blank. "We call this a pregnant pause," he said.

"Dude. Come on."

"Dude, tough day on the couch. Throw me a bone."

"Think about my fireplace mantel."

Liko did, picturing the stacked stone and the painting above the…

"Oh," he said. "Her boyfriend was Gideon Perfect?"

"Don't you love how this comes together so neatly?"

"I do."

"Unfortunately, the story has a slightly sleazy start because when she ran away with him, Maisie was sixteen and Gideon was twenty-two."

"*Slightly* is doing some heavy lifting here."

"Hence her reluctance to talk about it these days. Bring it up and her expression goes all sheepish and uncomfortable, and Huff pinches the bridge of his nose like he can't even. Sure, it was the seventies, different time, blah blah. But it wouldn't fly today and you can't help but project backward and think *no consent, statutory rape, end of story, goodbye and cancel.*"

"So she lost the baby, dropped out of school and took off with him?"

"Yep. Followed him on tour, disguised as a groupie. I think there was a cover story that she was the daughter or sister of a roadie or something. It was on the extreme down-low because of course my father was looking for her. It was kind of a miracle they managed to keep it all secret until she was eighteen. If that tour bus ever got pulled over in the wrong state, holy fuck, it would've been bad."

"How long did they stay together?"

"Eight years."

"Impressive."

"They were in love," Dane said. "Little by little, she became less his girlfriend and more of a best friend. Touring was a thrill, until it wasn't. Dropping out of high school was cool, until it wasn't. She was maturing, growing out of the lifestyle and eventually, out of the relationship. She and Gideon loved each other. I think they'll always love each other. They talk every day. He'd do anything for her. They're soulmates, but they're not life mates. So Maisie went home."

"To New York?"

"Yeah. Ten years of touring around the world, she'd amassed quite a respectable art collection, which was being kept in storage. She thought maybe she'd like to open a gallery someday. But she only had a GED she'd earned on the road. So she went to work at the bottom while going to college for art history."

"Who paid for her rent and education?"

Dane laughed. "If you miss *this* obvious answer, I'm hanging up."

Liko laughed along. "Everyone should have a rich, older, rockstar soulmate."

"It's not what you do, it's who you know. Anyway, lots of calendar pages blowing away in the wind. She eventually opened her first gallery in Manhattan. Then her second one in Norwalk. She was dividing her time between New York and Connecticut when I found her."

"How did you find her anyway?"

"I have an excellent feeling you will hear that story tonight. So drive safely."

MARIZABET, I COME YOUR ROOM

Liko tumbled into the pool, had a drink and a shower, and fell asleep in the cool of his bedroom for forty dreamless minutes, waking to the sound of loud laughter and Salma barking. He got dressed and fretted, because a bubble of festive joy was inflating in the kitchen, and he was going to pop it with the words *my son passed away.*

Liko Greenman, International Man of Misery.

"Just get it over with," he mumbled.

But when he came into the kitchen, Maisie simply put arms up around his neck and drew him close without a single word. Her hand rested on his head while Huff rubbed a few slow circles on Liko's back. They stood still, took one deep silent breath together, and Liko knew they already knew. He'd been spared. The bubble was pre-popped and it had been Dane's doing.

My friend is here, my friend has my back, my friend took care of it.

"We've been thinking about you so much," Maisie said.

"It's so good to see you," Liko said, meaning it to his bones.

The evening unfolded, soft and superb. The steaks were perfect, and the corn—renowned in four counties—didn't need a lick of butter or speck of salt. A mountain of gnawed cobs piled up as the wine flowed and the conversation twined and wove around the four people, dripping clusters of laughter.

"How'd you two meet?" Liko asked the Jensens.

"A Great Dane introduced us," Huff said.

Maisie raised her glass. "Thank you, Great Dane."

Dane waved a dismissive hand. "What are brothers for?"

"When was this?" Liko said.

"Same night I met Ethan and Nomi. At a rather momentous art show in SoHo."

"Life-changing," Huff said, running a hand lightly up and down Maisie's back. Though he was thoroughly stuffed, Liko found himself fixating on the intimate caress with a wistful hunger. Not missing Janelle, but a mate with touching rights. The partner who conveyed with a dozen little pats or pets, *You're mine, I'm yours, we're together and all is well.*

He felt Dane's gaze and glanced over. Dane looked back with his two-colored eyes. His face a gentle place for Liko to lay his head. He relaxed into the idea that two couples were at this table, and he put a hand on the back of Dane's chair. Dane moved his leg a little, and pressed their anklebones together.

He said, "Maze, Liko wants to hear how we found each other."

"I'm not demanding the tale be told," Liko said quickly. "I'm just curious."

Maisie twined her fingers and set her chin on top. "How much background do you have?"

Liko hesitated, his glance going around the table, and Dane gave a little encouraging nod. "It's okay, we're all friends here."

"Concise version," Liko said, keeping eyes on Dane. "I know after a long, abusive childhood where you were kept in the dark about way too many things, you were put into a private clinic. Among other horrendous suffering, you were forced to undergo top surgery without…"

"Informed consent," Huff said.

"And without reconstruction. You stayed in the clinic a while longer. More unspeakably horrendous things happened. That's where we left off the other night." Liko glanced at Maisie and Huff. "I slept rather badly afterward."

Maisie nodded and poured the last of the wine into all the glasses. "So Dane, have you introduced Paul Goldberg?"

"Not yet."

"He's a tricky one, Paul," Huff said. "Definitely the morally gray character in the story. But without him, God knows what would've become of Dane."

"Who was he?"

"Basically a minder," Dane said. "To call him a governor is very D.H. Lawrence, but it fits. So does supervisor."

"Handler," Maisie said.

"Coach is the most elegant way of putting it," Huff said.

"Basically my father hired Paul to make a man of me," Dane said. "To make sure I behaved the right way and, equally important, looked the right way. He took control of my clothes, my hair, my body, my looks, every scrap of food that went into my mouth. My schoolwork, my extracurricular activities, my transcript, the whole college admission process. Table manners, etiquette. He taught me to drive. He…" Dane trailed off, looking at little lost.

"Again, Paul's a tricky one to classify," Huff said.

"Did you know him?" Liko asked.

"Me personally? No, this is my hearsay analysis based on anecdotal evidence."

"I only met Paul once," Maisie said. "He came into the gallery and it was impossible not to notice him. He had such a presence. Aloof and intense at the same time."

Dane laughed a little. "Behind his back I called him the Sphinx. He was bald with sort of cat-like eyes. He almost never blinked."

"What was he like?" Liko asked.

"Formal and reserved and strict. I never kidded myself he was a friend, but next to my father, he was positively kind. Even though he was distant, he was handsome, and it was a time when I was discovering handsome men had an effect on me."

"He was predictable," Huff said.

"Yes," Dane said. "I never knew what I was going to get with my father. His rules changed on a whim. With Paul, there was a consistent code of behavior and I understood it. He was much more generous with positive feedback, too. If I did something well, I heard about it."

"What if you did something wrong?" Liko asked, thinking if it involved anything made of leather, he was leaving the table.

Dane shook his head. "Paul didn't put a finger on me. He didn't have to. He was a buffer between me and my father. If I pleased Paul, he reported back to Ivelaw, and I got left in peace. I got tiny allotments of freedom. I got to relax a little."

Liko looked at Maisie. "Why was Paul in your gallery?"

"I had no idea at first. He did a couple loops around the exhibit, then he came to stand at a painting right by my desk. I can still see him. His back to me, perfect suit, trench coat over an arm, just cool and slick and chic. He looked straight ahead at the canvas and said, *Is this by Marie Elisavette Strong?*"

"Dun dun *dun*," Huff sang under his breath.

"Who's she?" Liko said.

"Me," Maisie said. "Marie Elisavette Strong is my legal birth name, but I changed it to Maisie Montresor when I was twenty-one."

"How did Paul know it?"

Dane raised a finger. "From me. I never knew her as Maisie. Only Marie Elisavette, which I garbled together as *Marizabet.*"

"Marizabet," Maisie said softly, as if a little boy calling. "Marizabet, I come your room."

"That's what he'd say?" Liko asked.

"Can I come your room? I come stay your room, Marizabet." She exhaled long. "Anyway, my heart promptly fell out my asshole because anyone throwing my real name around had to be connected to my father. I literally had my finger on the panic button, ready to call security, but then he looked from the painting to me and said, *I have a message for Marizabet.* And Jesus Christ …" Maisie took her chin off her twined fingers and dropped a hand on the table to Dane, who took it. "Only one person in the world knew *that* name."

"Holy shit, what did you say?" Liko said.

"I said, *What message, how do you know that name, who the fuck are you?* Paul's hand came out from beneath the trench coat and held up a book. A copy of *The Secret Garden.*"

"Not just any copy," Dane said. "The Dell Yearling edition. Ninth printing. With illustrations by Tasha Tudor, who signed the title page: *To Marie Elisavette, may the magic always be in your garden.*"

Maisie was nodding, eyes bright. "For like a minute he was standing there, holding out the book, and I couldn't even move. Finally I took it." Maisie's hands mimed opening the book. "I saw the inscription from Tasha Tudor and almost fell out of my chair. This was my book from my old bedroom from my old life."

Dane put a hand on Liko's forearm. "Sidebar. Up until this time, Maze figured everything she left behind in Malba was gone."

"Thrown away, given away, chucked in the East River, burned," Maisie said. "*I have no daughter, she's dead to me, never speak her name within these walls.* So forth and so on."

"But nothing was touched," Dane said. "Her room stayed exactly as she left it. Clothes. Shoes. Makeup. Perfume. Stuffed animals. A poster of Franco Zeffirelli's *Romeo and Juliet.*"

"Oh my God," Maisie laughed. "Leonard Whiting, take me now."

"Did you give Paul the book to give to Maisie?" Liko asked Dane.

"I had no idea any of this was happening."

Maisie's hands mimed again. "I turned the inscription page and behind it were two pictures of Dane. One as a little boy, which I immediately recognized and—"

"You did?" Liko said. "You remembered him?"

Maisie didn't take her eyes off her brother as she drew a long slow breath in. Huff's hand returned to her back.

"I forgot his face," she said, "but I never forgot those eyes. How could I?"

Dane fluttered his lashes. "Heterochromia does have its perks."

"The other picture," Maisie began, but then stopped and shook her head. "That boy was unrecognizable. Both his eyes were brown and he was…"

"I was jacked," Dane said. "Porto had me on so much fucking testosterone."

"Growth hormones, anabolic steroids," Huff said. "Combinations that would make an endocrinologist stroke out. It was criminal."

"I went into the clinic a young prince," Dane said. "I came out a beefy, bloated, bad-skinned troll."

"School must've been miserable," Liko said.

Dane gave a sour laugh. "I made others miserable so they couldn't do it first."

"Our Dane, a bully," Maisie said. "Can you even picture it?"

"No."

"I was just an overly aggressive prick who would then go home and cry in his sister's pillows. How's that for a trope? To add to the bad boy image, I had quite a lucrative side business within my circle of elite peers and their parents." Dane glanced at Liko. "Huff did mention this story had morally gray characters. I was dealing drugs. I learned how from Paul. Despicable, yes. It also allowed me to bank a few grand into an account nobody knew about. So maybe it's a moral wash."

"Okay, put a pin in *that*," Liko said, his head spinning. "Go back to the gallery, Maisie. After showing you the book and the pictures, what did Paul tell you?"

"He said Dane was probably going to make a run for it. Could he come to me? I started to say *Of course* but he cut me off and said, *You need to look at something before you decide. What's been done to him isn't going to be fixed with room, board and a credit card.* Which I thought was obnoxious, but then he took out some papers from his inside jacket pocket and showed them to me." She paused and took a long drink of wine.

"What were they?" Liko asked.

"Xeroxed pages from his medical files. Post-op shots of the mastectomy. I didn't understand what I was looking at. I said, *What happened to him, is he sick, what's going on?* Then I got to the other pictures." Her eyes flicked to Dane.

"What I described to you the other night," he said to Liko. "The conditioning sessions. I didn't know it was photographed. Must've been a two-way mirror in the room. Or hell, maybe the person taking pictures was there the whole time and I blocked it out."

"Where'd Paul get them?" Liko said.

"My father kept copies of all my medical reports in his office. Paul had access to that office. He swiped them."

"I was almost sick on my shoes," Maisie said. "I told Paul, *You send him here. You tell him to come here.* Paul said, *If I can find you, Ivelaw can.* I said, *You just send Dane here.* Already my hand is reaching for the phone because I'm calling Gideon, I'm calling my lawyer, I'm calling my pipple."

"But what did you say to Paul before he left?" Dane asked, like a child insisting every detail of a beloved story always be told the same way.

Maisie smiled, "I said, *Tell Dane not to hide his eyes.*"

EVERY WOMAN IN WHITESTONE

1989

When Dane returns from the clinic, Diane retreats to some impossibly deep place in his soul. Dane covers the door with a brown contact lens and orders her to stay hidden and not make a sound. Like a switch being thrown, Diane goes silent.

Dane begins to consciously and systematically disassociate from his father. The abuse doesn't stop. The beatings and humiliation and bodily inspections continue, but Dane goes far away at such times, telling himself it's not important and will not be remembered.

This isn't important.

He's not important.

None of this is making memory.

This will be forgotten.

He depersonalizes his father, no longer thinking his name or the word *father.* Even *Sir* is ditched, until *(he)* is reduced to a mere cardboard cutout, speaking lines through a tinny squawk box. A decade later, watching *South Park* for the first time and taking in the two-dimensional characters with their horizontally split heads, Dane will sit up in rapt wonder, thinking, *Holy shit, it's what I did with (him).*

Dane continues to obey one law he learned from *(him):* Always get in front of a situation. You have to rob your enemies of attack by attacking first. Acknowledge your oddity before anyone else can.

You have to be your own bully.

First day of high school gym class, Dane strides nude into the shower and the first sideways glance he counters with a friendly, but aggressive glare.

"Digging my one ball?" he says. "Want a closer look, freak?"

The next gym period, he's confronted by a curious alpha male, "What's this about you only having one ball?"

Dane whips off his towel. "Yep. See for yourself. There it is."

"Hey, one-ball," the boys call in the hallway.

"I prefer Uno," Dane calls back.

When teased or jeered, he joins in the fun. He doesn't mind the below-the-belt humor because it keeps the focus off his mutilated chest. But he's got a good line for that situation.

"Nipple cancer," he says. "One day you're minding your own business, the next you're bleeding out your chest berries."

His peers exchange looks, not sure if he's serious.

"For real?" one says.

"I could've nursed a vampire. Then the shit got into my lungs. Nasty-ass time in my life. I look like a Ken doll, but better than being dead, right?"

He gets so far ahead of the potential hazing, he laps it. Soon his physical oddities become uninteresting. He can turn his back in the locker room to change, or create a screen with an open locker door, even pull a curtain in the communal showers, and barely anyone notices. Those who do and attempt to give him shit get nowhere.

Weak becomes Strong.

Diane stays safely hidden inside.

These are Dane's two laws in high school. Almost everything else he learns from Paul Goldberg.

Paul is in charge of Dane's diet, gym regimen, homework, meds and appearance. The academic load at Hunter is vigorous, and Dane isn't allowed any extracurricular activities except Mock Trial, Model UN, Speech and Debate, Congress and FBLA Parliamentary Procedure.

In between schoolwork and gym workouts are a plethora of life skills. How to get around New York City—first by mass transit, and after Dane learns to drive, how to navigate by car in and out of the tri-state area. There are lessons in classic fashion. Seminars in etiquette. And sometimes, judiciously, discreetly, things *(he)* might not approve of. A day spent working in a soup kitchen or homeless shelter. Museums. A movie. Avery Fisher Hall.

Paul also teaches Dane the basics of personal finance. He dispenses a cash allowance from *(him)* at the start of every month, and teaches the boy how to budget so it lasts.

"You have your own bank account?" he asks one day, as he's administering one of the slow-push injections in Dane's thigh.

"No," Dane says, breathing through the burn.

"You should." Paul's thumb on the syringe grows still and above it, his cat-like eyes look into Dane's, managing to be both distanced and dangerous. "You're going to want a bit of your own money. Personal money. Private money. But you're not hearing this from me." Ever so gently, he moves the needle buried in Dane's quadriceps with an expertise that's suddenly terrifying.

"I'll tell you how to do it, but you're on your own to keep it a secret. Statements will come by mail and you'll have to intercept them. Or open a post office box. Establish a line of credit and telemarketers start calling the house. Your father will know why. He'll ask me and of course I will deny any knowledge of what you've been doing."

The ache in Dane's thigh intensifies. Behind his left eye, Diane is crying wordlessly but Dane's face mirrors Paul's composed, aloof expression. He calmly fights the urge to blink and says mildly, "I understand. You can finish now."

Their eyes continue to hold as Paul depresses the plunger to the bottom and withdraws the needle.

"Most banks won't let you open an account without a deposit," he says. "Usually between five hundred and a grand."

"No point in it, then."

"I can lend you the money."

"I couldn't pay you back," Dane says, taking the shirt Paul holds out. "What are you always telling me—be impeccable with your word and your money?"

The corners of Paul's mouth barely move yet he definitely smiles. "I know one way you can make some cash. You move in the right circles."

Dane looks up from his buttons, brows wrinkled.

"Private school boys are always looking to get high."

Dane knows this is true in theory, but in practice, his only experience with hard substance has been with Paul. Another of the discreet lessons *(he)* would not approve of is an occasional, supervised joint or line of coke.

"You should know the limits of your tolerance," Paul says.

Dane's limits are exceedingly narrow. The frenetic, teeth-grinding high of blow is horrible, making his already tight-strung personality morph into electric anxiety. His brain explodes. Diane screams and screams and Dane can't get down fast enough. Being thoroughly stoned is just as disturbing. Now his brain implodes and the boundaries of his body seem to disappear. He has no *edges.* He's reduced to a pair of mismatched eyes, floating lost in space, looking in two different directions, unable to gain purchase on anything.

He experiments carefully, and finds he likes the comfortable, dependable buzz of two drinks. Any two will do. Three hits on a joint or bowl is just enough to make him feel cozy without leaving the confines of his existence and wandering around the astral plane. It's either pot or booze. Never both together.

"I don't want to get high, I want to get medium," he quips.

Up until now, he's been a chaperoned participant in heightened reality. Is it possible he could be the event coordinator? And make money doing it?

"The risks are higher than opening a little bank account," Paul says. "I'm not just talking about your father. It's a top-down game and you'll have to be more than impeccable with your word and money. You need to be immaculate. Screw a dealer and you could wind up with a broken arm, a knife in your back, or dead in a vacant lot. Your father finds any of your stash or cash, he'll beat you into next month. Get caught possessing on the street and you know where you end up."

His head moves imperceptibly in the direction of Riker's Island.

"And of course, I will deny all knowledge of what you've been up to. Implicate me, and there will be consequences."

"I understand," Dane says. Not for the first time, he asks his strange governor, "Why do you work for him?"

Paul doesn't answer. He never does. The Sphinx hardens to sandstone. "Finish getting dressed," he says smoothly.

DANE DRIFTS TOWARD SEVENTEEN, rising and falling on waves of aggression and passivity. Maintaining the perfectly masculine appearance and demeanor his father demands. Shrewd and scrupulous in his secret financial dealings. Utterly lost in his heart. Behind his left eye, Diane doesn't dare to speak, but she cries all the time. She ceases only when Dane takes the most dangerous risk of all and slips into his sister's bedroom.

Marizabet, I come your room.

He can't fit into his sister's old clothes anymore. To acquire new ones, he craftily combines a few of Paul's life lessons. He copies his minder's confident manners to engage a sales clerk at Saks Fifth Avenue. He charms her with a smooth cover story about a chronically ill girlfriend invited to a party. He gives measurements, orders a simple black dress and heels, and has them shipped to the post office box where his secret bank account statements go. Within two weeks, the elegant outfit hangs in Marizabet's closet and all the packing material is carefully brought to the dumpsters in back of Hunter Academy for disposal.

He repeats the process at Victoria's Secret and again at a small wig boutique. Yet when dressed in the new clothing, padded, made up and coiffed, Danelaw Strong looks in the mirror and sees the thing he dreads most: Danelaw Strong.

Diane peers over his left shoulder. She puts her cheek against his and shakes her head. It's a kind rejection. She's profoundly grateful he tried. She doesn't mind if he does it again. But it isn't what she wants.

He HAS TO BE supernaturally discreet when experimenting with sex. While *(he)* would probably be pleased if Dane fucked every woman in Whitestone, Dane's curiosity in men would not be tolerated. Plus he has a few quirks to explain, such as not wanting to take his shirt off. Hell, he'd rather not leave his pants altogether, what with his one ball, small dick and pathetic patch of pubes. It would be getting far, far behind a situation, which is against his law.

The few, furtive and fumbling encounters leave him with more questions than answers. He knows what feels good in general, but can't specifically pin down from whom he wants what. Everything is framed in binary, this-or-that options.

I like getting with girls. But I like getting with guys, too.
Which do I choose?
With guys I like being a top.
With girls I'm a bottom.
Shouldn't it be the other way around?
I want to look like a boy and feel like a girl.
I don't know how to choose.

The concept of *both* simply doesn't occur to him.

Once, at a party, Dane sees a man wearing a kilt. He's tall and built with tousled hair and a trim beard. He wears a tight, white T-shirt over his broad chest. Work boots, thick socks, and a goddamn *kilt.* A male adult in a *(skirt)* in public. It doesn't swish around his knees, but hangs from his lean hips in *(knife)* sharp pleats. It's *(silky)* soft, but it's hard.

Three buttons drop from the kilt's waistband, a row on either side of center.

A tantalizing trail, a chute, a funnel that pointed down—*This way! Hurry!*— without going anywhere. The buttons will frame the man's belly button, if he'd only take his shirt off. Dane wants it off. Wants the shirt off, the boots off, everything off but that amazing kilt. This is the most magnificent, sensational man Dane has ever laid eyes on. Dane wants him immediately and utterly.

I'm so hard for you, he thinks, staring.

I want to look like you.

I want to be handled by you.

I want to handle someone looking and feeling like you.

He grows dizzy, imagining the man unbuttoning the kilt, holding Dane's eyes. He'll unwrap it and hold the ends open like a bath towel. He'll be erect and sublime, shy and arrogant, entitled and beseeching, humble and proud. Rough and hairy in some places, soft and *(silky)* in others. Dane will go to him, put arms around the thick shoulders, press his clothed body to that miraculous nudity. The man will wrap the kilt around both their bodies and button them in safe.

"There," he'll say, and press big hands to Dane's back.

Dane blinks, feeling their hip bones bump and their erections collide. He's almost in tears.

The kilted man has a girlfriend with him. He touches and caresses her, wraps her hair around his fist, rubs circles on her back, nuzzles her neck. Watching them, Dane wants to die. As she leaves her kilted prince, the woman runs her hand down his arm and squeezes his fingers before exiting the kitchen. Dane watches her go. He wants to be her leaving. He wants to be the kilted man staying.

Come back. Stay here. Come back and stay here. Be with him. Be with us.

He wants to squeeze between their bodies and be adored. Wants them to want him just as badly.

Can you want a them? Is them allowed?

Then the kilted man speaks. He actually says something to Dane. Dane blinks, dry-mouthed and uncomprehending. "I'm sorry, what?"

A gorgeous smile breaks the beard, top and bottom. A beautiful laugh in his awesome chest. "My man, how old are you?"

"Seventeen," Dane says, too stunned to lie.

The man shakes his head, the smile turning a touch wistful. "Bummer," he says. He starts to leave the kitchen as well, and pauses to press his cold beer bottle against the side of Dane's neck. "Hope I see you again in your twenties."

Dane never sees him again, but he never forgets the sound of *my man*. He adopts it. "What's up, my man," he says. "My man, you look like hell. You are correct, my man."

If ever he meets a man who uses *my man,* Dane feels an immediate affinity, remembering an ice-cold touch on his neck and a bearded smile.

DANE IS IN MARIZABET'S room, dressed in his black dress and heels. He wears the long, blonde wig while sitting at the mirrored vanity, making up his face.

The doorknob turns.

Usually Dane locks it. Always he locks it. He hasn't tonight and later he'll wonder if it was on purpose. He thinks it's (*him*) coming in. Good. Maybe it will all end tonight.

But it's Paul who walks in. It's out of hours: Usually Paul leaves for the day at six. He's come back for some reason and he's posted at the half-open door, staring into the mirror, where Dane stares back.

A long considering moment passes. Time enough for Dane to realize he simply doesn't care anymore.

He has no practice feminizing his voice. He's never had a need during these secret, silent dress-up sessions in Marizabet's room. His throat is dry but he doesn't clear it. Rather he uses the dryness to craft a low, husky Kathleen Turner drawl.

"Come in or stay out," he says. "Either way, my man, close the door."

Close the door while you decide what to do, he thinks. *Whether it's turning me in or turning this to blackmail. If the latter includes fucking me, well, it'll be something new. I'm told I suck a mean dick. I bet I could make even a soulless Sphinx yell my name.*

Paul walks closer, looking at Dane's reflection the whole while. Dane can't fathom anything in Paul's expression. He has no idea how this is going to go down.

It's kind of exciting.

Paul studies the young woman in the mirror. "Red isn't the right lipstick," he finally says. "Not with your coloring. It's too stark."

Dane rolls his lips in and out.

"Change it," Paul says, in the same governing tone he always uses with Dane. *Get dressed, get in the car, start your assignments, finish your breakfast, fix your tie, do fifty pushups, stand up straight, don't use that fork, hang up your shirts properly.*

And now, *change your lipstick.*

So Dane does, reapplying a more natural peachy-pink. Paul nods approval, then goes into Marizabet's closet and finds a coat. He holds it out, like a gentleman. Dane puts it on, like a lady. They walk outside where Paul's car is waiting. He opens the passenger door for Dane.

"Sit first," he says. "Sideways. Then bring your legs in."

Later, Dane will marvel that him being dressed as a woman made little to no change in Paul's demeanor. Other than opening doors and holding out Dane's chair in the restaurant, Paul remains as impeccable and precise as always. His social control is absolute and Dane feeds off it, drawing a cloak of good manners around the bizarre circumstances.

Once or twice, as they make polite conversation about books—one of the few subjects on which Paul will share a personal opinion—Paul's expression morphs from cool observation to cool concern.

"Your father hired me to make a man out of you," he says over coffee for Dane, cognac for himself. "His words."

"You're doing a bang-up job." Dane longs for the days you could smoke in restaurants, just for the ritual of having Paul light it for him.

"What are you going to do when you're eighteen?"

Dane doesn't answer. Tucked in the back of his mind all this time is the idea this dinner could be a sting. He's half-braced for *(him)* to appear at the table.

"What do you want?" Paul persists. "What would be your ideal life?"

"I don't know."

"Living as a woman?"

"No. This is… This is just part of me. Something I do. No. Something I feel. A way I like to feel. And sometimes like to look. But it's private. It's for me. Being out in the world with you, as Diane, is—"

"Diane?" Paul says. "Is that your name?"

"It's a way I feel," Dane says carefully. "Out in public, dressed like this, maybe it should be a thrill or a dare or a big *fuck you* to society. All I feel is scared. If someone we know walks in and I'm seen like this, I'll lose it. I'll lose her. I'll lose myself. I've already lost so much. My body is barely my own. You dictate what I do, where I go, what I eat, how I look. And you take your orders from *him.*"

Paul looks at him hard. He elegantly signals the server for another cognac. Then he says, "Tell me everything."

It's the same way he would tell Dane to stop fidgeting or wear the blue sport coat. A steely order inside velvet courtesy. Dane sits up straighter, his wounded chest pushing out the padded lingerie.

"No, you first," he says. "Tell me why you work for him."

Paul blinks so infrequently that when he does, it's majestic. He finally answers, "Because I have to."

"Or else?"

"Or…" And Paul Goldberg hesitates. Something Dane's never seen. "Or he'll hurt someone I care about."

"I see. Thank you," he adds to the server, who has delivered the second cognac and topped up Dane's coffee cup.

"Now tell me," Paul says.

Dane does. As much as he can of his childhood, his mother, his illness, the clinic, the surgery.

"Do you believe you're as sick as they say?" Paul asks. "Is it even possible you've been walking around your entire life with chronic cancer?"

"How would I know?" Dane says through the wall of a toothy smile. "I'm just a kid. I live in a prison upriver from a prison. I don't know who or what to believe anymore. You give me those shots. You dole out the pills and stand over me until they're swallowed. Didn't anyone tell you what they were for? Did you never wonder yourself?"

Paul is blinking a little more rapidly now. "If I were you, I'd get out."

"How?"

"Just leave."

"And go where? Do what? Live on what? Survive how? I've watched my father destroy people's lives with one phone call, while he's sitting on the john. I don't just run from him, I run from a machine. You're a cog in his machine. What, are *you* going to help me run away and make a new life? More likely you'll take me home after this lovely dinner—thanks awfully, by the way—and tell him what went down. And speaking of which, is there a price for your silence? Do I need to suck your dick or anything? You want me to do it as Diane or Dane?"

"No," Paul says quietly.

Dane looks over Paul's shoulders, blinking back tears. "Should never have been born."

"Don't say that."

"It's true."

"It isn't." Paul folds his napkin and with a little jerk of his chin, indicates Dane should do the same.

ONE WEEK LATER, Dane comes out the front doors of Hunter Academy into a blinding blue winter afternoon. Usually Paul is waiting with the car, but he's nowhere to be seen. Another man approaches him, wearing aviators, carrying a thick folder and a small backpack. "Danelaw Strong?"

"Yeah?"

Christ, is he a Fed? Am I getting arrested?

Dane has an ounce of pot and five hundred in cash in his school bag. He considers dumping the lot and making a run for it. Then the man hands over the folder and pack, followed by a folded note.

"What's going on?" Dane says, his arms full.

The man only indicates the note.

> *Dane, I no longer work for your father. You shouldn't either. Don't ever go back to the house. What you need to know is in the folder. What you need to live is in the pack. What I taught you is yours forever. Use it wisely. Be careful. Hand this note back to Barry and don't attempt to contact or look for me. I will deny I know you or ever met you. Good luck. —PG*

Dane hands the note to Barry, who passes over a separate envelope. Inside is a clipping from the *New York Times* about a recent art show at the Montresor Gallery in SoHo. Another note clipped to it in Paul's handwriting.

> *The woman in the article, Maisie Montresor, is your sister. Go to her. Don't hide your eyes. Hand this note back to Barry. Do not ask him questions.*

Dane obeys instructions to the letter. Barry lowers his sunglasses a fraction to make eye contact. "Good luck," he says tersely, and walks away, leaving Dane clutching his school bag, a backpack, a file folder and a newspaper clipping. For five minutes, he stands still in the cold, in shock and unsure what to do.

What you need to know is in the folder. What you need to live is in the pack.

What I taught you is yours forever. Use it wisely.

First thing is to get to SoHo. No convenient task from Long Island but Paul taught him how to negotiate mass transit. So he starts hoofing it to the nearest bus station. Bus to the subway. Subway to Manhattan. Change for downtown. On the way he examines the backpack: It has his shaving kit, a couple changes of clothes, his birth certificate and a drawstring bag with prescription bottles, vials and disposable syringes.

He takes a quick peek at the thick file folder, too.

> *Subject, Danelaw Strong, was a 3.46-kg infant delivered vaginally at term; he had a normal right testis and an undescended left testis, with otherwise normal male genitalia. At the age of six months, the left testis was palpable at the inguinal ring...*

He absently touches his own left side. The scar where Dr. Porto took out a cancerous tumor.

He shuffles pages. Weird. In all the jargon, he can't find the word *cancer.*

> *...abdominal surgical exploration revealed a hernial sac containing an abnormal gonad and vas deferens. These structures were excised; they proved on histologic examination to be an ovary with a fallopian tube attached to a horn of uterus. Karyotyping of peripheral-blood lymphocytes then revealed two cell lines, one 46,XX and the other 46,XY.*

Ovary, Dane thinks, and it's Diane's voice in his mind, touching each word. *Fallopian tube. Uterus.*

She's back. She's here. She's talking to him. After months and months of silence.

He whispers carefully into the collar of his jacket: "Is it you?"

His left eye twitches at the corner. *Read it again,* she says.

> *These structures were excised; they proved on histologic examination to be an ovary with a fallopian tube attached to a horn of uterus.*

"Oh my God." Dane's mouth forms the words with no sound.

See, Diane says, reaching over his left shoulder to tap the page. *See, I told you. I was always inside.*

THE DISNEY RULE

The Jensens had brought a bakery box of treats, which they took into the living room with coffee.

"What was it like?" Liko asked. "Being reunited?"

"Surreal," the Strong siblings answered together, then looked at each other and laughed.

"Hey, *she* was prepared," Dane said. "I had no idea Paul had done reconnaissance. I thought I'd be walking into the gallery cold and introducing myself. Proving myself. By the time I got downtown, I was convinced all over again this was a setup and I'd be a moron to go into that gallery. I stalled for time by going to McDonald's." Dane rubbed his face. "Which, you have to understand, was an extremely subversive act. Fast food was *verboten*. My stomach didn't have the first idea what to do when I stuffed it with a cheeseburger and fries. I have no idea why I thought Mickey D's would stick it to my old man and give me courage."

"Hey, you were too young to get a scotch and soda," Huff said.

"I got to the gallery and was already feeling sick. I pushed open the door and barely had a second to look around when she was right there."

Maisie touched fingertips between her eyebrows. "Poor kid, I just kind of…*grabbed* him."

Dane spread his arms wide, then bent his elbows inward. "She *folded* me in. Like an envelope. And I don't know if I was connecting to her as a brother right then. Like I didn't feel this overwhelming recognition of *Marizabet, sister, yes, this is she, I remember this hug.* She was a stranger to me, but her energy was amazing. I didn't get hugged by too many older women at that time in my life, but Maze held me for a long, long time. A real Disney hug. You know the Disney rule?"

"You mean how character actors hug kids and don't let go until the kid does?"

"Exactly."

"Did you burst out crying?"

"I didn't," Maisie said. "I was too stunned, and my mind was far ahead, making plans."

"Me neither," Dane said, "because I immediately realized two things. One, this was the first day of the rest of my life. Two, I was about to throw up. I broke away from her and bolted toward a door, praying it was a bathroom."

The siblings were laughing now, and they finished together, "And *that's* how we met."

"Oh my God, what a shit show," Maisie said, wiping her eyes.

"I started crying between heaves," Dane said. "Even while puking, I hung onto those folders and papers like they were all I had left in the world."

"Where did you go then," Liko asked. "To Norwalk?"

"To my apartment that night," Maisie said. "On West Eighty-Sixth."

"Oh man," Dane said. "As if my head weren't already exploding…"

He told how when he got to Maisie's place, he was astounded to find Maisie had family pictures he'd never seen before, including a beautiful photograph of Helen deWinter with a three-year-old Dane on her lap. She was laughing at something off-camera, while Dane looked only at his mother, with his two different eyes and a big smile.

"It was on a little table as you came in the apartment door," Dane said. "I didn't even take my coat off or put down my file folder. I grabbed the picture and kind of stumbled backward against the wall. In the space of an hour I was reunited with the two most important women in my life. It was a lot."

More photographs were framed around the apartment. A shot of Dane alone, playing in a puddle of sunshine. Another picture of Helen, Maisie and Dane sitting on the floor in front of the kitchen fireplace: Helen and Maisie cross-legged, playing some kind of board game, and Dane tucked in Helen's lap.

Liko's eyes volleyed between the siblings as he shaped his next question. "Don't answer if it's too painful," he finally said, "but what actually happened to your mother?"

"She died in nineteen eighty-seven," Maisie said.

Liko barely breathed his next inquiry. "In jail?"

"In one of PHS's mental health facilities. Ivelaw had her involuntarily committed."

"I'm so sorry," Liko said. "I don't know if there's an encapsulated version of how Ivelaw Strong finally got his, but maybe it's enough to know he did."

Dane dropped his hand on Liko's leg. He ran it up a little, down a little. Then he seemed to come to a decision and he turned it palm up. Liko slid his against it, folding their fingers tight.

"What if I told you," Dane said, "that it was Fred who helped bring him down? First by bringing a class action lawsuit against Porto, which opened up a can of maggots in PHS."

"Dane's folder wasn't the only one Paul Goldberg swiped," Maisie said. "Kudos to him, too."

"And to Dane," Huff said, "who provided key testimony."

"Good on all of you," Liko said. "And fuck that guy."

They all reached for cups and glasses and toasted the sentiment.

"Can I request a story?" Huff said.

"Oh, babe." Maisie curled against him. "I'm sorry, you've gotten kind of sidelined during this whole saga."

He kissed her hairline. "Well, we haven't gotten to my chapter yet."

"It's one of the best chapters," Dane said.

"Wait, how *do* you come into all of this?" Liko said. "You said Dane introduced you and Maisie." He pointed between Huff and Dane. "You guys knew each other already?"

"Huff was one of my counselors at Kingpoint Academy," Dane said. He and Maisie did a round of finger snaps and Huff bowed his head.

"No shit," Liko said.

"During the course of our thoroughly professional relationship, I discovered Dr. Jensen was a huge Gideon Perfect fan. I thought to myself, *Well, well, let's tuck this information away for a more opportune time.* Fast-forward to nineteen ninety-three, I've graduated, and my sister is having a big show for a young, rising artist named Ethan Hasen. Gideon Perfect is going to be there, too, so I casually email an invite to my old mentor."

"It was an epiphanous event," Huff said.

Maisie ruffled his hair. "You have a low threshold for epiphanous events."

KNIGHT TAKES KING

Dane has seen his sister host at least ten shows at her SoHo gallery. Not once has he seen her with the jitters about an opening. The upcoming exhibit *Harefoot,* by the unknown artist Ethan Hasen, is making her distracted and full of sighs. Dane finds her fussing over the gallery program and chewing her thumbnail.

"Is this show something of a risk?" he asks. "Will you lose money?"

"Every pot has a lid," she says absently. "It's just…"

Dane studies the glossy brochure, which has small depictions of the photographs that will be displayed. "You've never hosted a photographer before," he notes.

"They're not photos. They're paintings."

"What?" He peers closer. "No, they're not."

"Those are canvases. Wait until you see them in person. His brushwork is unbelievable. His whole style is bananas. I'm still struggling to come up with a word for it."

"Realism," Dane ventures.

"It's beyond realism. It's hyper-realism. He calls it pathological perfectionism."

All the works are of rabbits and hares. Dane would be hard-pressed to recall the artistic details of past shows at the Montresor Gallery, but he's certain animal art has never been exhibited there.

"Why the fascination with rabbits?"

"I don't know, he just adores them. Their folklore and symbolism and legends. It makes no sense. There's classic animal depiction in art, but this? This is almost bordering on fantasy. He did start out in children's illustrations, but…"

"It's weirdly fascinating."

"It's evocative and I love looking at it. It makes no sense, but I absolutely love his work." She sighs, her thumbnail at her teeth again. "I'm just worried no one else will."

"Or maybe you'll have discovered a genius."

"I already know he's a genius. Which is another thing—he's supernaturally talented and brilliant, but he's a delight. An ego-less artist, what even *is* that?" She sighs a final time. "Oh well. I guess we'll find out."

"It'll be great," Dane says, patting her. "Dr. Jensen is coming. Did you tell Gideon?"

"Yes, yes," Maisie says. "He's coming to meet Ethan at the installation and get a personal walkthrough, then he'll do a quick appearance at the opening. He knows Huff is someone special to you and he's looking forward to it…"

"This is my sister, Maisie," Dane says. "Maze, this is Huff Jensen."

If Liko Greenman could time-travel to this introduction, he'd immediately recognize the look that passes between Maisie and Huff and counsel *Pump the brakes, you morons.*

Dane isn't quite as adept in detecting instant chemistry, but he senses Huff is no longer thinking about an introduction to Gideon Perfect. A feeling in Dane's young bones tells him he's executed an inadvertent but masterful gambit. Knight takes King to meet Queen. Check and mate.

The rest of the night, Huff and Maisie can't keep their eyes off each other. They tether immediately, drifting off to schmooze and peruse, then finding each other again. Each time standing a little closer together. Each time moving their little pod further from the mothership.

Dane tells himself he's happy for them. And he is. But the realization the one you adore will never be yours is never an easy thing. Nor a painless one. The bittersweet end of a dream is welling up in Dane's throat and nose and pushing on the backs of his eyes. Once again, he moves swiftly toward the gallery's small bathroom, where he once threw up McDonald's while clutching his medical file folder, knowing it was the first day of the rest of his life.

I guess it's the first day of the rest of their lives, Diane says dully as Dane wrestles his emotions. He runs the water cold and splashes his face. A little too vigorously because he washes the brown contact lens out of his left eye.

"Fuck," he cries, spying it balanced on the edge of the drain. His fingertips make a grab just as it slips away. "Fuck," he says again, looking in the mirror. His two-color gaze stares back.

The past three years have been a long, grueling and courageous journey of intense work. A lot of hours on the couch. A lot of behavior to unlearn and relearn. A lot of poison to dump at the feet of professionals and an immeasurable amount of bravery to sort through it all. A lot of feeling like absolute shit.

He's gathered vast amounts of knowledge, worked through dozens of issues—some resolved, some not so much. He's only just growing comfortable with what it's like to be Danelaw Strong and while he doesn't fear people being disconcerted, reviled or even rude about his appearance, he has enacted laws about who gets to see his natural eyes and when.

A knock at the door. "One sec," he calls. He stares harder at himself, digging deep to channel the Sphinx-like expression of Paul Goldberg, along with his absolute social control. It's time to be impeccable.

Nobody's looking at you anyway, he thinks. *And hey, if you get anxious, Huff is here. Might be hard to get his attention but at least he's here. Now go be there for Maisie.*

He unlocks the door with authority and strides out, instantly colliding with another man.

"Oh God, sorry," Dane says, catching a fumbled beer bottle just in time, directing the foam away from the man's jacket and tie.

"Whoa, nice catch," the man says. "Sorry about that."

"Here, mop it up before someone breaks their ankle." A woman Dane hadn't noticed drops a wedge of paper napkins on the spilled beer. As she moves it around with her foot, she puts a hand on Dane's shoulder to steady herself. He's barely registered her face but something about her touch makes his heart slow down, then give a flutter of flattered curiosity that this woman has chosen to lean on him.

I can trust you, the hand says. *In fact, I know you. We've been friends a long time, we just haven't been introduced yet.*

"That should do it." She scoops up the wad of napkins and heads toward a garbage can, and Dane looks at the man he bumped into.

The man looks back.

A tense, contemplative moment passes. Like the time between chess moves.

Whatever the opposite of Sphinx is, Diane says, *this guy is it.*

The man is dark blond with light brown eyes that are wide open and full of curiosity. Beneath their gaze is a broad, smiling mouth that slowly says, "Holy shit."

Dane can't yet speak, but he feels his mouth smiling back in agreement.

The woman returns, brushing her palms off. She's not smiling, and while her face is guarded, it's not hostile. Her hair is black and shiny, cropped tight around her ears and neck, with a tousled fringe of bangs above watery green eyes. She's dressed in what looks like a man's pinstriped suit over a white T-shirt.

Dane looks back at the man, who is a little taller. Then at the woman, who's just a bit shorter.

For another strategizing moment, they stand in a loose triangle, the woman on Dane's blue-eyed side and the man on his brown-eyed side. Each taking up the same amount of space. Each unable to simultaneously look at the other two, so the three gazes volley around, meeting and parting and meeting again.

Diane puts her chin on Dane's left shoulder, amused. *The Sphinx would be appalled at your manners right now. Perhaps say something?*

"Hi," Dane says.

"Hi," the man replies.

"Hi," the woman says, and gestures toward the bathroom, which Dane is still standing in front of. "Can I…?"

"Sorry," Dane says, and starts to walk away but the man's hand closes on his arm and stills him.

"Wait," he says. "Look at me."

Dane tugs his arm free but is unable to pull his soul away from that command.

Look at me.

He looks at the man, who stares deep in Dane's eyes. The look on his face is pure revelation, as if he's solved some great mystery.

Epiphany, Dane thinks. *The opposite of Sphinx is epiphany.*

"This is unbelievable," the man says.

"What?" Dane says.

"You're amazing," the man says. "I mean, you're perfect. Who are you? I need to talk to you. Can I talk to you?"

"You are talking to me. Who are you?"

"Sorry." The man switches his beer to his left hand and holds out his right. "I'm Ethan Hasen."

"Oh," Dane says, shaking. "You're the artist?"

Ethan looks back at the gallery a second, as if forgetting tonight is about him. "Yes. Who are you? What's your name?"

"Dane. I'm Maisie's brother."

"Brilliant," Ethan says, as the bathroom door opens and the woman appears.

"Good lord, can't you two find a better place to loiter than right outside the john?"

Her tone leans on Dane the same way her hand did before. She's teasing because she trusts him. She knows him. She's lumping him in with Ethan, making one and one into *you two.* Giving them shit because they're her friends. They've been friends a long time.

"This is Nomi Misteria," Ethan says. "Nomi, this is Dane Montresor."

"Strong, actually," Dane says. "My last name is Strong."

"Nome, we need to talk to him."

"We?" Nomi says. "I'm getting a drink and hunting down the waiter with the chicken satay thingies."

"Fine," Ethan says, and his fingers close on Dane's sleeve again. "Let's you and me talk."

"Shouldn't you be…" Nomi gestures toward the exhibit area. "You know. Artisting?"

"Shit." Ethan looks over his shoulder. Maisie is coming toward the trio, Huff Jensen trailing a few deferential steps behind, his gaze focused intensely on her back.

"Ethan," Maisie calls. "Don't wander off. I need you with me."

Ethan hands Dane's sleeve into Nomi's possession. "Hold this. Don't let him get away."

"No problem," Nomi says, then flicks her eyes sweetly to Dane. "Shall we go to Staten Island?"

"Don't," Ethan barks. "Maze, make your brother stay here."

"He has to," Maisie says. "I'm his ride home."

As she and Ethan walk off, she pats Huff's lapel and lets her hand trail down his arm. Huff lingers a moment, dazed and helpless, before looking back at Dane.

Thank you, he mouths.

Dane smiles and gives a slow, farewell wink. He's broken-hearted, but exhilarated, and he doesn't realize how longingly he stares after Huff until Nomi's palm cuts through his field of vision.

"Hello?" she says. "Wow, which one are you in love with?"

"I hope not Maisie," Dane says. "She's my sister."

"Ah. Then you must be pining for the lovely gentleman."

"I introduced them."

"Aren't you generous?" She releases her hold on his sleeve and puts her hands in her trouser pockets. "I'm starving. Can you pine and eat at the same time?"

They cram two little plates with appetizers and canapes, grab flutes of champagne and find a wide windowsill where they can munch and people-watch.

"I have no small talk," Nomi says. "You can jump immediately into personal questions, but I do love gardening, and I love books. Either of those topics interest you?"

"Books."

She smiles over her champagne. "What are you reading? Don't be shy. I never judge."

"I started Stephen King's *Misery.*"

"You read him before?"

"No, first time. It's freaking me out."

"I read *Misery* like this…" Nomi puts a hand in front of her face, then peeks through her fingers. The sea-green eye has flecks of gold around the pupil.

"I was kind of in a situation where someone had complete control of my life," Dane hears himself say. "It's not a good read for me right now."

"Absolutely not," she says, as receptive and unfazed as a good friend would be. As if she knew already what the situation was.

"I should put it down and come back after a few more years of therapy. Maybe read *Pet Sematary* instead."

Nomi vigorously shakes her head, chewing and swallowing. "You need a kinder, gentler intro to King. Try *The Eyes of the Dragon.*"

They stuff themselves and talk more about books. Anything Dane's read, Nomi has read or at least heard of. By the time they've finished their snacks, Dane has scribbled a dozen recommended titles on a cocktail napkin. He's tucking it in his pocket when the gallery noise ratchets up a few decibels. Gideon Perfect has arrived.

"It's the other man of the hour," Nomi says.

Dane cranes his neck to see Gideon hug Maisie hard enough to lift her off her feet, twirling her in a circle. He puts her down and she gestures to Huff beside her. The two men shake hands.

Dane smiles, his heart full of a thousand things. Huff steps back and looks around the gallery, finally finding Dane's gaze.

Thank you, he mouths again.

Dane raises his flute and finishes the last of the bubbly.

"I came with Ethan to the installation last night," Nomi says. "So did Gideon."

"Right," Dane says. "Tonight is just a quick appearance."

"I never met a celebrity before. It's weird to see them slouch around, look at paintings, drink a Pepsi, blow their nose. Do all these human things. He was so normal. And he reads."

Dane guesses he's just heard Nomi Misteria's highest accolade. He absently touches his pocket where the folded napkin is tucked.

"You and Ethan been together long?"

"We're not together," she says. "Just friends. It hasn't been long, actually, but…"

"But?"

"Ethan is one of those people who imprints. He decides he likes you… No, not even likes you. He decides you belong in his life. Immediately. And he follows you, tracks you down, grabs your sleeve and begs you stick around so he can talk to you. And pleads with everyone else not to let you get away."

"People like that can just as suddenly decide you're out of their life," Dane says.

"Tell me about it," Nomi replies sourly, and Dane will soon learn this is a woman who was thrown in a dumpster as a newborn baby.

The crowd has shifted in Gideon's direction, opening space around the paintings. Dane gestures ahead. "Join me down the rabbit hole?"

She fakes a yawn and a bored expression. "I've seen it," she sighs. "With Gideon Perfect on my arm."

Their sides bump and they lean a moment, laughing together. Nomi starts off and as she excuses herself between clusters of people, she reaches a hand behind for Dane. He takes it. All through the next hour, he thinks nothing of holding hands with this woman he's just met. Yet it's everything.

The evening will have much to remember. Much to think about later. It's an evening of bright color and photographic perfection that dissolves into impossibly fine brushwork. A tapestry of long ears and sleek heads. Round eyes full of wisdom, survival and longing. Triangle noses and delicate whiskers. The soft vulnerability of rabbits and the tough, elongated strength of hares. An encyclopedia of names and legends and tales across cultures.

"Check this out," Nomi says, stopping before a large canvas with multiple hares and rabbits forming the Iberian peninsula. "When the Phoenicians discovered Iberia, they found huge numbers of wild rabbits, which were unknown to them. They saw a resemblance to their native rock hyrax. The Punic word is *shaphan*."

Thinking the Iberian coast was simply a large island, the Phoenicians called the place *I-shaphan-im:* Hyrax Island. When the Romans conquered the peninsula, *I-shaphan-im* became *Hispania*.

"So Spain got its name because of rabbits," Dane says. "But it's actually the name of an animal that never lived there."

They travel along the exhibit, learning the word for *moon* in Sanskrit is *Śaśadhara,* meaning *the one who carries the hare.*

In Chinese folklore, female hares conceive through the touch of the full moon's light, or by licking moonlight from a male hare's fur.

West African trickster hares travel to North America on slave ships to transform into Br'er Rabbit and Compair Lapin. Native Americans have Nanabozho, the Great Hare. Wabosso the White Hare, the most powerful magician of all. And Ta-vwots, the Little Rabbit who destroys the world.

The Celtic goddess Eostre is a shape-shifter, assuming the form of a hare during each full moon. The Teutonic Holda and Norse Freya are both attended by hares. Kaltes, another shape-shifting moon goddess from Siberia, roams the snowy steppes as a rabbit.

Ostara, moon goddess of Anglo-Saxon myth, carries a white hare who lays brightly colored eggs, which are given to children at springtime fertility rituals. The forerunner of the modern Easter Bunny.

In Egyptian myth, hares are closely associated with the cycles of the moon: masculine when waxing and feminine when waning. All throughout ancient and modern cultures, across continents, hares are believed to be androgynous, shifting between genders.

Oh, Diane says.

Wow, Dane echoes.

The largest canvas is a trio of hares running in a circle. Each stretched long, noses to tails, their ears forming a triangle.

"It's an optical illusion," Nomi says. "Each hare has two ears, but it looks like they share only three."

Dane is overwhelmed. Slightly outside himself. The evening is spinning like those three hares, yet he's simultaneously grounded by the feel of Nomi's fingers and a list of her favorite books in his pocket. Maisie flushed with triumph, smiling as Huff moves a stray tendril of hair behind her ear. Ethan holding the tip of his tongue in his teeth as he writes his phone number on a piece of scrap paper, then makes a quick sketch of the three hares beneath it.

"Call me," he says. "Tomorrow, all right? Promise?"

Dane tucks the paper in his other pocket and promises. All the way back home to Norwalk, he keeps his hands in his pockets, each closed tight around the things Nomi and Ethan love best. Wishing he'd offered something for them to fold up and carry home.

You did, Diane whispers. *You gave them your eyes.*

TINNER WHEELED

"I loved this."

"What a great night."

"It was so good to see you."

"Let's hang out again soon."

Liko stood with Dane on the porch, waving after the Jensens' car. The red taillights floated along Oak Hill Road and winked out of sight. Then like a book closing, the two men folded toward each other and hugged.

"Hell of a party," Dane said.

Liko exhaled into Dane's hair and held on tight. Tired. Grateful. Suffused with belonging.

Dane turned his head and rubbed his brow along Liko's collarbone. Then he sighed and rested his cheek again. The hug went on. And on.

"I think we're both playing the Disney rule," Liko said.

"You let go first."

"No, you."

"Don't want to."

"Me neither." So they stood in arms for a long time. Stiller than a painting, except for the rise and fall of their breathing.

"You feel so good," Dane said. "In my arms and in my house."

"I love this place."

And I think I love you, Liko thought, but didn't say so. He took Dane's head and kissed him. No slow buildup like at the kitchen table. This kiss opened immediately and the Disney rule lost its G-rating. Their breath came fast and hard and their hugging bodies began to grind. Liko backed Dane into the shingled wall, fencing him in. His tongue curled around the stud in Dane's tongue, sucking at it.

"You like that?" Dane breathed.

"Yeah." Liko's hand spread wide on Dane's face, his thumb holding his mouth open and moving in little circles around the piercing.

"Someday," he whispered, "I want to feel this on my cock."

Dane groaned, his hands sliding into Liko's back pockets and pulling him in. "You wouldn't believe the things I want."

"Try me."

Dane's hips bucked against Liko's and they ground together again.

"God, man," Liko groaned, head tipping back as Dane's mouth went crawling up his neck.

"So hard for you," Dane said.

"Can we get off this porch before I get arrested for public indecency?"

"We're on private property." Dane's laughing mouth closed on Liko's bottom lip, bit a little, then let go slow. "Come on. Want to put you on my bed and do something."

Heading upstairs, Dane paused on a tread and reached to touch one of the dozen paintings hung in the stairwell. "I don't know if you ever noticed this one. But now you've heard its story."

Liko studied the painting, which reminded him of the White Witch from Narnia, though it had none of her sinister evil. This proud empress was cloaked in silver and white furs, snowflakes dotting her long hair. The light of a rising sun behind her, escaping in beams and rays that sliced through a tangle of leafless wisteria vines. Her arms cradled a beautiful child that could have been a boy or a girl. Tow-headed, their face pressed into the woman's sleeve, one eye peeking at the viewer. Three snow-white rabbits attended the queen: one tucked in her elbow, another on her shoulder, the third in the child's lap. The caption read *Tinner Wheeled,* with Ethan's signature EJH beneath.

"He based this on the photo of me and Helen," Dane said. "The one that was in Maisie's apartment."

Not a lot of blood was in Liko's head, but tonight he knew a little more about Dane, about Ethan and his unique way of expressing love, and about the secret words within people's names. His finger reached to touch the letters in *Tinner Wheeled.*

"H... E... L..." He felt his mouth stretch into a grin as he mentally rearranged and found it was all there. "*Tinner Wheeled* is the anagram of *Helen deWinter.*"

"Ethan was always smug about his goddamn anagrams, but this one? Even his jaw was on the floor." Dane's expression turned sly and he began backing up the stairs, pushing on the railings. "Now how about your clothes on the floor and your ass in my bed?"

Holding Dane's eyes, Liko pulled off his shirt and tossed it behind him. Dane pulled his off, turned and took the rest of the steps two at a time.

"Do we need condoms for this?" Liko asked, following into the bedroom.

"No."

Dane was stripping down in such a matter-of-fact way, Liko wasn't sure what was on the agenda. He pulled his own clothes off, watching as Dane closed the bathroom door, then lowered the shades on the room's tall windows. When the last one hit the sill, it wasn't exactly pitch black, but all was reduced to silhouettes and shadows.

"Along with my massive praise kink, I have a thing for the dark."

"I see," Liko said, blinking. "Except not so much."

Dane laughed. "Follow my voice."

"If I stub a toe and ruin the mood, it's your fault."

He crawled onto the big mattress where, as it turned out, Dane wanted them to kneel facing each other and touch themselves.

Liko's brows pulled tight. "You mean, me do me and you do you?"

"Yeah."

"Okay?"

Dane was reaching long for the bedside table drawer. "Need a minute to think it over?"

"No." Liko laughed. "I think I can manage what I've been doing since I was twelve. I'm just curious why."

"Because it's the first thing I ever fantasized about you." Dane said, pouring a little lube into his palm and passing the bottle.

"When?"

"Back in March. Not the night you rang the bell but the next. After you figured out who I was and drove home. That night, I lay in bed and thought about what you were doing, back at your house. It evolved into watching you jerk off." His shoulder rolled. "It was random but it was hot. So I joined in."

"Really," Liko said, settling down, letting self-consciousness slide off his back. "Just us touching ourselves. Not each other?"

"Each other was about a week later. Because, killing time."

"Were we talking this much during it?"

Dane laughed. "Is that a smooth way of telling me to shut up?"

"Not at all. Tell me everything."

"We were talking. Kissing. Confessing secrets."

Liko's eyes were adjusting better. He leaned and kissed a corner of Dane's mouth. "What secret did I tell?"

"I invented something. You and some buddies stole a car. Drove it into a bog in Scotland or some shit. Totally got away with it."

Liko laughed low in his chest. "It was a frog pond and I was grounded a month, but close enough."

They were quiet an intense moment, watching the shape and stroke of each other's hands.

"What are you doing with your thumb there," Dane said.

"I love this little sweet spot. It has a name but I can't think of it now."

"Frenulum."

"You're such a geek."

"It's where I'm gonna get you with my tongue ring. Someday."

"Fuck, man…"

They kissed a while, their hands moving, their breath drawing out long then quickening.

"Say more," Liko said. "About the first time."

"I started by imagining doing things to you. Making you come. I wondered what you looked like. What sounds you make. What you'd whisper. What you'd yell. But then all at once, I wanted to watch you do it to yourself. I wanted to watch you make it happen, not knowing I was there. I wanted to see what you do when you're alone with your hand. I wanted to see you make yourself come before I did it."

"I did rub one out that night," Liko said. He could feel it rising in him now. A tell-tale heat began to kindle between his shoulder blades, moving up his nape and across his crown.

"Tell me," Dane said, dripping a little more lube into each of their palms.

"I was in the shower. Thinking about you. The clue you gave me on a plate. The things I'd do to get more. And then you texted me at three in the morning."

"You gave me some bullshit about being too old."

"It's how I flirt."

The memory of feeling sought out and desired in the middle of the night sent another surge of blood into Liko's lap. He was past hard and approaching granite. The ache of not coming pulled him in all directions.

"Tell me what's making you smile," Dane said.

"One night he's texting me. Few months later, we're doing this."

"Your voice changes when you're coming around."

"Does it?"

"It gets this little rumbling, hoarse edge. Sexy as fuck."

Liko's head lolled between his shoulders. He slowed down the stroke of his hand, trying to match it to Dane's rhythm. Wishing he could match Dane's words, but his mind had gone as slick and slippery as his fingers.

"Watching you work up a nut is so fucking hot," Dane whispered.

"Keep talking to me."

"Can't believe I stopped the car to talk to you. When you were sitting on the stone wall."

"Looking for myself along the roadside."

"And it was my road."

"It was your car that slowed down."

"It was my house."

"It was the Green Man on the pillar."

"It was the guy from New Year's Eve."

"It was you at the door."

"Now it's you in my bed."

They kissed, swaying a little, their kneecaps pressed hard. Their mouths broke open together.

"Don't stop," Liko said, poised on a knife's edge. It was on him, opening like a flower, petals erupting out of his lap. He could feel it bringing Dane around, too, and then Liko's voice disappeared behind the wall of his teeth, while Dane's sling-shotted around the room, first a deep growl, then sailing up high into gasped laughter. They keeled over sideways, sending pillows flying. One knocked the bedside lamp over.

"Shit, my bad," Liko said, breathing hard.

"No worries," Dane panted. "Break a plate. Break a lamp. It's kind of our thing. Oh my God, man, that was fucking *sick.*"

"I approve this fantasy," Liko said. "Solid ten out of ten. Will there be others?"

"Only about six hundred." Dane shook his head hard, then slithered carefully off the bed and went into the bathroom. He came back and tossed Liko a towel, laughing as he wiped himself off. "Holy shit, you shot up to your collarbone."

"One chance to make a first impression. Jesus, it's on my neck."

"Show off." Dane came crawling along Liko's body, took the towel and tossed it away. He dropped down, his head on Liko's chest, an arm and a leg falling heavy and curling around. "This is fantasy number two of six hundred."

Liko closed his eyes and pulled Dane in tight. "Another ten out of ten. You're on a roll tonight."

His palms glided along Dane's back as his body and mind quieted down, shivering over the last of the pleasure. Then he gave an enormous yawn.

"You had a long day," Dane said drowsily.

"I did, didn't I?" His mind reached lazily backward, ticking off events that seemed a week ago now: the cemetery, therapy, meetings, lunch, and… "Oh my God," he said, laughing. "I thought a finger up the bum was going to be the best part of today."

"Day ain't over yet." Dane's hand slid down Liko's side and curved around one ass cheek. Liko laughed harder and batted the exploring touch away.

"One finger a day is my limit."

"Bullshit."

"Believe me, after the massive dinner we ate, you don't want to be near that end."

Dane yawned now, pulling the covers up and putting his head back down on Liko's chest. "I loved tonight."

"I don't have a word for tonight." Liko stroked his head. "Are you back in harbor?"

"Hm?"

"The other night, the conversation got heavy and you kind of got stuck at sea."

"I think I'm all right. Are you?"

Liko thought about it, assessing. "It got heavy tonight too," he said. "But you're also starting to tell about people who rescued you. Which is a better place to leave off than that hellhole clinic. You gotta move, my arm is going numb…"

Dane rolled off him and onto his side. Liko moved behind and wrapped an arm around, twining their fingers. "Tell me another rescue story. I want to fall asleep hearing about someone who helped you."

Dane hummed, his thumb moving across the edges of Liko's fingernails. "Let me think."

"What about… Who was the first doctor to treat you like a person?"

"Oh my God," Dane said, laughing softly. "That was Natalie Obrera. She was so fucking good to me…"

OBRERA

1990

"ALL RIGHT THEN," Dr. Obrera says. "Where should we start?"

"With everything in there," Dane says, pointing to the file folder Paul Goldberg stole from Ivelaw's office. "I've never seen any of this before. I don't know what any of it means."

"Weren't you told?"

"All I know is that I have cancer."

"Cancer?" She opens the file again and works through the papers. "You don't have cancer."

"Yes, I do. It's what they told me."

"Who?"

"Everyone. My father. Dr. Porto."

"What about other doctors?"

"I don't have any other doctors."

Dr. Obrera looks at him a long beat. "You do not have cancer. There is nothing in this folder indicating you have cancer now or ever had it in your life. What you have is tetragametic chimerism."

"What's that?"

"Nothing life-threatening. It means your genetic karyotype has two separate sets of DNA, one male and one female."

The room's edges swim and the blood behind Dane's eyes began to pulse. "What?"

"Sometimes, in cases of fraternal twins in utero, one twin absorbs the other and the result is a single birth. Often we don't even know this has happened until some unrelated blood test shows two different cell lines. Most cases of chimerism go undetected. It's not a disease. It's just a flukey thing that happens."

"I have a twin?"

"Well. You did. Once. It seems you started out with a fraternal female twin, which you then absorbed. I'm sorry, I'm making it sound like you intentionally ate her. This happens very early in pregnancy and like I said, often we don't even know about it. But in your case…"

She opened the folder and read, "…*Infant had a normal right testis and an undescended left testis, with otherwise normal male genitalia. At the age of six months, the left testis was not palpable at the inguinal ring. No further surgical exploration was recommended.*"

"That's right," Dane says. "I only have one. My mother says my body just forgot to make the other one, but the one I had was fine."

"So it is."

"What about my eyes?"

Dr. Obrera smiles at him. "They're stunning. And yes, it's a sign of chimerism. The proper term is heterochromia iridum."

"Not cancer?"

"No. Not cancer. It's harmless." Her gaze narrows. "You just lost all your color. Let me get you some water."

She brings him a drink and patiently goes through his records with him.

At age thirteen, child was in the 10th percentile for height and weight. No facial, axillary or pubic hair onset. At fourteen, he presented with severe gynecomastia and intermittent abdominal pain in the left quadrant. Mastectomy performed. Abdominal surgical exploration revealed a hernial sac, heretofore undetected, containing an abnormal gonad and vas deferens. These structures were excised; they proved on histologic examination to be an ovary with a fallopian tube attached to a horn of uterus. Karyotyping of peripheral-blood lymphocytes then revealed two cell lines, one 46,XX and the other 46,XY.

Dr. Obrera's face is flushed. The more she reads, the angrier she looks.

"What is it?" Dane says. "What's wrong with me?"

"Nothing," she snaps. She quickly touches her mouth and takes a deep breath. "I'm sorry. I'm having a hard time keeping my composure. So much about this is unprofessional and unethical and…" Her eyes press him. "You knew nothing of your medical history?"

"No."

"You must have been aware you were growing breasts."

He tells her what happened.

"You woke up and the mastectomy had been performed. It was done."

"Yes. And I had another scar. Here." He touches his lower abdomen on the left side. "Dr. Porto says he took a cancerous tumor out."

"He lied," Obrera says, again with that snappish tone. "Dane, you were lied to. They had no business performing a mastectomy until you'd finished puberty. They had a dozen other treatments in the meantime. Where the hell were your parents during all of this?"

Dane shrinks back a little, feeling at fault.

"I'm sorry," she says. "This folder has an appalling amount of malpractice, medical deceit and… Well, *abuse* is the only word coming to mind. I feel sick reading this." She rubs her face, appears to come to some kind of decision. "You've been treated so unprofessionally, Dane. I don't want to continue this discussion without you signing HIPAA forms and doctor-patient privilege in place. Do you understand?"

"Yes."

She leans forward in her chair. "I imagine the thought of any kind of medical exam must be incredibly frightening for you."

Dane's eyes swim. "I… Yeah, it's…hard."

She gives him a tissue. "Do you think you can come back and see me tomorrow?"

"And you'll tell me more?"

"I will tell you everything you want to know. And if I don't know, I will find out."

He's fighting like hell not to cry now. "I don't have cancer?"

"No."

"You're sure?"

"Positive."

"I've felt shitty for so much of my life and every time I asks why, I was told I had cancer. It was the answer to every question."

"I'm so sorry this happened to you," Obrera says. "It's vile. Unconscionable. I'll be honest and say I kind of feel like throwing up right now."

"Me too. I've been feeling so sick ever since I left home."

Her brows furrow. "Dane, are you on any meds?"

"Lots."

"What kind?" Her eyes close. "Please don't say you don't know."

"I don't know," he says, feeling swamped with fault again. "I didn't bring them with me. I forgot. I'm sorry."

Her head shakes back and forth. "Me too. I'm so sorry, Dane." She open her eyes. "Pills?"

"Yeah. And shots."

"Shots? Injections?"

"Yeah. Once a week."

"Subcutaneous or intramuscular?"

"I don't know what that means. I get them in my leg or butt?"

"And you left them all at home?"

"Yeah," Dane says. "No wait, not at my father's house. I mean they're home at Maisie's house."

"Oh thank God. All right. I want you to call me the minute you get back to your sister's house and read me what's on those labels."

"I will. Should I not take the pills anymore?"

"Don't change anything," she says. "I don't know what they have you on and I cannot discuss discontinuing until I know. For your sake. I cannot stress how badly you've been treated by your father and your doctor. I need as much information as possible before I start diagnosing or giving you advice."

"All right."

She reaches a hand and squeezes his fingers. "We will get through this."

"Okay."

"Is there anything you need to ask that cannot wait until tomorrow?"

"What's it called again? What I have?"

"Tetragametic chimerism. It's not a disease. You are not sick."

"Does it…make you crazy?"

"Crazy?"

"Like… I ate my twin sister, right?"

"Consumed during the embryonic stage," Obrera says. "You weren't *you* then."

"But she stayed. With me, I mean. She stayed with me. In like, half my body literally. This side." Dane feels all up and down the left side of his body. "The blue eye is her eye. The different skin color, that's her. The XX DNA. That's…her?"

"Yes."

Dane reaches to touch the paragraph in the report. "And they thought I had a missing testicle, but they found it later. In surgery. And it was an ovary."

"Yes."

"I have both kinds of parts. And I started to grow breasts. So am I really both a boy and a girl? What do you call that—intersex?"

Obrera exhales. "These are all excellent questions. And if I tell you I don't know enough to make a sound opinion right now, will you take me at my word?"

"I think so. You're the first person who's honestly explained all this to me."

"And you have no idea how sorry I am to be the first."

Later, Dane will regard returning to Obrera's office one of the greatest acts of physical and mental courage he's ever performed. He burns with anxiety, feeling at any moment he might throw up, pass out or weep.

Obrera examines him thoroughly but it's nothing like Dr. Porto. She asks about his comfort and gives him choices: *Would you like to have a nurse present? No one will come in during the exam but I can lock the door if you prefer. Feel okay? Are you ready to start? Do you need a minute? Sip of water? You're doing great.*

Her hands are gentle and her voice friendly and conversational as she explains everything she's doing and why. "You can ask me anything you want," she says. "If you think of questions later, we can always chat on the phone."

"I can call you?" Dane says, his jaw trembling a little.

"Absolutely." She reaches for a tissue and hands it to him. "You've had a terrible experience. You have no reason to trust doctors right now. No reason to take me at my word when I say you can trust me. So I'm going to put some more action behind the word. You can call me. At home. With any question."

"I never had anyone to call."

"I am so sorry for everything you suffered. Do you feel safe at your sister's?"

"Yes."

Safety is a novel concept and a tenuous one. Hunter Academy's attendance office was immediately on the phone to Paul Goldberg when Dane didn't show up to school. But Paul was oddly unreachable, so the school had to call the old man. Within days, Ivelaw Strong's machine had traced Dane's flight to Maisie

Montresor, but Maisie's team was ready and waiting, with the locks changed and the security system upgraded.

"Talk to Dane's lawyer," Maisie says on the innumerable phone calls from her furious parent. "Speak to counsel about it. You'll have to contact Dane's lawyer for that information. I have nothing to say to you, Ivelaw. Talk to Dane's lawyer. Goodbye."

Goodbye, along with *team,* is another word Dane is coming to appreciate. He's in awe of his sister's unflappable demeanor. She's not cavalier—she knows this is a precarious situation and for the two months left until Dane's eighteenth birthday, she could face charges of kidnapping and endangering a minor, unless her attorney successfully plays out the clock. Dane's medical file is being held in reserve as a bargaining chip. Multiple copies have been made and secreted. Dane's one job is to sit tight and turn eighteen.

"I'm afraid you've gone from one house arrest to a slightly more pleasant house arrest," Maisie says, sighing.

But switching from non-stop scrutinization to freedom hasn't been easy. Maisie's Norwalk home being so pleasant has Dane tied in a knot of survivor's guilt. He did nothing to emancipate himself. Paul orchestrated a safe passage and Dane was essentially passed like a parcel from his father's wealthy existence to his sister's wealthy existence. Gideon Perfect spun his mighty Rolodex of connections and now Dane is jumping waiting lists to get in with the best physicians and psychologists. He has an attorney on retainer and an interview with the headmaster at Kingpoint Academy—one of the best rehabilitation schools for troubled teens in the Northeast.

Meanwhile Fred and the others are still locked up in Porto's facility and there's nothing Dane can do while still a minor. His first therapy sessions are spent lamenting how he feels like such a privileged piece of shit who deserves none of these rescue efforts. It's a long time before he can frame himself as a victim within the big picture. A longer time before an idea of *himself* starts to take shape.

But all along the intense, agonizing, terrifying journey, the team is there. A pediatric urologist. The first of many psychologists. And always Natalie Obrera, wise, consistent and dependable as a head coach.

"Most intersex individuals are not chimeras," she says. "And most human chimeras don't have intersex traits. You happen to be both, but I can't definitively say one caused the other or that the two conditions are related. Are you intersex?

Yes, technically. You present as male. Your genitalia is not ambiguous. Would you agree?"

"Yeah. Except for the missing ball."

"That could happen to anyone. One percent of male infants have undescended testicles. It has nothing to do with being intersex. However, in your case, the undescended testicle wasn't a testicle at all. It was an ovary. And a bit of fallopian tube. And a scrap of uterus. You had female reproductive traits. None of them functioned properly. You weren't making eggs or menstruating. But when you hit puberty, your body started the normal fistfight between estrogens and androgens, and estrogens were winning. You experienced cyclical discomfort very much like period pains. You began to grow breast tissue. And unfortunately, you were kept completely in the dark. You received terrible care and guidance."

"Yeah," Dane says softly.

"You were abused," she says. "Don't dismiss it. Don't excuse it. You were appallingly mistreated."

"All right."

"Do you identify male or female? Have you thought about this?"

"Yeah. Mostly male. But sometimes… I never told this to anyone."

"You were never free to. But I'm listening."

He tries to explain. Mostly male. A little girl-ish. But definitely the sense of both. Always, always, he'd felt both.

"Finding out about the chimerism," he says, "actually makes me feel a lot better. It explains things. I feel like I make sense. Like I have a word for it now."

"Other words might resonate," Obrera says. "Gender fluid. Or non-binary. Are you familiar with those terms?"

"I think so. You don't feel one or the other. It's both."

"Yes. And let me reiterate: You might identify non-binary even if you weren't intersex, even if you weren't a chimera."

She starts writing words on Post-its and sticking them on the table. *Intersex. Chimera. Non-binary.* "These are mutually exclusive. You could be any one of these without the other two."

Dane hesitates, then writes *bisexual* on a Post-it and adds it.

Obrera smiles. "You're an extremely interesting person. I might even say one in a million but don't cite my study, it's not peer reviewed."

"I don't want to be someone's study. Ever again."

"I don't blame you. You deserved to be regarded with respect and dignity. You deserved to know what made you who you are. You deserved honest answers to your questions. You didn't have to suffer as much as you did."

"I feel so fucking lost."

"We'll find you, Dane. I promise."

Dane runs the back of a hand across his two-color eyes. "Up until now, the only *we* I knew was me and Diane."

"God, man," Liko whispered, holding Dane tight. "I don't think I've met a more resilient person in my life."

"Mm." Dane burrowed back closer and went still. He twitched once, then his body softened and his breath blew slow and soft on Liko's wrist.

"I loved tonight," Liko said. Soon he slipped under the dark, resting deep and undisturbed, except for a moment when he heard someone whisper, *I love you.*

But surely it was a dream.

Roof boss at St. Mary the Virgin church, Cheriton Bishop, Devon, UK

PART SIX
AY'LOUT ADAM

"Three is a magic number.
Yes it is, it's a magic number.
Somewhere in the ancient mystic trinity,
You get three as a magic number."
—Bob Dorough

AVERT YOUR EYES

Surely it was a dream.

Kyle sat in a glassed-in booth, surrounded by impressive keyboard consoles and wraparound monitors. Every display had a scene from the *Three Hares* game, and the floor was littered with collected pieces of art and architecture and cached jewels. The casters of Kyle's chair made little paths as he rolled from screen to screen, one earphone pushed back, cheek pressed against the cell phone tucked in his shoulder. He was talking fast, typing faster, consulting notes, gesticulating wildly. He was *on* and it was exhilarating to watch. Liko tapped on the glass, bursting with clues, dying to tell his son all he knew about the Green Man Chamber.

But Kyle couldn't hear him.

Liko's tapping finger turned to a knuckle. Then to a fist. Then his flat palms beat on the windows but Kyle couldn't hear him. Soon Liko was throwing himself against the glass, battering it with his shoulder as water began to drip from the joints, the rivulets growing stronger until they poured like rain and puddled around Liko's feet.

He called his son's name. Over and over, timed to the thump of his shoulder. Finally Kyle looked up. His eyes rolled around the Universe and he scowled, chucking his hair out of his face. He reached and touched his index finger to the window between him and his father. His mouth shaped words, *Get the fuck out of here, I'm busy.*

Then the booth went dark.

Liko's eyes popped open. He was on his side, his left arm twisted beneath him and his entire deadweight pressing on his shoulder. Outside the rain poured down.

With a groan, Liko rolled over, his heart pounding. The other side of the bed was empty. He rolled back and groped for his phone. Eight-thirty. A text from Dane was in his notifications:

Having a "Norwalk Day." Bunch of appointments and errands. Back later. Left you coffee.

Liko sat up, tilting his head away from his sore shoulder and wincing, reading the words again, a third time, feeling confused.

Confused and downright jellyfingered.

No *good morning,* no *you were great last night,* no *when I get home you're in trouble…*

He looked at *Nomi With Dusk Tiara* as if she'd have answers. She gazed back from the fabulous décolleté of wisteria blossoms and shrugged.

"Okay," he said to himself, taking a panoramic look around the king-sized mattress and all it had contained last night. He touched his collarbone and tried to give a careless smirk, but already a heaviness was descending into his chest. Thick and humid, like a rainy day. The dream about Kyle hopped in for the ride, replaying the part when the booth windows blacked out and the water rose around Liko's shins.

Get the fuck out of here.

Liko tried to get the fuck away from the dream but it piggybacked on his shoulders to the kitchen, where the coffee had gone cold and nothing in the fridge appealed. It dragged on his ankle as he went into the office and tried to work.

Where is my friend?

He alternated hot and cold. Throat tightening and loosening. His heart hurting. Feeling abjured, like he was suffering a throwing up and throwing down apocalypse with nobody to know or care. Feeling like an idiot because he was a grown-ass man, why didn't he just pick up his damn phone and text something witty? ***Nice try sneaking away, get your ass back here. Or at least share your location so I can stalk you like a needy lover.***

Were they lovers now?

"What is *wrong* with you?" he muttered, staring out the windows for the umpteenth time. "Just fucking call him."

I don't want to call, his heart sulked. *I want to* be *called. I don't want leaving, I want staying.*

He pulled on rain jacket and ball cap, took an umbrella and walked around the sodden farm. He sat on a boulder by the duck pond, holding a handful of peas, but naturally Jeffrey wouldn't come to him.

"Some emotional support duck you are." Liko flung the pods into the water and got up. If he couldn't get words on paper, he'd get steps onto his fitness tracker.

He took the path through the woods, only wanting to go back to bed.

Where is my friend?

Get in, get off, get out.

I don't want the get out part.

I don't want last night to be a service.

I want to see you right now.

Kyle touching a finger to the glass and the booth imploding with darkness. Dane pulling the shades, putting the bedroom into near-darkness.

Maybe he doesn't want to see me.

He's busy.

Get the fuck out of here, I'm busy…

By the time he strode to the middle of the Hare Ring and sat on the great, carved stone, he was feeling lower than low and twice as dumb.

You are fifty-five years old and surviving immeasurable grief. The snub of a dude you had a wank with last night is not going to kill you.

"It will if I want it to," he said, which was so pathetic he actually chuckled. "Go home, drama queen. Practice some self-care."

He mindfully started over with a hot shower, smart clothes and two scrambled eggs. Feeling nostalgic, he made tea instead of coffee. Nostalgia made him spontaneously call his parents for a chat. Hanging up, he still felt off-kilter and weirdly bereft, but he settled back down to work and banged out his chapters. He kept an ear peeled for the chime of his phone in the kitchen, but heard none.

In the afternoon, he took his laptop to the kitchen couch and opened *Three Hares.* He walked through the Green Man Chamber from the beginning, starting outside Paderborn and ending at the pine needle letters spelling out *Tinner Wheeled.*

He ignored how rearranging the letters to *Helen de Winter* felt like cheating, both at the game and on Dane. He dropped the last D into place—D for *defiant*—and watched what happened next.

An invisible breeze picked up the needles and blew them in a cloud toward the ceiling. They moved in a circle around the spinning hares, which slowly came to a stop. They sat in their allotted spaces, panting. Ears and noses twitching. Then they turned and began to run the other way.

From offscreen, a dog barked

From outside, Salma barked.

An explosion of sound in the front hall. Dane had come in like a teenager, asserting presence with as much noise as possible. Bundles dropped, shoes kicked off, the thwack of a jacket shook out. Gorilla footsteps into the kitchen. "Oh, hi."

"Hey." Liko toggled from the game to his email, as if he'd been caught surfing porn.

"God, it's fucking miserable out there." Dane flung a bunch of bags on the kitchen table.

Liko looked over the back of a couch, sure a snog would be forthcoming, but Dane was rubbing Salma off with a towel, baby talking an earful of praise and giving her a treat. Then he left and soon Liko heard a rumble of feet going up the stairs.

He sighed and went to the fridge. Last night's pasta was in one container, the caramelized onions and peas in another. He wasn't hungry at all, but he opened the pasta, sat down and took a cold bite.

"That's better," Dane said, coming back in. He'd changed into sweats and pulled the longer sections of his hair into an elastic. "Going in and out of seven different places, I got soaked. Then I got all chilled in the car." Walking past Liko's chair, he bent and kissed the top of his head. "Hey."

"What's up?"

Dane washed his hands, then stood at the sink a few minutes, kneading the small of his back and twisting side to side.

"Your back still bothering you?" Liko asked.

"The chiropractor was one of my appointments. He got some of the kinks out but the rain isn't helping. I might go soak in the tub later. Gotta take care of this first..." He sat and shook one of the bags out, dropping a small box and a disposable syringe onto the table. "T minus zero," he said, then frowned at the inside of the bag. "She usually throws in alcohol swabs. Goddammit..."

And he was gone again, leaving Liko with the same bite of pasta in his mouth and no desire to swallow it. He didn't want this. Didn't want perfunctory head kisses and excuses to get out of the room. Maybe from any other guy but not from Dane.

Maybe he doesn't want to see me.

Get the fuck out of here, I'm busy.

"Here we go," Dane said, throwing down a few pre-packaged alcohol wipes and a Band-Aid.

Liko went to the fridge for a seltzer. More invented business. Like the little sentences he often wrote between lines of dialogue to inject action into a conversation, or move his characters invisibly between here and there.

"The needles of my youth were nasty," Dane was saying. "When I was eighteen I switched to a transdermal patch. Then to a topical gel when I was thirty-two."

"Who prescribes it?" Liko asked. "GP or a specialist?"

"Endocrinologist. She's in New City which is a hike, but she's good so I don't mind too much. She started me on this stuff in twenty-fourteen. Testosterone undecanoate, suspended in oil."

"How often?"

Dane gave the syringe a few flicks. "Every twelve weeks."

"Taking one in the ass?"

"I can't jab my own butt without bruising myself, so it's the leg. Avert your eyes." He waggled his brows and slid his sweatpants down.

Liko put his jaw on the heel of his hand and stared. "You lube that needle or just raw dog it?"

"Little spit is all I need."

What the fuck are we doing? Liko thought, as the needle went into Dane's quadricep. *We made love last night and now it's locker room talk?*

One half his brain scoffed at *made love,* while the other insisted it couldn't be called anything else.

Please. You never made love with a guy in your life.

He's not a guy, he's a person.

You didn't even touch each other.

The fuck are you talking about, yes we d—

His thoughts stopped. He watched Dane's index finger slowly depress the syringe and his tangled thoughts followed it down.

You didn't even touch each other.

Down, down. Dane breathing deep. His eyes giving a little wince, then going smooth again.

The lights in the booth going down.

Avert your eyes.

You didn't touch.

Down. The oily, viscous solution going through the needle, under the skin, straight into muscle.

Digging my one ball, ya freak?

Get the fuck out of here, I'm busy…

"That's it," Dane said, withdrawing the needle and pressing the alcohol-soaked gauze on the mark. "T plus one."

"When will the antlers emerge?"

Dane smiled, dealing with the bandage. "In about an hour." His fingers pressed the ends of the adhesive. The skin of his thigh was smooth over corded muscle, with a down of fine hair lying close to the skin.

Avert your eyes.

I have a thing for the dark.

Dane slid his sweats up, then took the empty syringe to the sink. "In case you were wondering, I keep my sharps containers under here. Then they can go safely in the trash. Don't worry about jabbing yourself."

He flicked on the faucet to wash his hands again. Liko got up and moved behind him. Slid close, pinning Dane between his body and the cabinets, reaching an arm around his waist. The other he slid up Dane's chest, until the curve made by Liko's thumb and index finger cradled Dane's lower jaw.

"Hi."

Dane swallowed against Liko's palm. "Hi."

Liko was careful. He didn't want the guy to feel collared, just contained. He drew Dane back against him and put his mouth against Dane's hair. The scent of his skin made Liko remember last night, which started to get him hard. He pulled Dane closer and whispered, "Feel that?"

"Yeah." The water ran on, though Dane had taken his hands out and they were now fisted on the edge of the sink. Liko reached and turned the faucet off. "Open your hands," he said softly.

Slowly Dane's fingers unfolded. Water dripped off them, making dull plinks and plunks on the dishes. When the palms rested flat, Liko ran a hand under Dane's shirt, slowly across his stomach, then up between his pectoral muscles, pressing his heart. Dane sighed and swayed back a little, settling against Liko's growing erection.

"Still so hard for you," Liko said, kissing up the side of Dane's neck.

"Mm."

"Can't stop thinking about last night."

"Me too," Dane whispered.

"I want you to come upstairs with me. Something we need to talk about."

"You mean why I'm acting like such an ass right now?" Dane's head lolled from shoulder to shoulder, showing his nape, letting Liko's mouth reach it from all sides.

"I know why."

"Do you?" A faint smile was on his mouth, but the fingers on the sink ledge were twitching.

"Mmhm." Liko kept a hand pressed to Dane's heart. The other glided across his stomach until his fingertips slid beneath the waistband of Dane's sweats. Dane drew a deep breath in. His hands went to fists again, then opened.

"Don't be afraid," Liko whispered, sliding his hand a bit further. "We're going to talk about *this*. Okay?"

Dane closed his eyes and nodded.

"We won't turn any lights on. You can tap out any time. And truth or silence rules are in effect. Fair?"

"Fair."

"Don't be afraid." Liko put both arms around Dane and squeezed him hard. Held still through one shared inhale and exhale. "Come upstairs with me."

"Say the first part one more time."

Liko turned Dane around and gathered him in. "Don't be afraid."

UNO

Dane's heart thumped hard against the wall of his chest. It was stupid to be this nervous, still his eyes threw a glance at the windows. The cloud cover reduced the light to a dull blue-gray, but he was a hell of a lot more visible than last night.

It's all right, Diane said. *This isn't some stranger and this isn't a mindless hookup. You're invested. You trust him. I trust him. It's all right.*

"I meant it when I said you could tap out any time," Liko said, sitting on the end of the bed.

"I know." Dane clenched his hands once and drew a breath. He pulled his T-shirt over his head and pushed down sweats and shorts, kicking them off his foot.

Then he stood still, letting Liko look at him.

Liko shifted to put forearms on his knees. His eyes moved up and down Dane's body, a single index fingertip touching his lips. He looked serious and smoldering and unpredictable. Dane's heart was still beating hard, but his throat thrummed with wanting.

"I also meant it when I asked if you could give us average guys a chance," Liko said. His finger came off his mouth and made a rotating circle in the air. "Please," he whispered.

Dane turned slowly, showing his back. Then turned to face Liko again, who shook his head.

"Counter-clockwise," he said. "The best things happen when you're running against the order."

Smiling, Dane turned the other way.

Liko reached a hand. "Come here. Don't be afraid."

Dane stepped closer, exhaling as Liko closed gentle fingers between his legs. "Call me Uno."

"Shh." Liko's palm expanded and contracted. His thumb pressed slow circles. And then he shrugged. "I honestly can't tell the difference. Two, one, none—it feels good to me."

"Now you're just sweet-talking."

"I mean it. I'm completely underwhelmed."

Dane swatted his head. "Hey, don't be a dick when you're holding my dick."

Liko dodged, but his hand stayed where it was. "My bad."

Dane swallowed hard. "But since we're on the subject, you'll notice it's not very big."

"I will not notice because I literally do not give a fuck. Hey. Look at me." His free hand reached to hold Dane's chin. "I'm writing a story here, but it's not a romance novel. Or a porn script."

"So we shouldn't talk about my lack of pubic hair?"

"No. You want to talk about last night?"

"Badly."

"I loved it." Liko's hand opened and closed, warm and strong, getting Dane hard. "It was, I shit you not, one of the best nights I've ever had with a guy. Then I woke up alone and it killed me. You were gone all day, the fucking rain got into my head, I went around sulking like an idiot, abandoned and friend-zoned."

"I'm sorry."

"Dude, I'm feeling ten million ways about us but you gotta know, this is more than being a fuck buddy."

"I'm invested," Dane said.

"Yeah. So am I. And I'm telling you, your dick feels good in my hand because it's just like mine. We're two average dicks. Handling you feels like me. Feels like home. Now let go that breath you didn't know you were holding."

Laughing, Dane put his face into Liko's hair and exhaled. "Holy vulnerability, Batman."

"Along with your height, was this another failing in your asshole father's eyes?"

Dane nodded. "He'd just…fucking humiliate me about it. While he was swinging the belt, or else he'd barge into my bedroom or whip the shower curtain open. Berating me for both the size of my dick and never growing much hair. Then there was Porto, who would fucking *measure* it. Measure and loudly call out numbers to whoever was in the room, inches and centimeters. They'd write it all down and he'd sigh over the stats." He shook his head hard. "Anyway, then I found my life mates and my soulmates and my sex mates, and for twenty-two years I didn't worry about any of this. Now I'm on my own and out there and it's stirring up all these old ghosts. So I acted like one and disappeared this morning. I'm sorry."

"I understand," Liko said. "But now you're with me. I've looked at you and I can't stop. You're in my hand and it feels terrific. And I have just one more important question, and I need your absolute honest answer."

"What?"

"When talking dirty, do you prefer *balls* or *ball?*"

Dane picked up his head, laughing through the wet blur, astounded he could sport wood with all these emotions filling up his eyes and mouth and chest. "Balls," he said. "*Suck my ball* sounds asinine in the bedroom but I'll throw it down if a buddy's giving me shit."

"Try my shit. How's it going, Uno?"

"Suck my ball."

"Brilliant."

Dane put a knee on the mattress, then fell onto his side and pulled Liko along with him toward the pillows, kicking the covers open. They lay face to face, holding one another's heads. In the gloomy light, Dane couldn't quite see the color of Liko's eyes, but he felt their gaze in his soul.

"I'm sorry I ghosted you. I have no interesting explanation other than I got scared. When I get scared, I get stupid."

"I was over here being just as stupid. Let's just give each other grace."

Dane pulled Liko's shirt off. "Let's do what we did last night, but to each other."

"Potato, pohtato…"

They pounced, rolling from one side of the bed to the other before getting up on their knees. It was faster and rougher this time, forearms and wrists in a writhing pile and their wild kisses falling into rhythm with the slide and stroke of their hands. Outside the rain was hammering down again and thunder rumbled as they were nearing the edge. Dane came first, which sent Liko over. They collapsed onto each other's shoulders, breathing hard and laughing as a loud crack made the windows vibrate.

"Only nine out of ten," Liko gasped. "We didn't time it with the thunder."

"No lamps knocked over. Another point off."

"A respectable eight then. Holy shit."

They wiped off and lay down again. Liko turned on his side and ran a hand all over Dane's chest. "This feel all right?"

"Feels great."

"How much sensation did you get back after the reconstruction?"

"I never lost any up here on my pecs. Sternum down is where it went sideways…" Dane's fingers ran over one nipple and then on the underside of the muscle, all along the scar. "The feeling comes and goes. The right-side nerves still get confused. I'll get pins and needles all along the old scar tissue, then it'll go numb for a week, then it'll be super sensitive and I can't even stand a T-shirt."

"Is this okay?" Liko said, moving his hand around the right side with its gold hoop piercing. "Tell me what feels good."

"The wider the touch, the better. Wide and strong. If you do light touches with your fingertips or nails, like this? I don't really feel it. I like pressure more than caressing. You have big hands so… Yeah. That's nice."

Liko bent his head and closed his mouth around the silver hoop in Dane's left nipple. "Can you feel that?"

"A little," Dane said slowly. "Sort of. I can't exactly feel your mouth but I can *see* your mouth. It's the visual combined with the pressure of your hands and a little imagination thrown in."

"Team effort," Liko said.

Dane ran a hand through Liko's hair. "If it turns you on, it'll turn me on. Do whatever you like and if it bugs me I'll be quick to say so. Just know that something that feels good on my chest today might be a no-go tomorrow. It's not you, it's my nerves."

"Jesus, where was that line when I was having anxiety on dates? *It's not you, it's my nerves.*"

Dane started to roll toward him but his back gave a twinge of protest. "Oh man," he said, sitting up and pressing his hands into the small.

"Still giving you grief?"

"Yeah, you took my mind off it but now I think I need to soak some of this out." He looked over his shoulder. "Want to come with?"

Liko's eyes went toward the bathroom and something about his smile was fragile. "No," he said slowly. "No, but I hear good things about drinking in the tub. I can do you a G & T?"

"Do one for yourself while you're at it."

SHOTGUN

Dane lolled in the tub with the jacuzzi jets hammering his back. A half-smile twisting his mouth and a half-rise under the water as he planned the rest of the evening. A couple drinks in the tub, maybe lure Liko into the shower, a bite to eat, then back to—

"What the fuck?" A weird pounding noise had joined the bubbling rumble. Dane hit the switch, praying the motor wasn't on the fritz.

The pounding wasn't the tub, it was at the door.

"Dane?" Liko yelled.

"What?" Dane called back.

"You locked the door, dumbass."

"I did?"

"No, I'm kicking it for funsies."

He sounded legitimately pissed. "Hold on," Dane said, and got up and out, dripping across the tiles to flick the switch in the doorknob. "Take a chill, man, I didn't know I locked it."

Liko had a lowball in each hand, garnished with lime. He'd thrown on sweats and a heathered blue T-shirt that made his eyes pop out of his face. He stopped a few steps into the bathroom, gazing around. Looking gorgeous and still a little annoyed.

"Well, this is a religious experience," he said after a tight moment.

"Thank you," Dane said, easing back into the water. "I worked a long time on it."

"You painted the sky?"

"No, that was Ethan. All of it, actually. I did no work whatsoever."

"I've never seen bookshelves in a bathroom."

"After today, you'll wonder why all bathrooms don't have them."

Liko set one glass on the small table by the tub, looking everywhere but at Dane.

"So how many books have you dropped in the bath water?"

"Every book here earned its place *by* being dropped in the bath water. They're now counted among the righteous elite. Never to return to the hoi polloi of the living room shelves."

Liko still stood with his back to Dane, hands on hips, perusing. Dane sipped his drink and watched. A weird energy was coming off him and Dane couldn't pin it down.

"Did I ever mention you look good from the back?"

"You did. Thank you."

Is it me, Diane said, *or is he the one acting strange now?*

Not sure, Dane thought. Liko definitely seemed tense. Even from the back. Dane let a few moments pass, then said, "Why don't you sit down and have a drink? You brought two of them."

"I did." Liko came and sat down cross-legged on the mat, but it was as if he were lowering himself into liquid nitrogen.

"Are you okay?" Dane asked.

"Yeah."

"You're not. Look at me."

Liko looked over, with a faint, wobbling smile.

"Don't be afraid," Dane said. "Tell me what's going on."

"Me and bathrooms aren't friends."

"Oh?"

Liko stared down into the depths of his drink. "Kyle died in the bathroom."

Then Dane felt like shit. "Oh my God, that's right. I'm so sorry."

"Nothing to be sorry about."

"No, it was thoughtless. I forgot." He closed his eyes, miserable. *He found Kyle in the tub, you moron.* "I'm really sorry," he said.

"It's not you, it's my nerves. It's dumb, but I can't help it."

"It isn't dumb. Please don't torture yourself by sitting here. Thank you for the drink but God, don't stay if it's making you upset."

Liko drew his knees up and sat still. Eyes looking at nothing in particular. Hand still jiggling the ice in his glass. "No, this is okay," he finally said. "I mean, it's a good place to face the fear. I can pretend it's a library with a tub in it. But will you do me a favor?"

"Anything."

"The real trigger is I had to break the bathroom door down that night. It's not so much the room itself as the closed door. But a closed, *locked* door with the sound of running water behind it makes me irrational. I'm not asking you to forfeit all privacy, just… If you're in the shower or tub, don't lock the door. Okay?"

"Done." Dane finished his own drink and set the glass on the table. Liko looked back and smiled up into his eyes. "How about the other half, as the Brits say?"

"Lovely, as the Brits say."

When he was gone, Dane pulled the plug with his toe and let a third of the water drain. Then he turned the hot tap on and fretted, still embarrassed at his careless gaffe.

Liko came back with the drinks, then perused the bookshelves again. "Here's an ode to manly love," he said, taking down a battered copy of E.M. Forster's *Maurice.* He sat against the tub and read out loud. He stopped after a few chapters and brought up the whole bottle of gin, a bowl of ice and potato chips. As the sun went down and the bathroom grew darker, he lit the bathroom's various candles.

Dane rested an arm on the ledge of the tub, cheek on his bicep, damp fingers playing with a fold of Liko's shirt. The walls of the room drew close. Even the fixtures seemed to lean on their elbows and listen.

"This is nice," Dane said softly, drawing up Liko's neck and behind his ear.

Liko smiled and let the book rest open in his lap. "I might become friends with this bathroom."

Dane closed his eyes. "Wow, I'm drunk."

"Same."

He opened his eyes and they stared a long time. Then Dane slid his hand around Liko's neck. "Come here…"

Liko's head tipped back in Dane's grasp. Still holding the book, he let Dane kiss him. Nudge his lips apart and taste him. Sweet with gin and lime, salty around the edges, sharper in the breath exhaling into the back of Dane's throat.

"Give me your tongue," Dane murmured.

With a little moan, Liko followed Dane back into his mouth. He sighed as Dane's other wet hand undid a button and slid under his shirt, stroking his chest, his palm making circles on Liko's heart. The book toppled onto the tiled floor and now Liko was rolling up and onto his knees and pressing Dane back into the tub, nestling his head down on the ledge. His other hand found Dane's cock, hard under the soft water, and gathered it into his fist. Dane groaned in Liko's mouth, his knees and his kiss opening wider.

Liko pressed their brows together, breathing hard. "You coming out or am I coming in?"

"Sounds like you're asking who's gonna top."

Liko drew back with a side-eye. "You wanna talk about this now?"

"Speed-dating style. Thirty seconds. Go."

"I don't have a ton of experience, I'm vers, it's been a while and we have no condoms. I'm fine with either tabling indefinitely or making a run to CVS. Go."

"I think I'm vers but don't have any experience to make an informed opinion. Let's table literal topping and explore spiritual topping."

"Is the state of your back conducive to being thrown around a bed tonight?"

"Gentle rolling on the bed would be preferable."

"And you definitely want me to drive."

"Not to CVS. Just in bed."

"Got it," Liko said. "Either way, call shotgun."

Dane laughed. "Shotgun."

Liko pulled the plug and yanked a towel from the track. "Out. Free swim is over."

A minute later they were wrapped in arms and kissing like each was the other's dinner. The edges of their mouths blurred and bit, Liko groaning every time he felt Dane's piercing on his tongue.

"God, you and the kissing," Liko said. "You might have to start locking doors just to get away from me."

From far away, Salma barked. Dane heard it, then forgot it as Liko rolled again, getting Dane under him, knocking extra pillows aside, getting Dane's legs around his hips. He poised on his forearms, palms cradling Dane's head.

"Buckle up," he said. "I drive crazy."

"And you drive on the wrong side of the road."

Smiling, Liko kissed him, then whispered, "Wait until I turn you over."

Downstairs, a door slammed.

"Shh." Dane tensed up and his finger pinned Liko's mouth. "Wait."

"What?"

"Shh."

Dane's ears strained, wending their way down the hall and the stairs and the little bit of domestic noise that…

Salma barked.

"Dad?" A woman's voice called.

"Oh for fuck's *sake*," Dane hissed.

First Liko's eyes bulged. Then his captive mouth bulged against contained laughter. "Guess who's coming to dinner?"

DAD, YOU SLUT

"Can't believe I'm the one asking," Liko said, "but is the door locked?"

"No."

"Great. Hope you're not a barge-in family."

Saskia was coming upstairs now and Dane was frozen like…well, like he was caught in flagrante. Liko grabbed a handful of covers, hauled them over their naked bodies, and rolled off Dane just as knuckles rattled on the door.

"Dad? I'm home. You in there?"

"Hey honey," Dane called. "Give me a minute, okay?"

"You sleeping?"

"I was. Just getting dressed. I'll be down in a sec. Can you let Salma out for me?"

"Sure thing."

Dane threw an arm across his face and counted footsteps down the stairs. "Fuck my life."

"Want me to hide?" Liko asked. "I won't be offended. Once I had to help a date crawl out the window when Kyle came home early from a sleepover."

"You and your fuck buddies."

"It was a *date,*" Liko said huffily. "Do you want me to disappear?"

"No," Dane said. "No, Saskia asked me to wait at least a year before I dated. It's been two and change." He flipped the covers back and sat up, exhaling his frustration and ignoring his pouting erection. "All right, let's just do this." He looked back. "I mean, only if you want to. If you'd rather hide…?"

"Fuck it." Liko got up. "I'm still drunk. Let's have some fun. Where are my clothes?"

"I might have thrown them in the bathtub."

He strode off and Dane looked longingly after, mumbling, "Shit."

"You want to go down first?" Liko called. "Give a little backstory, make sure my reputation precedes me?"

"No," Dane said sourly. Then, "Yeah. Actually, yeah, I'll go down first."

"Good, because my clothes are soaked."

Dane pulled on his clothes and pushed his hair back into place. He tried a casual expression in the mirror. Fat chance. His lips were puffy and his face was red from Liko's beard. No hiding he'd been vigorously kissed recently. He ran a cold washcloth and pressed it to his cheeks and chin, hoping it would take some of the rawness out. If not, to hell with it.

"Let's go, Green Man," he said.

Liko followed in a towel, holding the bundle of his wet clothes. "This is like a Blake Edwards movie."

"You're having way too much fun."

Dane opened the door and looked up and down the landing. Liko slid a hand down the waistband of Dane's sweats and grabbed his ass. "Damn, you're going into this situation commando?"

"Jesus," Dane hissed, but leaning back into Liko's palm at the same time, wanting nothing more than to close and lock the bedroom door.

"Sorry, I'll behave," Liko said. "All clear?"

With an exchanged glance and a nod, they were off, Liko timing his sneaky footsteps down the hall with Dane's loud ones down the stairs.

"Saskia Helen Mary Ruta Hasen-Strong von Schoenfeld," he said, striding into the kitchen. "As I live and breathe."

"Deddy," she said, throwing arms around him. "Who's the grandest Deddy of the Danelaw Deddies?"

"I am."

She kissed his cheeks and fussed with his hair. "You're all tousled."

"I was napping."

"Sorry I woke you up."

"No worries. It was just a surprise."

"I know. I pinged but you didn't answer. I guess you slept through it."

"Right." Dane drew out a chair and sat down.

"I'm so hungry." She opened the fridge. "What's going on in here?"

"Pasta with onions and peas. Other assorted veggies. And there's burrata."

"Ooh. Perfect." She emerged with a stack of Tupperware and kicked the door shut. "So what's new?"

"Well…"

"Is the Pub doing open mic tonight or is it too rainy?"

"Probably too rainy. Hey, listen—"

"Oh, I saw Margy Kulleseid when I got gas in town. She says hi."

"Sask."

"What?"

"I kind of have a friend here."

She glanced back, licking her fingers. "Where?"

Dane lifted his gaze to the ceiling, then looked directly at his daughter.

"Oh," she said. Then she turned all the way around. "*Oh.* A friend like a… *friend?*"

Dane blinked back and lowered his chin on a fist.

"Oh my God," Saskia said. "And I just barged in like… Well, fuck a duck. I'm sorry."

He turned a hand over in the air. "This is awkward."

"Oh my God, I'm mortified." She looked at her half-assembled plate, then at the fridge, then at Dane. "This is so bad. I'll go."

"Stop."

"No, no. I'll go get a drink at the Pub and come back when you're both ready. Or if she's embarrassed and wants to leave. Holy hell."

"Nobody's going anywhere," Dane said. "Fix your plate and sit. *He's* going to come down in a minute. You'll meet. We'll have a drink and all be mortified together."

"He?"

"He."

Saskia crossed her arms. "Dad."

"I know."

"*Dad.*"

Dane pointed a finger. "You said a year. Male or female."

Her arms unfolded and her palms went up. "I know. This is not *Dad,* like *Dad, how could you?* This is…"

"Dad, you slut?"

"Shut up." She came to hug his head and smack a kiss on his crown. "I'm happy for you."

"Thanks."

"And oh my God, Dad, you slut."

Dane sucked his teeth and swatted her butt. She camped a little shriek and went back to her food.

"So how long has this friendship been going on?"

"We actually met over a year ago but forgot we met. Then we met again because... It's kind of complicated. Forget it. The answer is we've been friends a few months."

"A few months and he's upstairs," she said, putting her plate in the microwave and hitting some buttons. "Sounds more like an interest than a friend."

Dane pretended a mysterious stain on the table required all his concentration.

"Dad." Saskia pulled the word into two sing-song syllables.

"I heard you."

"Are you pleading the fifth?"

"No."

"You don't have to tell me. It's fine. I respect secrets."

"He is a friend." Dane scraped at the mark with his fingernail.

"Well, that's lovely for you."

"With benefits."

"*Dad.*"

"You asked."

"I know, but this is bananas."

"Tell me about it."

"Tell *me* about it."

Dane's phone pinged a text from Liko. ***I'm coming down. Stop talking about me and gird your loins.***

"All right, he's coming down. Act casual."

"I'll need a G & T for this level of subterfuge."

"I'm out of gin," Dane said faintly, thinking of the almost empty bottle upstairs by the bathtub. Thoughts of the bathtub made his face flame. He was still blushing when Liko walked in, fresh and handsome in jeans and a black T-shirt.

"Tempt me with fiber," he called.

Saskia whirled around. "Oh my God, that's Cora's line."

"I'm Liko and it's now my line."

They each took two steps forward and shook hands.

"I'm Saskia. So nice to meet you."

"And you as well."

"Are you from around here?"

"Connecticut."

"That explains your accent."

They both laughed. Dane could practically see a little bubble of instant rapport forming around them, and his whole stomach and chest collapsed in relief.

"Have you guys eaten?" Saskia said.

"We tarted up our happy hour with some potato chips," Liko said, pulling out a chair. "Hardly a balanced meal."

Saskia opened the fridge again and took out more Tupperware. "How about cold potluck. I'll just throw it all on the table."

"There's a loaf of ciabatta in the bread box," Dane said, still feeling a little dazed.

"You have any wine? Oh wait, here's some chardonnay. Liko, can you get glasses? The credenza over there. Left-hand side."

Liko knew damn well where the wineglasses were kept, but he made a show of finding his way and opening a wrong cabinet. When his back was turned, Saskia shot Dane a wide-eyed look and mouthed, *He's gorgeous.*

Dane crossed his eyes and mouthed back, *I know.*

You slut.

You're grounded.

"Done talking about me?" Liko said.

"We're done," Saskia said. "You pass inspection. You can come back."

THEY HAD A LOVELY little feast, and Saskia produced surprise dessert from the freezer.

"What *would* you do for a Klondike bar?" she asked, breaking open the seal and passing them out.

"Oh my God, they come in dark chocolate?" Liko said, grabbing.

"I do unspeakable things for these," Dane said, pawing for one but Saskia held it out of reach. "Gimme."

"Go get Ethan's postcards," Saskia said.

"Now?"

"Now."

"We're having a nice supper and you're going to put my ex on the table?"

"Yes. Go get them and go slow so Liko and I can talk about you."

Liko went on eating his ice cream, dancing in his seat a little, expression innocent.

"You're both grounded," Dane mumbled, pushing back. "I do this under duress. The record needs to reflect my protest."

He took his time getting the cards from the file drawer in John's old study. Liko's laptop, notebooks and papers were on the desk, and one of his flannel shirts draped over the back of the chair. Dane paused to put his nose to it and inhale the scent of the Green Man.

Only you can write the laws that keep your peace.

Back in the kitchen, he arranged the cards in rows on the table, then polished off a Klondike bar while Saskia looked them over, ending with the last roof boss of St. Mary the Virgin church in Cheriton Bishop.

"Three more locations in Devon," Dane said. "Then he goes back to the continent."

"He asked if I'd meet him in Paderborn the first week of December," Saskia said. "To mark the end of the pilgrimage."

"All right."

"And he asked if you'd come too."

Dane was so calm, he wondered if he'd been expecting this. "I see."

Saskia sat down. "I'm going no matter what. Will you think about coming? Not for him or me. For Mammu."

"I know," Dane said. He looked at Liko, who was elegantly licking the chocolate off his fingers. He looked back at Dane and in the light of the kitchen lamps, he sparkled white, silver, black and purple. He was dazzling, yet so quiet and unobtrusive. Attending to Dane like a hare to a pagan god. He smiled, and the smile could only have been saying, *I will go to war for your peace.*

"Will you think about it?" Saskia said.

Now Dane looked at his daughter, whose piebald hair was exactly like his, shining in an ombre of blond and copper and sable. She had a constellation of freckles across her nose, just like Nomi. Diane's blue eyes stared back at him. The keen intelligence behind that gaze had humbled Ethan's.

"I will think hard and seriously about it," Dane said. "I'll take all of August to think, and make a decision in September."

"That's fair," she said.

"I'm bringing Liko, so the trip also depends on his schedule."

Liko smiled, blushed, and busied himself with his Klondike wrapper, folding it into precision quarters.

"One more thing," Dane said. "It's not fair for you to keep being the go-between. You're our daughter, not the ambassador carrying messages. If Ethan wants me to come, Ethan should extend the invitation. And asking you to relay one last message to him is a spectacular self-own, so fuck my life."

They all laughed and Dane exhaled, pleased.

"You are a Great Dane," Saskia said, rising half out of her seat to hug him.

"The greatest," Liko said quietly.

THE MEN HESITATED IN the upstairs hall, not sure whether to boldly go to Dane's room together, or part ways and sneak around later.

"Good night you two," Saskia called from her bedroom. "Sleep well."

"Fuck it," Dane muttered, and led Liko by the wrist to his room.

"Lock it," Liko said.

"No shit." Dane turned the switch in the knob, then pretended to push the dresser across the doorway.

"That went well," Liko said. "Splendid, as the Brits say. What do you think?"

"I thought splendid."

"Saskia's terrific," Liko said. "I mean it. I'm partial to people with Ks in their names, but even if she were Annabel, she'd be fabulous."

"She is," Dane said, painfully conscious of his daughter's presence in the house. How the energy always changed when she came and went. The complete privilege of having her. This only child, this beautiful soul around which three hares had chased each other. This treasure, this blessing, and she was not only terrific, she was alive.

Liko had had such a fabulous treasure and it was gone. Offensively, inexplicably, cruelly and unjustifiably gone.

"The night we met," Liko said, "I made you promise to keep living for her. One more year."

Dane nodded.

"You keep doing that."

"I will."

Liko sat on the end of the bed. He rested forearms on his knees and laced his fingers. He looked at Dane a long time. "I know what you're thinking."

"Do you?"

"I pick up on it all the time. This little frisson of guilt from other parents. Maybe not guilt, more like a heightened compassion that makes them hold back. It's for my sake and I appreciate it so much. Really. But you're allowed to enjoy your daughter. I don't resent you. Love her, talk her up, brag about her, take joy in her mere presence, cherish every breath she takes. Clutch and cling to her because she's your only child. Yeah, it's bittersweet. Seeing anyone adore their child is bittersweet to me now. How I cope… Well, one of the ways I cope is when I see a terrific kid, I say so. It's not just for you. It's for me. I'm kind of borrowing her a few minutes. Parenting by proxy. I indulge in their terrificness and help myself to a bit of the adoration. Sometimes it works, sometimes it doesn't. It's my thing to cope with, not yours. Make sense?"

"Yes."

"That's all." Liko twisted his fingers. "Life is too goddamn short and there's precious little I give a fuck about. You love her with everything you got. I'd be more offended if you didn't. Just like you'd be if you saw someone not unabashedly adore their spouse for your sake."

"I'm kind of adoring you right now."

Liko let go his hands and set his palms behind him on the mattress. He held still. Vulnerable yet commanding. His body telling Dane, *Get over here,* but a tremor around his eyes adding, *but be careful.*

Dane went, and knelt between Liko's feet. He ran careful hands up the long thighs, planed them along Liko's chest and up to his head.

"I'm also concentrating on doing the next thing."

Liko's beautiful smile unfolded in his beard. "I'm a thing. And I'd like to be next."

Their next kiss was different. Something between them had shifted. Settled down. Horses were being held and flavors savored. The kiss had a slow softness within an urgent rhythm. Liko still leaned back on his hands, and Dane set his own palms down on the mattress, canting onto Liko's chest as he got lost in it. Tasting everything Liko had put in his mouth tonight. He thought about tasting himself in Liko's mouth and the front of his sweats rose into a point.

Liko kissed all over Dane's neck. Ran his tongue up Dane's throat, then drew him close and wound arms around his waist. He put his forehead against Dane's stomach for a long breath in and out. He looked up and Dane held his face, thumbs stroking his cheekbones.

"Green Man, you are so fucking beautiful."

"Great Dane, you give me so much peace."

Dane started kissing him, stopped to pull Liko's shirt off, then went deep back into his mouth. Following the foliage resurrection back to the seed under his tongue, back to the Tree of Life, back to the first being who was both man and woman.

Adam androgynos.

You have formed me behind and before, and laid your hand on me.

Let us make love in our image.

Liko trembled then, and pressed his forehead to Dane's stomach again.

"You all right?" Dane said, running a hand through his hair.

Liko nodded. "Never been this emotional with a guy. It's…a lot." He took another deep breath, in and out. When he looked up, he was dazzling.

"Shotgun," he whispered.

Dane pulled him up, stripped him down, then pushed him back on the bed and went crawling up his body. Boxing Liko in with knees and elbows, kissing with both sides of his soul.

"So hard for you," Liko whispered. "God, I haven't wanted someone like this in so fucking long."

Dane reached for lube, slicked up his hands and gathered their cocks together, sliding and squeezing them side by side.

"God," Liko moaned, his head tipped back on the pillow, writhing in between Dane's thighs.

"Like that?"

"Love that."

"You're so fucking hot."

"Tell me the story."

"Once there was a Green Man in my bed," Dane said. "And then I fucked him with my hands. And then I fucked him with my mouth. Until finally he came hard enough to topple a cathedral. And then…"

"And then," Liko whispered, breathing hard.

"And then you write the next part." Dane moved back and dug his hands under Liko's body. Happiness enclosed him like a leather vest, passion crisscrossing up his back and pulling him tight. His edges perfectly matched. Diane dreamily narrating the inner monologue. Nomi beyond the stars, clothed in wisteria with Dusk Tiara, pleased for him. And Ethan, wherever he was. Not part of now, but part of all the *thens* that brought Dane to now, here, in this bed with the Green Man. The farm and the land and the intersection of two roads cupping the house in its fertile palm. The house thrumming happily because Saskia the Knife was here. Safe in her bed, alive and terrific. Changing the energy just by walking through a door, because three would always be the most magic number.

"Are you here?" Liko whispered.

"All here." On a mission of desirous peace, Danelaw Strong was purely present and utterly himself, as he lifted up the overflowing bowl of Liko's hips and drank him down.

THE NAOMI ROAD 40

Ornamental plasterwork Treasbeare Farmhouse, Clyst Honiton, Devon, UK

GARDENS, NOT LAW

Over breakfast the next morning, Saskia caught her father up on Oxford, travels around Europe, and her current internship at the Broad Institute, in their new research building on Kendall Square.

"How many years left at Oxford?" Liko asked.

"Two," she said, licking strawberry jam off her knife. "I might be able to squeeze it out in one though."

"You can't rush genius," Dane said.

Liko peeled a clementine. "You'll graduate with a…?"

"PhD in mathematics."

"Then she'll be Dr. Hasen-Strong," Dane said.

"What's your thesis?" Liko asked, as if he were well-versed in the philosophy of math when he'd barely scraped by in high school trig.

"Algebraic coding theory and symmetric block designs. More specifically, combinatorics and applications of representation theory to coding theory."

"I have on matching socks," Liko said, and glanced under the table to be sure. "Tell me about your internship?"

"Right now I'm learning to catalogue the genomic alterations responsible for cancer, using genome sequencing and bioinformatics."

"Now she's used up all my memorized buzzwords," Dane said. He reached and lovingly jostled Saskia. "I need a crib sheet to brag about her properly."

"You do all right, Deddy. Just don't call me a mathmagician."

Dane winked at Liko. "She still mixes up D5W and WD-40."

Saskia gasped. "Bitch, that was a secret."

They took the last of their coffee into the den to do the next clue of the Green Man Chamber.

"I haven't done this in years," Saskia said. "Go from the beginning."

Liko did, feeling dumb as he demonstrated his little gaming quest in front of a Rhodes scholar, but Saskia beamed as if they were watching home movies.

"You know, I'm in this chamber," she said. "Do you see me?"

"You?" Liko peered. "No. But I'm sure I'm missing the obvious."

She got up and walked toward the screen, pointing to the windows behind the Green Man's altar. Between two of the arched frames, a large knife hung on the wall.

"Saskia means *knife.*"

"That's right," Liko said. "Dane told me. A kiss A."

"Look at you anagramming like a champ."

"You do *not* want to play Scrabble with this one," Dane said, flipping a thumb toward his daughter.

Liko rearranged *Tinner Wheeled* to *Helen de Winter,* which turned the ceiling motif in the other direction and woke up the sleeping dog.

Liko paused the game. "I always wondered why the dog isn't an actual Great Dane."

"You ever meet a Great Dane?" Dane asked.

"No."

"They're the worst."

"Harsh, Dad," Saskia said.

"Sorry. Many people adore them. I do not. They're big and slobbery and not my kind of dog at all. *That* dog is Parker."

"May he rest in peace," Saskia said.

Liko resumed the game. The dog stretched, yawned again and walked away from his blanket, which lifted off the floor like a flying carpet. It rotated to fill the screen, revealing itself to be a map of the Danelaw. A replica of the one that hung in the front hall of the farmhouse.

"This part of the game is a little simplistic," Dane said absently. "To me, anyway. I think Ethan anticipated me and Nomi getting frustrated if the puzzles tried to be too clever. It's a love note, after all. He wanted to please us, not show off."

"Your whole voice changes when you forget to be mad at him," Liko said.

"Right?" Saskia said, laughing.

"You two aren't allowed to be friends," Dane muttered, pulling his ball cap lower.

Across the top of the map, letter tiles spelled out *Danelaw Strong.* Across the bottom, thirteen blank squares waited for their anagram.

"Do you have a middle name?" Liko asked.

"No," Dane said.

"As you'll soon see," Saskia said, "Dad having a middle name would've ruined everything."

Dane dumped out the bag of Scrabble tiles. "I'll do it on the table. Liko can have the honors on screen. Now gird your loins, Greenman. If you thought *tinner wheeled* was fucked up, wait until you see this."

He spelled out his name first. Then Saskia came to lean on his shoulder and together they rearranged the letters into three new words.

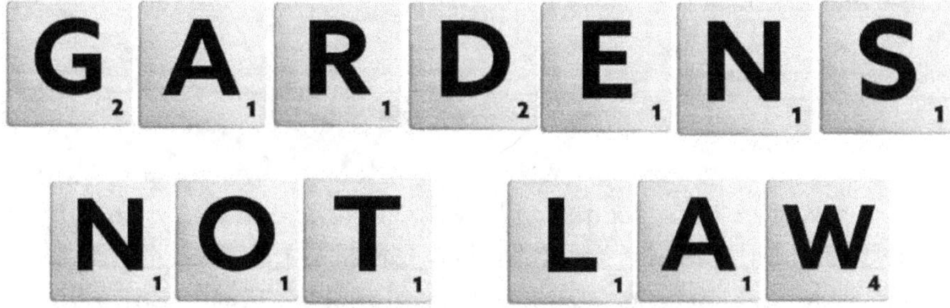

"Stop," Liko said.

"Bananas, right?" Saskia said.

Dane turned up his palms. "I'm the scion of a legal family. But my destiny is gardens, not law."

"You could've been named something else and had a whole different life," Liko said. "No, not a different life. A different destiny?"

"I like to think so. Most people won't be onboard with the idea but I believe in it. So…" He gestured to the TV. "Anagram me, baby."

Liko started moving letters. "You make it sound so dirty."

"Get a room," Saskia murmured.

As the phrase *Gardens, not law* locked into place, the drawn lands of the Danelaw began to burgeon with growth, life and harvest. Animated crops sectioned off the map into patches of green and gold. Grains. Wheat. Corn. Fruit trees exploded with blossom, then drooped from boughs weighted with bounty. The produce accumulated until it fell off the map. The game perspective pulled back to show the cornucopia piling up on the floor of the Green Man Chamber. Parker the not-Great Dane circled around it, barking and wagging. The caramel-colored duck, who up until now had done nothing in the game, followed behind him, sniffing with interest at the mound of fruits and vegetables.

Above the horn of plenty hovered the expected letter tiles, spelling out *Naomi Misteria*.

"I have to tap out here or I'll get all weepy," Saskia said. "Plus I need to hit the road, but not until I raid the veggie garden. Liko, I hear you've adopted a duck?"

Liko closed the laptop and bolted off the couch. "You can't leave until you've met my duck…"

LIKO HAD NEVER BEEN good friends with August. He'd always found it an oppressive month of extremes, from the weather to the psychological end of summer. He could never get completely comfortable, either sweating through his clothes or shivering from overzealous air conditioning. His mind wanted to be on vacation while his soul was bracing for back to school.

This August was magical, rolling by in long weeks of hard work, beautiful weather and Dane. Being at home together, being raunchy at the Pub, profound on the porch, electric in bed.

Dane was a powerful lover, which was a revelation Liko couldn't quite understand because what had he been expecting?

Get in, get off, get out, he answered. *That's the only way you knew with men. Clumsily flinging yourself into the moment any which way, having a grand old time, but you didn't think about it too much. Didn't dial into what* he *was getting out of it. Didn't linger afterward.*

The dog days became wolfish nights when the moon blushed at the howling coming from the master bedroom. Dane could do things with his hands and mouth Liko never dreamed. To go from a smartass who smugly thought he was the more experienced, to a humbled wreck thinking that last orgasm caused irreparable brain damage, was a humbling journey he hoped would never end.

"God, don't let this end," he whispered to the dark of Dane's bedroom, the words almost soundless. His heart immense. His body inside-out. Dane's hair falling through his fingers, Dane's head lolling by his thigh, Dane's throat humming against his cock, Dane's tongue stud getting the sweet spot and his fingers finding sweeter spots. Knees wide, heels digging furrows in the mattress, Liko died a thousand little deaths, then resurrected and resolved to keep living. He still grieved. He still battled the words and argued with clients. He still had indescribably bad days. But God, at least the steady endorphin stream from consistent sex kept him from crouching on the bottom of the pool, wondering if he could drown himself.

"How are you?" kind friends still asked.

"Hanging in there," he'd answer, thinking *I'm bouncing.*

I'm just awful, but I'm not alone.

He's awful too, and we're in it together.

He's my best friend and we get each other.

Some days suck out loud, but being with him doesn't suck.

This little life at Schoenfeld's does not suck.

The farm work was in panic mode, with produce rolling off the fields. Cora was making flatbreads out of everything. Dane sent Liko frantic texts every morning: *Pick the zucchini before it turns into a porn star.*

The kitchen garden was a jungle of green beans, herbs and cucumber vines, plus one rogue melon plant in a shocking relationship with the cherry tomatoes. Dane introduced Liko to standing salad, which meant a lunch break on their feet, eating straight off the plants. Folding lettuce leaves into their mouths, popping tomatoes and matchstick beans, crunching cucumbers down to the stems, finishing with a sprig of parsley and a drink from the garden hose. Such lunches gave Cora's fibrous temptations a run for their money.

September rolled around. Liko finished William Shepherd's book and started another. He glanced out the study window one morning and saw a school bus ambling down Oak Hill Road, flashing red lights as it stopped for a pick-up.

This would have been Kyle's senior year.

It was a hard, suck-ass day. But Dane was around. Dane would come back to the house. Dane would listen. Dane would know.

Dane would hold him all night.

THE NAOMI ROAD 41-44

Postcards sent August 9, 2017 – September 7, 2017

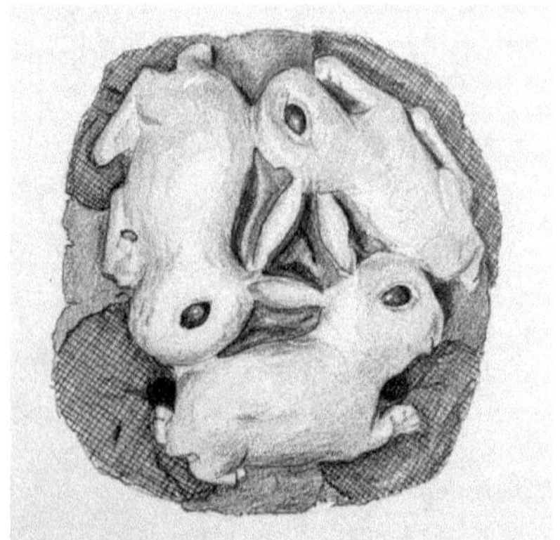

Roof boss, St. Eustachius' church,
Tavistock, Devon, UK

Roof boss, St. Hubert church,
Corfe Mullen, Dorset, UK

Roof boss, Chapter House, Église Saints-
Pierre-et-Paul, Strasbourg, France

Plate, Musée Alsacien de Strasbourg, France

THE MOST COMPASSIONATE WAY

ONE MORNING, AS THEY were about to solve the next clue in *Three Hares,* Liko got a call from Janelle's sister, Angie. This was Kyle's favorite aunt and the in-law Liko had gotten along with best. But divorce always drew tough lines, and he'd had little to no contact with Angie the past two years, the last time at the memorial service in April. He'd entirely forgotten her number was still in his phone.

"I'm so sorry to bother you," she said, "but I'm really worried. I can't find Janelle."

"Can't find her?"

"She's not answering calls or texts. We've always shared our locations but I don't know where she is. I mean, the beacon shows her at home, but I'm here and she's not."

"You're inside?"

"I've looked everywhere."

"Do you see her phone?"

"No."

"What about her car?"

"That's gone. Lee, I'm really worried," Angie said again. "She got fired two weeks ago."

"Oh shit." Liko stood up, a hand to his forehead. "What happened?"

"It's been bad, she's just been spiraling. She gave up on therapy and I think she stopped taking the meds. I've been trying to get her to check herself into Four Winds Hospital for a two-week program. She needs professional help. I'm sorry, I know it's not your concern anymore, I'm just rambling out loud because I'm not sure what to do."

"No, no, I'm glad you called," Liko said, bringing up Janelle in his contacts. They'd turned off location sharing years ago but he tried anyway, only to be directed to turn the feature on in settings.

"God, something set her off," Angie was saying. "I don't know what."

"Back to school," Liko said. "I'm almost sure of it. I saw kids getting on a bus the other day and broke down."

"Fuck. All right. I'm going to wait here at the house and I'll keep calling and texting. It has to be twenty-four hours missing before I can call the police, right?"

"I think so. I'll try texting her too. Keep me posted, all right?"

Dane tactfully shut the laptop as Liko brought him up to speed. The morning turned heavy and ominous, filling Liko with a dozen conflicting emotions.

It's not your concern.

"But it is," he said. "In context, she is my concern."

"Of course," Dane said. "The soul portal you told me about? You and Janelle keep it open together. She's your concern because she's necessary. Try texting her."

Liko sent a couple, but *read* didn't appear under them. Dane stayed calm and reassuring. "Let's take Salma on a walk before it gets too hot. Just a quick one to the Hare Ring and back. You'll still be in cell range if Angie calls, and it'll feel like doing something."

So they did. They sat with their backs against the carved granite block and watched Salma flush out rabbits.

"Thanks for being understanding," Liko said.

"I've been kicking an idea around my head a few days," Dane said. "Basically, you and I are a pair, but each of us has one ghost—Kyle and Nomi—and one loose end—Janelle and Ethan."

"Wow," Liko said. "Go on."

"This next part I can't quite pin down. We're two hares with an open space for a third. Not literally. Not polyamorously. It's like the ceiling motif in the Green Man Chamber, before you figure out how to put the third hare into it. You and I are going round and round, but at any given time, Kyle, Nomi, Ethan or Janelle is joining the chase."

Liko stared, the concept turning in his mind. "Maybe," he said, "when they join, it turns the triskele the other way. Not the wrong way but the most compassionate way."

"Exactly," Dane said. "One day soon, Ethan's going to email or call me. I really don't know what it'll be like, but he'll be running with us a bit. He'll chase me while I'm chasing you, and you'll chase him because you have my back." He got up and brushed off his butt. "Something like that anyway. Point is, when one of our ghosts or loose ends is turning us the other way, we're understanding about it."

"It's a great theory. I like it." Liko got up too.

Dane took his hand. "I don't know, man. Maybe we all operate in threes, even if we're not aware of it."

THE DAY PASSED, sober and silent, with no updates from Angie. In the late afternoon, Dane and Liko resumed the game, returning to the gigantic cornucopia of produce and the letter tiles hovering over it, reading *Naomi Misteria.*

"The anagram of Naomi Misteria is *O Mister Anima I,*" Dane said, arranging Scrabble tiles on the coffee table. "Anima is Carl Jung—the inner feminine side of man. Mister is one of the many names Nomi suffered in middle and high school. It was so like Ethan to pull out of your name something that caused you so much pain, and see the profound, beautiful thing in the letters left behind."

Liko moved the letter tiles into place beneath the cornucopia. The tiles turned a bright, springtime green. Then they lengthened and grew skinnier. The tips further elongated into points.

"Asparagus?" Liko said carefully.

"Yeah," Dane said, smiling as the stalks gathered together in a pretty clump, ready for display at a grocery store or produce stand. "Nomi got all teary at this part. It's a really sweet story. You'll know because I use my nice voice to tell it."

"The voice that forgets to be mad at Ethan."

DUCK EGGS

1991

WHEN NAOMI MISTERIA IS seventeen, she's assaulted for the second time by a foster father. She promptly declares to her social worker she is done with family placement, and puts on the desk an article about a facility outside Poughkeepsie.

"It's called the Mid-Hudson Juvenile Resident Facility," she says. "The locals call it Lark House. It's geared toward kids transitioning out of foster care to independent living. I want to go here. I can finish senior year and learn the skills I need."

It's perhaps one of the happiest years of her life, at least by Naomi Misteria standards. Lark House is situated in a quaint village called Guelisten, high on a bluff over the Hudson River. Naomi can walk everywhere at any hour of day or night. The politics and drama of the local high school are no different from the half-dozen she's attended, but perhaps something is in the local water system for nobody bothers or bullies her. She works weekdays at the public library, weekends at a small bookstore. She builds a vegetable garden for Lark House and takes cooking shifts in the kitchen. She doesn't make friends, but she grows comfortable with being friendly.

The career counselor at Lark House first reads about Schoenfeld's in the *Poughkeepsie Journal,* and promptly shows the article to Naomi. "This place looks right up your alley. It's a bit far but I wonder if they'd do a work-study with us?"

Naomi reads the feature again and again. Goosebumps rash up and down her arms and her toes curl tight. This place isn't just up her alley, it's her Somewhere. Her eyes blink rapidly as they devour the history of the Black Dirt Region, which sounds like something in a fairytale.

Once upon a time, somewhere in the Black Dirt Region, a witch grew a garden…

She reads about Mary Schoenfeld, whose German immigrant ancestors first bought the land. The CSA and partnership with local food banks. The flocks of chickens and ducks. The fields and crops. A pergola covered with wisteria vines—scions of plants that had survived Hiroshima.

Oh please, she thinks, the newsprint trembling in her hands. *Please. Please…*

She cuts the article out and hangs it over her bed. Imagines herself living in such a place. Working there. Belonging there. She's never prayed in her life, but every night before turning out the light, she reads the article and entreats whatever divine power may be: *Please.*

This is my Somewhere.

I know it is.

Please.

If they don't already know how, Lark House teaches all residents to drive. Getting a license is priority, as it's the first step to independence. Cars aren't abundant, so four to five residents form a pod to share ownership of a clunker. They learn to change oil, check tire pressure, handle the maintenance and take turns.

Naomi patiently waits for her scheduled day on the calendar, and on a brilliant Saturday afternoon she drives across the Mid-Hudson Bridge and down the Palisades to Orange County. Heart beating thick in her bound chest when she sees the sign reading, *Schoenfeld's: Farm to Market*

At the end of the long drive is a covered stand, the day's produce laid out in colorful piles or arranged in bushel baskets. Jars of honey line up warm and golden.

"Hello." A young woman is arranging bouquets of wildflowers in tin buckets of water. "Can I help you with anything?"

"I read the article in the *Poughkeepsie Journal.* I was in the area. I just wanted to visit."

"Did you now? That's wonderful. Welcome." The woman waves a general hand around. "Visit away."

Naomi hesitates. "Do you work here?"

"I do."

"Do you love it?"

The woman throws arms wide and smiles even wider. "Best summer job ever."

Naomi takes her time walking the farm, checking off each thing she read in the now-memorized article. The sprawling farmhouse. The barns. The greenhouses. The fields. The flower gardens. The chicken coop and the duck pond. She ambles down the path to the three renovated cottages which host artists every summer. On the little patio outside one house, someone is painting at an easel.

This is Somewhere, Naomi thinks, holding her elbows tight.

This is Here.

A long walkway connects the farm to the house, with a pergola built over it. Posts rooted in concrete, iron bars reinforcing the cross struts. The vines winding around the base of the posts are as thick as her wrist. Hercules and the Nemean lion, locked in combat. More delicate vines near the top, foliage like ferns.

At the far end she sees the man and woman from the article's pictures. The Schoenfelds. John and Mary. Such absurdly generic first names. And yet they're perfect. Naomi has to talk to them. But she can't be one of the many faces who come visit. She has to make an impression. She has to make them not just see her, but remember her.

She ducks behind an outbuilding and takes off her sweatshirt. Underneath is a T-shirt and under that, the Ace bandages binding her flat. She unwinds and stuffs them in her bag. Just this once, she will let her breasts be her calling card. They are the bane of her existence, but they are *unforgettable.* If they speak of her later as the Girl with Big Tits, so be it. As long as they remember her.

She ties the sleeves around her waist, adding some padding to her hips and a bit more balance to her overall figure. She squares her shoulders and begins to walk down the vine-covered pergola, letting her hand trail on the foliage.

This is Somewhere and I am here.

I am a granddaughter of Ruta Skadi and you will remember I was here.

"Hello," she calls. "Are you the Schoenfelds?"

"We are," they say.

Mary is a rail: lean and straight and strong. Her graying hair hangs in a braid down her back. No makeup or adornment except a pair of dangling, silver earrings. John is softer. Slouchier. Also with graying hair and a beard, and bright, curious eyes.

Naomi has rehearsed her pitch, honing it short, simple and to the point. *This is who I am, this is what I want.*

"So if you think it's possible," she finishes, "the career counselor at Lark House asked if you'd call her." Naomi hands over a business card. "I wrote my name on the back."

"I think it's more than possible," Mary says, studying the card.

"Didn't we do a farmer's market in Guelisten a few years back?" John asks his wife.

"Hudson Bluffs," Mary says. "And it was I, not we."

John smiles at Naomi. "It was the royal *we*."

"Beautiful area but a bit of a shlep for us," Mary says. "So it was just the once. I remember Guelisten though. Holy cow, that town was a picture postcard."

Naomi laughs. "Right? There's got to be at least one Satanic cult in all that Normal Rockwell charm."

Mary beams at her, and if she'd touched each of Naomi's shoulders with a sprig of cloud pine, Naomi couldn't have felt more anointed.

"Well, thank you for your time and the tour. I hope we talk soon." Naomi gives Mary a conspiratorial glance. "The plebeian *we*."

Mary gives a sisterhood wink and on that good note, Naomi shakes their hands and sets off down the driveway. She unties the sweatshirt from her waist and drapes it over an arm. Pins her shoulders and raises her face into the oncoming wind. She knows she looks very, very good from the back.

So concentrated is she on her rearguard action, she leaves her front open for attack. A boy is at the covered farm stand. A boy around her age. A good-looking boy dripping competent confidence who is going to take one look at her from the front and make decisions.

He's not important, she tells herself sternly. *He's not part of the plan. Walk by and nod. "Hi" is all that's required.*

The boy is taking bundles of asparagus from a Radio Flyer wagon and stacking them on the shelves. Gold brown hair fluffs out from under a backward ball cap. Dark brows and lips that look, dammit, sculpted. Beyond annoying, a guy with a chiseled mouth like that. It looks rock hard but no doubt it would melt under a kiss.

Whatever.

"Hi," she says. Brusquely. Like a challenge.

"Hey, how are you," he says, a single mosh of sound through those ridiculous lips. "You like asparagus?"

"Sure."

"Just picked. Still warm from the sun." He separates a slender spear from a bunch and breaks it off at its natural sweet spot. He gives her the part with the tip, takes a bite from the bottom half, and goes back to unloading and arranging, the spear tucked in his mouth like a green cigarette.

"Hey, could you set this on the top shelf there?" He hands her a piece of cardboard nailed to a block of wood to make it stand up. "Put that rock on top of the wood so it doesn't blow over. Thanks."

The sign reads: *Asparagus. Picked today. $2/bunch or 3 for $5. Try it steamed with fresh, poached eggs. And think of us later when you pee.*

"I will literally put a poached egg on anything," Naomi says.

"Holy crap, same," the boy says with a gigantic smile. His teeth, thank God, are far from perfect. Impeccable chompers on top of the beautiful lips would be too much to bear. "You ever have a duck egg?" he asks, eating the last of his asparagus spear.

"No."

"Want one?"

"How much?"

"Free for a first-timer. Hold on. Be right back." He takes the handle of the wagon and sets out along the driveway, but stops after a few steps. "Hey, can you put this out by the road?" From the bottom of the wagon he takes a large sandwich board, also advertising the fresh-picked asparagus. Naomi takes it, pleased to be assigned these tasks. Her first job at Schoenfeld's.

Remember this, she thinks, setting the sign carefully at the driveway's edge, weighing the center down with a few rocks. *Remember this day. It starts here.*

She closes her eyes, meditates on the date. *This day next year, I will be eating fresh-picked asparagus and duck eggs in this place.*

Her prediction is off by fifty-one weeks—by the following Saturday, she will be at the farmhouse table, enjoying this exact meal. But for now, she breathes in sunshine and dirt and dreams of a Someday Lunch in Somewhere.

A stacked stone fence runs along the two-lane highway, tiny wildflowers and thyme growing in the crevices. Where each length meets the driveway, the stones are built up into a pillar, squared off at the top with slate. A round planter on each puffs up high with red geraniums and spills down yellow and orange nasturtiums. A mailbox is built into one of the pillars. On the other is a circular plaque: a man's face carved out of leaves, with two clusters of acorns dripping off his mustache. Naomi noticed this foliate head in other places around the farm and wonders what it means.

"Here you go." The boy is back. He holds half an egg carton in one hand,

and under the other arm is a duck. Behind him trots a small menagerie: a puppy on a leash, a cat, two chickens and three rabbits.

This is getting a little precious, Naomi thinks.

"I brought you two" he says. "How long do you normally poach your eggs?"

"I'm a four-minute kind of girl."

"These are bigger than chicken eggs so you'll want to give an extra minute or so. Actually, I prefer to hard-boil my duck eggs. Ten minutes. But you do how you like."

Naomi points to the caramel-colored fowl in the boy's arm. "Do I thank her?"

He grins. "This is Maple. The best duck ever." His free hand strokes the bird's sleek head and she seems to enjoy it, so Naomi reaches gentle fingers and rubs the beautiful feathers.

"Thanks for lunch, Maple," she says. "I'm Naomi."

"Nomi," the boy says, mishearing her. "Wow, I love that name. Nomi."

All at once, so does she.

Nomi.

Know me, she thinks. *You know me. You, Nomi.*

"I'm Ethan," he says.

"How long have you worked here?"

"I live here."

"Oh. You're a Schoenfeld?"

"Yes and no. John and Mary are my parents. But I'm called Ethan Hasen."

"Hasen?"

"It's German for hairs."

Confused, she touches the ends of her hair where they lie on her sweaty shoulder.

He laughs. "Not hairs on your head. Hares like rabbits."

"Oh," she says slowly, happily. "Like hasenpfeffer."

"Schlemiel, schlimazel, Hasenpfeffer Incorporated."

They laugh and Maple flaps out of Ethan's arm, heading up the driveway in a dignified waddle. He peels a few leaves of lettuce from the heads on display, crouches down and feeds them to the rabbits. The puppy starts to jump around Nomi's legs, panting and yipping.

"Parker, sit," Ethan says. "Sorry, he's just a baby. The training is torture. *Sit.* Good boy." He feeds the dog a lettuce leaf.

"Why are you called Hasen?" Nomi asks.

"It's a long story I won't bore you with," Ethan says.

Please do, she thinks. *Bore me. Know me.*

Name me.

"I'm listening," she says, and eases the pressure by putting the egg carton carefully at the bottom of her bag, then moving to pick three bunches of asparagus.

"I'm adopted," Ethan says. "My real mother left me at a fire station when I was a baby."

Nomi almost drops her bag as she looks back. "What?"

"I was abandoned at a firehouse. John and Mary fostered me, eventually adopted me, but they felt strongly I should be able to choose my last name. Rabbits and hares are my favorite animals. The Schoenfelds are German. So *Hasen* covers all ground. And I liked how it sounded with Ethan."

"I do too," she says. "Each takes different effort to say. *Ethan* is like pushing uphill. *Hasen* is like rolling downhill."

He looks at her and blinks twice. His beautiful mouth slowly exhales, "Wow."

They stare at each other. Nomi hasn't been so at ease in someone's gaze since she was eleven and still flat-chested. She's never stood with her breasts unbound in front of a boy and forgotten they were unbound. She knows nothing except this boy might be Someone.

"What's your last name?" he asks.

"Misteria." She hesitates, her heart beating fast. If this place is Somewhere, it must pass all tests. "I was abandoned too. In a dumpster, not a firehouse. Someone put Misteria on my birth certificate but I have no idea who or why."

"For real?" Ethan says.

"For real."

He goes on staring into her eyes. Naomi holds still as Parker nudges the hand at her side and the rabbits sniff at her feet. Finally, she asks, "Do I give you the money?"

Ethan points to the large jar on the top shelf of the farm stand. Like everything else, it's clearly labeled with a little sign: *Honor system. Don't be a jerk. If you have no money, leave SOMETHING.*

Amid the bills and coins are little bartering tokens: polished stones, a toy soldier, a Charms blow-pop and a pair of gold hoop earrings.

Nomi's purchases come to five dollars. She drops in a ten and takes out the earrings. "Fair?" she asks.

"Fair," he says, and holds out a dusty hand. "It was nice to meet you. Please come back again?"

"I will," she says.

Oh I will, she thinks.

She drives away from Birch Island feeling accomplished. In a few hours, she's in the large, industrial kitchen at Lark House, steaming her asparagus. She piles them high, adds a swizz of olive oil, salt and pepper, and hands the plate around to the other workers. The spears are devoured and fingers press the plate to pick up the salt crystals. Naomi then goes out to her vegetable garden, gathering greens to make a giant salad for the Lark House residents' dinner. She decides to hard-boil one of her duck eggs to put on top. Breakfast tomorrow will be a poached duck egg with soldiers.

She hums as she works, unaware that across the Hudson, back at Schoenfeld's, Mary is shouting at her husband and son to come look, come see, they won't believe it. She stands under the pergola, her fingers holding a vine, pointing, laughing, almost in tears. She's found a bud. The wisteria vines have been here fifteen years and never bloomed. But they are now.

"Misteria," Ethan says, the M turning over to a W, then turning back.

Next morning, a staff member comes into the Lark House kitchen and conveys someone is at the front desk, wanting to see Naomi Misteria.

"Who?" Nomi says, anxiously minding the poaching of her egg.

"Some guy. Blondish hair, nice-looking. Kinda weird though."

"Weird?"

"He's got a rabbit with him…"

"THAT'S A LOVELY STORY," Liko said. "Especially when told in your nice voice."

Dane hummed.

"So the dog in the game is Parker. I assume the duck is Maple?"

"Yes," Dane said absently, his expression still in the long ago. A single stalk came free in Liko's cursor. He tried giving it to the Green Man, who shook his head politely. Parker didn't want it. But of course, Maple ate it delightedly.

"Good girl," Liko said under his breath.

As if she heard, Maple quacked twice, turned in a circle, and laid an egg.

"Do I poach it?" Liko asked.

Dane laughed. "It's a gift." He sat back in the cushions and leaned his head against Liko's arm. "As are you."

Liko's hand dropped on Dane's knee. It jostled his leg a little. Held still. Then it slid up Dane's thigh, under his shorts.

"This a gift for me, Uno?"

"Suck my ball," Dane whispered, closing his eyes. His knees moved apart, giving Liko more to work with.

Then the doorbell rang.

"You gotta be fucking kidding me," Dane said.

Liko rolled off the couch onto the floor. "This is *not* happening," he groaned, arms over his head.

"If it's Saskia, she is disowned," Dane said. "Jesus H, I can't answer the door with a hard-on."

Liko rolled over. "I'm no help here. Look."

"That's barely a rise."

"Hey, a little respect please."

"You started it, handsy. Go. You're on."

"Christ, you are an insufferable boss." Liko got up and adjusted as best he could, then headed to the door just as the bell rang one more time.

"Coming," he called, then mumbled, "Or I was about to, so this better be important."

He pulled open the door. The sun hit him in the eyes and backlit the woman who had apparently given up and was starting to walk down the porch steps.

"Hi," he said, shielding his eyes. "Sorry about that. Can I help you?"

She whipped around. Lost balance and stumbled back against the railing. Then sank onto the stairs.

"Are you all…" Liko trailed off and stared, not recognizing her at first. Then recognizing but unable to put her in this context.

"Janelle?"

LOOK GOOD
AND FEEL BETTER

Oh my God, *it's her,* Diane said.

Holy shit, it's you, Dane thought, flung backward in time to a cold March night when his doorbell rang and he opened it to a broken, weary traveler from the past. Now, exactly as then, time slowed down as a dozen thoughts battled their way to a decision.

First the prism of abandonment dropped on top of the situation and refracted it into beams colored the red of *you can't have him,* the orange of *get out* and the green of *he's mine.* Diane had her kitchen knife in hand, hackles up and teeth bared, reaffirming her vow to go to war for the peace of the Danelaw.

Dane gathered everything he had ever learned from everyone he had ever met. He called on his strength, dug deep for his grace, and breathed through the irrational, frightened moment. He let every color have a say, then he moved the prism and let the colors meld back into a simple truth: Here was someone in distress, the victim of an emotional shipwreck, coming to the haven of Schoenfeld's. Here was a grieving mother at rock bottom. A woman who undoubtedly knew actions had consequences, and by a combination of bad choices and bad luck, she'd lost everything.

One ghost and one loose end, he reminded himself. *Two hares with space for a third. At any given time, one more comes in and for a little while, we run the other way. Not the wrong way, but the most compassionate way.*

Janelle was here. She had come running here. Looking for refuge in the one person she knew would answer her cry for help. In context.

She had sunk onto the porch steps and Liko crouched beside her, his hand moving her tangled hair off her flushed face. Dane came out and crouched down too.

"Hey," he said softly. "I'm Dane."

She looked at him, then put her face in her hands. "I'm so sorry."

"No," Dane said. "No, it's good you came. A lot of people are worried about you. Come inside where it's cool." He stood and reached firm hands down to take hers, draw her to her feet.

"Come on," he said. "Come in the kitchen. Let's get you a drink."

Janelle sat at the kitchen table with a glass of water while Liko, pale but calm, made some phone calls. Dane sat kitty-corner and peeled an orange. It seemed a pathetic, inadequate offering. What this woman needed was *sustenance*.

Dane stared at the coiling peels, remembering this kitchen on a long-ago night, when Nomi should have been sitting in the chair Janelle now occupied, but never would again.

Maisie and Huff set plates before Dane, Ethan, and Saskia. On each was a single baked potato, skin split to reveal fluffed insides and a pool of melted butter. A constellation of coarse salt and ground pepper.

If Dane had been at all amenable to the thought of food, a baked potato would be the last thing on his mind. He stared at the random, almost absurd snack, then picked up his fork and took a bite.

Butter, salt and peasant sustenance filled his mouth. His stomach closed gentle hands around the simple food, sighed, and wondered if there were more.

"This is perfect," Saskia said.

"Just what I wanted," Dane said.

"What I didn't know I wanted," Ethan said.

They ate the potatoes, eyes closed and little whimpers beneath their hearts. When Maisie said, "Eat the skin, it's good for you," they ate the skin, obedient as children, and licked trails of butter off the sides of their hands.

"Want another?" Maisie said casually.

They held up plates like three Oliver Twists. "Yes, please."

Diane, in spite of herself, put her blade down and looked closer at Janelle. Took in the wrinkled clothes. The dry tangle of her hair. The pale, lined face ravaged by unfathomable grief and the consequences of actions.

My man, Diane said. *My man, this is a lot.*

She needs help, Dane thought.

She needs armor.

Dane put his hand on Janelle's. Jiggled it to get her attention. "Hey," he said softly. "I've got the mother of all bathrooms. A hot shower or a cold washcloth will make you feel better. Want to look?"

She stared back at him a bewildered moment and Dane feared the offer was a mistake. Then she nodded.

"I'm going to help her wash her face," Dane said to Liko, who nodded and mouthed, *Thank you.*

Holding hands, Dane led Janelle upstairs. He put out clean towels and his spare terrycloth robe. "My wife's old stuff is under the sink," he said. "Body wash, sugar scrub, lotion, the works. Use whatever you want. I don't want you to lock the door, all right? I'm going to sit out there on the bed. I won't come in, but if you're not out in ten minutes, I'll have Liko check on you. Is that fair?"

She nodded. Dane put down the bathmat and showed her how to work the various shower heads. "I'll be right out there," he said again.

It was a short shower though it felt like days, during which Dane chewed his nails and prayed Janelle found nothing under the sink to slit her wrists. The water turned off and after five minutes, Dane knocked politely.

"How you doing?"

Janelle opened the door, swathed in the robe with a towel turban on her head. Her eyes looked a little more lucid. "Better," she said. "You're so kind. Liko said you were such a great guy and this place was healing and I'm sorry I…" She was crying again. "I didn't know what to do."

"Shh," Dane said. "You're safe here."

Confident now, sensing she trusted him, Dane got a comb. He had Janelle sit on the edge of the tub and got the snarls out of her hair, parting it on the side and combing it sleek and smooth behind her ears.

"Want me to put some makeup on you?" he asked.

"You?"

"Me." Dane took out his phone and scrolled through his pictures until he found the ones he took back in May, wearing Nomi's lingerie top and the Dusk Tiara.

"I learned from the best," he said. "My daughter was the only girl in her class whose father did her makeup for prom. Her friends used to book me solid."

Janelle looked at the phone, at Dane, then back at the phone. Just the way Liko had, down by the pool. She inhaled deep and let it out slow, a bit of curiosity in her face as she said, "Okay."

He lit some candles, put some music on his phone, and had Janelle sit on the counter so he could work standing. He did a beautiful, subtle job. No dramatic smoky eyes or winged liner or plumped lips. Just a thin layer of armor. A self in pieces pulled together.

"You're so much stronger than you know," he said.

"No, I'm not."

"You are."

"I fucked up my life."

"We all make bad decisions, but we all deserve a second chance." In the mirror, Dane saw Liko in the door. "Hey, you."

Liko said nothing. He sat on the floor, his back against the tub, arms around knees, and watched Dane work.

"You deserve a chance," Dane said. "A second chance, a third chance, a seven hundredth chance. As many as it takes until you find peace. You deserve peace. You deserve to look good and feel better. And you will. You're so much stronger than you know."

When he was done, and before Janelle turned to look at her reflection, Dane got the Dusk Tiara and set it on her head.

LIKO DROVE JANELLE IN her car, and Dane followed them back to Norwalk to keep the peace.

He helped and aided and precipitated as Janelle's sister and girlfriends took her in hand.

He drove past Liko's house, because Liko wanted to show him where Kyle lived, once upon a more peaceful time.

He drove to the cemetery, because Liko wanted to show him where Kyle rested in peace.

He drove them back to Birch Island. No music or radio, just peaceful silence. Liko cried a little, his face in his hands, his head against the window. Then he put the seat back and fell asleep, his fingers twined with Dane's on the console. Dane held their hands to his mouth and gave a bittersweet sigh. The car felt full of love and grief. Divinely shotgunned with ghosts and loose ends. His eyes kept glancing to the rearview mirror to check the backseat. He sensed Ethan and Nomi dozing in the middle row, holding hands. Janelle and Kyle in the back—the mother sleeping fretfully and the son plugged into his music.

Up ahead, the towers of the Tappan Zee Bridge pierced the sky like the masts of a mighty ship.

"And then," Dane whispered against Liko's fingers. "And then. And then. Until finally. And then…"

THIS EPICUREAN FROLIC

Liko's love was full of power that night, his power fueled by love.

"God, you're so good," he whispered against Dane's mouth. "You're like the greatest thing I've ever known."

The room was lit by a dozen candles, flickering shadows on *Nomi With Dusk Tiara.* In the middle of the king bed, Liko had Dane under him. Dane's heels in his palms, Dane's knees tucked tight against his ribs. Liko was inside him, just a little, hyper-attentive to Dane's breathing and sounds and the fingertips curling into Liko's skin.

They were good at each other, getting better each time. Easily saying and showing, discovering moves, taking risks, changing minds and setting limits. Figuring sex out slow and careful, like the most intricate and detailed of paint-by-number kits. Dane still didn't quite trust what his body could do, how far he could open, how much he could take. Liko barely moved past the tip, but just that much could make his cells melt like wax. He held still and burned like another candle, hanging by the moment and thinking of nothing else. Expecting no more than what was happening, right here, right now. Just as he was letting go of binaries and roles and constructs, he was letting go of criteria and definitions. Letting these nights of lovemaking create themselves. Quick sketches, huge murals, abstract impressions, surreal allegory. A different masterpiece each time.

Tonight, back home in the farmhouse, naked in bed, the day's events turning them dire, desperate, tender and bonded, Liko eased inside Dane and right away, something was different. The night trembled as both men drew an identical, surprised breath and stared at each other. Wondering. Contemplating. Feeling it through.

"Oh my man," Dane said.

"Is it all right?"

"Come in more."

"Can I?"

"Feels so good tonight." Dane's hips curled up as he exhaled and Liko could feel a letting go, a surrender. Permission granted for a body to do what it could. Dane's trust opened and Liko slid into that faith. It was like moving into the heat of an open oven door. A ferociously tiny, fevered kiln, both crackling and smoldering.

Dane's knees came up to hug Liko's sides tight while his arms flung wide and loose.

"Christ," Liko said, putting his forehead against Dane's heaving chest. "I'm gonna lose my mind."

"Holy shit, Lee."

"You all right?"

"I'm unbelievable." Dane's arms dropped over his face, then dropped back out. "How is this… What is *happening?*"

Euphoria hugged Liko from all sides, buttery warm and snug like a leather vest. Softer than the down of a duckling. Tough and resilient like a trampoline. He ran fingers up the midline of Dane's body, tracing the border where the wisteria blossoms did not cross.

"I'm falling in love with you," he said. "I swear, it started the night we met and it never stopped."

Dane kissed him. "I know your memory had to let that night go a little while, but I kept holding it. I never forgot. I thought about it every day. When I opened the door and it was you, I almost died."

"Don't you dare," Liko said hoarsely. "You stay alive." Thrumming and crackling, he slid arms beneath Dane's back. He put his heartbeat against Dane's. Pressed his stomach against Dane's hard cock. Set their brows together. Looked for everywhere they could fit.

"All right?"

"So all right," Dane whispered. "Keep giving it to me just like that."

Liko gave all he had, moving slow and easy, but with long, deep strokes. Dane stayed relaxed and open, taking it, eyes closed and smile magical against the candlelit night. Liko took his head and nudged Dane's lips apart with his fingers to drop a secret on his tongue.

"I love making love with you."

Dane caught Liko's chin and whispered back, "Right now, you're fucking me." His tongue ring slid along Liko's lip. "Like nobody and nothing I ever knew in my life."

"Think you can turn over?"

"You want me to?"

"You wouldn't believe the things I want." He slid out carefully and Dane rolled over. Liko pulled a pillow under his hips, got him tilted up a little, then he sank back in, stretching out long, putting his heart on Dane's glistening back.

"All right?"

"Yeah." Their fingers twined tight and they made love for a long, slow, timeless time, letting it pile up around them.

"Do something for me?" Dane said.

"Hm?"

"Just for a few seconds, fuck me the way you want to. I mean the way you really want to. Not so careful. Let me feel you be selfish for a minute, and don't ask me if I'm sure."

So Liko let the wind take his caution and he closed his eyes and he fucked. Blindly, wantonly, varying his strokes hard and fast with the slow ones, selfishly finding the best angle and heat and friction. When Dane closed tight fingers around his wrist in an unmistakable signal, it was an effort to stop. Liko lay still, poised on the edge, breathing hard, tadpoles swimming before his eyes.

"That's how I want sometimes," he said thickly.

"Okay," Dane said, breathing just as hard. "Okay."

"All right?"

"Yeah. That's just…too much tonight. Not too much ever," he added. "Just too much tonight. Jesus…"

He shifted a bit, squeezing around Liko's cock, either inadvertently or on purpose, and Liko came. It fell out of him. Fainted out of him in a few swooning pulses and then one great shudder out his ears.

"Fuck," he gasped. "The hell you do to me, man…"

Dane's hand came up and back and curled around Liko's head, cradling it on his shoulder. "I swear, I had no idea it could be like this."

Slick and spent, his head spinning, Liko turned Dane over and finished him off with hands and mouth, humming and groaning deep in his chest as Dane's back bowed off the mattress and his voice bounced off the walls.

"God, I love making you come," Liko said.

"Holy hell," Dane gasped. "I can't feel my face."

Liko laughed and kissed him, then went to chuck the condom and grab towels. They cleaned up and wandered naked down to the kitchen. There they scavenged the fridge like hyenas, eating with their fingers straight out of jars and containers. Cold steak, limp grilled vegetables, all the cherry tomatoes, burrata piled on heels of bread, balsamic drizzled on everything. Taking sloppy bites over the sink, kissing between bites, passing a bottle of Malbec back and forth. A Klondike bar each to finish. It was a debauched, Tom Jones bacchanal and if Liko had experienced something like it in his sexual career, he couldn't remember. This epicurean frolic was going in his hall of fame.

"I love food," Dane mumbled around a mouthful. "I love sex. I love food. I love growing food that I can eat after having sex."

"It's so cliché, but I could totally go for a smoke."

"I got some around here. Jackie or Pao always leave packs behind and I'd keep them for the bad nights when I was drinking alone and sobbing."

Liko considered, licking the last bits of chocolate off the Klondike wrapper. "This is a good night," he said. "And more kissing is to be done."

Salma had been exceedingly gracious all this time, but her expression around the chew toy in her mouth grew more and more woebegone. The men let her outside and dove into the pool, throwing the ball to her from the cool water as they talked and talked.

"Who do you think sent me the letter?" Liko asked.

"I'm keeping all theories simple. Either someone at Henshe Games has an eye on the forums, or enough gamers contacted Henshe to tell them about Kyle and your post. Eventually it got to someone who wanted to do something."

"Someone who not only knew who Jonathan Henshe really is, but where he lives. Lived. Once."

"Where was the envelope postmarked?"

Liko laughed. "You know, I was thinking about the postmark the other day and I have no idea what it was. I kept the letter, but I guess I put the envelope in the recycling."

"It's entirely possible Ethan sent it," Dane said absently.

"This is true."

They stared a thoughtful beat.

"You didn't send it," Liko said.

Dane smiled and shook his head. "I don't go on those forums. I'm not a gamer, and I already know about everything that's in *Three Hares.* Including the mystery at the end."

"Fair."

"Do you believe me?"

"I do." And because it felt good in his heart, Liko said it again. "I believe you." He dove under the water and surfaced by Dane. Took him under the arms and hoisted him up to sit on the pool's edge.

"Smooth," Dane said, squeezing Liko's sides with his calves.

"I just believe you," Liko said, taking Dane's head in his hands. "I believe you."

Dane's hands closed around his wrists. "I believe you."

"I believe in you."

"I believe for you."

"I believe this night."

"I believe in the Green Man."

"I believe you're the Greatest Dane."

"I believe I'd like to fuck you again."

Liko sucked his teeth drew back. "You know, we were having a nice moment and you had to get all filthy about it."

"You know, when you get huffy your T-H turns into an F. *Filfy.*"

"Yeah? Get out of the pool. I'll show you what else turns into an F."

THE DAY BROKE WITH a sunbeam stab to the eyes and the sound of a rooster screaming with his whole face.

Dane rolled over with a groan. "Which god do I thank for being a country boy?"

"Who do I gotta fuck to get a cup of coffee?" Liko croaked.

Dane sat up with a visible effort and yawned. "You got fucked last, so I guess I'll make the juice."

Liko caught the yawn and stretched with it, joints cracking. "I don't really care about the coffee. I just want to see you walk around naked."

"Given the recent spate of people barging into this house at inconvenient moments, I'll put clothes on."

"Take your time."

Dane obliged by walking slowly into the bathroom, then out again. His back to the bed, he opened a dresser drawer. Closed it. Held still a long moment, which allowed Liko to cram his eyes.

"Want to see something?" Dane finally asked.

"I don't know, the view's pretty good right now."

"I got a better one. But you might not be able to handle it."

"Try me."

Dane brushed all his hair over to the left side of his head. Then he slowly turned, giving a three-quarter profile. Enough for Liko to see he had tucked his genitals between his thighs.

The girl trick.

Liko had pulled it on Janelle every now and then. Busting out of the shower or closet with his junk tucked away, striking an exaggerated diva pose with crossed legs. Janelle either ignored him, rolled her eyes, or murmured something diplomatic like, "Yes, dear, that's lovely. Did you put the recycling out?"

Liko stared now. Not being at all diplomatic as he thought, *Oh my God, she's lovely.*

Diane stood still, a hand on the dresser. The other smoothing a few long strands behind her ear. Miles of smooth skin, interrupted only by the whorls and spirals of a Blaschko's line.

A thousand spirals, Liko thought. *A kilo-koil.*

He stared. An immeasurable moment passed.

"Hi," Diane said.

"Hi."

"Close your mouth."

"Can't."

Her hand went from her hair to her hip. "Handling it?"

"No."

"The correct words are, *you were right.*"

"You were right," Liko said. "I was so unbelievably wrong."

She smiled. A lopsided, closed-mouth smile. Its curve was a little skeptical, a little amused, and a little cautious. Yet it lifted up into the blue of her eye, deepening to sapphire in the sunshine.

"It's nice to see you again," Liko said.

Her chin tilted. "That's right, we've met before."

"I didn't really like you."

"I wasn't myself that day."

And Liko just sat with that a long time, mesmerized and astounded.

"Show me…" He trailed off and shook his head. This moment was a privilege, not a trick to be performed on demand. But Diane smiled, and turned toward the dresser. Continued turning until she was three-quarter profile on the right side. And she was no longer Diane but Dane. Untucked and brown-eyed, his hair lying close and tight along his head. Inked and adorned with a brazen, toothy smile. "Handling it now?"

"Barely."

Dane turned and Diane looked at Liko. She turned and then Dane looked.

"Funny," he said. "Remember how I told you how they/them pronouns never quite fit me?"

"I remember."

Dane's expression was far off and intent. "They fit right now. I mean, I feel…*them* right now. In a way I usually don't."

They turned back to Diane's side. Looked at him with that Mona Lisa smile and that impossible blue eye. They crossed their arms, laughing, and said, "You can barely even."

"I literally can't."

They turned to face dead-on, shook their head and raked hands back through their hair, breaking the spell. Then it was only Dane, all Dane, standing naked in a splash of sunlight, saying, "I'll stop before your head explodes."

"You're so beautiful."

"Who?"

"You. Both of you, any of you, all of you."

Dane's eyes started to roll, then dropped and settled on Liko's. "Thanks," he said.

"Does Diane ever want to go out?"

"Out?"

"Like…to dinner."

"You mean a date?"

"Yes," Liko said. "Exactly. A date."

Dane slowly unfolded a T-shirt. "No. I love the invitation," he added quickly. "Thank you for asking. Maybe someday, but right now, no."

"You don't have to explain. And you really are beautiful."

Dane's head popped out of the collar. He came over, took Liko's face and kissed him. "It's just the company I keep."

THE NAOMI ROAD 45-46

Stone boss at Lausanne Cathedral, Switzerland

Engraving detail from a consecrated bell at the
Haina Monastery, Frankenberg, Germany

YE THEN

They returned to the game, where Maple the duck had just laid an egg.

"You said it's a gift," Liko said.

"A poached egg on anything is a gift. Especially when fed to a Greenman."

Liko clicked on the egg and brought it to the Green Man's mouth, but nothing happened.

"Don't feed it," Dane said. "Just offer it."

Liko put it in the foliate god's hand. The Green Man tossed it from one palm to the other, then like a food network chef, rapped it on the stone beneath him and separated the two halves of shell with a flourish. A showy cloud of gold, sparkling dust cascaded down the front of the altar, covering the inscription. When it cleared, ten random letters within *And ye then deign to know me* were lit up.

On the floor, ten square slots opened: a group of four, a single, and a group of five, ready to receive.

"I know you're so excited," Dane said.

"Well I'm learning what kind of sexual favors you like, so I don't think this'll be too difficult." Liko picked out Scrabble tiles and started playing around.

After a minute, Dane asked, "Would you like to phone a FILF?"

"Silence, please."

"That's Saskia's line."

"She gave me permission. Okay, I got it."

"It was on a plate."

"Don't harsh my vibe." Liko dragged the letters down, feeling his smile widen as each clicked into place, spelling *Nomi* and *Ethan* with a single letter N between:

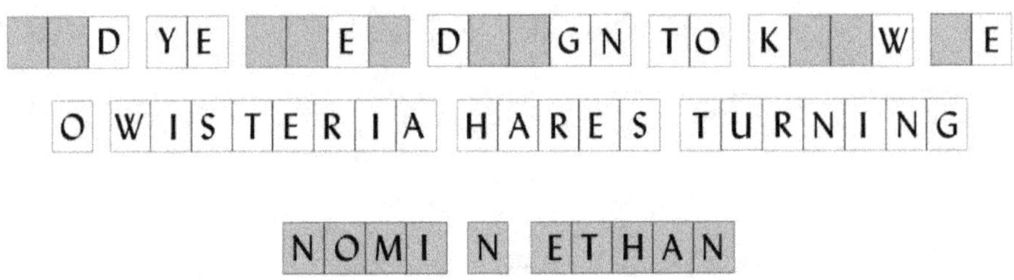

"Yeah, it's on a plate," he admitted, "but let the record show I did it on my own."

Dane was slowly shaking his head. "Of all the things in the chamber, Nomi and I found this first line the weirdest. Not weird, just puzzling."

"Why?"

"It's so… Ethan was romantic as fuck but he wasn't cutesy or precious. He was a chisel-in-stone kind of guy. *Ethan 'n Nomi* is like something you'd draw on your notebook in middle school. I remember lying in bed with her and talking about it. Was it a nod to her and Ethan having met first? To them being married? Is the N just *and* abbreviated or does it mean something else?"

"You didn't ask him?"

"No, because after we solved the other two lines, we realized Ethan must've been getting tired. He was under huge pressure to launch the game and the developers couldn't wait around for him to finish his Easter eggs much longer. He put the most thought into the other lines and just did what he could with the leftover letters. It probably bugged the fuck out of him, having to use a cute little N between names. So Nomi and I never mentioned it."

"N for *never.*"

"N for *not everything needs to be said out loud.*"

As they'd been talking, another golden, sparkly swirl revealed more letters illuminated in the inscription. A lot of them. Liko's eyes widened and he sighed darkly as he counted twenty-two letters to rearrange in a six-word sentence.

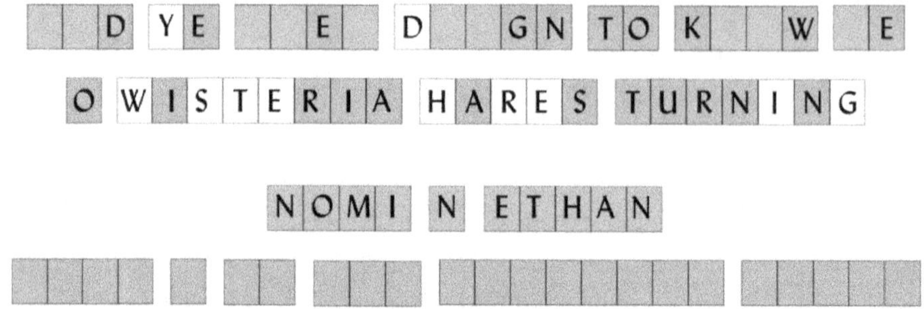

"This one's gonna be hard," he said.

"That's my line," Dane said.

"Ha ha."

"No, literally. This next line is about me. I cried my face off when I solved it. I'll probably cry it off when you solve it. Or we solve it. Fuck a duck, I'm crying already. God *dammit…*"

Liko almost laughed before he realized Dane was genuinely upset. He shut his mouth and watched as Dane got up abruptly, collected plates and cups and went into the kitchen. Liko stared after, at a loss.

So much loss to be at, and Liko knew only too well how deep the reservoir ran. How it bubbled up between the cracks of your daily life. Grief was sneaky and devious. It hid around corners and under couches, stifling giggles as it waited for you to settle into a peaceful moment. Then it pounced on you. It staked out your house. It laid an ambush. It waited. A perpetually packed rolling suitcase by the door. The last thing you collected on your way out: *Spectacles, testicles, wallet, watch, grief.* Then you drove off with grief riding shotgun and your coffee cup on the roof of the car. Life went on somehow.

"Grief is a bandit," Liko said under his breath, as if trying out an opening line for a story. "Time is a thief. Grief is a bandit. Love is…"

He sighed, gaze fixed on the open laptop, letting the beautiful, pathologically perfect artwork of *Three Hares* blur in and out of focus. Staring at the N between Nomi and Ethan.

Not everything needs to be said out loud.

He sat up.

He got up.

He went into the kitchen, where Dane was washing dishes.

And he said out loud: "I love you."

The water went on running but Dane's hands went still in the sink and his head bowed.

"Come here," Liko said, going to him. "If you're going to cry your face off, cry it onto me. Because I love your face. I love your crying. I love all of you. Come here."

He turned the faucet off and turned Dane toward him. Dane didn't cry. He put his face against Liko's chest and exhaled, his wet hands holding onto Liko's shirttails.

Time is a thief, Liko thought. *Grief is a bandit.*

Love is a creator.

Love did things. Love was a noun and it took action. Love crunched and crushed. It dripped butter and sugar then it glinted bare-boned, stripped down and ready to fight. Love reclined on a chaise. Love ran marathons. Love planted a garden, love devoured like locusts or reaped the harvest. Love took your breath and gave you life. Love pushed. Love pulled. Love coaxed you in and turned you out. Love fucked with your head and love told you the truth.

Love is an artist, Liko thought. *Its medium is the truth. Just tell Dane the truth. This is the friend of your life. Your life is right now. Tell him the truth. Truth or silence.*

"I love you," he said against Dane's hair. "You gave my life back to me. You gave *time* back to me. I don't want to waste or kill it anymore. I want to spend it."

Dane's arms tightened around Liko's waist and he sighed. "Lee, my man, this is a lot."

"I know. There's precious little I give a fuck about, and this lot is in the little."

Dane lifted up his head. "What?"

"I don't know. It sounded good until I said it out loud."

"Oh my God, who are you?" Dane was laughing as he pretended, sort of, to bash his forehead against the wall of Liko's chest.

OUR GREATEST DANE

"ALL RIGHT," LIKO SAID. "Twenty-two letters into six words. Let's do this."

"Start with—"

"No, no, let me do it myself."

"Have at it." Dane opened a book and put his feet up.

Twenty minutes passed.

"Goddammit," Liko said, "give me a hint."

Dane shifted the book to one hand and unzipped his shorts with the other.

"You know, I'm feeling a little objectified while on this quest."

Laughing, Dane zipped again and set the book aside. "Me trying to give hints will be torture. I'll do the first four words, you take the rest. We're a team, right?"

"Yeah."

"They say there's no I in *team*." He started moving letters. "But in our case…"

When he was done, the first four words were *Know I in our.*

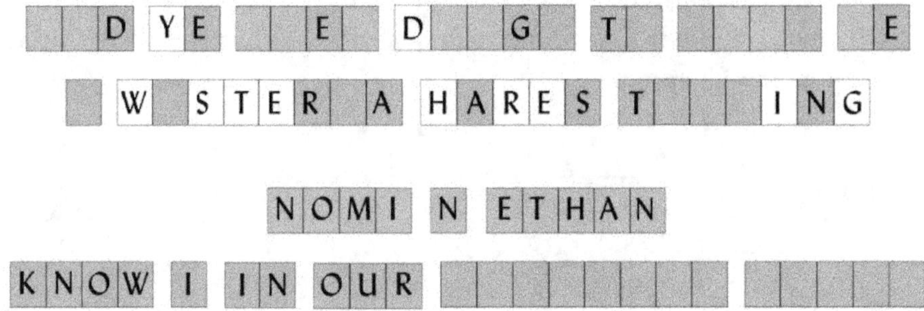

"Holy hell," Liko said. "I'd never get that on my own. How long did it take you and Nomi to solve?"

"Dude, it was so bad. For real, we were a pair of idiots working it out with our Scrabble tiles."

"I feel better knowing even you insiders were struggling. Okay, this eight-letter word is gonna be a bitch."

"Eight rhymes with…?"

"Hate? *Plate.* Which clues are served on."

Dane raised eyebrows and pointed at himself.

"Well, I know it's not straight," Liko said slowly. "Fate? Wait…"

"I'm rethinking this entire relationship now."

"Great," Liko cried. "Oh my God. Duh."

Dane made a backhanded swat against Liko's arm. "Dipshit."

Liko moved the five letters to spell *great.* Then he made a superlative quantum leap and added E, S and T. Not great but greatest.

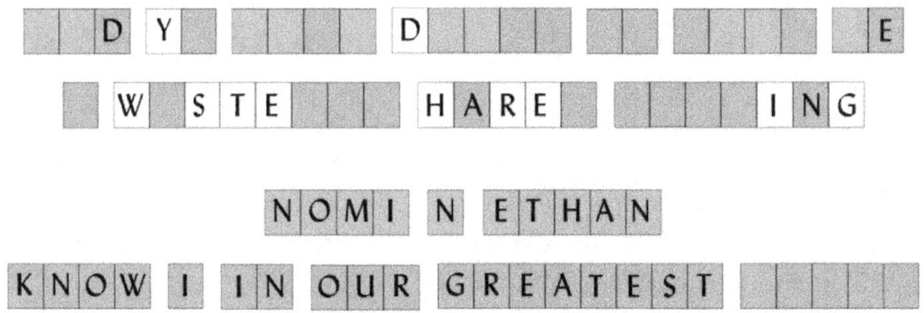

"This last part killed me," Dane said softly.

Obviously the remaining four letters spelled *Dane,* but the space waiting for them had five letters.

"Know I in our greatest Dane," Liko said. "No, no, don't tell me. Let me do it…"

His eyes flicked left to right and back again, looking for it. The part that killed Dane. It was right at the edge of his mind. He knew he was looking right at it, but he wasn't *seeing* it. He always missed the obvious.

"Know I in our…"

Then he saw it.

Two homophones.

Know and *no.*

I and…

He looked sharply at Dane, who had his hands steepled around his mouth and nose. Over his fingertips, one blue eye and one brown eye looked back at Liko.

"No eye," Liko said, tracing one of Dane's brows. "No *eye* in our greatest Dane. But there is. Both eye and… Put an I in *Dane* and you get Diane. Wait…"

He clicked over to the Green Man, with his brown-and-blue gaze. A strange and incredulous trepidation made the hair on Liko's nape stir. He felt exactly as he did when he watched Kyle drop the hare into the fire, all those months ago. Doing something beneath his dignity. Deigning.

Kyle's presence stirred over Liko's shoulder now, leaning close, awed and astounded. *Hell, yeah, Dad. This is* sick. *Do it. Don't wait. Do it now.*

Liko clicked the Green Man's blue eye.

It came free in the cursor and went into his cache.

"You got it," Dane said under his hands.

"Holy shit," Liko said. He returned to the letter slots. He left the D where it was, skipped a slot, and moved the A-N-E to the end.

"I love this," he said under his breath. "Oh my God, I fucking love this."

"Same," Dane whispered.

Liko took the blue eye out of his cache and put it in place.

An eye for an I.

The remaining letters of the inscription lit up but Liko barely noticed. He reached an arm and drew Dane close. Wrapped the other around and pulled Dane against his heart. Reading the words over and over.

Know I in our greatest D(i)ane.

"Unbelievable," he murmured. Marveling at the time and the effort and the creativity that went into this entire chamber. The hours to forward engineer and reverse engineer all the clues and solutions, all the causes and effects. And to make it all mean something to only two people. The only two people that mattered. Because three was a magic number.

And love is an artist.

"It's amazing," Liko said, holding Dane harder. "Oh my God, man, what a..."

He trailed off. He had no word for what it was.

A love letter, he thought, open-mouthed and staring, half laughing around a lump in his throat.

Love letters.

Letters of love.

THE KNIFE

Now TWELVE LETTERS were left from the original inscription *And ye then deign to know me, o wisteria hares turning*. The last slots had opened in the floor, grouped in four words.

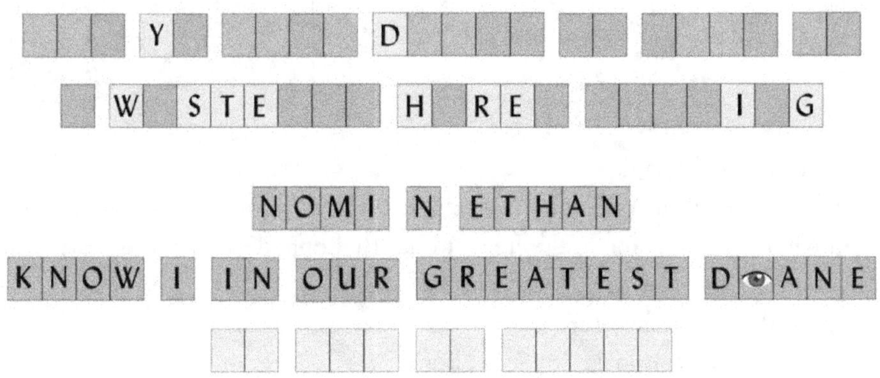

"How many clues to solve after this is done?" Liko asked.

"Just one." Dane opened his book. "Good luck."

Liko pulled together letters to make the last two words *is* and *three*. He shuffled the W, D, G and Y around but with no more vowels, he couldn't make any words. Also he had five slots to fill, but only those four letters left.

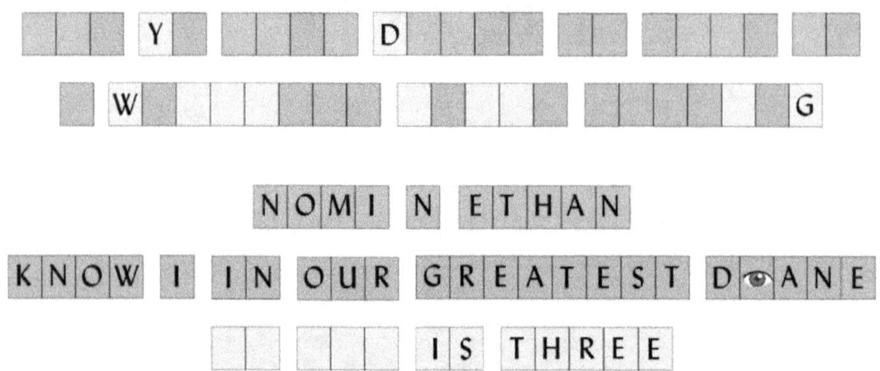

"I'm stuck," he said.

Dane lowered the book to see. He looked so delicious, Liko leaned to snog for a while, before Dane broke free and lightly bopped him on the head with the book. "Work with the D and G a bit."

"I need a vowel though."

"What could you make if you had one?"

"Dig," Liko said. "Dug. Dag? *Dog.*"

Dane touched his nose. "Dog spelled backward is…?"

"God." Liko moved the G and D into the beginning and end of the three-letter group. "But I still need a vowel."

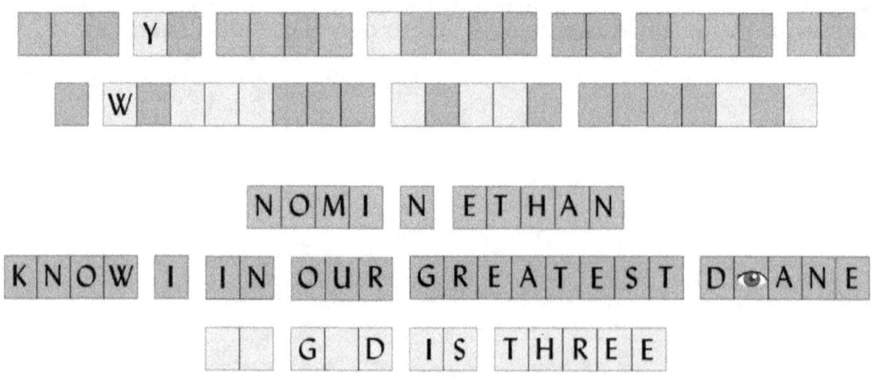

"Would you like to buy an I?"

Once upon a time this hint would have sailed over Liko Greenman's head. But not today.

"Ah," he said, "in this game, an I is never just an I." He clicked over to the Green Man and circled the cursor around his one remaining eye. The brown one.

"May I, sir?"

The eye came away and Liko dropped it between the G and D.

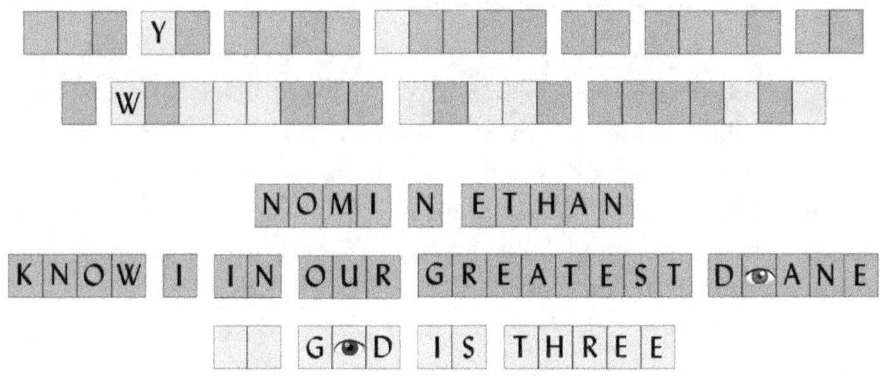

Which left just the W and Y. Liko moved them into the last slots, thinking it was an abbreviation of the word *why.* Another cutesy concession that would've annoyed Ethan to pieces.

"Why God is three," he said.

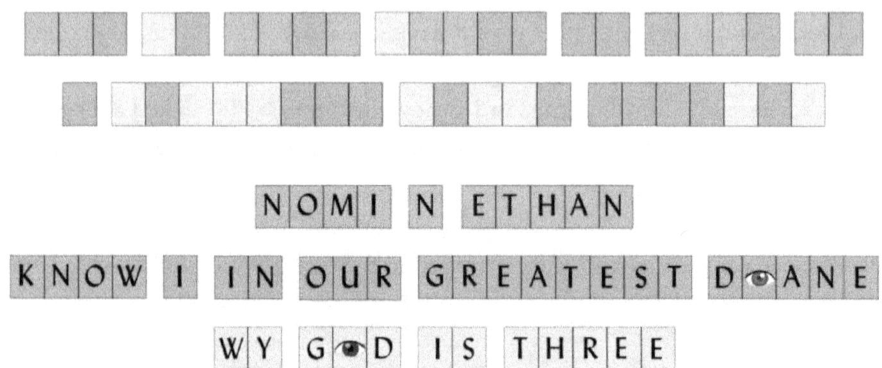

Dane smiled, rubbing circles on Liko's back. "Remember Nomi and I had a rule in Scrabble. A way to cheat against Ethan."

"So the score wouldn't be two thousand to six. I remember…"

It took Liko a few tricky clicks to turn the W upside-down and make it an M. It locked into place and all the letters of the anagrams lit up bright. Liko paused the game. Just to take it all in.

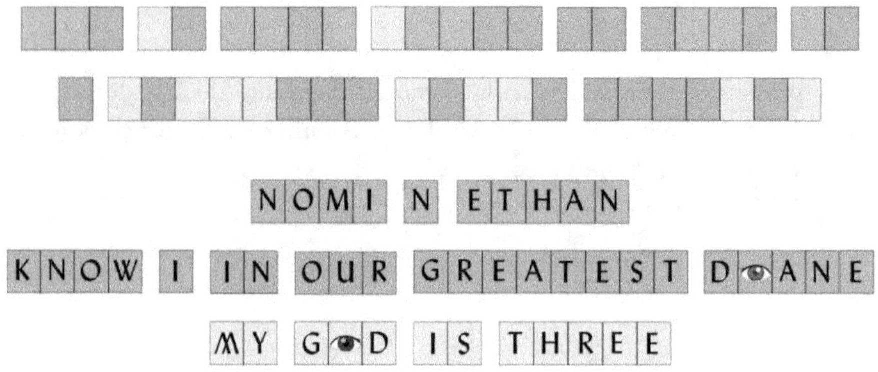

"My God is three," Liko said.

"Well, yes," Dane said slowly. "But the eye is still an I."

"My *guide* is three?"

Dane smiled. "Ethan could be a little ham-handed in his romantic gestures."

"All in, how long did it take you and Nomi to solve this?"

"Weeks. And truth be told… God, we sound like such dicks when I tell this part of the story."

"What?"

"We loved Ethan but we didn't *think* like him. Nobody thought like him. And neither me nor Nomi was a gamer. We wouldn't obsessively play something until all hours, never resting until we could solve every puzzle. So Ethan does this great unveiling of the chamber and says it's a mystery just for us. When I say we stumbled through it, I'm being kind. We weren't indifferent or unappreciative, we just weren't *good* at this kind of stuff. Ethan had to prompt and hint us through what he thought were obvious clues, and he'd get all huffy."

Dane put fingertips to the bridge of his nose, shaking his head. "It was a beautiful thing. He worked so hard on it and he loved that only we would know what it all meant. We *appreciated* it. We just weren't good at it. *Oh. The wisteria. Got it. Cute. No no, not* cute, *sorry, I mean brilliant.* Oh God…"

Dane's face came up and his eyes were liquid. He sniffed. "Whoa, that hit me." He ran the back of his hand across his face and sniffed again. "Okay, watch what happens next, and then we stop for the day. Because I need to ask you something."

Liko tapped the space bar and the animation continued. The view pulled wide to take in the chamber as a whole. For a moment, nothing happened. Then Saskia's knife, hanging on the wall behind the Green Man's altar, disengaged from the stones and clattered to the floor. At the same time, the ceiling motif stopped spinning and the hares came to rest. Liko clicked over to collect the beautiful weapon and put it in his cache. Then he shut the laptop, turned sideways on the couch and looked at Dane.

"So, Green Man," Dane said. "You have one thing left to do. One more romantic gesture to behold. And then the game is done. And then. And then. Until finally."

"And then?"

Dane took his feet off the coffee table and tossed his ballcap aside. He crawled on top of Liko, kneeling across his thighs. "Then it's October, when Schoenfeld's is a scream. The CSA is finished but the pumpkins start rolling in. Apples and cider start rolling in. Week days are nuts, weekends are indescribable. I'll be running around like a headless chicken and falling into bed at night, calling shotgun. Will you still be here?"

"Yes."

"November is when I collapse and do nothing but eat, sleep, read, get drunk and screw. I'll start to think about Thanksgiving—making plans with Huff and Maisie, who to invite, what to make. Will you still be here?"

"Wouldn't miss it."

"December is booked. We're going to Paderborn."

"Then to France," Liko said. "Then to London, for Christmas with Basil and Bootsy."

"For the first time in twentyish years, I won't be decking the halls of this house. I'll miss the tree lighting at the pond, and the hootenanny at the Pub. We've even given up New Year's Eve at Huff and Maisie's house, and the chance to finally kiss on the roof, because we'll be in Devon, looking for Tinner's Hares."

"I'll live," Liko said, running his hands up and down Dane's legs. "It was the resolution, after all."

"Then we come home. What does that look like?"

"You tell me," Liko said, feeling slightly outside himself.

"I want you to stay. End of story. End of game. I want you here all year. All the time. I want you to stay."

Liko stared, unable to speak.

"I'm in love with you and I want you to stay," Dane said. "Stay here, Henry Greenman. Henry Hugh Liko Greenman, the anagram of which, by the fucking way, is *please stay with me.*"

"I thought it was *tempt me with fiber,*" Liko said softly. He grabbed Dane around the waist and toppled them sideways onto the couch. "Fine, then."

"Fine?"

"I'll stay," Liko said, hugging and wrestling and gnawing on Dane's earlobe. "You will?"

"I'll be your Valentine. Your St. Patrick's Day hangover mate. Your April Fool. And next May Day you can dance around my flagpole and decide if—"

"Okay, shut up now."

Liko laughed and wrapped both arms tight around his magnificent Great Dane, rolling them off the couch onto the rug. The coffee table lurched and a plate fell onto the floor.

"What is with you and the fucking *plates,*" Dane said, muffled in Liko's grip. "I can't have one romantic moment without you breaking something."

"It's part of my brooding charm."

"Jesus Hernando Christ, you're lucky you're cute…"

Postcards sent October 1-31, 2017

*Plaster Ceiling detail, Burg Breuberg
Castle, Odenwald, Germany.*

*Painted panel, Unterlimpurg Synagogue,
Schwäbisch-Hall, Germany*

Reliquary at Trier Cathedral, Germany

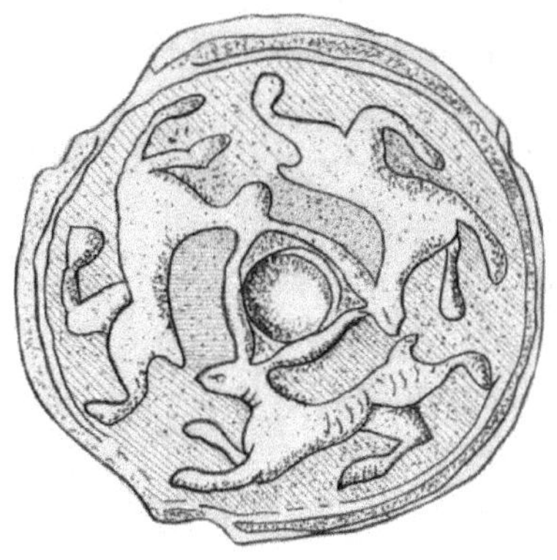

*Blue Glass Medallion, Museum für
Islamische, Berlin, Germany*

AMIABLE PROXIMITY

Despite the bacchanal of harvest and fall festivities, October was a tough month for Dane since he'd been on his own. The changing foliage and crisp air evoked so much bittersweet nostalgia for his first months at Schoenfeld's. When he was all of twenty years old, tentatively emerging from a chrysalis into the company of people who thought he was miraculous.

"I'll never forget opening weekend of that first fall season," he said to Liko. "It's when Ethan gave me the leather vest. So I'd feel braver in crowds."

He fetched an old photo album and showed pictures taken that day, when, for the second time in his life, Dane appeared in public as his inner chimera. His eyes out and his face bisected. He made up the left side himself, his blue eye stunning beneath false lashes with a small row of spangles beneath. Ethan airbrushed the right side of Dane's face with leaves and twigs and clusters of acorns, making him half Green Goddess, half Green Man. But it was the clothing that made Dane feel fantastic that day: he wore Ethan's gifted leather vest with a kilt and motorcycle boots.

"My man," Liko laughed over the album page. "What did that guy you met say? *I hope we meet again in your twenties?*"

"His loss," Dane said.

"Captivating and ghosting older men at parties is like a thing with you."

Nomi was dressed as a witch. But what a witch. A wild wig of auburn tresses. A velvet pantsuit with high-waisted, wide-legged trousers. Platform boots and a gnarled broomstick taller than she was. She radiated power and magic. Photographed together, walking through and engaging the crowd, she and Dane were pure dynamite. Charmaine DuJour would've gagged, gooped, shat twice and died.

"Liko needs to hold still now," Fred sang, moving their body between Liko and the photo album. "Close your eyes, my love. They're a terrible distraction."

Liko smiled and closed his eyes, holding perfectly still as Fred adjusted the stencil across his cheekbones, then began airbrushing.

"Did Ethan teach you how to do this?" Liko asked.

Fred snorted. "I taught him. Ethan hasn't cornered the market on artistic license."

"And he never needed to be the smartest guy in the room," Dane said, with all the peace in his heart.

He and Ethan had finally spoken on the phone. Ethan emailed first, asking if he could call. Then texted to confirm the date and time. By the time the formal appointment rolled around, Dane was joking he didn't have a thing to wear to this job interview. Liko laughed along, but tactfully vacated the house and went for a walk with Salma.

The ring of the cell phone sent an icicle into Dane's heart. He inhaled deep through the second ring and picked up on the third.

"Hey," Ethan said.

"Hi."

Dane put his forehead in a palm, shaking his head. *So that's all it takes,* he thought. *One word brings it all back.*

One word could render them both silent, too. A long, breathing moment passed before Dane finally spoke. "Where are you?"

"Germany. I got to Odenwald this morning. I mailed you a postcard from Frankenberg."

"Didn't get it, but I haven't checked the mail today." Dane got up from his seat on the porch and walked down the driveway.

"Trees must be starting to turn," Ethan said.

"Yeah, it's going to be a pretty fall."

"Is the CSA over?"

"Last boxes get picked up on Thursday." Dane collected the mail and rifled through it. "Ah, here it is. Haina Monastery. The engraving on the consecrated bell."

"Sketched from memory," Ethan said. "I couldn't get near the bell."

"You know what these postcards have made me appreciate?"

"What?"

"How many bad medieval artists were in the world."

Ethan laughed.

"Seriously," Dane said. "What the hell are these—they look like mutant deer on steroids."

Ethan's from-the-belly hilarity kept tumbling over the line. Dane smiled coolly at the sound, and Diane carved a satisfied notch in their shared soul as the laughter softened into thoughtful quiet again.

"How are you?" Ethan asked.

"Truth or silence rules in effect?"

"Yes."

"I'm good. Farm's doing well. CSA in the red. We only lost four chickens to foxes. I grew some veggies for myself. And I met someone."

"Saskia said."

"You?"

"It's been a journey. Grief isn't linear but processing grief on a linear path is… I don't really have a word for what it is. Starting in Cave 407 where my parents saw the Three Hares for the first time. Progressing along the route, leaving a little of Nomi in each place. It's like a long goodbye. At each stop there's just a bit less to hold onto. More room in your heart for new things to grow. I don't know."

"It's a beautiful thing to do," Dane said.

"Truth or silence," Ethan said softly.

"I mean it."

"Will you come to Paderborn?"

Dane drew a deep breath. "Before I answer, I need to say something."

Ethan gave a little laugh. "I figured you'd have many somethings to say."

"I need to say I'm sorry."

A surprised beat. "For what?"

"What I said the night before you left."

"Oh God, Dane, I don't even remember wh—"

"I bet you do," Dane said. "Your eyes and ears never turn off and you have an eidetic memory. You remember."

"All right, I remember, but…"

"But nothing. It was shitty and I've regretted it since. I'm sorry. I was upset and angry, but it's no excuse for taking such a cheap shot at your identity. You wouldn't do it to me."

A shaky breath and a sniff. Then silence again on the other end.

"I'm sorry," Dane said.

"Thank you."

"You didn't believe you could be man enough for me, and it broke my heart."

"Dane…"

"It made me feel I didn't do a good enough job making you believe it."

"You have no idea what your love meant to me," Ethan said thickly. "Meant to me, means to me, and will go on meaning the rest of my life. I want you to come to Paderborn for so many reasons. Because it's the end of this pilgrimage and I want you and Saskia to be there. To sprinkle the last ashes and end it with me. I need three people to be there. The three most important people to Nomi. But I want you to come because I just want to see you. I miss you so much."

"Why?"

"Because you're a soulmate. Because I equate seeing you with peace. Because I still love you. I'll always love you."

But, Dane thought. *But, but, but. Which is the birthplace of all our arguments and I am* not *going there. Not today, not ever again.*

I give a fuck. I can't relegate this to the Meaningless Scrapheap. But if Paderborn is the end for Ethan, it has to be an end for me.

These are the terms of peace.

"I'm coming to Paderborn," he said. "Flights are booked, itinerary is set. Liko is coming with me, which is non-negotiable." He winced at his terse delivery and lowered his voice. "I want to see you too. Despite what you might think, or how I act, I do miss you too."

"Do you?"

"So much. So many ways. But for me to move on with Liko, I need to hear something from you. Not now, not on this call. I want to hear you say it in Paderborn."

"Say what?"

"With truth or silence rules in place, I need you to say you're not in love with me anymore."

"Dane, I—"

"Don't do it now," Dane said. "Come on, my man. You are the king of the concept-to-creation pipeline. A master of the romantic gesture. Let an average schmuck have his chance."

Ethan laughed, but Dane could tell he was in tears. "God, I missed hearing *my man*. No one else says it."

"Only men who are much men can be *my man*. Anyway, those are the terms of Paderborn. The Paderborn Protocol."

"You know I'd do anything for you."

"I need this," Dane said. "Those words. That place. It'll be the end of both our journeys and the start of new ones."

"What will be your new journey?"

"Remains to be written. Yours?"

Ethan hesitated, inhaling slow. "I'd like to come home."

Dane didn't say anything.

"Not to your house. Not even to the farm. I'm a misanthropic son of a bitch, but I can read a room."

"This I know."

"Birch Island is my home. That land is in my soul and the Black Dirt Region is where I've grown my best ideas. I don't regret any of this pilgrimage but I'm so homesick, it hurts. So can you think about amiable proximity between now and Paderborn?"

Dane's eyes were wet but he smiled into his cheeks. "I can do that."

They were unaccustomed to goodbyes. After twenty-odd years, their typical way of ending a conversation was falling asleep mid-sentence. But those days were over. They made a little small talk, cracked a few jokes, klutzily decoupled and hung up.

Peace negotiations concluded, Dane texted Liko. ***Terms favorable. Treaty to be signed in Paderborn.***

FRED MADE A LAST pass with the airbrush, stepped back and scrutinized their efforts. "I believe my work here is done."

Liko turned his head and looked at Dane. His violet eyes gleamed from a painted, foliage mask.

"It would be twice as magnificent if you'd shaved the beard," Fred said.

"I would've been murdered." Liko reached and jostled Dane, who was staring open-mouthed. "What are you, the butler? Say something."

"You're gorgeous," Dane managed.

"It's the company I keep." Liko slid down from the vanity and turned around to view himself in the bathroom mirror. He turned his head this way and that, admiring the intricate foliage design from temple to temple, hairline to beard line.

"Next year, full face," he said. "For my debut, I'll play it safe."

"You're gonna cut a bigger swathe than Pao," Fred said. "Get a move on, Green Man. Fame awaits at the fall festivities."

They posed on the porch first so Fred could take a picture, which Dane would frame and hang in the kitchen: Liko with his horizontal half-mask of leaves, and Dane with his vertical one. Their other-worldly eyes two bucks circling, each believing they were the fairest of all, and they ought to take it back inside.

Or upstairs.

THE NAOMI ROAD 51

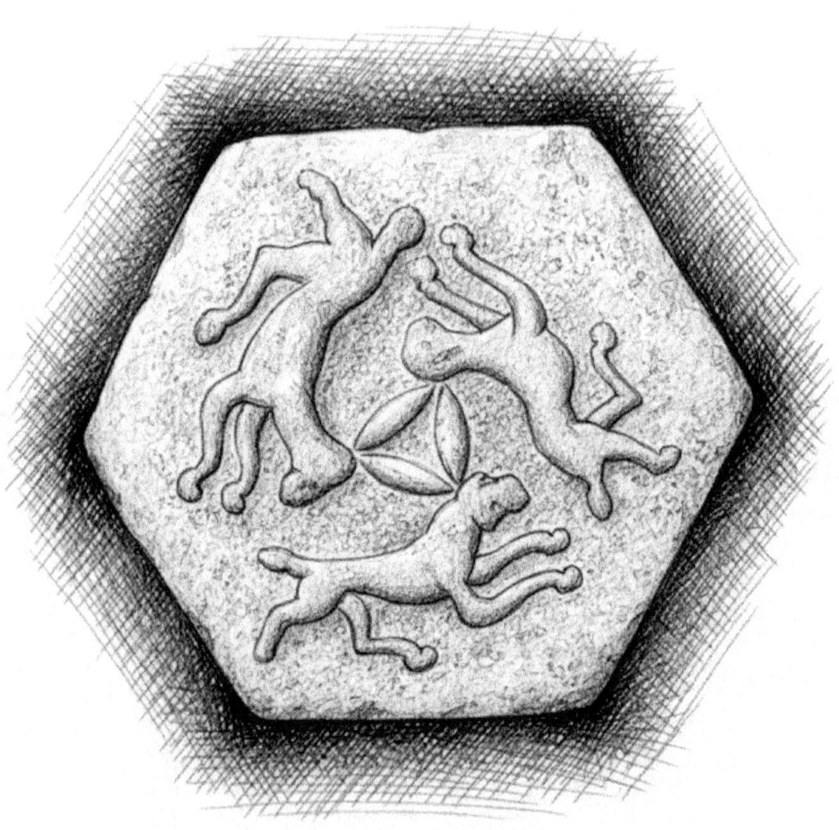

Terracotta tile, Museum für Islamische Kunst, Berlin, Germany

ALL THE FAITHFUL ATTENDANTS

Dane collapsed the first two weeks of November. He slept late, roused only when Liko brought him a cup of coffee in bed. They went for hikes in the afternoon, enjoying the last of the foliage. If he had the energy and motivation, Dane tidied up garden beds or raked leaves. But usually he was napping at three o'clock and Liko usually came in with him. They snoozed and shagged, or shagged and snoozed. Got up, went out or stayed in as it suited them.

Thanksgiving was held at the Jensens. Dane and Liko spent the night and while it wasn't a New Year's Eve reenactment, they did discover the rail of the widow's walk could support the weight of two men. They noted the observation and wisely vowed never to attempt the experiment again.

"One and done," Dane said as they tiptoed back downstairs. "Too old for that shit."

"Tell me about it," Liko muttered, sucking the base of his index finger. "I got a fucking splinter…"

Dane was mildly pissy about the farmhouse not having a Christmas tree. He piled the kitchen mantel with pine branches and white lights, and cut snowflakes for the windows, because certain holiday décor mandates in the Danelaw were non-negotiable.

The postcard from Paderborn arrived. Ethan did an exquisite job with the arched majesty of the Drei-Hasen-Fenster. Dane settled it carefully in the pine boughs over the fireplace, then he and Liko opened a bottle of Grand Marnier—an early Christmas gift from Fred—to finish the chamber mystery.

"Damn, I'm feeling all thumpy," Liko said, touching his chest.

"Raise your glass and lower your expectations," Dane said. "Then take Saskia the Knife and cut the ceiling motif into thirds."

"That's it?"

"That's it."

Liko felt all kinds of bittersweet as he glided the knife along the seams between the Three Hares.

Kyle, my man, I wish you were here. I wish you were here. I wish you could see…

The ceiling panels slid apart, taking the rest of the chamber with them, until the screen was filled with…

"I told you it was anti-climactic," Dane says.

Liko gazed on a painting of Schoenfeld's three worldly hares. They were in the Hare Ring, and yet everything from the Green Man Chamber was also present: all the objects and symbols and animals and flowers that made up the story of *Ye Then Deign to Nomi.*

The three lovers knelt in front of the granite block altar. Not the haphazardly carved one from reality but the game's pedestal of perfection. A fire burned in its circular depression and next to it lay Saskia the Knife.

Dane and Nomi knelt facing each other, she clothed in wisteria flowers with her arms up around Dane's neck. Her head adorned with the Dusk Tiara and her chin on Dane's shoulder. Her eyes were shut but her open-mouthed expression could have been laughter, tears, or both.

Ethan was painted naked as birth, kneeling behind Nomi, his arms reaching around her to hold Dane's face. Drawing his head close, close enough to kiss but forever paused in the magical moment before lips touched.

Dane was cloaked in his leather vest. His chest pressed tight to Nomi's, the broken cages for their hearts made whole. He had one hand in Nomi's hair, the other on Ethan's face. Of the three, only his eyes were fully open. Only he looked as they all leaped.

Nestled in the grasses and wildflowers were all the faithful attendants: Parker, Maple, chickens, barn cats and ducklings. The Green Man lounged against a tree in the foreground, watching the lovers, composing the story. Ruta Skadi stood at his side, proud and pitiless, a hand on her cloud pine broom. Opposite, shimmering silver and white, was Helen of Winter in her furs and snowflakes, her arms full of eggs. At her feet was the Jade Rabbit, holding his mortar and pestle. In the background, silhouetted hares sat still, bounded high, or got up on their hind legs to box.

And of course, across the face of the burgeoning moon, the motif of the Three Hares. Running, Liko noticed, counter-clockwise. The wrong way.

The most compassionate way.

"It's beautiful."

Dane smiled. "It's beautiful to me. No one else will have an orgasm over it."

"Where is this painting now?"

"It used to hang in the living room but Ethan took it when he left."

"Ouch."

"No, it would've hurt more seeing it on the wall every day. If I ever miss it, I know how to find it in the game. Weird how nobody knows this work by Ethan Hasen exists, yet anyone who downloads *Three Hares* has a copy." He ran a hand through his hair, brows furrowed. "We kind of belong to the world now."

Liko was quiet a long time.

"Is this a letdown?" Dane asked.

"If I didn't know the story behind it all, maybe."

"It's nothing that means anything to anyone but me."

"It was made it for you. And Nomi."

"I'd erase this game from existence if it would bring her back."

"Yeah," Liko said. "Fair. I'd do a lot of things to get Kyle back."

"What would he have thought about all this?"

Again Liko was quiet.

Once upon a time, a grieving father was quiet.

And then he thought.

And then he thought some more.

Until finally he said "I don't know. Kyle was never in love."

"He will be."

"You think?"

"I do. So do you. Kyle will come back. He's already reborn. He's a new spirit with an old soul and he'll find you and Janelle. Same with Nomi. She'll find me and Ethan and Saskia. We won't know it, but she will."

"Maybe… Never mind."

"No, tell me."

"Maybe Kyle and Nomi will meet."

"Why not? Maybe you and I making love opens some kind of cross-reference portal for them. It's a woo-woo theory but it sure fucking beats the alternative theory of everything being meaningless."

THE NAOMI ROAD 52

Cloister window at Paderborn Cathedral, Germany

PADERBORN

December 2017
The Cathedral of Saint Mary, Saint Kilian and Saint Liborius
Paderborn, North Rhine-Westphalia, Germany

ROLF, THE NATTY YOUNG man who'd made the viral video on the cathedral's website, gave a private tour from one end of the nave to the other, across, up, down, beneath, and finally outside to the Drei-Hasen-Fenster.

"Is it me," Liko murmured, "or can young Rolf not take his eyes off Ethan?"

"Right?" Saskia whispered. "He's about to sing 'Sixteen Going on Seventeen.'"

Dane didn't know what calls had been made or strings pulled, but the cloisters' inner courtyard had been roped off for half an hour. He, Ethan and Saskia stood in front of the window together, undisturbed by visitors. Saskia held the little box with the last of Nomi's ashes, while Ethan and Dane held up their hands as a screen so the cold winter wind wouldn't crash the ceremony.

"Love you, Mammu," Saskia said, pinching a bit of the fine, gray dust and rubbing her fingers to release it beneath the window. She said it again in Latvian, "Es tevi mīlu."

Ethan took the next bit and scattered it with no words. He'd done this fifty-one times before and all he needed to say to Nomi had been said.

Dane went last, running a fingertip around the inside of the box to corral enough to pinch. He stepped a little away from his family, looking up at the Three Hares.

"Katherine Jones," he whispered, "this is Danelaw Strong with a message for Ms. Nomi Hasen. The message is, *I love you.* And please will she call me back?"

He let go his fingers and the ashes dispersed, floating up across the window. Saskia put arms around him from behind, and Ethan put an arm around them both.

Dane looked down at the box still in his palm, and the little bits of ash left. He looked over his shoulder and kissed Saskia's head. "Baby, give me a minute with Ethan?"

Her eyes were bright and liquid, her fine freckles like copper magic in the thin sunshine. She kissed each of their faces, then went over to stand with Liko, who was talking with Rolf by the fountain.

Dane motioned with his head toward the buttress next to the window. Ethan smiled, and they walked toward it together. They slid their fingertips around the inside of the box, getting every last bit, then rubbed the ashes on the buttress, in the approximate place of the loose stone in the *Three Hares* game. A stone memorializing a loose brick in a chimney, where a girl called Silver had hidden treasure.

"I miss you so much," Dane said.

"All day every day," Ethan said.

They stood, their hands on the ashy brick. Their free arms came up to drape on shoulders. Their heads rested together as they made their peace, remembering all they did for a woman they loved.

Ethan's hand moved and his fingers slid in Dane's hair. "You are the friend of my life," he said. "My soulmate. A Great Dane who knocked me over and gave me peace. I'm not in love with you. I am beside love with you." His caress in Dane's hair became a hold, and he turned Dane's head to face him. "Understand? I am *beside* love with you."

Ethan's chin tilted one way, indicating the buttress. Then toward Liko, who was ambling along the cloisters alone. "Beside love."

Dane's eyes flooded warm, turning cold crisp on his cheeks.

"Beside love," he said. "Because your autobiography is called *The Sider House Laws.*"

"Oh, my man," Ethan laughed, and he kissed Dane's wet face.

"Apparently giving average schmucks a chance at romantic gestures is *beyond* your capabilities." Dane rubbed one cheek, then the other on his forearm. "Thanks for nothing."

Ethan hugged him hard. "Thanks for everything."

From the cathedral, the little party made their way to Städtische Galerie, Paderborn's art museum, where Ethan donated the beautiful painting from the end of the game. A long time spent viewing their story in its new home. Then another private, exclusive tour behind the scenes, of the kind only Ethan could arrange.

Outside, there were suggestions of an early dinner, but Dane felt his emotional and social tanks running on fumes, and Saskia looked a little tired and pale. Possibly she was relieved all had gone so well. They hugged goodbye in front of the Schloss Neuhaus and parted to their separate hotels.

"That went well," Liko said. "Splendid, as the Brits say. What do you think?"

"I thought splendid."

Liko put an arm around him and bussed a kiss on Dane's crown. "It was beautiful. I legit got choked up watching you three. And I saw Rolf slipping Ethan his digits."

Dane laughed but said nothing.

"You guys all right?"

"More than all right," Dane said, sliding his hand into Liko's back pocket. "We're beside ourselves."

EPILOGUE
ADAM ANDROGYNOS

"I love you," Big Nutbrown Hare said to Little Nutbrown Hare. "I love you to the moon…and back."
—Sam McBratney, Guess How Much I Love You

"The body sleeps when the story ends."
—Saying among the Kaluli tribe of Papua New Guinea

THE GREEN MAN'S PEACE

r/Three Hares Mystery
*Walkthrough for Green Man Chamber, in memory of Kyle Greenman
(@kgr33n) •May 11, 2018•*
Lkgr33n

Hey gang, it's the Greenman.

So it's been a hot minute but I'm back as promised and I've solved the mystery. I didn't do it alone. Far from it. I don't know if one of you beautiful people brought my story to Henshe Games or if they found me themselves, but they were kind enough to reach out and provide me with one single clue to start me on a journey. The clue eventually led me to a beautiful farm in New York. Besides being a thriving agro-tourist business, it's an artist colony, a haven, a refuge, and a museum of sorts. Jonathan Henshe once lived there but no more. Now only a Great Dane lives in the farmhouse. He took me in. He told me he could show me the solution to the Green Man Chamber in ten minutes, but it wouldn't be satisfying or even interesting because I didn't know the stories behind the chamber and everything in it. Didn't know the stories behind the entire Three Hares game, which, at its essence, is a love letter.

The Great Dane suggested I treat the mystery as a paint-by-number kit, and I wisely took his advice. I spent the entire summer on his farm, listening to stories and solving clues. And in the end, it was not only satisfying and interesting, but I felt like one of the recipients of the love letter.

A promise is a promise. I can't please everybody but I'll offer options. I'm attaching the walkthrough with no explanation. If you get to the end and find yourself disappointed or confused or let-down or wanting more, then I have a love letter for you in the form of a novel called The Great Dane. *All is explained in its pages. It has lots of pictures. Proceeds will go to the scholarship fund at Kingpoint Academy in Sherford, Connecticut.*

If neither of those options appeal and you want to continue solving the chamber on your own, I'll simply tell you that the anagram of Jonathan Henshe is Ethan John Hasen, and leave you to it.

My quest to solve the mystery of the Green Man Chamber was—still is—dedicated to my son. The novel The Great Dane *is dedicated to all of us.*

At one point or another, all of us have wondered who we are.

All of us have scratched at a label put on us, feeling it didn't quite fit.

All of us have felt pressured to be something we're not.

All of us have wished we were someone else—whether in envy or despair or admiration.

All of us have looked in a mirror and been confused at what we see.

All of us don armor to do brave things: a change in voice, a different accent, a favorite sweater, high heels, a good luck charm.

All of us are fluid.

I used to think all of us hear a voice when we talk to ourselves but I've since learned this is only some of us. But whether or not you have an inner monologue, the book is for you. The journey is for you. The quest and the game and the mystery and the solution: all for you.

For Kyle Dalusio Greenman.

For the Great Dane.

And for me.

With love and wonder at everything life can be,

Henry (Liko) Greenman

Liko's phone pinged a text from Dane: **Open mic starting in ten min. Better hurry bc Brian's here and it's SRO.**

Leaving now, Liko texted. He read over one paragraph of his post, then abruptly hit *publish* and walked away from the laptop.

Spring had been chilly this year, grudging to get over itself, but tonight felt like the first breath of summer. The air was soft as Liko walked down the driveway. Waiting for cars to pass on Oak Hill Road, he admired the rising full moon, then glanced across Route 34, to where Ethan's tiny house was finished, cozied up to the refurbished barn that was his new studio. The house's one-man porch was strung with lights, and within their cozy glow, Ethan sat in a lone Adirondack chair.

No more cars came along Oak Hill Road, but Liko kept standing and staring. Remembering.

Looking for myself along the roadside.

Magic at the crossroads.

Not sure why, Liko turned away from the Pub, crossed 34 and made his way over to the tiny house.

This quadrant of the crossroads had been re-parceled, rezoned and sold to Ethan. Like a true child of divorce, Saskia split her time between the farmhouse and the tiny house, not yet wanting any sort of communal, middle ground. She liked both her fathers in one place, but in separate abodes.

Dane was being a bit of a Sphinx toward his new neighbor. He paid no attention to the legal real estate transactions, never wandered across the road to look in on construction or peek in the new studio. Once Liko saw Dane throw a quick wave from the mailbox, across the road to where Ethan was raking leaves. Ethan waved back, then both men returned to their business.

Ethan made no sudden moves. No requests to see the old homestead or have dinner together. No works of art as peace offerings. No emotional ambushes, no little notes or sketches left for Dane to find. Ethan asked permission to take the back road up to the Hare Ring, which was granted. Otherwise he kept to his property and when he put a foot on the farm, it was either to work, or do a little chiseling on the granite block.

He wasn't part of Dane and Liko's life.

He wasn't with them. He was barely visible.

Yet Liko couldn't help an almost amused feeling that like it or not, they still made a threesome. And he was weirdly all right with it.

Because Ethan and Dane are beside love, just like Janelle and I are in context.

We each have one ghost, and one loose end.

And maybe we all operate in threes…

"Hey," Liko called.

Ethan raised a hand with his wide smile, but didn't reply. In addition to his scarce presence, he seemed to be under a strange vow of silence since his return to Birch Island. He spoke a necessary amount and no more. He had a new dog, a rescue mutt called Silvio. If anyone had made BFFs around here, it was Salma and Silvio.

"Coming to open mic?" Liko asked.

Ethan got up and shooed Silvio inside. Then he beckoned Liko, pointing toward the studio.

Liko's heart kicked up a notch. A month ago, also for reasons unknown, he'd broken the rules against emotional ambushes and left a picture of Kyle in

Ethan's studio. No explanation, just the photo and a piece of paper with his son's name.

Maybe it was diplomacy. Maybe a peace offering. Maybe terms of surrender. Or just a father's entreaty to an artist: *What beauty can you make of this tragedy?*

Liko followed Ethan through the double doors, into the beautiful vaulted space. The skylights were covered and the smell of oil and turpentine hung thick in the air. Ethan was walking to his large easel where a canvas was turned backward. The piece of paper with Kyle's name was tacked to the frame. Ethan unpinned it and handed it to Liko.

KYLE DALUSIO GREENMAN

Ethan circled a finger in the air. Liko turned the paper over and read:

KYRIE ELEISON AD LUNAM
Kyrie Eleison: Greek, "Lord have mercy"
Ad Lunam: Latin, "To the moon"

"Oh my God," Liko said.

Ethan made a soft, appreciative sound in his chest, then pointed to the I in *eleison.* He seemed about to say something, then changed his mind and only pointed to the letter I again, then to one of his own eyes. Liko wrinkled his brow, turned the paper over and back. Then he got it.

"His name only has one I," he said. "From Dalusio. The other one is an eye."

Then Ethan gave a tremendous, wistful sigh and pointed to the G in *Greenman,* which hadn't fit into the anagram. His shoulders made an exaggerated shrug as he cleared his throat. "Pretend you can turn a G upside-down and make it an I."

Liko laughed. "I heard how extra letters can make you lose sleep."

"I did my best," Ethan said. "Maybe G will stand for something in your heart."

Greylock, Liko thought, but aloud he said, "It stands for *good enough.*"

"A lesson I'm forever learning," Ethan said with another sigh. "Anyway, Lunam is also an old Anglo-Saxon name. Comes from a Norman word, *laund,* which means an open space in a forest or lawn."

He turned the canvas around.

Before Liko was the Hare Ring under a moonlit starry sky. The laund in the forest, its perimeter of trees clogged with wisteria blossoms. Kyle Greenman sat cross-legged on the granite block, beautifully rendered in silver and gold and bronze. He gazed upward in three-quarter profile, with just one eye showing. Not the deep brown the boy possessed in life but Liko's smoky purple iris. The father's eye in the son's face, fixed on the moon, which was plump as a peach, the motif of the Three Hares delicately painted on its surface, almost too fine to see. On the side of the granite block, Ethan had painted bold, chiseled letters spelling out Kyle's anagram:

KYRIE ELEISON AD LUNAM

"Dude, it's beautiful," Liko said, and trusted himself to say no more.

Ethan walked to the wall where another large canvas was leaning. He turned it around. A second composition of Kyle sitting in the Hare Ring was roughly sketched out. Slightly different, but all the same elements: the moon, the anagram, the three-quarter profile gazing up.

"For his mother," Ethan said.

Overcome, Liko closed a hand around his face a moment. He looked up through tears at his son.

Kyrie eleison ad lunam.

He would accept this gift. He'd load Kyle's contemplative magnificence into a syringe and plunge it into his veins. He'd hang this painting where he could see it every day. He'd make a masterpiece of gazing at his beautiful boy in the light of the Jade Moon.

And he'd make his peace with Ethan Hasen.

A separate peace, he thought. *The Green Man's peace.*

"Thank you," he said.

Ethan nodded and pressed a closed fist to his heart.

"Did you send me the letter?"

Ethan smiled at his shoes and his hands went into his pockets. "I wondered if you'd ever ask."

"You did? It was you?"

"It was Saskia. She saw your post on Reddit and told me about it."

"Shut up."

Ethan nodded. "I sent the letter purely as a gift for your son. No matchmaking intentions. Although I did Google you, and I found your LinkedIn page. When I looked at your picture, I kind of felt the way I did when I first met Dane. Maybe you've heard I tend to get strong feelings about people at first sight, but it doesn't usually happen with photographs. It's always an in-person thing. But I looked at your picture and immediately felt something. I thought, *This is a…*"

Ethan freed a hand and turned it palm up. "I couldn't pin down what you were or what I was feeling. I kept coming back to *This is a Green Man*. The more I looked at your face and your name, the more I had a weird vision the Green Man on the stone pillar had torn himself off, walked away from Schoenfeld's and gotten lost. I had to send him home. Home to the Danelaw." His shoulders hunched once and relaxed. "It's dumb."

"Dude, it's so far from dumb," Liko said. His arms and neck shivered as the beginning of his story slid into place. He'd been focused so long on the quest and the mystery and the end of the game, the prologue had been forgotten. Now he shook his head, stunned at this third act reveal.

"I didn't know you," Ethan said, "but I knew my own instincts. I knew I could do something for you, not to make it better but make it different. I thought maybe by sending you here, I could also do something for Dane. Something to remake the peace I broke. Make a new peace."

"I see."

"But make no mistake, it all started with Saskia. She showed me your post. I wouldn't have known otherwise."

Liko backtracked through all his interactions with Saskia, marveling at the kid's poker face. "She's a sly boots."

"She's the sharpest knife in the drawer, all right." Ethan looked at his watch and apparently talked out, pointed in the direction of the Pub.

"Coming?" Liko asked.

Ethan shook his head, but his smile said he appreciated the invitation.

Liko looked again at the painting. "I love it so much," he said, extending his right hand. "Thank you."

Ethan blinked at the overture. Then he shook hands, whispering, "No, thank you." He gripped Liko's hand an extra second. "I'll always love Dane. I'll do anything for him. Even leave. You don't have to worry."

Liko smiled and his other hand patted Ethan's shoulder. "I'm not worried and I don't want leaving. I want staying."

With a last look at Kyle, Liko left the studio and walked diagonally through the crossroads toward the Pub. A roar of applause and raised voices floated from the patio area. Followed by a familiar stomp-clap beat and the now-famous Brian launching into "Thank God I'm a Country Boy."

A man stepped out of the Pub into the floodlights. He stood hands on hips, looking up at the farmhouse, then to left and right.

Looking for myself along the roadside, Liko thought.

"Lord have mercy to the moon," he whispered to Schoenfeld's. This beautiful land. This refuge. This haven. This home.

Then the Green Man's laughter touched the stars as he was run down by a Great Dane.

GREEN MAN CHAMBER WALKTHROUGH

CLUE ONE

Pull the loose brick in the buttress next to the Drei-Hasen-Fenster. Flip the switch and ascend the stairs to the Green Man Chamber.

CLUE TWO

Click the wisteria bloom until it ages and turns to a pod. Cache the three seeds.

CLUE THREE

Pick up the rabbit hiding in the wisteria and move it to the ceiling motif.

CLUE FOUR

Pick up the rabbit at the base of the altar and move it to the ceiling motif.

CLUE FIVE

Pick up the rabbit in the Green Man's lap and drop it into the fire. The smoke will turn into a third hare which will join the others in the ceiling and start the motif spinning clockwise.

CLUE SIX

Take one wisteria seed and feed it into the Green Man's mouth. He'll chew it up and spit out leaves that form a tiara.

CLUE SEVEN

Return to the stairwell and click the mortar and pestle in the painting of the Jade Rabbit. Use them to grind up a second wisteria seed. The dust will fly out the window and circle the moon, which becomes a pearl.

CLUE EIGHT

Put the last wisteria seed and the pearl into the tiara. Put the tiara on the Green Man's head. One of his eyes will turn blue, the other brown. Pine needles will spill from his mouth to form the words TINNER WHEELED.

CLUE NINE

Rearrange TINNER WHEELED to HELEN DEWINTER. This will make the Three Hares motif reverse direction and the sleeping dog will wake up.

CLUE TEN

The dog's blanket is a map. Rearrange the words DANELAW STRONG to GARDENS NOT LAW. The map will grow animated crops, which will pile up on the floor.

CLUE ELEVEN

Rearrange the words NAOMI MISTERIA to O MISTER ANIMA I. The letters will turn into asparagus spears.

CLUE TWELVE

Feed asparagus to the duck. It will lay an egg.

CLUE THIRTEEN

Give the egg to the Green Man. Certain letters will light up in the altar inscription.

CLUE FOURTEEN

Move the first batch of lighted letters into the floor slots to spell NOMI N ETHAN.

CLUE FIFTEEN

Move the next batch of lighted letters into the floor to spell KNOW I IN OUR GREATEST DIANE. You're missing the second I in Diane. Take the Green Man's blue eye and place it between the D and A (eye = I).

CLUE SIXTEEN

Take the leftover letters and spell MY GOD IS THREE. You have to turn the W upside down to make an M, and take the Green Man's brown eye and use it as the O. (Or if you prefer, the eye remains an I and the phrase is, MY GUIDE IS THREE).

CLUE SEVENTEEN

The knife on the wall will disengage. Use it to cut the ceiling motif into thirds. Behind it is the end of the game.

*Point of personal privilege on Clue Five: Hours before he died, my son discovered how to drop the third hare into the fire. He thought of it from the word **deign,** which means to do something beneath your dignity. And so, a confession: I knew how to solve this clue when I wrote the post that eventually went viral. I deliberately didn't share what I knew with the community. At that time, I was very angry with the world. Hoarding the clue was revenge for what had been taken away from me. I kind of regret it now, so I'm trying to give it back a little better.*
—LG

AUTHOR NOTES

Sorry this book took so long. I wrote it myself.

I can't even remember where or when I first saw a depiction of the Three Hares, but I became mildly obsessed with its threefold symmetry. Every time I looked at it, I heard an echo of *Schoolhouse Rock:* "Somewhere in the ancient mystic trinity, you get three as a magic number."

Researching the motif, I learned that wherever the Three Hares appear in churches, the Green Man is close by. Another (sigh) rabbit hole, another ten books, another obsession.

But no story.

In 2020, I wrote 80,000 words of a new *Venery* novel, decided it was a lazy, cheap shot at the Larks, and put it away. Then I was diagnosed with breast cancer and it was like my brain put itself away. The next four years are a fog of treatment, Covid, Tamoxifen, the appalling state of events in the US, and menopause. I wrote words and liked none of them. I researched my themes, I did interviews, I collected anecdotes. My characters were interacting, and eating a ton of great food, but they weren't telling a story.

I wondered if I was done. Maybe I'd told all my tales. I always joked that my greatest success (*A Charm of Finches*) was behind me, but maybe it was true. The scary thing was, I kind of didn't care. Javier Landes had reached this point, too: "He grew comfortable in the apathetic complacence. This was how things were now. If they changed, they changed. If they didn't, whatever… Then he woke up one day with an idea."

So did I. I attribute the fog clearing to Veozah, but my study is not peer reviewed so ask your doctor if it's right for you. All I know is a light suddenly went on, the Thing sat in my lap, the hares started spinning the other way, and this book came *pouring* out of me in eight months.

I'm a big fan of picture books for grown-ups and I was thrilled to combine my wordsmithing and my artwork in this novel. Finally an excuse to take that ProCreate course! As you know, I love drawing mandalas, and recreating the Mogao cave ceilings was right up my sacred geometry alley. Still, you wouldn't believe how many drafts I trashed trying to get it to look like a pencil sketch by an artist whose style could be described as pathological perfectionism. Curses, hoisted with my own petard.

Some of the sketched postcards came out well because the source photos were excellent. Others are pretty damn bad, either because the source photos were poor, or the artefact itself is damaged and/or inaccessible (also, Dane is right—a lot of these rabbits look like mutant frogs). For example, the nave tile of St. Mary's church in Long Crendon is crumbling and peeling. In these cases I used AI to assist filling in/finishing out details I could then "draw." I also used AI to change the date on the Ukrainian postmark in the chapter "A Minor Hullabaloo," because these details matter.

Louie Martin designed Gideon Perfect's *Two-Faced* album cover.

Adriano Bezerra created the map of the Danelaw.

Nima Verzone drew the Drei-Hasen-Fenster postcard, and the full-size window with its adjacent buttress in "Deign to Know Me."

My inspiration for *Three Hares* was the *Hidden Objects* series by Big Fish Games, which I used to play for hours on my phone when I was commuting to work in Manhattan, and the *Myst* series from Cyan Games. I love casual, single player, non-linear games with beautiful art and an interesting story, with puzzles to solve, clues to collect, no adversity except your own frustration. I moshed it all together to make *Three Hares*. If any developer wants to make it for real, call me.

When I was in third grade, my friend Michelle Franks and I put some random treasures in a metal box and buried it in her back yard. We never saw it again. We dug and dug but either we forgot where we buried it, or it got little feet and walked away. To this day, we laugh about that box and wonder if anyone ever found it.

Schoenfeld's is a composite of two local establishments in my neck of the woods: Harvest Moon Orchard and Tilly Foster Farm. Everything Cora serves at the Pub is based on everything my husband and I ate at Il Salviatino outside Florence, Italy.

My husband and I also spent a debauched forty-eight hours in New Orleans, during which we hit one bar that served pork rinds and cabernet, which is an inspired combination. Then we tried to get dinner reservations at another bar that had champagne and French fries on the menu, with anything from a $250 bottle of Grand Cru to a six-pack of Miller High Life.

There was once a commercial for some kind of cereal, toasted bran flakes or whatever, and it had this nerdy guy dressed like *The Book of Mormon,* going around to open-air markets to see if any vegetables could equal the tastiness of his cereal. "Tempt me with fiber," he said as he swooped down on an Asian proprietor, who handed him a cabbage. I seem to be the only person who remembers this commercial. My brain is a weird place.

The provenance of Frombé and Buttercup will never be disclosed.

Philip Pullman fans and purists will rightfully note that *His Dark Materials* was not published when Naomi Misteria was in her teens. I know. I intentionally tore a hole in the space-time continuum and took outrageous poetic license. Apologies. If you haven't read this series, get on it. Also, if you have a very young person in your life, buy them a copy of *Mud Pies and Other Recipes* by Marjorie Winslow. If you do not have a young person, buy yourself a copy. Thank me later.

And now the unpleasantries. Dr. Porto is loosely based on Dr. John Money, a psychologist and professor at Johns Hopkins. Dane and Fred's experience at Porto's clinic is loosely based on the ordeal of David Reimer, whose parents were advised by Money to raise David as a girl after a botched circumcision. Ivelaw Strong's fictional company Paumanok Health Services is loosely based on Universal Health Services. Loosely based or not, these things happened. Don't Google them on a full stomach.

So here we are and here it is. A long time coming, and a lot more I can get wrong than right. Time is a thief, grief is a bandit but love is a creator. Don't give up. Follow your curiosity and keep feeding the beast. If you feel like you're going in the wrong direction, you're not. You're going in the most compassionate direction. Put on your armor. Give yourself grace. Be specific when you petition the Universe. Call on your pipple and make gentle places to lay your head.

Thanks for waiting.

Kyrie eleison ad lunam.

—SLQR

Somers, New York

October 31, 2025

ACKNOWLEDGMENTS

Multitudes of thanks to…

Michelle Cooke, who went to extraordinary and hilarious lengths to help me get a copy of *The Three Hares: A Curiosity Worth Regarding,* by Tom Greeves, Sue Andrew and Chris Chapman. It's the definitive work on the subject, but tragically out of print. Michelle contacted the Edinburgh Library and asked if she could take pictures of their copy, but they snootily refused. In the end, I found a used edition which I had to ship to Michelle, and then she sent it to me along with some amazing snacks and a big box of Yorkshire Tea. These are the friends of your life. (As of this writing, the book remains out of print. If you want to look at my copy, you come my house, Marizabet.)

Ask a librarian anything and they always take it seriously. Whether I send Hannah Henry 80,000 words that go nowhere, or the finished work, I ask for candid, honest, sensitive feedback and Hannah always takes the ask seriously. I value what she tells me like a pearl. She makes me a better writer and a better person.

Dr. Jen Greenberg, who helped me back into harbor and carries my love in a tourmaline. She read an early draft of *Dane,* gave valuable feedback and advice, and told me about Dr. John Money, which helped shape Dane's story. She also ran Dane's story by an endocrinologist who confirmed, "Gonads gonna nad."

Candie Platel, who has the mother of all bathrooms. She reminds me that it's never too late to make new friends. "You smell your own," she says, and it's true: I walked into her house and immediately felt at home. I wrote about 5,000 words sitting at her desk while she did her housecleaning. She drives crazy. Shotgun, baby.

Corey Stewart, both new friend and new co-worker, for her no bullshit, big sister approach to editing; also for being a Master of Divinity and telling me lots more about Elohim and Adam.

Michelle Fewer, for love, sanity, social sageing, and for making a community of fabulous pipple.

Simona Meloni, for interior formatting, and Tracy Kopsachilis, my treasured cover designer.

Darren Eliker, my narrator, my friend and ally, father of Adam, curator of coffee and sandwiches, shameless potato chip thief, and he who makes a gentle place just by saying "Hi." This will be our sixth audiobook, but it's the first I wrote with your voice in my head. It was a collaboration from the start. Dammit.

Special shoutout to Joyce Hiebert who works at Michigan Crop Improvement. It's a fascinating job that at one point might have been Nomi's job, so I sat Joyce down in the dining room at Turf Valley Resort and picked her brain for an hour. I filled 20 pages in my notebook with fabulous stuff, but often as these things go, it just couldn't be worked into the final manuscript. But I have it, and I will use it someday. Best of all, I have the memory of Joyce enthusiastically giving me her time and expertise, and I love her with all my heart.

Emma Scott, for picking up where we left off. For drinks at the bar, placing wasabi peas to hold a thought ("Put a pin in that!"). For MoMA and a hungover breakfast, laughing at the permeable membrane between our ideas. For the ever-growing gallery of brazen email pitches. For half-ass interior décor descriptions. For surviving the unimaginable. For all the minutes. #LABU

My readers near and far, and everyone in Suanne's Read & Nap Lounge for patience, support and constant encouragement.

I'd be remiss if I didn't thank Pat McGuinness, who dropped "Thank God I'm a Country Boy" at a party, made the place go apeshit, and created an instant family memory.

My beautiful kids, Julie and AJ. She was at a playdate and he was beside himself: "I'm getting in love with her and I want her to come home *now*." The mission of the Suannelaw was always to make a gentle place for them to lay their heads. May they always know they can come home.

And no end of gratitude for my husband JP: soulmate, life mate, fellow traveler, the friend of my days. He makes me psychologically visible every hour and treats everything that comes out of my supremely weird head as normal. I am forever in and beside love with you.

ABOUT THE AUTHOR

A former professional dancer and teacher, Suanne Laqueur went from choreographing music to choreographing words, writing stories that appeal to the passions of all readers, crossing gender, age and genre. As a devoted mental health advocate, her novels focus on both romantic and familial relationships, as well as psychology, PTSD and generational trauma.

Laqueur's novel *An Exaltation of Larks* was the grand prize winner in the 2017 Writer's Digest Book Awards and took first place in the 2019 North Street Book Prize. Her historical fiction novel *A Small Hotel* won a silver medal in Foreword Reviews Book of the Year. She lives in Westchester County, New York with her husband and two children.

ALSO BY SUANNE LAQUEUR

The Great Dane

A Small Hotel

THE FISH TALES
The Man I Love
Give Me Your Answer True
Here to Stay

VENERY
An Exaltation of Larks
A Charm of Finches
A Scarcity of Condors
The Voyages of Trueblood Cay

SHORTS
Love & Bravery: Sixteen Stories
An Evening at the Hotel
Tales from Cushman Row
A Plump of Woodcocks